3.25.22

MAR   2022

W9-ARE-811

The Mirror Dance

Catriona McPherson

The Mirror Dance

HODDER &
STOUGHTON

First published in Great Britain in 2021 by Hodder & Stoughton
An Hachette UK company

3

Copyright © Catriona McPherson 2021

A CIP catalogue record for this title is available from the British Library

Hardback ISBN 9781529337921
eBook ISBN 9781529337938

Typeset in Plantin Light by Palimpsest Book Production Ltd,
Falkirk, Stirlingshire

Printed and bound in Great Britain by Clays Ltd, Elcograf S.p.A.

Hodder & Stoughton policy is to use papers that are natural, renewable
and recyclable products and made from wood grown in sustainable forests.
The logging and manufacturing processes are expected to conform
to the environmental regulations of the country of origin.

Hodder & Stoughton Ltd
Carmelite House
50 Victoria Embankment
London EC4Y 0DZ

www.hodder.co.uk

This is for Ann Mason and Julie Weidman, with love.
(Who's the stalker now?)

Chapter 1

August Sunday afternoons, in my fond childhood memories and therefore still in my hankerings, are golden, with lawn chairs – nay, hammocks – set out in the graceful shade of a beech tree and bumblebees providing a lullaby. Full of lunch, one waits for tea, turning the pages of a book and banishing all thoughts of Monday.

On *this* Sunday afternoon, the first day of August, I was huddled over a fire in my sitting room with the windows shut tight against a squall of chilly rain, lamps lit already and the next day, a bank holiday, promising the same again. What is more, since no one expects to light a fire in August, the wood was not quite seasoned and offered more smoke than warmth.

I clicked my tongue to encourage Bunty, my Dalmatian, to join me on the sofa. She is large and Grant, my maid, tells me her stiff white hairs are the very devil to brush out of tweed, but she is a furnace in any weather and marvellously comforting. At that moment she remained on the hearthrug, curled into as small a ball as a spoiled Dalmatian can curl into, grunting a little as her well-fed middle constricted her lungs, not deigning to move away from the fire despite my entreaties, although she gave me a regretful look from under wrinkled brows, in compensation.

The telephone bell was a welcome intrusion. I stood and fairly scuttled over to my desk. Reaching for the earpiece, I expected to hear the voice of Mallory, my daughter-in-law, with a plea for help. Her twins, at fourteen months, had just got their legs under them and were now proving daily that

Mallory and Donald's modern view of child rearing was exactly the muddle-headed nonsense I had known it to be from the day the twins were born and she began rumbling about their swaddling clothes. It was all very well when they could be put on a blanket and left to kick their legs, and it was hardly more trouble when the worst they could do was shuffle around the parquet on well-padded bottoms, gazing at stairs and doors as though at iron gates. Now, though, all was lost. As soon as Lavinia first hauled herself to her feet with fistfuls of curtain silk clutched in her fat little hands and took a wavering, staggering step towards her brother, the need for a sharp nanny increased threefold. These days, hand in hand and thereby acting as mutual ballast, they charged about day nursery, night nursery, downstairs and garden like a four-legged dervish, Mallory trotting after them, issuing ineffectual threats that sometimes shaded into begging. I had given both Mary Poppins books as presents, one for each twin on the first birthday, but the hint was too oblique.

'Hello?' I said kindly but firmly into the mouthpiece. It was quite a revolution in life at Gilverton when Pallister, our butler, decided he did not mind the master, and even the mistress, answering the telephone after all. When we had first installed the contraption years ago, he would not have countenanced such a thing.

'Is that Mrs Gilver?' The voice was brisk and cheerful, easy to place in the upper-middle-class of Scotland.

'It is,' I said. 'To whom—'

'Thank the Lord. I'm Miss Bissett, Sandy Bissett, ringing you from Dundee with a job, if you'll take it.'

'Go on,' I said, winding a bit of lead out of the end of my propelling pencil and turning over a fresh sheet in my writing pad.

'You wouldn't mind if it were tomorrow?' Miss Bissett went on. 'August bank and all that, you know.'

'What's the nature of the investigation?' I said. How

contrary we are. I had been lamenting the tedium of the Monday holiday a moment before – servants on a jolly, cold luncheon, shops shut and no post – but here I was resenting an offer of work to get in its way.

'Not really an investigation,' Miss Bissett said. 'More a scolding. I thought I could take care of it myself but I'm quailing.'

'And whom would I be scolding?'

'There's a puppet show in Dudhope Park,' she said, 'a mean little thing really. Punch and Judy. Only the chap's got a wheeze. I imagine he does it wherever he tramps to, but I don't care about anyone else. I care about what he's got up to *here*. He has worked a couple of my characters into his play and I want him to stop. Or pay me royalties, but I wouldn't imagine he could afford it out of the coins in the hat.'

'Your characters?' I said.

'Rosie Cheeke and her little sister.' There was a pause. 'You know.'

'I'm not sure I do,' I said. In truth, I was certain I did not.

'He tried Oor Wullie and The Broons first. Last weekend this was.'

'Ah! Now, I'm with you,' I said. 'Rosie Cheeke is a comic character from the *Sunday Post*?'

'No,' said Miss Bissett. 'But the principle is the same. As I was saying, he had an Oor Wullie and a Maw Broon puppet when he got here last weekend but someone from the legal department at D.C.T. was round there before you could say knife and got it shut down. That's when he moved on to us. So now I'd like you to go and shut him down again. Cease and desist.'

'Wouldn't you be better with a lawyer?' I said, even though no solicitor I had ever met would be willing to wander a municipal park on a wet bank holiday to deliver a threat.

'Can't afford a lawyer,' Miss Bissett said. She had not

paused, which is admirable, but the embarrassment of her admission had turned her voice gruff.

'Would you like an estimate of my fee?' I asked, hurriedly. I am no fan of not being paid for my work.

Miss Bissett made a sound that might have been a sniff and might have been a dry laugh. 'If I was planning not to pay I'd not pay the lawyer,' she said, which made me laugh too.

'Dudhope Park, in Dundee,' I said. 'And you're sure he'll be there tomorrow? It's not forecast to be much of a day.'

'He was there yesterday and he's there now,' she said. 'Hiding in his little tent, leering out at everyone. He's a rather nasty piece of work, but it's not just you, is it? Your partner is a gentleman?'

'Alec Osborne,' I said. 'Nasty pieces of work a speciality. Don't worry about me.'

'Thank you,' said Miss Bissett. 'Very well then. Miss Bissett of Doig's, number three Overgate, Dundee. Cease and desist the wrongful appropriation of copyrighted property.'

I was scribbling madly, knowing that I could not come up with any better-sounding words on my own. 'Might I have your telephone number, Miss Bissett?' I said. 'To report at the end of the day.'

'Why not pop round?' she said. 'I can write you a cheque on the spot if you bring an invoice. Until then, then. Goodbye.'

'Until wh—' I managed to get out before she rang off, leaving me wondering.

Oor Wullie and The Broons had begun appearing in one of the lower Sunday papers some time last year, and I had seen them peeping out from under the kindling on Tuesday mornings, so hoped that someone in my household had the relevant subscription. Therefore I made my way to the servants' door. Perhaps no one on the other side would have given it a moment's thought but these were the rules I lived by. If I wanted tea, coal or sherry I rang for Becky. If I wanted

4

to pick the brains of one of my staff in the course of detective work I went to them, just as I would go to any other witness. Besides, the kitchen and servants' hall are always warm and cosy.

Even at that, I hesitated to disturb them as I looked at them through the half-glass. Pallister was at the head of the table, in his shirtsleeves with his waistcoat hanging open and a pair of very small gold-framed glasses clinging to his nose as he perused a book review; Grant sat with her back to the fire and her writing case open before her, a pen in one hand and a cigarette in the other, gazing at her half-written letter as she composed her next thought; Becky, still known as head housemaid even though there was nothing but a regiment of daily women for her to be head *of* these days, was leafing through a picture paper. She had her shoes off and her feet up on an empty chair that would once have held an under housemaid. She scratched one instep with the toes of her other foot and looked the picture of ease.

Drysdale, the chauffeur, was nowhere in evidence; keeping Hugh's Rolls on the road was a labour of love that stretched over most Sundays and into the evenings too. My little Morris Cowley had not begun to cause much trouble yet, but when it did we would either have to start using a garage in Dunkeld or accept that Hugh's time as the owner of a Rolls Royce was over.

Strangely enough, despite the fact that the retrenchments we had made heretofore had fallen on me – closing then selling our London house, giving up Paris trips, sacking maids – I dreaded Hugh's first true step towards the harshness of the modern age. To date, he retained his steward, his farmer tenants, his gamekeeper, his butler and Drysdale and, so long as he never caught sight of Mrs McSomeone in her pinny and hat sweeping the stairs, he did not have to face much in the way of reality. One did wonder how it would take him, when the day came.

As I touched the door handle to let myself in to the servants' hall, my good Mrs Tilling entered at the other side, rather hot and dishevelled from her kitchen.

'Madam,' she said, spying me.

'Don't get up,' I told the others. Pallister alone did not heed me. He shot to his feet and started fumbling with his waistcoat buttons, the gold-rimmed glasses trembling on the very point of his nose in a way that made me want to cup my hands to catch them. I sat down in one of the empty seats. 'Does anyone know who Rosie Cheeke is?' I asked.

Pallister frowned but the three women nodded and Becky started stirring the heap of discarded papers and magazines that had colonised the table over the course of the day.

'She's . . .' said Mrs Tilling. 'It's hard to explain. She's not real. Is someone teasing you, madam?'

'There she is,' Becky said, plucking a coloured paper out of the pile and pushing it towards me. The magazine was one of those strenuously cheerful organs, promising thrift without want and entertainment without corruption: drying flowers and quiet games for after tea were mentioned on the cover of the current issue, the type running along under an illustration of a young woman of thumping good health. Her hair was red and curled into glossy billows under a straw hat; her eyes were green and dancing; her teeth were pure dazzling white and rather large; and her cheeks were indeed as red and as round as two apples. *The Rosy Cheek* was written above her in twining letters, which looked as though they had been formed by manipulating a length of red ribbon.

'There's always a strip cartoon about her inside the front page,' Becky said. 'Not much in the way of a story, but you know how it is.'

I did not know how it was. My sons' fierce devotion to Buck Rogers and Popeye had been as bewildering to me as it was tiresome. I had even tried waving Rupert Bear, that

6

odd little creature, under their noses for a while, thinking at least he was English.

I now ran my eyes over the page of squares depicting Rosie Cheeke's latest adventure and discovered, to my amazement, that she was Scottish! In the first little box she was setting off on a walk in the Lomond Hills. In the last, she was back home in a grey sandstone villa with a saved puppy.

'And the woman I spoke to mentioned a sister?' I said, looking up.

'Freckle,' said Grant. 'It's a girls' comic. There's sometimes an advertisement for it in the back of the *Cheek*.'

I turned to the inside of the back cover and saw that she was right. There was indeed a black-and-white but otherwise very splashy whole page devoted to enticing readers to buy or subscribe to *The Freckle* for some young relative. 'Wholesome, cheerful, Scottish fun!' it declared in a banner along the top above a portrait of a child clearly related to the cover girl of the *Rosy Cheek*, only with curlier hair, pinker skin, dimples and, right enough, a dark smattering across her upturned nose.

'*Has* someone been teasing you, Mrs Gilver?' Mrs Tilling said. She had begun to return to her normal brick-red complexion now that she was away from the range that had seen her grow as purple as a turnip and as shiny as a billiard ball.

'Not at all,' I assured her. 'Someone has been intruding on the ownership of these fictional girls and the writer, or artist perhaps – well, in any case, the copyright holder – has asked me to step in and see if I can't stop him.'

'Forgery?' said Grant.

'Plagiarism, they call it,' Becky put in.

'Theft by any name,' added Mrs Tilling.

Pallister had kept his own counsel throughout the discussion, perhaps deeming women's picture papers and girls' comics beneath his attention, but he unbent now. 'Something quite different for you, madam,' he said. 'I don't recall such a case coming under Gilver and Osborne's purview before today.'

'You don't know the half of it, Pallister,' I said. 'The plagiarists are not publishers; they're puppeteers. I'm engaged to go to Dudhope Park in Dundee tomorrow to persuade a travelling puppet man to stop – to cease and desist, in fact – from featuring Rosie and Freckle in his show.'

'Truly?' Grant said.

'Quite,' I assured her. 'He started with Oor Wullie and The Broons, apparently, but the might of D.C. Thomson's lawyers cooked that goose quick enough, so he's lowered his sights a bit.' I was looking closely at the magazine again, searching for a publisher's address. It was a matter I had never considered before and so I did not know where such a thing might be found.

'Oh!' Becky said. 'I'd have loved to see a puppet of Joe Broon. And Maggie.'

'But the Cheeke sisters would be a treat too,' Grant said. 'I shall come with you, madam.'

'We could make a day of it,' Mrs Tilling said. 'Eh, Becky? We're all promised a half-holiday, Mrs Gilver. Cold cuts of what I'm busy with right now.' She consulted the fob watch on her apron and, assured that nothing needed her urgent attention, sat back again.

'Yes, yes, that sounds lovely,' I said. 'A day at a park on an August bank holiday Monday. Except that it's raining cats and dogs and chilly with it and I'm going expressly to shut the thing down, not to watch from the stalls.'

'But you'd have to watch for a bit to be sure there was a case to answer,' Grant said. 'Otherwise how do you know that this chap who rang you isn't a rival puppet man making mischief?'

'Trying to use you – excuse me, madam – to queer his rival's pitch,' Becky added.

'Now, now,' Pallister said, very mildly for him. I had never expected him to mellow; he was terrifying at the age of forty and, as middle age began to add the gravitas of silver hair and a frontage, I had expected him to end up quite Zeus-like. In the face of my detective agency, however, he was close to surrender.

'Very well then,' I said. 'After luncheon. We can go in the Cowley. There's no need to trouble Mr Osborne with such small fry, I shouldn't think.'

The look that passed among the women was mostly anticipation, but it was mixed with just a pinch of amusement, which I decided not to see.

Chapter 2

For the truth of it all was that Alec Osborne was otherwise engaged that summer. Not quite literally yet but I could see the path ahead of him and I was keeping off it, keeping out of his way. It was fifteen years now since the beginning of our professional collaboration and personal friendship, on the case during which his fiancée had died and her father had left him the neighbouring estate to Hugh's and my own. In that fifteen years, there had been many attempts on his bachelorhood – from what Teddy, my younger son, calls 'the near Misses' – as why should there not be, for Alec was presentable, comfortable and available (which was all the mamas cared about) and was also clever, funny and kind, which was more and more what made the Misses themselves take an interest these modern days.

Just after Easter this year, over a great deal of throat-clearing and easing of his collar with a finger as though it were strangling him, he responded to my casual dinner invitation – such an invitation as I offered twice a week, an invitation that barely needed to be made at all – by asking if he could add another to my table.

'Unless it's pigeons and they're already dressed,' he said. 'Fools in their cups and counted.'

'Mrs Tilling would gladly turn dressed pigeons into a stew for you, Alec dear,' I said. 'And fools to trifle. Who is it?'

'Her name's Poppy,' said Alec. 'She's the niece of a neighbour of my brother in Dorset. She's stopping in tomorrow on the way to some shooting.'

'Of course,' I said. 'You needn't have asked. Lucky for you to be able to offer some entertainment, such as it is. I shall ask Donald and Mallory over too and see if I can't scare up a girl for Teddy to ignore. Make a party of it.'

'Well,' Alec said. 'Of course it's up to you, Dan. But I'd actually rather we were *en famille*.'

'Is she in mourning?' I asked, wondering why she was headed to the Highlands for a shooting party if so.

'No, no, nothing like that,' Alec said. 'Her parents are barely fifty. It's more that . . . well, I'd like you to meet her. Properly. Take a sounding. Tell me what you think. I value your opinion greatly, as you know.'

'Oh?' I said, then all in a rush the truth about this young woman broke over me; her significance in my future and the favour conferred by Alec bringing her here for inspection. He had finally taken the plunge. 'Oh! Oh well then yes of course certainly.' I said it just like that, in one long string of tumbling words. They rang again and again in my memory all the rest of the day, warming my cheeks. Meantime, I spent an hour with Mrs Tilling planning a menu at once fit for a king and at the same time casual enough to pass as nothing special. I spent much more than an hour with Grant, discussing my frock and letting her pluck quite five hundred hairs out of my eyebrows as she had long been pleading to.

'I look astonished,' I said when I viewed the result.

'You and me both, madam,' said Grant. 'I never thought I'd see the day.'

It was an excruciating evening. The food was delightful and Miss Lanville ate sensibly and conversed with Hugh about country matters. Alec conversed with me and at no point turned cow eyes across the table or fell silent while he gazed upon her perfection. He might have; she was certainly perfect enough. She had black hair, sleek and polished, and olive skin so carefully protected that she looked like a geisha – I have noticed some olive-skinned girls recently grown as

11

dark as gypsies, what with tennis and the lido – and she was dressed in one of those bias-cut gowns that look like nighties, with no more than a clip in her hair and a single gold bangle around one wrist as adornment. She made a fuss of Bunty, and no fuss at all at the mention of twin babies, and asked questions about Europe that caused Hugh to nod approvingly before he answered her. The excruciation arose from quite another quarter. In short, she spent the evening being kind. She gave me an excess of kindly attention that was both familiar, from when I used to have quiet dinners with elderly acquaintances, and quite horribly new, for no one – not even Mallory – had ever before treated me that way.

As I sat at my dressing table, wiping off my pitiful attempts at beauty with a smear of cold cream, Hugh walked in.

'Fine girl,' he said. 'Didn't you think so?'

'Perfect,' I said. 'A poppet. A catch. It's a terrific idea.'

Hugh sat down on the stool at the end of my bed and regarded me in silence for a while.

'She looks like you, you know,' he said in the end. 'Same colouring, same way about her.'

'I didn't notice it,' I said, beginning to pat vanishing cream under my chin as Poppy Lanville might have to do in about twenty years.

'Oh yes,' Hugh said. 'I thought so right off. Quite a compliment, I thought. And you know, Dandy, I'd make the most of it if I were you. Because that's going to have to do.'

I looked down into my lap and willed the two tears that had formed in my eyes not to fall. 'Nonsense,' I said. 'What rot are you peddling to tease me?'

'I wouldn't tease you,' said Hugh. 'Not tonight. But I did want to say this.' Then he stopped for so long that in the end I looked up again and caught his eye. 'Poppy or no Poppy, it would never have come to pass.'

'Good God!' I said. 'Do you think I don't know I'm fifty? There's no need to rub it in. *Especially* tonight.'

Hugh rose and came towards me. This was becoming rather a torrid scene, for us.

'You misunderstand me,' he said. 'What I meant was I wouldn't have it. I wouldn't have taken it. Pistols at dawn, if need be.' He put his hands on my shoulders and patted them. 'I thought you'd like to know.'

So there had been not just a coolness between Alec and me, born of delicate feelings on his part and tact on mine, but a matching coolness between Hugh and me too, born of mortification. I barely saw him some days unless the babies were there; they made a very effective solid little buffer.

After luncheon the next day, which I took alone in the dining room and Hugh took out of waxed paper standing up in a distant field, I asked Drysdale to bring the Cowley to the back door, for a change, and the four of us women packed ourselves into it with a measure of holiday spirits to go along with our picnic tea, Mrs Tilling having proved unable to foresee a trip even as far as Dundee without some catering of provisions. They bickered a little over the front passenger seat, Grant pressing the question of hat size since hers was a cartwheel, but Mrs Tilling pointing out the inarguable fact that she would have some trouble stuffing herself into the back, even if they all took their hats off and put them in the boot with the picnic.

'Look, *I'll* go in the back if I must,' I said in the end. 'Grant, you've often said you'd like to try your hand.'

'Can you try for the first time when I'm not here, Delia?' Becky piped up. 'I'm all my mum's got now after my brother went in the war and I'd hate her to be left with no one.'

Grant was still sulking when we arrived an hour later on Dudhope Terrace and I pulled into the kerb outside the smart park railings. I still did not believe that a puppeteer would be plying his trade this cheerless Monday afternoon. It was not quite raining – a category of weather that Scotland has raised to a fine art – but rolling banks of thick grey cloud were showing their displeasure at the holiday and the gay display of summer bedding just inside the railings was being threshed like cornstalks by a stiff wind. I saw a shower of petals, blown clean off the marguerites, go scudding off down the slope of lawn, for Dudhope Park had a fair rake to it, here in surely the hilliest little city north of Rome.

Despite the inclemency, a fair few of Dundee's townspeople who were lucky enough to be given a holiday from their work were taking the air. Kites were being flown, hopscotch beds were being chalked into paths (surely until the park keeper saw them and ordered them to be rubbed off again), and indeed an audience was beginning to gather upon thru-penny deckchairs and ha'penny benches set on a particularly steep slope with the red-and-white Punch and Judy tent at its foot. The flags atop it cracked in the wind, and its striped skirts were flapping too, showing the wooden substructure as a thin frock shows off a girl's legs on a windy day.

'Deckchair, madam?' Grant said, with an innocent air, gesturing to four empty seats in the front row.

I dug a shilling out of my bag and handed it to the chap who was jingling a coin bag and ripping little pink tickets off a roll. 'These will do nicely,' I said. Grant is beyond a joke but it did gladden me to see how much pleasure Becky took in plumping down in the front row with a glance behind at the lesser mortals. Mrs Tilling let herself drop, causing an alarming creak in the skeleton of the deckchair, and set the picnic basket on her lap with the air of a court reporter ready for the proceedings.

'Ten minutes,' the ticket man said. I gave him a close look, wondering whether he was an employee of the park or was attached to the puppet show. He wore no uniform; he was dressed in barely respectable corduroy working trousers and a knitted jersey, with a scarf around his neck in lieu of a collar and tie. On the other hand, surely an itinerant puppet

14

show could not travel the roads with this collection of benches and chairs. It would take a motorvan at least to haul it around, if not an out-and-out lorry.

Ten minutes later, the four of us had cups of scalding hot tea from Mrs Tilling's thermos flask and the other three had napkins on their knees and buns clutched in their hands. I could not face removing a glove and so had decided to do without. The audience behind us on the benches and a few children cross-legged on the grass before us were busy with bottles of ginger beer, lollipops, sandwiches (I could not imagine which meal they constituted at quarter to three in the afternoon) and even one or two hot meat pies eaten straight from paper bags transparent with grease.

The music started as though it were drifting across a distant hill, a faint air unfamiliar and yet instantly recognised. It was the sound of the fair, of the circus, of the Pied Piper of Hamlyn, of the Morris Men and the Mummer's Fool. It was not quite innocent, despite its lilt, and if it had been a voice instead of a pipe it would have been mocking. I shivered and then told myself it came from sitting still on this chilly day and took another sip of tea.

A cheer went up from the crowd as the music grew louder, then they settled, agog, to watch the show.

With a quack of kazoo, that old reprobate Mr Punch came jogging on from the left-hand side and the children clapped and hooted at the sight of him.

'Oh what a day, what a day, what a jolly holiday,' he cried. 'And who is this come to see me?'

It had been many years since I had watched a Punch and Judy show and either they had grown darker, or I had been a ghoulish child. First a little dog bit Mr Punch on the nose – 'Oh my nose, my pretty little nose, my perfect little button of a nose!' – and was roundly kicked for it. Then Mr Punch, having offered to tend his crying child, bashed the infant on the head and threw it to the ground. When Judy complained,

15

reasonably enough, he hit *her* with a stick and sent her fleeing. Through it all, the children rolled with laughter and the grown-ups shouted only encouragement, exhorting Punch to 'Whack her a good 'un' and 'Give him what for', all joining in at the tops of their voices whenever the puppet cried out in his cracked sing-song, '*That's* the way to do it!'

But the nastiest moment of all came twenty minutes in when a new character, silent and drab, appeared and stood in the middle of the stage, separating Punch from Judy.

'How does he do three at once?' Becky said. 'There's never room for two people in there, is there?'

I shrugged. 'Pulleys?' I said vaguely. 'A contraption worked by foot?' I was perhaps thinking more of a one-man band than a Punch and Judy show, but evidence of some cleverness or another was certainly before us. Punch stood, quivering with thwarted rage, on the left and Judy stood, quivering with maternal indignation, on the right and, in the middle, the new puppet stared out blankly towards us. Then, as we watched, his head shifted upwards in a little jerk, leaving his body behind. To oohs and aahs from the crowd, his neck continued to grow, unfolding from tight pleats like an accordion, until his face was looking down from just under the top arch of the stage and his neck was a smooth column of cloth, printed I noticed like giraffe skin. The children adored it, screaming with laughter and pointing, but I found it unsettling in a way I could not begin to explain. Mr Punch and his Judy were with me. They tipped back as the neck grew, following the upwards climb of the strange puppet's face and, when he reached his zenith, they too grew still, making a tableau.

When nothing had moved for a moment or two, I turned to Grant. 'Is this the intermission?' I said.

'I don't know,' said Grant. 'Where's that ticket seller? They usually pass a hat at half-time, don't they?'

'I wonder when Rosie and Freckle are going to appear,' said Becky. 'We can't really do anything until they have, can we?'

'They can't come too soon for me,' said Mrs Tilling. 'I don't care for that giraffe fellow. I don't care for it at all. What's it supposed to mean? Is it funny? Because I don't get the joke.'

The joke, if such a thing existed, was beginning to pall for the rest of the audience too. The children were losing interest and turning back to teasing and lollies. The adults, who had paid the ha'pennies, were grumbling.

'Is that it?' someone piped up from a good way back.

'Ho! Mr Punch?' shouted a wag. 'Are you on holiday too?'

'Come on. Get on with it!'

'Give us what we paid for.'

'This int the way to do it' got the loudest laugh of all.

It was when a rough-looking sort with his cap on the back of his head and an untidy cigarette clamped in the side of his mouth made his way forward and knocked on one of the kiosk's wooden legs that I first thought to step in.

'Wakey-wakey!' the man shouted. 'Or I'll come round there and give you a taste of what you're dishing out.'

I stood, hurriedly, giving my teacup to Grant to hold for me.

'Let me,' I said, striding to one side of the kiosk. 'I've got some business with the puppeteer on behalf of a client and perhaps I should take care of it now and find out what the hold-up is too.'

'Suit yourself,' said the man in the cap. He flicked his cigarette to the grass rather near my feet, in a gesture that was as insolent as it was hard to pin down. I would look prissy if I complained. I ignored it for that reason and went around the corner of the kiosk to the rear.

The hangings were grubby this close up, especially at the join, where fingerprints darkened the canvas and the edge was patched and mended. The two flaps were held shut with three pairs of tape ties at top, middle and bottom and all three were done up in double bows.

'Excuse me,' I said loudly, to the gap between the tapes. 'I don't know your name, I'm afraid. And I'm jumping the gun rather. But I've been sent to talk to you. The . . . owner of a copyright you seem to have been infringing is rather keen for you to stop.' I waited. 'Can you hear me?'

There was silence and stillness from inside the tent. Even the wind seemed to have died away.

'Now listen,' I said. 'There's no point ignoring me. You can't get away with it, you know. Well, you *do* know. Because the newspaper's solicitor told you in no uncertain terms. And now I'm telling you too. Cease and desist. I've got a letter to make it all official.'

I fished the letter out of my deep pocket and poked it into the join between the two flaps as though posting it through a vertical letter box. I heard it fall and hit the ground on the inside.

'Do you hear me?' I said again. 'Heavens, you're rude to ignore someone this way.'

At that I finally heard a sound from the other side of the canvas. Two dull knocks rang out and there was a ripple of tittering from the audience on the far side of the kiosk. After another moment of following silence, Grant appeared.

'He's dropped them,' she said.

'Who's dropped what?'

'The professor.' She jerked her thumb at the tent. I had quite forgotten Punch and Judy men were given that nickname. 'He's dropped Punch and Judy. They toppled onto the ground outside the tent. What did you say to him?'

'Nothing much,' I told her. 'And he said nothing at all to me.' I turned to face the tent. 'Are you all right?' I asked in a louder voice than I had used until now. 'Hie! You in there? Are you well? Are you ill?'

Grant's eyes had widened and now she caught her lip in her teeth.

'I'm going to come in if you don't answer me,' I said.

18

Silence met my words and so I took a firm grip on each grubby canvas edge and tried to prise them apart.

'You'll have to undo the ties,' Grant said.

She was right. I crouched and worked on the lowest one, near the grass, while she reached and took care of the uppermost one. Then I tugged at the middle of the three. When it gave, the two sides of the kiosk gaped open, giving us a view into the dim little cubbyhole where the puppet man practised his sorcery. It made me think of the inside of an old and ill-kept pianoforte, such was the cat's cradle of strings and rods.

From a shelf tucked under the level of the stage, a row of little faces stared at me, their glass eyes gleaming and their jaws gaping. And on the ground, slumped against one of the corner supports, the professor sat, all dressed in black, with his head bowed and his leathery, chestnut-brown hands limp in his lap.

'Are you drunk?' I said. There was an odour, but it was no spirit I had smelled before. 'Are you sleeping?' I stepped inside and shook his shoulder. 'Are you ill?'

At my touch, he rolled sideways, shouldering the bottom of the canvas hanging that fronted his tent and coming to rest on his back with his head out on the grass. Grant and I gaped, only very slowly coming to see that his black jersey hid an enormous apron of dark stain that spread from collar to belt and that his hands were not chestnut brown from the sun but from a soaking. While I was staring dumbly at his neck, trying to make sense of the second thick black line above the edge of his jersey collar, the people outside beat me to understanding. There was a rustle of whispers, a rising chorus of concern and then one long, pure, piercing scream.

Chapter 3

Either there were policemen in the park already or the park keeper had a whistle of his own but, within a very few minutes of the summoning note ringing out, a keen-looking bobby had arrived to take charge. He kneeled outside the tent and took the puppeteer's pulse by pressing two fingers against the base of the man's throat. It seemed unnecessary to me, but nevertheless the very act of sticking to protocol instilled faith.

When the young policeman stood and took his handkerchief from his trouser pocket, I thought it was to wipe his fingers and I felt a frown begin to form. I despise fastidiousness in men; women cannot escape blood, what with one thing and another, and I do not think men should seek to capitalise on their good fortune. I had wronged him though. He flapped his hanky out and, bending, laid it gently over the dead man's face, causing an outbreak of consternation in the gathered crowd. Now it seemed regrettable that the hilly nature of the park afforded everyone such a grand view.

'Now then,' he said, straightening again and facing them. 'I'm going to have to ask you all to stay where you are, while I take myself off to the nearest box and ring up my sergeant.' He had a calming effect on the crowd, for one so young. Some of the children continued to weep and a few young women saw their chance to repose upon a manly bosom but most of the picnicking audience appeared, at his words, to put back their shoulders and lift their chins. 'Nobody's to touch him, mind,' the constable added. 'Nobody's to touch ocht. I'm Geordie Adams from Powrie Place, and you can bet I know all your grannies, so don't cross me. Stay in your seats and I'll be back before long.'

He did look down at his hand for a moment at the close of his little speech, and one could forgive him regretting the red tips to his fingers. Then he set off at a fair pace. I remembered having heard that those blue police boxes had various facilities inside. The idea, I suppose, was to spare policemen the indignity of queueing up with ne'er-do-wells at the public places but washing off the blood of a murdered man was a boon too.

When he had disappeared from view, Becky and Mrs Tilling both got to their feet to join Grant and me beside the kiosk.

'Oi!' one of the few men piped up from the back row of benches, where he was holding a little girl on his knee and letting her bury her face in his neck. 'What did he just say? We're to stay in our seats.'

'We weren't in our seats,' Grant called back pertly. Then she turned to her colleagues. 'You two should sit down though.'

'And when you do,' I added in a low voice, 'take a look and tell me what you can see. I'm going to walk behind the tent again. Let me know when you spot me.'

'Hey!' shouted that same man, as I started off. 'We're not to go in.'

'I'm not going in,' I said. 'I'm going behind.' I was as good as my word. When I had got the kiosk between them and me I turned and looked down the park to the south. A path crossed it diagonally and there were trees aplenty planted up either side, but unless I was greatly mistaken, they did not answer the current point.

I began to walk away from the back of the tent, keeping it between the crowd and me. After ten paces, Mrs Tilling called out: 'Madam? I can see you.' I turned and faced the front again. The deckchairs and benches were not set out in straight rows, but rather in an arc like the stalls of a theatre and Mrs Tilling, right at one edge, had a fair view down the side and around to where I stood.

I shuffled along until she was hidden from sight but the courting couple in the deckchairs at the other edge of the front row had cottoned on. '*We* can see you now,' the male portion of the pair cried out.

I shuffled back again. 'No good, madam,' said Mrs Tilling, who had come back into view. Walking backwards, rather precariously since I was going downhill, I made towards the path and the trees but before I was halfway there I could see both of them at once. Puzzling, I returned to my seat.

'How was it done?' Grant said. 'How did anyone get in and out without being seen?'

'We were watching the puppets,' Becky said. 'He must have walked up the green, bold as brass.'

But a woman of young middle age who had been quiet up until that moment now leaned forward and cleared her throat. 'Excuse me,' she said. 'But *I* wasn't. My chum's late, you see. Look, I've got this empty seat all ready and waiting for her. She gets off her bus at the corner of Barrack Road and Infirmary Brae – down there,' she added, pointing to the south-east corner of the park. 'I was watching for her. And I saw nothing.'

'Suicide,' said an elderly woman in the third row, her voice rich with scorn. 'What a wicked thing to do. All these bairns here to see it.' She had a fair gaggle of grandchildren gathered around her. One was too small to care what was happening as long as there was a blob of sugar left on the lollipop stick, but an older girl looked anxious at the word and a boy aged somewhere between the two said: 'What's soo-side, Granny? Is he just playing, that man?'

I gave her a look, intended to say that she had made her

bed and must now lie upon it, then I turned round to face the front again.

'It wasn't,' Grant said quietly. 'It couldn't have been.'

'Not a chance,' I said. 'No one could do that to himself and anyway, the weapon would have been lying there. Which it isn't, unless he's sitting on it, which doesn't seem at all likely.'

'Do what, madam?' said Mrs Tilling, leaning in close and talking softly. 'What kind of weapon?'

I hesitated to reply. The police constable's handkerchief made a very small and rather innocent-looking bump at the base of the puppet kiosk. If one did not know what it covered one would walk by without a glance. Indeed, people *were* walking by, their interest only piqued by the fact of an audience sitting almost silent in a ring of seats, as though entranced by a show, when no show was happening.

But the handkerchief was far from innocent. A man lay dead feet from us, killed by the most brutal means imaginable. Chatting about it struck me as disrespectful and ghoulish. Neither was it lost upon me that the woman behind with her grandchildren was quivering like a radio antenna. I would only provide her with fodder for gossip.

'Remember Miss Rossiter?' I said, recalling an investigation from 1926 when not one but two members of a respectable Edinburgh household had been found with throats slit from ear to ear.

'How could we forget?' said Grant, with a burble of amusement in her voice. I had been undercover as a servant for the duration of the case and Grant had found everything about my disguise – hair, clothes, vowels and laundering prowess – entertaining.

'It's the method employed there that's been employed here,' I said. I thought I sensed the grandmother behind us sit back in her deckchair with a huff of disappointment.

'Nothing very big to be hidden then,' said Becky. 'He might have fallen on top of it.'

'He might,' Grant said. 'But he's left-handed.'

'How do you know—' I began, then I realised. Thinking back to the scene inside the kiosk I remembered a detail I had noticed almost automatically. The man had worn a wristwatch and it was buckled around his right wrist.

'And the murderer is right-handed,' Grant said.

'Why's that then?' said Mrs Tilling.

'Because he – the professor – was facing the front, working the puppets,' I said. 'And the only way in is through the tied flaps directly behind him.'

'Well, that too,' Grant said. 'But also, there's no way the man could have walked off through a park if he'd done that to someone facing him.'

'Why not?' said Becky.

I knew. The gush of blood from the slashing of a man's neck is a deluge, not a trickle. To reach over a shoulder and do the deed, with the victim's body acting as shield, is one thing. To lunge forward and unleash that deluge on oneself is something else. I shuddered. I might even have groaned.

'And I tell you what else isn't in there,' Grant went on. 'Besides the murder weapon.'

'What?' I said.

'See if you can work it out,' she said, infuriatingly, as we heard a police klaxon and saw a motorcar enter the park gates and begin to drive, surely to the outrage of the gardeners, up the lawns to where we were waiting.

The sergeant had brought an inspector with him and two more bobbies, all of whom made short work of the gathered audience. I wondered if the aim was to send us packing before the police doctor arrived and began the necessarily grisly business of examination and eventual carting off to the mortuary.

Grant and I gave our evidence. We told of the stilling of the three puppets and the long hiatus with the crowd jeering.

We told of going around to the back of the tent and calling out, and of untying the ties and entering.

'Oh yes?' the inspector said, glowering down at us. He was immensely tall, with a high-domed forehead and a knobbly skull sparsely covered over with wisps of pale hair so that it looked like a celeriac root before the gardener has had a chance to tidy it for the kitchen. 'You disturbed the scene of the crime?' he enquired, sepulchrally. He would have made a wonderful bit-part actor filling in a crowd scene behind Bela Lugosi.

'N— well, yes,' I said. 'Before anyone knew it was the scene of a crime, we did.'

'And how were the ties fastened?' the inspector said. It was a sensible question and he rose in my estimation, from 'only in it for the golf' where I had first pegged him.

'Neat double bows,' I said. 'Which is interesting, isn't it?'

The inspector gave me a severe look. 'Ah,' he said. 'You *are* that Mrs Gilver. I wondered. Well, just mind and leave this to us, won't you madam?'

'Of course,' I said. 'I've never done otherwise. Not once.'

'And so,' the inspector said, 'since you *are* that Mrs Gilver, can I ask you what you're doing here? Anything we should know about?'

I should have told him. I cannot quite account for the fact that I did not tell him. 'I've brought the female members of my household,' I said instead, not quite lying. 'My housemaid and lady's maid and cook. It's a holiday Monday after all.'

'Good for you, madam,' Grant said, when he had gone. 'Client confidentiality is nothing to throw away lightly. Have you worked out what was missing?'

When she put the two ideas together in that way, it was easy. 'Oh!' I said, thinking back over the row of glass eyes staring at us from the shelf inside the kiosk. 'I wouldn't swear to it, Grant, but now you happen to mention it . . .'

25

'*I* would swear,' Grant said. 'I paid close attention: the doctor, the policeman, Pretty Polly, Jack Ketch, the devil and the blind man. And of course Punch, Judy and Scaramouche were onstage.'

'Scaramouche?' I said. 'The man with the neck? I found that rather disturbing. I'm sure it wasn't in the show when I was a child.'

'Me neither,' Becky piped up. 'The one I saw had a crocodile and sausages.'

'Bastardisations,' Grant said. She has a theatrical background, both parents still on the boards, and can become very proprietorial about anything with a whiff of greasepaint. 'But you see what I'm saying, madam? There was no Rosie Cheeke and no Freckle.'

'Not on the shelf ready for their big entrance,' I said. 'Perhaps they were packed away in the professor's case. Perhaps Miss Bissett made more of an impression than she thought she had.'

'Perhaps,' Grant said. 'Or perhaps . . . you know.'

'I don't think I do,' I said. We were standing off to one side of the seats now, watching the last of the crowd disperse. With typical contrariness, the sky had lightened and the weather had turned almost warm enough to be pleasant just as everyone traipsed homewards, and the policemen were determined to prevent new arrivals from unpacking picnics and skipping ropes. In fact, they were shooing hopeful townspeople off like so many chickens.

'What I mean,' said Grant, 'is if, despite employing detectives, someone came to stop the misuse of the characters and things got out of hand, no doubt that someone would take the puppets away. Wouldn't he? Or indeed she.'

'Hm,' I said. 'That puts rather a different complexion on things. If you're serious about suspecting Miss Bissett then I can't keep her name from the bobbies.'

Before Grant could stop me, I strode over to the huddle

of inspector, sergeant, doctor and the original constable and cleared my throat to attract their attention.

The inspector turned. 'Now, Mrs Gilver,' he said. 'I know you think you've a role to play here. But you really don't want to be on hand for this, dear lady. I'm afraid there's a very dreadful sight to be seen and I wouldn't like you to faint.'

'I've seen it,' I said. 'And I'm fine. Besides, I'm not over here to gawp for a second time. I wanted to tell you something. A clue. Perhaps. The puppeteer – the victim – has made enemies in Dundee, you see. He had to be told off by a lawyer for D.C. Thomson over a matter of puppets based on their characters. And apparently he moved on—' I stopped, for the inspector was holding up a hand as if directing traffic.

'Dear lady,' he said again. It is an epithet that has always irritated me. 'Are you suggesting that someone from our own good D.C. Thomson's has had a hand in this?'

'No, not at all,' I said. 'Not a bit. Because they told him off and he took heed. But then he tried the same game from another angle. Have you heard of Rosie Cheeke?'

'A puppet?'

'Yes,' I said. 'Well no. Not usually. And not legally. But allegedly yes. Only it's nowhere to be found.'

'I fear, dearest lady,' the inspector said, 'that the shock of the nasty scene you happened upon has caused you more distress than you'd like to think. You are not making a great deal of sense.'

The worst of it was, he was right. 'Well, in any case,' I said, 'the real puzzle is how it was done.'

'A blade,' said the sergeant.

'No, I mean how the murderer got away,' I said. 'With the tent out in the open like this and the audience all facing it. There's no blind spot, you see. I tried it while we were waiting for you to arrive.'

'I really do advise you to go home, have a strong cup of

27

tea and put your feet up,' the inspector said. 'Let us worry about the murderer and how he got away.'

'It's a question of angles,' I said. 'And sightlines.'

'Or talk it over with Mr Osborne,' the inspector said. 'He'll explain it to you.'

With those few words he snuffed out the last embers of my desire to help him. 'I will,' I said, with a smile so sweet and so insincere I felt sure he would see through it. Instead he met it with a smile of his own, kindly and avuncular. I would not have been surprised if he patted me on the head. He, in contrast, would have been extremely surprised by my reaction.

'Do you know how to get to Overgate?' I asked, sweeping up Grant and the others as I headed for my motorcar. 'I want to meet this Miss Bissett who brought us here.'

'It carries on from the High Street, I think,' Becky said. 'But if you believe she's a killer, madam, should we go on our own? Or maybe should you and Mr Osborne go together?'

'There are four of us, Becky,' I said grimly. 'None of us is alone. You can wait outside by all means.'

Overgate was indeed right in the middle of the town, rather a scruffy collection of old buildings, leading from a wide bit of road that might pass as a square, or might just as easily be put down to poor planning. The buildings' uses had gone through many revolutions in the time they had stood, but I could tell from a cursory study that none had ever gone up in the world. The old signs painted directly on the bricks said things like 'Hatter and Milliner', 'Music Lessons within' and 'Gentleman's Outfitter' while the new signs painted on sheets of board and nailed above the doors said things like 'Tobacconist' and 'Lodging House: clean rooms, good food', even 'Cash for clean rags'. Number three Overgate had held its place down the years, though. The old painted sign on the gable end said, albeit in rather chipped letters, 'John Doig and Co., Printers and Publishers', and the new sign above the smart black door and wide plate windows said 'Doig's Publishers, est. 1872' in gold paint of impressive solidity and shine. In each of the windows flanking the door stood propped a large mock-up of a magazine cover, much in the fashion of a single soigné hat on a stand, or a single strand of pearls draped over a chiffon scarf.

'It's shut,' Grant said, from beside me. 'I thought it would be. A newspaper office would be open, or even a weekly paper. But a monthly magazine wouldn't be paying staff double time on a bank holiday.'

I had to agree. The black-painted door was locked up tight and there was no light showing behind the gauze curtains that formed a backing to the magazine covers in the windows.

'Let's go home,' I said. 'I'll ring her and come back in the morning.'

'Yes, let's,' said Mrs Tilling. 'I'm chilled to the bone and I've got a pot of chicken broth ready to warm through. I knew how it would be, sitting in a park in Dundee on an afternoon like this.'

'Lovely,' said Becky. 'Just what the doctor ordered. But can you drop me in Dunkeld madam, please? If I'm not needed I might see if my chum wants to go to the pictures.'

There was a tiny hesitation before the word 'chum' and a strange little silence of held breath and wide eyes from the other two and, with a slump, I deduced that Becky was courting. Of course she was – a pretty, cheerful soul and just turned thirty-five – and I was pleased for her, but it was yet another death knell for Gilverton. When we lost her, as we would, I could not see persuading another young woman of her talents to come and live out in the quiet with us and serve as the drill sergeant for a squadron of surly chars. Grant would never leave me. Pallister would see out his days polishing our silver and disapproving of my shenanigans, I was sure. And Mrs Tilling would just as soon depart Gilverton as she would let bottled salad cream into her larder. But as I glanced at her now, noting her stoutness and shortness of breath, the way she sat with hands planted on her knees, rubbing them a little for comfort as though they ached, I tried not to think about her age or the stone floor of the Gilverton kitchens, much less the winding staircase to her attic bedroom.

'Chicken broth sounds perfect, Mrs Tilling. We can have it for supper with some anchovy toast. In the library. It's only the two of us.'

'It'll make a good meal with a bit of toast, right enough,' Mrs Tilling said. 'It's fairly stiff with barley and I've used the very last of the Swedish turnips out of store too.'

In the light of that information, I took myself off to Alec's for supper, under cover of filling him in on the frights of the afternoon.

Chapter 4

It helped that Poppy was in Dorset. Of course, she would be up at the end of the week to play hostess for the shooting, but then Alec always disappeared into a cloud of grouse for the twelfth anyway and I had learned not to rely on him for a while around then. This, I told myself sternly, would be no different from any other year. I did not believe myself, because Poppy was bringing her parents with her on the planned visit and Alec was bound to ask her father the all-important question and then announce the thing at the party he had planned for the end of his shoot. I would do well to make the most of this evening, I told myself even more sternly, for these cosy sessions in his summerhouse with supper on a tray, or in his library with supper on a card table, would not survive the coming upheaval.

When Barrow, his butler-cum-valet, let me in I thought I could detect a look upon his face that spoke of new thoughts, far from welcome. That is to say he greeted me like an old friend of the house, much to be treasured, instead of looking down his elegant nose at me and silently blaming me for the trays and card table (for he would have liked twelve feet of white linen over mahogany every night no matter what, and flanking footmen to serve). I was sure it was not me per se that roused these tender feelings of regret. It was more that the event that would see me reduced to tea with Mrs Osborne in her drawing room would also see him answering to her maid and her cook instead of running the show.

I passed through the house and out of the orangery doors

into the garden, with Bunty racing ahead. She adored Alec and even the demise of his fat spaniel Millie had not seemed to reduce the joy of a visit to Dunelgar. At Alec's whistle from the distant summerhouse, she forgot her ancestry as a carriage dog, stopped prancing and instead fairly bolted for him.

It did not take long to furnish Alec with the necessary facts regarding the new case. He had never heard of the various newspapers, magazines and comic strips, of course, but he proved a surprising fount of knowledge about Mr Punch and his merry gang.

'Scaramouche, eh?' he said. 'A purist then.'

'Hardly, if he's added local colour like a touring pantomime. I didn't care for Scaramouche, Alec. Even though I didn't understand him. Or perhaps the more so because I didn't understand him.'

We broke off then to let Barrow serve us our bowls of chilled cucumber soup. He does pride himself on his chilled soups. I mentioned them to Mrs Tilling once and the hint went down exactly as well as expected.

'I'll leave this here, sir, if it's all the same,' Barrow said, setting a perfectly roasted cold chicken on a side table, under a fly net. 'It's jointed. And a potato salad,' he finished, gesturing towards a covered dish. 'If that's all?'

'That's all,' Alec said, then watched the man's back as he made his way across the lawns to the house. I was keeping an eye on Bunty, as she shuffled, in that way of hers that she no doubt believes to be surreptitious, closer and closer to the chicken. 'Barrow seems to have thrown in the towel at last,' he said. 'Leaving us to shift for ourselves instead of standing there like Hamlet's father.'

'Hmm,' I said. I thought it rather more likely that he was ingratiating himself by any means available, before the coming nuptials.

'As to Scaramouche,' Alec went on. 'I think he's a portent.

His stretched neck is supposed to foreshadow what's coming to Punch if he doesn't mend his ways.'

'Does he mend his ways? I can't remember the plot, such as it is.'

'No he does not. He hangs the hangman and then outwits the very devil.'

'Heavens,' I said. 'And the children just keep laughing and licking their lollipops throughout?'

'That's children for you,' Alec said. 'Give me a dog any day.' He said this even though Bunty was now sitting with her nose not quite an inch from the fly net, quivering with anticipation and drooling rather.

'You say that now,' I told Alec. 'But just you wait.'

I thought I was being insouciant and thought insouciance was called for, but to my surprise Alec retreated to silence and did not meet my gaze until he was asking me what I wanted from the chicken.

'As if you don't know by now!' I said, but that reference to our long friendship and perhaps the number of suppers we had eaten *à deux* down the years only made matters worse. Bunty was the winner for our awkwardness: she was fed more scraps of skin and gristle and a few slices of juicy breast to boot, since fussing over her was such a ready-made distraction.

'Bright and early in the morning then,' I said, standing at the end of the meal. 'And we'll see if Miss Bissett has read the late papers or found out on the grapevine.'

'Why not ring her?' Alec said.

'I tried. I asked for Miss Bissett of Dundee and the girl could find nothing. Then I tried Doig's but it rang out. Not so much as a caretaker, evidently. No, nine o'clock tomorrow morning is the best bet, I reckon.' I clicked my tongue for Bunty and headed back to the house, passing Barrow on my way.

'Leaving already, Mrs Gilver?' he said, with a note of strain in his voice. I was sure I was right; he really had hoped that if he left us alone in the twilight with a cold chicken and a bottle of Riesling I might throw myself at Alec's feet and beg him never to marry.

As is typical after a holiday Monday, the next morning dawned clear and warm and I regretted the days when I could pull on a dress of lawn and ribbon, put a straw hat on my head and call myself ready. I have never understood the thinking behind wearing exactly the same garments in August as in February – tweeds and a shirt with stockings and brogues – only in paler shades.

'I'll boil,' I said to Grant as she handed me my gloves.

'Or freeze later,' she said, as though in sympathy. And that was true too. Gooseflesh is as much a part of evening dress in Scotland as diamonds and silk. I have never been in a Scottish dining room that was not arctic in any month of the year.

Alec was waiting in my sitting room when I came downstairs, sitting with Bunty's head in his lap while he perused the issue of the *Rosy Cheek* I had purloined from the servants.

'Better than most,' he said. 'I like a comic strip, for one thing, and there's an actual route for a walk in the hills. Did you notice, Dan?'

I had not.

'Clever,' Alec said. He turned a page. 'Ooh, and an instructional article on tipping. Very sensible idea. I look forward to meeting the publishers of this organ. It's a lot less silly than the papers—' He stopped, like a horse refusing a fence. I carried on, like an unseated rider sailing over without him, and supplied the words 'Poppy reads' in my mind.

It was a very different Overgate we arrived in an hour later, pulling Alec's Daimler to the kerb. The tobacconists and greengrocers were open for business and the pavement was lively with delivery bicycles, early shoppers and gaggles of children. The black door at Doig's had been thrown open to show a glass and brass affair and, even before we passed through it, we could feel a rumbling through the soles of our feet, a distant but insistent hammering that made me think of *Götterdämmerung*.

'Printing,' Alec said. 'Perhaps we should make an appointment for another day.'

'Let's press on,' I said. 'We can melt away if need be.'

It was the first of our many mistakes regarding the magazine business, as we were shortly to learn.

Inside the front door, a dazzlingly modern young miss, who was patting her curls and gazing at herself in a compact glass, looked over the top of it as we approached the desk she sat behind.

'How may I help you?' she said in refined tones, then spoiled it by hastily adding, 'Can I! How *can* I help you? And "good morning". Oh dear.'

'We won't tell,' Alec said, with a smile for the girl. It worked on her like sunshine on a daisy, causing her to beam back at him. 'We've come to see Miss Bissett. She's expecting us.'

That was somewhat overstating the casual request that I stop by to have a cheque handed over in payment for seeing off the puppet man, but the girl did not question it. She lifted a telephone receiver, one of the new models with a rotary dial and a single listening and speaking device, like a dumb-bell. Tucking it into her neck, she turned to a little switchboard mounted on the wall behind her desk and pondered the various pegs waiting to be clipped to any of the dozen switches. I glanced at her desktop while she hummed and hawed and saw that she was no better a typist than a tele-phonist, for there were discarded sheets and carbons everywhere and the page still wound into her typewriter at this moment showed a blob of ink from heavy-handed pounding on the keys. I wondered if Miss Bissett was a collector of lost lambs, or a philanthropist who gave work to orphanage alumni; there was no other explanation for this girl's employment.

'Um,' she was saying now. She had gone as far as to unhook one of the pegs and was now hovering over the switches, darting from one to another like a dragonfly, never landing on any. I thought I could hear her whisper 'eeny-meeny' under her breath.

At last, she made a decision. She clipped the peg and spoke into the mouthpiece. 'Miss Bissett? Oh sorry, Miss Findlay.' Then she hung up, a picture of defeat. 'Perhaps I'll just pop up to her office,' she said, rising. 'Quicker.'

Teetering on high heels and hobbled by a tight skirt – I really did think those had passed out of fashion and I was concerned to see this evidence that they might be coming back again – she walked along a corridor leading into the bowels of the building and began climbing a set of stairs.

When the sound of her heels had finally died away, a door behind her desk opened. 'Fion— oh,' said the woman who was leaning through it. 'Any idea where Fiona's got to?' she asked. Glancing at the girl's desk, she added: 'Gone to the stationery cupboard, has she? She's very hard on ribbons.'

'She's off to find Miss Bissett to announce us as visitors,' I said. When the woman smiled and rolled her eyes I was unsurprised, for her hair was russet curls and there were freckles on her arms, showing below her three-quarter sleeves, even if those on her face had been covered with powder to match, in smartness, her scarlet lipstick. This, I deduced, *was* Miss Bissett and the magazine was more personal to her than I had imagined.

'That girl!' Miss Bissett said. She stepped smartly over to the telephone and switchboard and clipped a peg without a moment's hesitation. We could hear the bell ringing out both from the receiver and from wherever it sat in the building. It echoed in the stairwell. 'I'm Sandy Bissett. Alexandra,' she

36

said, holding out her hand to shake. 'And I assume you are Mrs Gilver?' She turned away. 'And of course she won't answer it in my office! I give up.' She disconnected the call, replaced the receiver and came round to the front of the desk. 'How did it go?' she said. 'Have you raised an invoice for me? It doesn't matter, if not. You can jot a few lines on a sheet of scrap. Just so long as there's something to show the accountant.'

'You haven't heard then,' Alec said. 'I'm Osborne, by the way. The other partner.'

'Heard what?' said Miss Bissett. 'Did he cut up rough?'

I looked around the bare reception foyer. There was nowhere to sit except the desk chair of the missing Fiona and it was one of those revolving affairs, worse than useless as a refuge after a shock. On the other hand, Miss Sandy Bissett did not strike me as the easy-to-shock kind.

'The problem has resolved itself,' I said.

'Jolly good,' Miss Bissett said, but with a wary note in her voice.

'Inasmuch as the professor is dead,' Alec said. 'And so can no longer misuse your property in his ventures. But—'

'I rescind my "jolly good",' said Miss Bissett. 'Poor chap.' She ran her tongue around behind her lips. It could have been in response to the sudden news drying her mouth, but could just as easily be meant to make sure none of her lipstick had become stuck to her teeth. I had often wished every devotee of bright red lipstick would develop the habit.

After a moment, evidently thinking over Alec's words, she added 'But what?'

'He was murdered,' I said. 'He had his throat cut.'

I was right. She was not the swooning sort. She swallowed hard once or twice and pressed a hand to her throat but her eyes stayed sharp. 'In the pubs?' she said. 'In a fight at closing time. He did strike me as a drinking man and so *very* rude.

Locals in the public bar wouldn't put up with the way he spoke to me on Saturday.'

'Not in a drunken brawl, I'm afraid,' I said. She frowned at my words. 'Yesterday afternoon, in the park. In his kiosk.'

'How horrid,' said Miss Bissett. 'Have they caught the man?'

'They have not,' I said. 'And I don't see how they're going to, at first blush. So we thought, Mr Osborne and I, that we might at least find out a little more from you, in case it's helpful.'

'*You're* going to solve it?' she said. '*You're* going to catch him?' Miss Bissett's face was a picture of frank incredulity. I mistook her tone for disbelief and bristled instead of replying, but she took the wind completely out of my sails when she added: 'Can I have an exclusive when you do?'

'Is it the sort of story the *Rosy Cheek* would run?' said Alec, sensibly enough. 'I'm not disparaging you, I should hasten to add. I've only read one issue but I liked the hill-walking comic strip very much indeed.'

'You're hardly the reader we keep in mind when we're laying out the forward issues,' said Miss Bissett. 'But thank you. No, I still do what I can freelance for the dailies. Owning a magazine doesn't keep me in tea and buns, I'm afraid.' She smiled. 'So can I?'

'Certainly,' I said. 'But for now, might we ask you a few questions?'

'It doesn't have to be this morning,' Alec said. 'I hear the presses and deduce that it's a busy day.'

'For the printers,' said Miss Bissett, 'and later for the packers and the drivers. But press day is the next thing to a holiday for the rest of us. The die is cast – well, the formes are bound and the proofs are passed. You couldn't have caught me at a better time, actually. Come up to the conference room and I'll get us some early coffee, if Fiona ever resurfaces.' She went to the same doorway the girl had disappeared

38

through and held it open for us. 'She's very friendly,' she went on, trying to herd Alec and me through the open door like a cowman with skittish cattle. 'Which is not to be sniffed at in a receptionist. I remember the dragon who used to sit behind that desk when I was a child, rebuffing scoops, customers and everyone else who tried to breach the sacred threshold.'

'When you were a child?' I said. 'Did you inherit the *Rosy Cheek*?'

'From my grandfather and my father,' she said. 'But don't tell my uncle. We don't speak of the precise details of ownership in his hearing. Mind you, I don't think he's in today.'

Alec, trying to recover from going through a door held open for him by a woman, looked as though he was instantly on this touchy uncle's side. He stood at the bottom of the stairs like a hotel doorman, ushering Miss Bissett and me up ahead of him and wearing a severe frown. Miss Bissett grinned as she passed. 'You'll live,' she said. Then she set off at a clatter up the staircase, her feet ringing out on the metalled edges of the steps. I followed her as fast as I could, resenting it since the stairs wound around a little self-service lift in a wire cage and I saw no reason we could not be in it. Alec started to puff as he came up behind me too. And Miss Bissett did not stop on the first floor. She swung around a landing and kept climbing. I was breathing like a bull by the time we were halfway to the second-floor landing.

'Yoo-hoo!' We all looked up as we continued to climb. Fiona was bending over the banisters to begin haranguing her boss at the earliest opportunity. 'Miss Bissett?' she said. 'Is that you? Yes, it is. Oh good. Well, there's someone here to see you. I've left them in recep— Oh they found you. Good.' Then she stepped inside the lift, pulled the door across and descended, passing us with a wave.

'Coffee, Fiona!' Miss Bissett called as the girl went by us.

'Coffee for three in the boardroom, please.' There was no reply.

'I'll just fetch the notes I took,' Miss Bissett said, when we were on level ground again. 'Once a reporter, you know. I jotted down quite a lot. Go in, go in. I won't be a minute.'

'Yes, sir!' said Alec under his breath, opening the door opposite Miss Bissett's office. Inside was a gloomy chamber that would have been at home in a bank, solicitor's office or indeed undertakers, were it not for the outsize prints of magazine covers hung upon the wall here and there in between the more usual Victorian gentlemen in their high collars with their pocket watches in hand. There was no furniture beyond a long table, set about with twelve chairs whose seats were upholstered in the same green as carpeted the floor and draped the narrow windows.

Alec was inspecting the prints. 'Look at this Dandy,' he said. 'January 1887. The *Rosy Cheek*, volume 1, issue 1. If that's not a coloured photograph of Miss Bissett then I'm her little sister Freckle.'

'It can't be,' I said. 'It must be her mother. How old would you say she was anyway?'

That impertinent question was hanging in the air between us when we heard Miss Bissett approaching across the bare polished boards of the landing. Guiltily we sprang away from the wall and drew out a chair each to plump down into.

So it was that all three of us saw it together. In Alec's chosen seat, bent in the middle and hard up against the back, its feet not quite reaching the front edge of the cushion, was a red-haired, pink-cheeked hand puppet, its head lolling and its wide mouth mocking us with a leering grin.

40

Chapter 5

The worst thing of all was the fact that the puppet was held in place at the chest with a skewer driven into the pad of the seat back.

'What is that?' I said. 'A hat pin?'

'It's a bodkin,' said Miss Bissett. 'The compositors use them to winkle bits of type out of the formes.'

'Don't touch it,' Alec said, as the woman reached out a hand. 'Don't touch anything. Where's the nearest telephone?'

'My office,' said Miss Bissett faintly. 'Why?'

'To ring up the police, of course,' I told her. Perhaps the shock had dulled her wits, but it struck me as an odd question. I was walking around the table squinting into the shadows where the rest of the chairs were pulled in and, right enough, I found what I was looking for. At the foot, the chair set across the other short end contained the other puppet.

'Is this Freckle?' I asked Miss Bissett. 'It's hard to tell but I don't want to strike a match. If you crouch down and look . . . Here, take my hand.'

But Miss Bissett squatted, rather more effortlessly than was ladylike, bringing her knees around her ears and her face under the level of the tabletop.

'Yes, that's her,' she said.

'Can you see another pin?' I said. 'A bodkin?'

'No,' said Miss Bissett. 'It's a shooting stick this time.'

'A shooting stick?' I said, thinking helplessly of country walks and leather seats. I crouched down beside Miss Bissett but she was in my light.

'What the compositors use to shoot type along the line in a forme,' said Miss Bissett. She straightened and gave a mirthless laugh. 'If the bodkin's a stiletto to a little puppet, then a shooting stick's pretty much a stake through the heart.' Her lip wobbled.

'Come away,' I said. 'Come and sit down. Is there a key to lock this door?'

'No,' said Miss Bissett. 'Or if there was it was lost long ago.'

'I'll wait outside,' Alec said. 'You two go into the office and – yes indeed, Dandy – sit Miss Bissett down and give her a glass of water.'

But even as he said it we all heard the lift again, bringing Fiona and the coffee tray. I met her, took it out of her hands and told her to go back downstairs again. It was brusque and it clearly puzzled the girl, but not as much as seeing Alec stationed outside the conference room door like a guardsman would have puzzled her.

Miss Bissett's office was as unlike the room across the landing as could fairly be imagined. It was on the sunny side of the building and light poured in through three windows and a skylight, making dust dance in the air. There was a desk heaped with the expected paper, but also with swatches of fabric, various toys, a mystifying number of small devices that might be fob watches of several designs, and a collection of teacups and sandwich plates the like of which I had not seen since my last visit to Teddy's college.

'You'll have to excuse the mess,' Miss Bissett said, sitting in an ancient chair behind her desk. It was made of leather and greatly flattened, then made up with a sheepskin and a stuffed pillowcase to somewhere near comfort again. 'It builds up over the month. I was going to attack it this morning.'

'Plenty time for that,' I said, although to be frank the question of where to set down the tray was challenging me. I nudged at the nearest edge of the muddle on Miss Bissett's

42

desk, somewhat in the manner of a snow plough clearing a railway line, and managed to get it stable enough to let go, with only a few items dropping off the far side. Miss Bissett kicked absent-mindedly at a crocheted nightdress case until it was under her desk and less likely to be tripped over.

'Now then,' I said, lifting the coffeepot.

'I can't,' she said. 'Fiona makes filthy coffee. I can only drink it with a biscuit and I couldn't possibly swallow a biscuit. I feel as if my throat's closed over. Could you just fill my cup with water, please? There's a little cloakroom through there.'

There was indeed. I hesitated on the threshold but it was spanking clean. Perhaps the char who was no doubt forbidden to touch Miss Bissett's desk made up for it buffing taps and scouring porcelain. I ran the water until it was cold, filled the teacup and took it back.

'And now I really must ring up the police,' I said. 'Can I get an outside line without young Fiona being involved?'

'From here you can,' Miss Bissett said. 'Not from everywhere. We wouldn't want the print staff chatting to their sweethearts all night when no one's around to check up on them.'

She lifted the receiver – another modern one; it would have outwitted me – and dialled once, then handed it to me when the girl on the exchange was already squawking.

'Dundee police station,' I said. 'Or if you've got names, I'm looking for an Inspector . . . D'you know? He never *said* his name. Well, I'm looking for an inspector, anyway.'

It took an unconscionable amount of time to track down any inspector at all, and when someone did finally lift an extension set somewhere deep in the heart of the Dundee police station it was not the chap I had met the previous day. This individual, breathing so heavily down the line that it buzzed and rattled, and in between breaths sucking at his teeth with a great deal more enthusiasm than he showed for listening and making notes, did eventually take in the information that I was ringing up with new developments in the Dudhope Park murder case.

'I shall pass the message on, madam,' he said grandly.

'Oh please don't,' I said, foreseeing Alec spending the entire morning on sentry duty. 'Please try to get Inspector . . . or Sergeant . . . Oh, this is too infuriating! Or even Constable . . . Powrie? No! Constable Adams. George Adams. I don't suppose you could lay your hands on Geordie Adams and send him along here, could you?'

After a scolding about ordering up one's favourite policemen like mannequins in a dress shop and a prolonged episode of whistling through his teeth while he consulted the duty roster, the man let out a cry of triumph. 'You're in luck, madam,' he said. 'Constable Adams has just come back to the station for his tea break. I'm looking out of the window at him now.'

'If he doesn't mind missing his tea and bun,' I said. 'I'd be most awfully grateful.'

'He can fill up on biscuits,' said Miss Bissett behind me.

'Not long now, Alec,' I said, sticking my head out into the corridor. Alec was standing four-square in front of the closed doorway, guarding it against a non-existent onslaught. The landing was empty, the lift cables still and the stairwell as quiet as the grave. 'Someone's on his way.' Then, at a cry from inside Miss Bissett's office, I wheeled round just in time to see her emerge from her little cloakroom, staggering and pale.

'What is it?' I said.

'What is it?' Alec's voice echoed from across the landing, sounding rather plaintive as the door swung shut against him.

Miss Bissett sank into her chair and mumbled through trembling lips: 'In there. On the mirror.' I must have frowned. 'Behind the door. It's mine. It's definitely mine.'

It had not struck me before that there was no glass above

the sink, but only a hook there as though waiting for a glass to be hung from it. Perhaps it was left over from when this cloakroom was the preserve of Mr Doig. But of course the glass these days was hung on the back of the door itself, opposite the window, shining clear symmetrical light on the face of the young woman who used it to rouge her cheeks and black her lashes. And indeed to paint her lips with her bold red lipstick. I gazed at the message written in that very lipstick, filling the rectangle of glass with jagged letters, leaving only patches here and there to reflect my own shocked face back at me.

THATS
THE WAY
TO DO IT!

'Where do you keep it?' I said, joining her in her office again.

'Dandy?' Alec called out. 'What's going on?'

'I keep one in my bag and one in my desk,' said Miss Bissett. 'Here.'

She had wrenched open the shallow drawer just under her desktop before I could stop her. But I managed to stay her hand before she started rummaging.

'Fingerprints,' I said. I suppose I was once as carefree about these things as Miss Bissett, but enough time had passed in my detecting career that her actions struck me as foolish and bewildering. These days, to clamp a hand on top of possible prints at the scene of a crime was as unthinkable to me as the habit of those monstrous doctors in days of old who passed down a ward of patients, with never a drop of water nor a whiff of soap, and broadcast disease like a wedding guest strewing rice.

'Is it there?' I said to Miss Bissett. I was studying the innards of the shallow drawer as closely as anyone could but there was such a jumble I could barely pick out individual items. I saw pencil stubs, hair ribbons, foreign coins, nubbins

45

of chalk, broken combs, railway tickets, envelopes with notes scrawled on them, chips of soap, inky handkerchiefs screwed into balls, dice and playing cards, powder puffs and eyebrow tweezers, safety pins and hat pins, a dog collar rolled into a tight spiral and held with pink tape, a suspender strap missing its hook, a compass with a ball of sealing wax speared on its points and a mousetrap.

'No,' Miss Bissett said. Then, unbelievably, she set her hands flat against the front of the drawer and pushed it shut again. I bit my lip on the word that sprang into my mouth, and thanked my stars I would not be in charge of this scene of the crime for much longer.

For I could already hear the steady tread of what were unmistakably a policeman's boots climbing the staircase and, after a moment, I heard Constable Adams' voice enquiring: 'And who might you be, sir? You look like you've been roped in as a special, the way you're standing there.'

Alec explained in the sort of spare, clean words that would well befit an officer's report. I sidled out and added my tuppenceworth, trying for the same style.

'And whoever it was, was in Miss Bissett's private office too, writing nasty things on her vanity glass in lipstick.'

Constable Adams looked to one side and then the other, spoiled for choice, before plumping for the puppets in understandable preference to a lady's cloakroom and the tools of her wiles.

Soon we were banished. Such is the way of it these scientific days. We repaired to the foyer and watched a fingerprint man, with his stout case of mysterious equipment, a photographer grappling a tripod and an even stouter case of lenses and plates, and the inspector with his entourage of sergeants pass through and tramp up the stairs. Miss Bissett had been enveloped in the inquiry and was now lost to Alec and me. We still had Fiona.

'So you've been here at your post since the front door was

opened at nine?' I said, confirming what she had – with countless asides and rephrasings – just told me.

'Yes, and you were the first two in. Except the staff. And the post. The print men have been here all night, but Advertising came in and a few from Features who're already working on next month's issue. Nobody in Art. They don't have anything to do until there's a story to illustrate, you see?'

'Is that it?' I said. 'Print, Art, Features and Advertising?'

Fiona gave me a kindly look, suitable for the elderly and infirm. 'What?' she said. 'Hardly. There's Editorial, Fashion, Letters, Home and Garden. Then there's Payroll, Accounts, and Deliveries. And the Freckles.'

'The same again for the sister paper?' I said. The premises had appeared commodious but now I began to wonder how many people could possibly be stashed away in the various departments of the building.

'Not, not nearly,' Fiona said. 'It's mostly the same – Payroll and Deliveries and all them. Print too. All that. It's just two specialists in the Art department who draw the comics and three of them in features who only work on the kiddies' side. Maybe six?'

'Out of how many all told?' Alec said.

Fiona started counting on her fingers but lost track when she had been round both hands a couple of times. Next she tried with a pencil, jotting down her tally, but gave up again. 'It's somewhere about thirty-seven,' she said, at last.

'But all are known to you and to each other?' I said. 'There aren't strangers coming in and out?'

'Strangers? Of course not. What is it that's happened anyway? Strangers? Do you mean a thief? What's happened?'

It had taken her a good ten minutes to wonder but now the thought had struck her it appeared to have struck her hard.

'Someone put something in the conference room that doesn't belong there.'

'A stranger got all the way to the conference room?' she said. 'Put what?'

'I meant members of the public, I suppose,' I said. 'Do they drop off letters by hand? Or hand in . . . I don't know, competition entries? What about renewing subscriptions?'

'We're a national magazine, not a local daily rag,' came a voice from behind Alec and me. 'And so necessarily all of that is done through His Majesty's mail. Not round the back of the allotments on the way to the steamie.'

That was our introduction to Mr Syme of the Art department. His entire personality was contained in that one strange little outburst: pride in the *Rosy Cheek*, especially in relation to the other publishers in town, an absurd level of pomposity about perfectly neutral matters like the post, and wild flights of scorn out of absolutely nowhere.

'Sorry, Mr Syme,' Fiona said, shrinking down into her collar. Heaven knows what she was apologising for.

'Allow me to introduce myself,' I said. 'Mrs Gilver of Gilver and Osborne.' Alec waved as I said his name. 'I take it you know about the puppets?'

'I've given up getting any work out of any of the girls upstairs,' Mr Syme said, with a purse of disapproval. 'I'm going out for my coffee. I am unavailable for comment.' And he swept out of the front door and away along Overgate, holding his umbrella – quite unnecessary today – in front of him like a shield.

'Should staff be popping in and out?' Alec said, watching him go.

'I'm not running after him to tell him otherwise,' said Fiona. 'He's only the second in command in one department, you know. "The girls" are none of his business to get work out of or not. But you'd never know it.'

'He's been here a long time?' I said.

'In with the bricks,' she confirmed.

'Why are those coppers not gathering the staff?' Alec said.

48

He was standing near the stairwell, looking upwards. 'It's a rum old way to run a mur—'

I cut in, hastily. 'When does the char go off?' I asked Fiona, thinking again of how Miss Bissett's little cloakroom gleamed.

'She doesn't,' said the receptionist. 'She changes her pinny and does the tea trolley.'

'When would that be?' I said.

'Oh, before nine,' Fiona said. 'She always has everything lovely for us coming in. And then she takes good care of us mid-morning. She'll be out getting the buns now.'

'Excellent,' Alec said. 'I could murder a bun, if you'll pardon the expression.'

'Someone else nipping in and out!' I said. 'And when was anyone last in the conference room?'

'Friday for the last of the layouts,' Fiona said. 'Friday afternoon about two-ish. But Mrs Miller would have been right in after them. You'd not believe the mess they leave after the last of the layouts.'

'And does Mrs Miller come in this way, with her buns?' I said. 'Can we wait for her here? Or is there a back entrance?'

'At the back and downstairs,' Fiona said. 'I don't know how she stands it on press days but her kitchen's right near there and she finds it handy.'

'Let's start with her,' I said.

'Down two flights and follow the noise,' Fiona said. We were well on our way when she called after us. 'You wanted to know about strangers.' We wheeled round and waited. 'There was a man with a plant.'

'A potted plant?' Alec said.

'It might have been a bouquet of flowers,' she said. 'It was done up in florist's paper. Only it looked too heavy for flowers.'

I returned to her desk. 'When was this?'

'Five o'clock on Friday,' she said. 'I wasn't at my desk. I had gone down to the staff entrance to draw the overtime line in the book. You know, to show who was working late. Miss Bissett's supposed to do it, but she rang down and asked me on Friday. Well, when I got back this man, with a pot plant, was in the lift, going up.'

'And when did he come back down?' I said, trying my utmost to hide what I thought of Fiona's powers of recall.

'I didn't see him leave,' she said. 'But, if he found himself locked in, there's the back door to the bins, and the loading door for the vans and the staff door, as well as this one. He'd have to be very stupid to get locked in for the whole weekend.'

'Can you describe him?' I said, shuddering rather when I remembered the look on the puppeteer's face when *I* saw him.

'He was an ordinary sort of a man. He wasn't wearing an overall or an apron or anything. If he *was* from a florist.'

'A strange man, carrying a parcel, just as the office was closing and you didn't see him leave,' Alec said. He too was boggling at the utter dimness of the girl. 'I think I'll pop up and mention him to the police, just in case. Dandy? Would you like to track down Mrs Miller and see what she's got to say about the looking glass? No raisins for me, mind.'

'Yes, she should be back by now,' Fiona said. 'And it's plain scones on a Monday. Oh! But this is Tuesday. It's cherry loaf on a Tuesday. Gingerbread sometimes.'

I did not think it had occurred to the child that the strange man with the paper-wrapped parcel too heavy to be flowers might be anything to do with all the policemen; it must be very comfortable to live such an unthinking life.

Alec and I shared a shake of the head and roll of the eyes as we parted at the stairs, he to climb up and spread the news to the police and I to descend into the bowels of the earth to the roar and shudder I had to remind myself was only a printing press and not the monster its clamour brought to my already rattled mind.

Chapter 6

The noise was not helped by the stink, oily and sharp, that grew and grew as I approached the presses until it threatened to choke me. I peered through a kind of porthole into the belly of the beast itself and saw a hammering, rattling machine as big as some beach huts I have changed in and an endless flashing white hurtling through and round it, up and down, tended by a pair of red-faced men in blue dungarees, with cotton hats on the backs of their heads. They stood at the ready, leaning on long poles, occasionally stepping forward to wipe a portion of the behemoth with a flick of a black rag. I could not bear to watch them. I supposed they knew what they were doing but at any moment I expected a corner of the rag to be caught and bear the man who held it off into the guts of the dragon.

'You shouldn't be down here,' came a voice close to my ear, making me jump. I turned to see a man, dressed in the dark blue overalls and matching cap of the printers. He had retreated to a more polite distance and was holding open a door to what looked like a store room. He cocked his head to invite me in and then closed the door behind both of us, shutting out the worst of the roar. The vibration continued; if anything it felt worse without the accompanying sound.

'Excuse me raising my voice, madam,' the man said. 'But it was shout in your earhole or shake your arm and you wouldn't want that.' He held out a hand liberally stained with ink. The hairs that should have been reddish to match his moustache and the sideburns under the little cap were instead pure black and as stiff as quills.

51

'There was no need for either,' I said, but with a grin to soften the scolding. 'I'm here with the permission of Miss Bissett.'

'You're *here* at the invitation of yours truly,' the man corrected me. I grinned again. 'Here' was indeed a store cupboard; reams of paper the size of staircase runners stood on end and tin cans of ink as large as steamer trunks were neatly stacked on stout wooden shelves. The atmosphere was delicious, all the new paper making it quite unlike the pall that hung over the rest of this basement. I saw that the window of the room was made of a fine metal mesh, like that of a larder, letting in a little fresh air too.

'I'm at Doig's, I mean,' I said, playing along with his mild waggery. 'And down here on my way to the kitchen.'

'But "Miss Bissett" hasn't got the say-so to let people go wandering round down here when the press is running,' the man said. 'Whatever laws she lays down up there in the offices.'

'I see,' I said. 'That does make sense. It's a question of safety, I suppose.'

'It's a question of jurisdiction,' the man said. 'Separate magisteria.'

I must have looked as surprised as I felt at this startling phrase on the man's lips.

'I'll introduce myself,' he said. 'Johnny Doig. I'm Sandy's cousin. I'm in charge of printing.'

'Ah,' I said. I had been taken in by the boiler suit. But, setting it aside, this man might well be the son of a doctor, banker or indeed newspaper proprietor, with a yen for the practical end of the business, just as Hugh likes to deliver the odd calf or even dip the odd sheep just to keep his hand in and retain the respect of his tenant farmers.

'Well, no doubt you know all about me,' I said. 'Mrs Gilver, of Gilver and Osborne.' No glimmer of recognition met my words. 'I'm looking into the matter of the puppets.'

Mr Doig's face fell. He stared at me for what felt like a full minute, then swallowed. 'What puppies would these be?'

'Not puppies. Puppets.'

His grin reappeared as he hit himself on the side of the head. 'Printer's ear. Worse than housemaid's knee, any day. But thank God for that; Sandy's menagerie is beyond a joke already, and she might be hard-nosed as a businesswoman but she's putty with a dog. So, what *puppets* would these be?'

'She didn't tell you?' I said. Johnny Doig shook his head. 'That's odd. If you're a partner in the business.'

'Ah,' said Mr Doig. 'Well, no. I'm not. I'm the grey lamb of a black sheep, you see. Slowly bleaching myself white again through hard work, and trespassing on the kind heart of my cousin meantime. In short, I'm not a partner. Sandy owns the whole show, not that we could ever get my dear old black ram of a father to admit as much. When I said I was in charge down here I meant that I get to breathe oil and sweat ink, because it saves Sandy doing either.' He smiled as he spoke and it seemed without rancour. 'So what is it I should know?'

I hesitated.

'I'm a very *pale* grey lamb, Mrs Gilver,' he said. 'Pearly grey, not gun metal. And I am family.'

'Forgive me,' I said. 'I'm being overly cautious. There's a – at least, there *was* a – puppet man, a Punch and Judy man, who came to town and added local colour to his show by copying the characters from your cousin's magazines.'

'What a good idea,' Mr Doig said. 'Free advertising.'

I opened my mouth to argue but then the thought struck me that he was right and instead I gaped.

'Where do you come in?' he went on. 'You don't look like a woman who earns pin money handing out coupons at a Punch and Judy show.'

'Coupons?' I said.

'That's how I'd do it. Dish out money-off chits for new subscriptions at the curtain. Or even off individual issues.

But that gets the local newsagents and bookshops roped in and they're notorious stick-in-the-muds. Sticks-in-the-mud, I mean. WH Smith's act as if they're allergic to money whenever someone comes up with any kind of wheeze. I suppose they're too big to trouble themselves with the kind of scheme that would be a boon to a little outfit like the *Cheek* and *Freckle*.' The way he said it made it sound like a coaching inn; there was insolence about it somewhere.

'Miss Bissett took a very different view,' I said. 'She wanted me to ask the professor to cease and desist. She was annoyed by his infringement of copyright.'

Mr Doig stared at me, frankly dumbfounded. As I watched, enlightenment broke over him like a cracked egg.

'Let me guess,' he said. 'I know exactly what happened. No puppeteer would land in Dundee and immediately think of our game gals as the two brightest stars. Who did he try first?'

'Oor Wullie and some of The Broons.'

'I knew it!' Doig slapped a tin of ink to punctuate his cry. It made a very satisfying fat smacking sound. 'Of course! DCT are far too high and mighty – no, that's unfair, just too big and successful – to need the help of a tinpot little travelling puppet show. So they cooked his goose and he moved on to us and Sandy couldn't help herself.'

'It's understandable,' I said, helplessly defending a woman from the scorn of a man, even though I quietly agreed with him and felt foolish for not thinking the same until he thought it for me. I would take great delight in bearing this new angle back to Alec and watching him agree and feel a fool in his turn. 'I mean, if Miss Bissett is trying to bring Doig's up, then following the lead of the premier publisher in town isn't the worst idea.'

Mr Doig clutched his chest as if receiving a severe shock, even as his eyes danced. He sat down on a crate, took off his cap and fanned himself with it. 'My oh my, Mrs Gilver. Let me count the bricks you just dropped and beg you never to

54

drop them on Sandy. They'd flatten her. "Bringing Doig's up"? "Following the lead"? "The premier publisher"? Dear, oh dear, oh dear. You see the thing is, last century, the two companies were about upsides. Nowadays there's a chasm between Thomson's and Doig's. Thanks, in large part, to my dear papa, I'm afraid.'

'Oh?'

'He never had much of a head for business. Never had much of a head for anything except ponies, cards and dancing girls, actually. But my Uncle Bissett never had the heart actually to sack him and Sandy's no better. So he still works here, the old scoundrel. He's off to Bournemouth on his holidays, right now, and no doubt I'll get a telephone call asking for cash once he meets enough chaps to start a poker school at his hotel.' Johnny Doig shook his head, but fondly.

'And so Miss Bissett staged a coup?' I asked.

'Indeed,' said Doig. 'Enough reminiscing! Back to our tale! Just as the brothers were all ready to throw in the towel, Cousin Sandy announces she's not going to finishing school after all. She's going upstairs to the boardroom and it's onward printing soldiers!'

His words were scathing and bordered on blasphemy. I was moved to a defence of the intrepid young woman he described. 'Such vision,' I said.

'Such sentiment,' Mr Doig said. 'Such stubbornness. That woman on the front of the magazines was her mother, you see. The whole enterprise was no more than old Grandpa Doig's gift to his beloved daughter.'

'I thought the cherub who graces the *Freckle* was Miss Bissett,' I said.

'She is now,' said Mr Doig. 'When Sandy came along, an adorable little red-headed granddaughter, she inherited the mantle, more or less.'

'Even more reason for her to make sure the magazines

both thrive,' I said. 'For her grandfather, her mother and herself. They are thriving, aren't they?'

'*Are* they? She's got schoolfriends who don't need the money working for free, and pensioners who want to keep their hand in working for a pittance. Well, I mean to say, she's even got me in running the presses to keep that bunch of old lags in line.'

'Old lags?' I said, with a glance towards the printing room.

'Grateful and therefore conscientious,' he told me. He put a hand on the door handle. 'They need watching, mind you.'

'Might I ask one last practical question before I let you go?'

'Have at it,' said Johnny Doig. 'Are you considering a new career as a typesetter?'

I ignored him. 'How easy would it be for a chap, locked in here after five on a Friday, to let himself out?'

'I should say he'd have to dig a tunnel,' Doig said. 'Who's been saying otherwise?'

'Well, Fiona.' We shared a look. 'Quite,' I added. 'Silly of me. I hope for better things from Mrs Miller. Could you point me her way?'

There was no need; as we exited the store room, a stout woman came towards us, swinging a tower of four baker's boxes tied together with string. She wore a red straw hat bedecked with cherries, and an open mackintosh over an apron.

'Mrs Miller?' I said, or rather yelled, over the din of the printing press. 'I was on my way to talk to you, if you have a moment.'

'I'll have one of my headaches by dinnertime,' Mrs Miller said. 'What with the racket and the smell of the ink. I'll be hanging over a basin before the end of the day.'

'Dear, dear,' I said. 'Let's step away by all means. Where's your kitchen?'

'Kitchen?' she said. 'Kitchen! A kitchen would be a fine

thing. I've no more than a pantry. Never stops them asking for the moon and the stars for a long meeting though, does it?'

I shrugged, which earned me a sour look. I was no better than the rest of them, whoever they were.

Her quarters *were* snug, to be fair. She walked in ahead and I had to shuffle to the side to get the door shut behind me. It had a deep sink, with a geyser set above it and a cold tap at its back and overlooked a dark yard full of dustbins through a barred window. Its fittings were a set of shelves that stretched from floor to ceiling, filled with thick green china and piles of dishcloths and tea towels. And its furnishings were a tea trolley, complete with urn. I deduced from the breadboard and tea caddy on top of it that this was her work bench for as long as she was busy with preparation, and was then transformed into a vehicle when the time came for distribution.

'Have you heard what's happened?' I said.

'Heard?' said Mrs Miller. 'Heard! I can't hear a blessed thing on press days. They could be hacked to lumps by an axe-wielding lunatic up there and I'd not know.'

'It's not quite so bad as all that,' I said. 'But there's been some trouble. In the conference room and in Miss Bissett's little cloakroom.'

'What? No! I don't believe it,' said Mrs Miller. 'What is it this time? A party? I've only just got it back to rights after that orgy they call a layout meeting. I'll give my notice. I will. And then they'll all be stuck with a gas ring and a packet of biscuits. Because no one else would put up with it, down here getting a sick headache in this cupboard and chasing around for fancy cakes for them. They're like a lot of children, Mrs—' She broke off and took a breath. 'Who are you?'

'It's nothing like that,' I said. 'The conference room is still perfectly brushed and swept and Miss Bissett's lavatory is dazzling. You are a conscientious woman, Mrs Miller. I can hardly believe you do it all alone every day. And then turn on a sixpence and go out shopping for cake too? Cherry cake, young Fiona said.'

Mrs Miller was soothed by this outrageous sucking up. 'And me with corns like hens' eggs,' she said, easing off a shoe to display one to me. It was indeed a whopper.

'Now then,' I said. 'Did you do the conference room at the end of last week or this morning?'

'This morning?' Mrs Miller said. I was beginning to catch her habit of speech and I waited for the second helping. 'This morning! I couldn't have gone home for my holiday and left that midden. Coffee cups and teeming ashtrays, enough paper to make another magazine out of and sandwich packets lying all over. Mr Doig's cigar ends everywhere. And one of those so-called editors that think they're so hoity-toity doesn't eat crusts. We'd have had rats by now if I'd left crusts of cheese sandwiches lying under the table all weekend, wouldn't we?'

'Well, ants at least,' I said. 'In this warm weather. So you had to go rummaging right under the table to fetch them out again, these crusts?'

'And me with my knees,' said Mrs Miller.

'So you would have noticed if there was anything left lying on any of the chairs,' I said.

'Noticed?' said Mrs Miller. 'Noticed! I'll say I noticed.' I felt myself perk up. 'There's always something left lying everywhere after their so-called meetings. I had to brush crumbs and ash off *half* of them upholstered seats and take greasy fingerprints off every last *one* of the polished backs.'

'Excellent,' I said. 'That's very good news. A lot of work for you, of course, but no end of helpful as things stand now.' In truth, it was no help at all in regard to timing, leaving as it did the whole three-day weekend. But it sounded as though Mrs Miller had removed all fingerprints from the chairs before the intruder placed the puppets. 'Did you do Miss Bissett's cloakroom on Friday afternoon too?'

'I'm no fan of doubling my work,' she said. 'That girl wouldn't know a day off if she met one in her porridge. So I do her Friday morning like I do everyone and then I do her Monday morning too. Or Tuesday as it might be, with the holiday.'

'Now that's *very* interesting,' I said. 'So you cleaned there this morning? At what time?'

'I'm a Methodist,' said Mrs Miller, unexpectedly. Her next words made her meaning plain. 'I work from top to bottom, strictly methodical. I start up in the art studios in the roof and work my way down through Miss Bissett's level, to the offices on the first floor and then the offices on the ground floor and finish up down here. So I would have been on the second floor about six o'clock.'

'And you didn't notice anything out of place in the cloakroom?'

'I don't know what you're expecting me to tell you about Miss Bissett's habits, madam,' Mrs Miller said. 'Who did you say you were?'

'Of course not!' I said, shuddering at the very notion, and thinking – not for the first time – what excruciating intimacy one has with one's servants. 'But here's the thing: someone, at some time since Miss Bissett last used her cloakroom, has written a nasty message in lipstick upon her vanity glass.'

Mrs Miller's face fell. She stared at me with her eyes wide and her mouth dropped open.

'Well, not nasty exactly,' I hurried to add. 'Not profane and not threatening. Just odd. Taken in conjunction with everything else. Just rather odd.'

'On her vanity mirror?' Mrs Miller said.

'Behind the door,' I said. 'You couldn't have missed it. Bright red letters an inch high.'

'It wasn't there at six o'clock this morning,' Mrs Miller said very definitely.

'No, I shouldn't have thought so.' Perhaps the florist really was a florist, I thought. Or perhaps he was someone's young man, bringing a posy for her and leaving at her side.

'No need for you to think,' she said. 'I'm telling you. I'm everywhere in this place between five and nine of a morning. Ask that girl on the desk, if you don't believe me.'

'Of course I—'

'*Fiona,* or whatever she's supposed to be called. Until the minute we open up for the day and everyone's at their desks or their typing machines. I'm not one of these cleaning women you'll see dragging a mop bucket round under everyone's feet. I'm in charge till that red line goes in the book then I'm gone. Five o'clock, the place is mine again. I don't stand for argument on that score.'

'It's a long day for you,' I said, hoping to quell any more irrelevant details.

'I only empty bins at five o'clock,' Mrs Miller said. I was out of luck, it seemed. 'For the rats, like I said. And I go off home for my dinner at noon and try to put my feet up till tea time. Not that I get a bit of peace or rest, not really. *He's* off his work with his back. Been under the doctor for years and it never alters.'

'Poor thing,' I said. Then hastily clarified: 'Poor you. A bit of peace after lunchtime isn't much to ask.'

'So,' Mrs Miller went on, in a conspiratorial tone, getting to what I sensed was her point at last, 'between tea and closing I have a bit of time to myself. Like you say, madam, it's not much to ask.'

'Certainly not.' I gave her a smile. I did not give her any encouragement to carry on.

'If it's a good day,' she carried on, nevertheless, 'there's a nice bench by the church there. I sit and have a fag and look at the papers. When it's foul I go in. I don't get my smoke, but you can't have everything.'

'That's one good thing about the Church of England,' I said. 'There are so many candles no one would notice a hardworking woman having a puff.' But I had overstretched the cord of friendship that had begun to grow between us.

60

I had shocked her. Minutes before, that would have served my purpose, ending our conversation, but now an idea had occurred to me. Perhaps all of this was not irrelevant after all. 'What did you do on Friday afternoon?' I asked. 'It was nice weather.'

'I sat out.'

'On which side of the church?' I said. 'Where's your bench?' for I had glimpsed spires and buttresses and a couple of shady trees as we drove by the previous day. 'I don't suppose you could see any comings and goings, could you?'

'Exactly,' said Mrs Miller. 'Like you said. Even when I'm off, I'm still on. Besides, there's no point me trotting back over to start cleaning before the bosses are out. So. There's a bench opposite that cut-through and I can just see the front door.'

This was splendid news. 'You watch the door while everyone leaves at five?'

'Even on my wee break to myself.'

'Did you see a man with a parcel done up in florist's paper? He would have been headed in right on five o'clock. He might have walked in with you.'

'With me?' said Mrs Miller. 'With me! I go out the door there through the yard. I go in and out that way for dinner and for my little rest. Mornings I come and go through the staff door to the corner of Union Street. Lovely baker's on the corner of Union Street. Spotless. Everything very dainty.' She gave a beseeching look at the stack of baker's boxes tied together with string, where sustenance for the staff awaited her attentions.

'I imagined this chap coming in the front door,' I said. 'At least, Fiona saw him heading upstairs from the ground floor.' I waited. 'But if you didn't see him, perhaps not.' She scowled at me. 'Thank you, Mrs Miller. You've been very, very helpful. Conference room chairs clear on Friday evening, cloakroom glass unmarked at six this morning, no one in the front door at five.'

She gave me a hunted look. 'I brush those chairs with a stiff brush and then smooth the nap with a chamois,' she said. 'And I shake out the curtains every month and shift the folds.'

'Splendid,' I said. 'I shall pass that on to my own girl when I get home. We've just had new curtains in our dining room. The old ones were faded into stripes from no one ever disturbing the folds. I shall suggest that trick, Mrs Miller. Thank you.'

It was not the first clue I missed in this case, and it was by no means the last. I was already quite a ways down the wrong path, if only I had had the wit to look around and see. I might have realised it if I had had leisure to think over all that I had heard that first morning at Doig's. I might have felt it bothering me, for I have often experienced the troubling, yet faint, sensation of something missed, something seen but not observed, something learned but not remembered. I call it an eyelash on my cheek. Alec, less poetically, calls it a bout of indigestion that recalls the taste of a meal. But then Alec always does think of his stomach first and probably considers eyelashes seldom if at all.

Unfortunately, that Tuesday morning, events within and without were just about to overtake all of us and drive such wisps as eyelashes and indigestion from our minds. As I climbed the stairs away from the pounding of the press and the anguished looks of Mrs Miller – seen but not observed – the sight that greeted me was Miss Sandy Bissett, in handcuffs and with a police sergeant holding her hard above one elbow, being borne across the foyer, while young Fiona shrieked and squawked behind the reception desk. The inspector strode ahead of them, looking terrifically pleased with himself. Alec and Constable Adams brought up the rear, both looking angry, incredulous and quite, quite stunned.

Chapter 7

'This is preposterous,' I said, watching the police motorcar with Miss Bissett inside go off along the street. A gaggle of onlookers had gathered and were not dispersing. Rather they stood in clumps looking to Alec and me for further excitement.

'I need to talk to you, Dandy,' Alec said.

'But what *happened*?' I asked, giving him a look no less severe than that I turned on Constable Adams, who was still beside us. 'What's the charge?'

'Murder, madam,' the policeman said. 'You should know. You were there.'

Some of the nearest bystanders had heard the word and every man Jack of them was now silent and aquiver, waiting for more. The life of Overgate – its grocers and drapers, its hawkers and loungers – had ground to a halt. The very air above us seemed to hang heavy and, when the klaxon – quite unnecessary – with which the inspector accompanied his progress had died away, there was silence.

'Exactly,' I said, turning aside and whispering to Adams under my breath. 'I was there. I was asked by Miss Bissett to be there. She would hardly press a detective to watch a murder, now would she?'

'It would be bold,' said Adams. 'That's for sure.'

I raised my eyes to heaven at this response and, in doing so, spotted the staff of Doig's gathered at the upstairs windows, watching appalled the aftermath of what had befallen their boss out of nowhere, or so it must have appeared anyway.

'Foolhardy,' I said. 'And how exactly was Miss Bissett supposed to have got into the kiosk and out again without anyone seeing her?'

'To be fair, Dan,' Alec said, 'that's a problem for any murderer.'

I glared at him. 'Let's discuss this inside,' I said. 'Our client, Alec, has just been hauled off in chains—'

'Cuffs,' Adams put in, then evidently wished he had not when he saw my look.

'—and our job has accordingly just increased in urgency. Do you really think she did it?' I asked Adams.

'Motive, evidence, opportunity,' Adams said. 'It looks quite black for her.'

'But,' I began again, then bit my lip. 'Surely there hasn't been time yet to gather all suspects and consider their motives. Perhaps he had just run away with someone's wife. Or perhaps he was locked in a feud with someone. How much do you know about him?'

'Me?' said Adam.

'The police,' I said.

'Nothing. We don't even know his name.'

'Well then,' I said. And I repeated my opinion of the whole silly mess. 'Preposterous!' Then I marched up the steps and banged the front door of Doig's shut behind me. As if the sound itself had jolted the thought into my head, I had a sudden shuddering realisation. I opened the door again. 'Adams?' He looked up. 'Has this place been searched?' He frowned. 'Because someone walked in at five on Friday and no one saw him leave.'

'A convenient passing stranger?' Constable Adams said. I stared him down and at last he softened. 'Well, we'll have to go over the place anyway. I'm sure we'll notice him when we open the right cupboard.'

I banged the door even harder this time.

Alec slipped in quietly behind me. The foyer was jammed

full of people: Mr Syme was there; Fiona was still wailing like a train in a tunnel and Mrs Miller had stumped upstairs and now stood with one hand against the wall for support and the other pressed to her chest. I hoped it was an expression of her feelings rather than a practical measure, but truth be told I did not care for her colour. As well as these three, at least another five men and as many girls were rumbling and twittering, beseeching Fiona for information and scolding her to stop her silliness, which only spurred her on to greater hysteria until she sounded more like a kettle than a train. Johnny Doig was nowhere to be seen. Indeed, none of the print men had joined the crowd in the foyer and I could still hear the great beast thrashing away under my feet.

'Ladies and gentlemen,' Alec said. 'Please, ladies! If I could have your attention?'

Fiona did not so much pipe down as run out of breath but the effect was the same. She hiccoughed and sniffed but caused no more uproar.

'My name is Alec Osborne, and I am a detective,' Alec went on. 'I and my partner, Mrs Gilver here, were engaged by Miss Bissett, before this morning's unfortunate occurrence, to look into the very matter which has taken such an unexpected turn.'

'That looks bad,' said Mr Syme. 'She took you on to fix it before it blew up? That looks like guilt whichever way you slice it.'

There was a flurry of comment at that. I could not tell whether it was shocked dissent or shocked agreement.

'Were I a solicitor,' Alec said, 'perhaps. But we are private detectives, as I told you. The police have made a grievous error and it is lucky that my partner and I are on hand to help them correct it. Now then, we are going to have to talk to all of you, but the last thing we want to do for our client is disrupt the smooth running of her business. Miss Bissett

65

is going to need the magazine, both magazines, ship-shape and Bristol fashion when she comes back.'

'*If* she comes back,' said one of the girls, a rather slovenly-looking creature in artistic linen and bagged stockings.

'And besides,' Alec said, 'there are other aspects of the case requiring our urgent attentions. So, we would like you return to work and by and by either Mrs Gilver or I will be along to speak to you. What do you say to that?'

'But you haven't told us anything,' a young man said, standing with his hands on his hips, looking at Alec the way I would look at a broken dish.

'Who's the second in command?' Alec said. 'Who takes over as editor with Miss Bissett otherwise engaged?'

'Mr Doig,' said a voice.

'He's away on his holidays,' said another.

'Well then, me I suppose,' said a third from the back of the gaggle. 'But if someone else wants to make a bid I shan't fight for it.' She was a writer. I knew it without asking. Besides the ink on her cuffs and the pencil in her hair, she wore a look of detachment, almost of amusement. If this was one of the *soi-disant* old pals who was working for peanuts, then Miss Bissett had misjudged her. She was no friend of the woman, she who could lift that one eyebrow and shrug off her commitments at a time like this.

'I think you'll find I have seniority, Miss Cameron,' said Mr Syme. 'I have been here longer than anyone else. Besides, my war record speaks for itself.'

I frowned. A war record did not seem to me to be terribly relevant to the current crisis. A smothered giggle from one of the girls told me that, quite contrary to Mr Syme's words, his war record never got the chance to speak for itself and that it was not unusual for him to bring it up willy-nilly.

'Young Mr Doig is surely the obvious lieutenant,' I said. Alec cocked his head in interest. I cocked mine back to indicate the noise from below us. 'He's the printer,' I said. 'Busy

66

today, of course. Miss Bissett's cousin and, I'd imagine, very much concerned with the family business and its fortunes.'

'Good, good, jolly good,' Alec said. He is the mildest of men when caught unawares in public. A marvel, really. 'His Christian name wouldn't be Johnny, would it?' At the murmur of assent, he added: 'Miss Bissett only said one thing as she was being brought downstairs and that was, "Don't tell Johnny till the print run's done".'

'I second that,' said Mr Syme. 'I'm not sure I could do my day's work after all this commotion. If we don't tell print and packing until the vans are off, so much the better.'

'I don't think I can agree to that,' I began, but was shouted down not only by Mr Syme but by a perfect chorus of others in agreement with him.

'It's a delicate creature,' Mr Syme said. I frowned, thinking of the printers downstairs, who were burly to a man. 'The magazine,' he explained. 'It must be printed before the end of the packers' shift and out in the vans in time to catch the trains to get to the shops and stands at the same time as every other month. Our subscribers won't mind, but the casual lady traveller at the station kiosk won't cancel her journey for the *Rosy Cheek*; she'll simply pick up a *Good Housekeeping* and be lost to us forever.'

'I'm in charge of payroll, Mr Syme, as you well know,' said a severe-looking chap frowning over a pair of pince-nez glasses whose lenses were so narrow, one wondered whether they served any purpose. 'If the packers need time-and-a-half, I'll answer to Miss Bissett for it.'

'But still and all,' said the artistic-looking girl in linen. 'You know what Johnny's like. Let's wait till after the run, shall we?'

It struck me as callous, but I could see the sense in it. I shrugged at Alec. He shrugged back at me. 'Now then,' he said. 'Before you all disperse: how many of you knew about the Punch and Judy man?'

Blank looks spread over the gathered faces.

'Punch and Judy?' said Mr Syme. 'Is that a riddle? It's hardly the time. Not with all this going on.'

'But all *what*?' said the arch woman he had called Miss Cameron. 'What's it about? What did Sandy *do*?'

'Yes, we owe you an explanation,' I said. 'The Punch and Judy man was using Rosie Cheeke and Freckle puppets in his act. Miss Bissett engaged us to deal with the matter.' A twinge of unease plucked at me; Mr Doig had spoken such sound good sense on that score. 'But he was murdered yesterday and whoever did it has tried to implicate Miss Bissett in the crime.'

'A frame-up?' said one of the younger men. 'How did he manage that then?'

'He hid the two puppets here in the building and left a . . . note of congratulation regarding the crime, for Miss Bissett to find when she came in this morning.'

'And the police think it's a double bluff, do they?' that same young man asked.

'So the one thing we do need to ask everyone, right now,' I said, 'is about a chap who came here with a parcel, wrapped up the way a florist wraps a bouquet or a potted plant. He went upstairs. Did anyone else see him arrive, and perhaps even more to the point did anyone see him leave?'

Some of the staff stared at the floor, in efforts to remember, and some gazed at one another, hoping that someone else would cry out and smack himself in the forehead as the memory struck, but no one said a word.

'I really did see him,' Fiona said tearfully. 'I'm not lying. I never lie. I was brought up by the nuns and I'd rather pull my tongue out than tell a lie. Ask anyone.' Her voice was rising again and her face was colouring too.

'Nuns?' said Mr Syme. 'I never knew that about you. Well, well.' He was more shocked to hear that a member of a different church worked in his office than he had been to

68

hear that his boss was arrested for murder. There are some details of Scottish life that never become less shocking.

'When was this anyway?' someone asked.

'Oh!' I said. 'Forgive me. Five o'clock on Friday.' Fiona stopped crying at long last. No one else spoke in the silence. 'No?' I said. 'No one saw him leave? I'm rather afraid, you see, that he's still in here.'

Fiona jerked as if from electricity and shrieked – there is no other word for it – '*Friday?*'

'Yes,' I said calmly. 'You told us so.'

'But but but,' Fiona said, making someone giggle, 'you think he's still *in* here? Since *Friday*? A murderer? Still *in* here?' Then she gathered her gloves and other belongings from behind the reception desk and made for the front door at a clip.

The rest of the staff divided cleanly between those who appeared relieved that Fiona and her hysterics were gone, those who were now considering hysterics of their own if there was a day off in it, and those genuinely fearful on account of the intruder.

'Shall we search?' said Mr Syme, rather heroically.

'You could start,' said Alec, 'but the police are coming back to do it thoroughly, we believe.'

'Anyway,' said Miss Cameron, 'I rather think that chump Fiona *did* see him leave and doesn't have the sense to come clean about it. There was something terrifically stagey about the way she took off just then, wouldn't you say?'

They all began to bustle away to their departments, at that, perhaps to work or perhaps to show how unlike chumps they were.

I took a file card from a packet of fresh ones on Fiona's desk and printed upon it:

With regret, Doig's is
closed to the public today.

I tried not to think of that horrid little message smeared on the cloakroom glass as I stepped outside the front door and pushed in the drawing pin.

'Do *you* think he's still in here?' Alec asked. I shrugged.

'Do you think Mrs Miller will come round?' he asked with equal interest, five minutes later, when we were settled in Miss Bissett's office with the door shut.

'I expect so,' I said. 'That's a lot of cherry loaf to go stale otherwise. Besides, I imagine she'll want to regale them all.'

'Should we have shut it all down and interviewed them instead of letting them mingle and make up tales?'

'Not a bit of it,' I said. 'Unless you think Sandy Bissett actually did it. You don't, do you?' Alec did not dignify me with a response. 'No, what we need to do is find out who the poor chap was, find his next of kin, be given permission to keep digging, and then find out about his life and his troubles. Find out who would want to kill him, who had a real motive. A motive stronger than questions of copyright. It's ridiculous. I can't believe the police gave it credence. She was dealing with it. She engaged us.'

'The inspector took that as helpful evidence,' Alec said. 'She cared enough to put detectives on the man, and it's just a step from there to caring enough to kill him.'

'Well then the inspector's a fool,' I said.

'You didn't see her, Dandy,' Alec said. 'She was very angry. She shied a paper-punching machine at one of the sergeants. Missed, thankfully. And then there was the lipstick.'

'But she kept one in her drawer; she admitted as much,' I said. 'Anyone could have taken it out and written on the glass with it.'

'But she had it on her hands,' Alec said. 'Smears of it all over her hands.'

'I'm sure she did!' I said. 'If she had managed to see that note on her glass and *not* clap her hands to her face in

70

horror then I might be willing to think she's a cold-blooded killer.'

'Fair point,' Alec said.

'Although,' I went on, 'one would think a woman who wore red lipstick would be well-drilled in the habit of not touching it.'

'And a woman who wore red lipstick would also be able to put it on herself without a lot of mess and wiping up,' Alec said. At my look, he added, 'There's a wastebasket in that cloakroom that had various bits of . . . well, paper, you know . . . all covered in more of the red muck.'

'Really?' I said, turning to look at the closed cloakroom door. 'Well, well. I'd have thought lavatory paper would hold prints quite nicely, wouldn't you? Have the police taken it all away for testing?'

'Every last scrap,' Alec said. 'If they find fingerprints and they're not Miss Bissett's she might be in luck. Mind you, what self-respecting crook these days doesn't know to wear gloves when he's out writing odd notes on ladies' glasses?' He was going to say more but stopped, for we both heard a noise, growing louder, a kind of hammering and a buffeting along with it. In a moment we each realised that it was the sound of feet on the stairs as someone charged up towards us. We only just had time to brace ourselves before Johnny Doig came bursting in at the door.

'Is it true?' he said. He was breathing raggedly and his face shone with sweat. 'We stopped for tea and Mrs Miller—'

'Yes, it's true,' I said. 'Miss Bissett has gone with the police to answer questions about the professor.'

'Mrs Miller – the old ghoul – said she was handcuffed.'

'Well, yes,' Alec said. 'She was rather upset and started to get boisterous.'

'And I heard from the tea lady!' Johnny Doig was barging about the room, searching for something. He found it in the bottom of a cabinet: a bottle of whisky, three-quarters full.

He drew a deep breath as he straightened. 'Boisterous!' he said and made a harsh sound close to a laugh. 'I can believe it.'

'But still thinking straight,' I added. 'It was your cousin who asked that you be left in peace to finish printing the magazine.'

Now Johnny Doig really did laugh. 'I can believe that too.'

'She won't be held,' Alec said. 'There's only the merest wisp of circumstantial evidence against her.'

Doig slopped a goodly measure of whisky into a nearby teacup and, calming a little, looked at Alec and then at me. 'What are you doing about it?' he said. 'Anything?'

'The very best thing we could do,' Alec assured him. 'We are going to find out who else might have done it and trail his scent past the policemen's noses. We've found in the past that's the best way to distract them from a suspect, haven't we Dan? Certainly there's no point arguing. Once they've got an idea in their head they do grow enamoured of it, and pretty quickly.'

'They didn't give a fig for the man with the florist's paper, by the way,' I said. 'I told quite a clever constable the whole tale and it merely annoyed him.'

'But she can't just languish in a jail cell while you rustle up distractions,' Doig said. He went to take a second swig from the teacup but appeared to realise, looking down into it, that he was downing whisky at ten o'clock on a Tuesday morning. He shuddered and set it aside.

'Might Miss Bissett have rung up her lawyer?' I asked. 'If you know the name of the most likely firm, you could check.'

'It's been a lot of years since the Doigs and Bissetts had tame solicitors to ring up,' the man said. 'I don't think you quite understand the sort of budgets we've been running on recently.'

'The pals and old-timers, quite,' I said. 'But don't tell me none of those artistic girls has a brother in the law. Surely.'

He nodded and then tilted his chin and half closed his eyes. 'They're on the cover,' he said. 'I can hear it. Seven coloured inks and glossy stock. I better get back down there.'

And he was gone.

'Talk about the princess and the pea,' Alec said. 'Can you believe he could hear the difference between a page of print and a picture going through the press, three flights up?'

But I was barely listening. 'Where would a Punch and Judy man rest his head?' I said. 'Theatrical digs? Men's hostel? Room above a pub? He's been in town for a few days. He must have been staying somewhere.'

'Not a hostel,' Alec said. 'Where would he put his tent and his case of puppets?'

'Perhaps he had a van,' I said. 'Or a cart,' I added, when Alec looked askance at the notion of a wandering puppeteer running a motorvan. 'And slept underneath it. Or under canvas.'

'Would Grant know?' Alec said.

'Oh no doubt. And she'll be thrilled to tell us. I wonder if I'll be able to make this contraption connect me to the outside world. Unless you'd like to try.'

Alec was filling his pipe. He might be an unusual man but he was still a man and grappling with a strange telephone while I watched him was beyond his patience to endure.

Chapter 8

Grant, for once in her bumptious life, was stumped. I tried not to enjoy it too much, or at least too obviously.

'I couldn't say, madam,' was all she came up with after a long pause, during which her frantic thoughts came clearly down the line from Gilverton. 'If he was attached to any sort of circus or fair, that would be one thing. Even if he was at the seaside. Because they have huts, for the men who do the donkey rides. I think. If he was a ventriloquist, of course, it would be theatrical lodgings. I had a bad scare from a ventriloquist in digs in Paisley when I was a child. They never are content to leave it on the stage. Unprofessional.'

It was, I knew, the harshest criticism of any act.

'But as things stand?' I asked.

Grant repeated herself: 'I couldn't say.'

Once I had rung off, Alec and I regarded one another a while. He spoke first. 'Must we wait then?' he said. 'Must we simply wait until the police find out who the chap was or discover him under a desk at Doig's? Go home and read it in the papers over breakfast?'

'Papers!' I said. 'Alec, you are a genius. There might have been something in the paper announcing his show, wouldn't you think? If not signs pasted up on lamp posts. We could at least get his name.'

'Worth a try,' said Alec, knocking out his pipe and standing. He loves a visit to a public library more than almost any other act of detecting. He had forgotten all about the cherry loaf and the tea trolley with the prospect of a reference reading room in store.

Scotland is hopeless at cottages and not much better at whole villages, being a stranger to duckponds and pretty churches. But banks, libraries and parish schools are something of a speciality, for these are at their best when worked up along austere lines, and austerity is Scotland's watchword, whether in a building fashioned from large lumps of grey stone, or a landscape fashioned from even larger lumps of grey stone, with cold water in the valleys and funereal pines along the roadsides. All that said, Dundee's reference library was something else again: an enormous block of decorated stone, although rather more ecclesiastical-looking than municipal. Still it was impressive and since it sat on one side of an expansive square, one could easily step back far enough to be impressed.

Commanding from without, it was revealed upon on entering to be staggering within. The foyer had a vaulted ceiling with stone ribs held up by pink marble pillars and the reference room itself, when we were directed upstairs and through a pair of red velvet curtains, was a veritable cathedral, with a dazzlingly high barrel ceiling and stained glass everywhere.

'Where would we find yesterday's papers?' I asked the uniformed chap watching over it all from his high desk. He sucked his breath in over his bottom teeth and shook his head.

'Today's papers are in the periodicals reading section,' he said. 'A week and older are back from the bindery and shelved forever more. But yesterday's? Tricky.'

Alec put a hand inside his coat, feeling for his wallet, but the man's haughty stare stopped him. Library janitors, the look said, were not waiters or barmen, to be sweetened with a tip. Library janitors were as one with the careful archivists who served the books and journals of this august place, protecting them from marauders like us.

'Thank you,' I said. 'And where might the reading section be?'

'*Periodicals* reading section,' the man corrected. 'We have several.' He waited in vain for sounds of admiration and then waved an arm at a distant counter.

'You never know,' I said to Alec as we proceeded towards it. 'Yesterday was a holiday. Perhaps they're behindhand. Or perhaps the professor meant to stay all week and next week so his notice will be in today's paper too.'

We had to wait our turn for that morning's *Courier & Advertiser*. A painfully respectable old gentleman was subjecting it to close scrutiny, sucking peppermint after peppermint as he read every word on every page. Even when, after twenty minutes, he drifted off into what I considered a terribly early nap, he slept with one hand spread proprietorially over the page he had been reading and left no possibility of anyone taking his prize unless by the kind of tablecloth trick that would surely awaken him.

I went up to the desk and whispered an enquiry in the ear of the librarian who was at work there, cutting out press clippings from a *Scotsman* with a fearsome set of brass shears.

'What?' she said, not whispering at all. 'Take material away from a patron who's consulting it? On what grounds?' She had pale blue eyes, rather protruding and excellent for glares.

'On the grounds that he's not consulting it,' I said.

'Ssh,' she said. Clearly the relaxation of the whispering rule was for staff alone.

'On the grounds that he's hogging it,' I said, lowering my voice. 'He's fast asleep and practically drooling on it.'

The protruding eyes bulged at that and the librarian rose from her seat to see this enormity. She still held the shears, giving her movement a threatening air. When she was upright, she blinked and let herself fall back into her chair again. 'It's the colonel!' she said. 'Drooling indeed. Hogging! The colonel reads the *Courier* every morning, very thoroughly.'

'And thinks over the implications of the day's news with his eyes closed,' I said. 'I see.' The librarian was not used to impertinence, I surmised. Certainly she did not seem to have identified my words as such. She inclined her head and, in doing so, caught sight of the confetti of press clippings strewn over her desk. She returned her attentions to them.

'No good,' I said to Alec, who was poised at the next table to the colonel, like a cat at a mouse hole. 'He's a favoured patron and not to be trifled with. She's got a handy-looking pair of scissors she doesn't mind brandishing so I'm not inclined to argue with her.'

'Scissors?' Alec echoed. 'One would think scissors of all things would be banished from a library like matches from a firework factory.'

'She's doing the clippings,' I said. 'Your favourite reading matter doesn't spring fully formed from a deity's fingertips, you know.' He would not mind the teasing, or if he did there was no help for it. For Alec's admiration of those squat volumes of library press clippings was amusing in its fervour. He did not look annoyed at my words. If anything, he looked smug. I realised the source of the smugness one heartbeat too late to undercut it with any triumph of my own.

'Press clippings?' Alec said. 'The means by which the archivists of Dundee life gather, organise and preserve the notable events of this fair city? Such as the travelling entertainers who're passing through perhaps?'

'I doubt it,' I said, but Alec was already striding towards the elevated sarcophagus running up the middle of the periodicals room, that oracle of minutiae, that pinnacle of subdivision: the card catalogue.

'Puppets, puppets, puppets,' he said, selecting one of the little leather index books that huddled on a shelf below the wooden bulk of the catalogue itself. 'Here we go. Puppets: finger, marionettes, shadow— Oh!'

'Nothing between M and S?' I said.

Alec turned a page. 'Ah,' he said. 'A separate section, owing to the multitude of them. Punch and Judy, classmark PN 1979: sub-entries for Christmas, fairgrounds, municipal parks . . .' He stopped, staring down at the page.

'Well done,' I said. 'I've already blotted my copy book with the keeper of the shears. If one of us is going to ask to see what she's clipping out of yesterday's *Courier*, it should probably be you.'

'What? Oh yes,' Alec said. 'Sorry. I was distracted by the next sub-entry under Punch and Judy. It says "murder", Dandy.'

'That was quick.'

'Fifty years ago. Punch and Judy, murder, Dudhope Park, August 1887.'

'Bound to be a coincidence,' I said, but I had had to swallow hard before speaking. 'Odd, mind you. Let's get the volume and see.'

The 'Crime: city: 1887: Jun–Dec' volume of clippings was not, unsurprisingly, near at hand and Alec and I had plenty time to stare at the colonel during the second half of his extensive nap, willing him either to wake or to move his hand off the sheet of newspaper it was anchoring. It was a dead heat, in the end. The uniformed library porter brought the volume just as the old gentleman snorted, roused and smacked his lips, blinking awake and refastening his attention on the national news as though he had merely glanced away to look at the clock or greet an acquaintance.

The porter set the volume down on the table where we waited and produced a snowy white dusting cloth, with which he wiped the front and back cover and the page edges too before releasing the book into Alec's stewardship.

'Very good of you,' Alec said. 'It was pretty mucky.'

'And careless users have been known to spread dirt onto the pages themselves,' the porter said. Once again, it seemed that the collection was king and those who would use it and soil it were the danger.

The story was as measured and dry as were all stories in respectable Scottish newspapers of half a century previously:

Yesterday, in Dudhope Park, a visitor to the city met with an untimely end, by violent means of person unknown. A popular summer fixture along the Tay and down into Fife, Albert 'The Professor' Mackie, was done to death in his Punch and Judy stand, while his audience awaited the spectacle of the puppet show. Witnesses were unable to furnish the constabulary with any description. The police investigation continues.

The following day, an even shorter article had been published:

Police remain baffled by the murder of Albert 'The Professor' Mackie, who was killed on Monday afternoon in Dudhope Park. Anyone with information is urgently requested to report to the constabulary or to the editors of this publication.

Two days after that came a piece so tiny it was a waste of a whole page of the thick white press-volume paper to which it was pasted:

The funeral has taken place of Albert Mackie. The inquiry into his murder remains open.

'And that's that,' Alec said. 'The next piece is about a robbery in a smithy in Lochee. What do you make of it, Dan? It can't be nothing, but what is it?'

'An oddity,' I said. 'An unsettling oddity.'

We stared at one another for a moment, each wondering if the other was going to say more.

'I'm glad to hear you're unsettled too,' Alec plumped for in the end. 'My gooseflesh has got the willies. But it gives us an "in".'

'Does it?'

'Two ins, actually. Possibly three. For a start, we can go to the police station and make sure someone there knows about this earlier case. Fifty years, after all. There won't be anyone who remembers from his experience. And we can surely strike up a conversation with the bulldog on the strength of it.' He jerked his head in the direction of the librarian at the desk.

It was not a kind description of her unfortunate countenance, but if she had not had the attitude to match I daresay it would never have occurred to him, for he is not one of these men who routinely rank women according to their looks and disparage those at the bottom of the league table.

'And the third?' I said.

'It's a faint hope,' said Alec, 'but I was wondering if Punch and Judy tends to be a family business. All that equipment and tradition, you know. Because if so, maybe our professor is a Mr Mackie too.'

It was useful practice for the bobbies, I suppose, but Alec got the shortest of shrifts with the librarian. He sauntered up and leaned against her counter as though it were a gate and she were a milkmaid. 'Was there anything in the late edition about the Punch and Judy man?' he said. 'It's a strange coincidence, isn't it?'

'Are you addressing me?' the librarian said, turning the fullness of her round blue gaze upon him.

'We were just looking at the report from fifty years ago,' Alec said. 'About *that* murder. And, I suppose, it got us thinking. What do you do if a story begins somewhere – entertainments, say – and ends up somewhere else entirely? Crime, for instance. Do you have a spare? Or do you cross-reference? There must be endless calls for fine judgement in your game.'

'My game,' said the librarian, in withering tones, 'is a matter of adherence to principle and meticulous execution of very clear rules. Disturbances are a constant irritation, mind you.'

I could not help a snort escaping me. Alec's mouth dropped open.

'Look,' he said. 'I'll talk plainly. Has a notice about the Punch and Judy show in Dudhope Park come under your blades in the last few days? And, if so, was the man's name given?'

'And I shall talk just as plainly back,' the librarian said. 'We offer *today's* newspapers as a benefit to the people of Dundee who wish to read *today's* newspapers. My job would be easier and more pleasant if countless strangers had not read them, marked them, and even torn items out of them before they came to me on the following day. But I make no complaint about the vicissitudes of my job. However, it is not my job to offer corrective aid to those individuals who neglected to read the day's papers when they were freely available. If you desire yesterday's newspaper today, I can only direct you to the fiction lending library and the works of Mr H.G. Wells.'

I gave a shout of laughter and even Alec found more delight in the quip than insult in the scolding. He put his hat on, expressly to tip it at the woman, and then left, arm in arm with me, his eyes dancing.

'I don't care if she's said it a thousand times before,' he said, as we passed back through the velvet curtains. 'Her delivery was perfect. She should be on the stage.'

'She'd never leave the colonel,' I said. 'Slow down, Alec, before you tumble. Where are you going in such a tearing rush anyway? The police station surely doesn't shut for luncheon.'

'The police can wait,' Alec said. 'That woman gave me an idea and if we don't skedaddle, "luncheon" will overtake us.'

We crossed the foyer, and passed out through the door into the bustle of the square again. 'What idea?' I said.

81

'I'll give a clue,' Alec said. 'Yesterday's news.'

'You're headed to D.C. Thomson's to quiz the layout editors who blocked the page of notices?' It was remarkable how an hour or two in Doig's had put the jargon in my mouth. 'It's not a bad idea. We should speak to them anyway, after all. About the puppets. Where are they? Do you know?'

'They don't read it,' Alec said. 'It's back to front and inside out when they do what they do. And even after they've done it they don't read the meaning. They only look at the letters and spacing. That's how the howlers get through with such gratifying regularity.'

'Well, what then?' I said.

'Mind you, they don't know that we know that,' Alec said. 'We could certainly pull off an act of ignorance. And it would give us a reason to go and pester them. I've no idea where they are, by the way.'

'Yes, but what was your idea?' I said.

'Oh come on, Dan,' said Alec. 'What do people say about yesterday's news? Or rather what do people say about where today's news will be tomorrow.'

'Lining budgie cages?' I said. 'Are we headed for a pet shop?'

'Close,' said Alec. He put his chin in the air and took a deep sniff. 'I can't discern one right now, but surely there must be one. And it's just gone noon. We better get our skates on.'

I followed him, still puzzled, down the broad expanse of Reform Street, as he muttered, 'This is all a bit too swanky' and sniffed once or twice more. He gave one final sniff, smiled, and sped up as we reached the Overgate again. Light dawned upon me as we arrived on the doorstep of Delnevo's Fish Restaurant, just as a black-haired man in a white apron turned the sign from closed to open.

'Ah,' I said. 'What a brainwave.'

We were Delnevo's first customers of the day and, I daresay, best customers of the week. Alec, of course, purchased a full complement of fried fish and chips. I asked for a fillet of fish, planning to knock the batter off it before eating. But it was our side order that lifted us out of the realms of the everyday. Having ascertained that Mrs Delnevo wrapped her husband's fragrant, piping efforts in the *Courier & Advertiser* of the previous morning, Alec offered her two shillings for the pile she had waiting on the counter if she would let him replace it with today's paper instead.

'I'll help you rip them up into separate pages,' he said. 'I wouldn't want you to get behindhand.'

'For two and six I'll rip it up myself,' Mrs Delnevo assured him, sound businesswoman to her core and an asset to her husband, who stood beaming behind her.

Chapter 9

I am glad every day that the strictures of Victorian life have loosened the deadly grip they had on me and my chums when we were girls and young women. Life these days is one long endless riverboat cruise by day and a longer, even more endless cocktail party in the evening. I would not have it any other way. There are, however, limits to the bacchanalia, and eating fried fish in the street was beyond those limits by a mile.

Alec disagreed. 'It's piping hot and crisp,' he said. 'If we don't eat it now, it'll be inedible. What a waste of food, Dandy.'

That was a low blow. Alec had heard enough of Nanny Palmer's edicts, remembered from my childhood and shared liberally, to know that 'wasting food' was just about the only concern that could hope to compete with 'eating in the street like an urchin'.

'Let's compromise,' I said, 'and take them to a park bench. I'm sure I've eaten an ice on a bench before now. This isn't so very different, really.'

As to the park: where else but Dudhope? It was the nearest of any size anyway and the only one where trees and grass were more to the fore than soot and the sound of motorvans. Alec was still displeased. Fearing the collapse of the batter and the softening of the chips to gelid lumps, he retrieved his Daimler from outside Doig's and drove at a fearsome pace. When we arrived, he plumped down onto the nearest bench inside the gates and I saw steam rising from the parcel as he opened it.

'Poetry,' he said. 'I do love the haddock and chips of Scotland, Dan.'

'I know,' I told him. 'You've mentioned it once or twice before now. Might I borrow your handkerchief for a napkin, please?'

Alec gave a glance at the stack of newspapers he had laid on the bench beside him but did not make the suggestion aloud. Instead, he shook out his hanky and passed it over.

'I should have bought a bottle of ginger beer,' was the next thing he said, after wolfing down half the contents of his package. 'Dandy, if you've finished picking that poor fillet to death, you can choose between tracking down an ice cream seller and starting in on the newspaper sheets.'

Since I had consumed less salt than Alec and was not in a state of thirst that demanded instant relief, I wiped my hands on his handkerchief, screwed up the discarded batter into a parcel I hoped would outwit the gathering pigeons and began studying the many, many pages of the previous day's local rag.

If I had been looking for international, national, local or parish news, or even for sporting commentary and the starters at Ayr, I should have known where to find them. Notices for puppet shows, however, struck me as the sort of little titbit that might be tucked in anywhere, in the fashion of those obscure Bible verses I have never really understood, or those brief advertisements for one-day sales of household linens (if it is not blasphemous to mention these two categories of item in one breath).

There was indeed a Bible verse – 'Oh that you would bless me indeed and enlarge my territory', Chronicles 4:10 – which was certainly obscure enough. There was a sale too, on 'second-best-quality glass cloths 10/- a bundle'. I hoped the bundles were of some considerable size, since the price seemed steep otherwise.

'Are you reading advertisements?' Alec said, for all the

world as though he had not, in the past, been caught up in the telling of a years-old rugby football match when supposed to be searching for reports of crime. I turned the sheet over and scanned the next one. It was the obituary page. At least, it was births, marriages and deaths all together, but the burghers of Dundee seemed to do a lot more dying than anything else, even in August.

'I don't suppose anyone will put in a piece about the professor,' I said.

'Not in the local news of the town where he happened to die,' said Alec. 'I wonder where he came from.'

But I was no longer listening. I had seen something. The mystery of the epidemic of summer deaths had resolved itself upon closer study: these were not all obituaries. Some of them, indeed most of them, were 'In Memoria', recalling obituaries of the same day in years gone by. And there, in the middle of the alphabetical run, was Albert Mackie:

On this day, fifty years ago, by foul means at Dudhope Park, Albert Mackie, a visitor to our fair city. We have not forgotten. 'Their foot shall slide in due time, for the day of their calamity is at hand.'

'Listen to this, Alec,' I said and read it out to him. 'Is that the Bible? It's rather nasty.'

'Gleefully nasty,' Alec said. 'Deuteronomy, I think. One of that lot anyway.'

'Do you think it's worth pursuing?' I asked, leaving aside the question of who, along with Deuteronomy, constituted 'that lot'.

'Telling the police, you mean?' Alec said. 'No. I wouldn't like to see the expression on that inspector's face if we tried. But do I think it's worth finding out, from the paper, who placed the item and then asking what their interest is in a decades-old crime and what they might know about its reprise yesterday? Of course I do.'

'Will the paper tell us?' I said. 'Isn't it confidential?'

'We have connections in the periodicals publishing business in this town, Dandy,' Alec said. 'I rather think Johnny Doig could help us, don't you?'

'"Could", certainly,' I said. '"Would" is another matter.'

'But we've got to try,' said Alec. 'It's too odd to ignore.'

He was right, but just at that moment I found that I *was* ignoring him. My attention had been caught by another individual in the park. Of course, there were a fair few people walking, whether with or without dogs; still more standing in groups chatting and, while it was quieter than it had been on the holiday Monday, the nannies and mothers alone made quite a crowd as their charges ran about like chicks. Perhaps it was the fact that this man stood, still as a marble statue, while the toddlers and children played around him, ignoring them as though they were gnats, while they in their turn ignored him as though he were indeed the statue he so closely resembled. That alone would have made him remarkable but, added to it, I felt sure that he was standing upon the very spot where the Punch and Judy tent had been pitched, and therefore upon the very spot where the professor had died.

'Alec,' I said. 'You've sharp eyes. Is that chap down there crying?'

Alec squinted and then raised his brows and nodded. 'Are you going to see what's wrong with him?' he said. At my look – for I had not missed the easy way the job had fallen to me with no discussion – he added: 'Best for us not go in mob-handed after all. Poor thing. One wouldn't want to embarrass him in his anguish.'

I was already off the bench and squaring my shoulders for the encounter.

The man did not notice me until I cleared my throat, then he swung round to see who was bothering him, his cheeks awash with tears and his eyes brimming with more.

'Are you unwell?' I said. 'Can I be of any help?' He was

an odd-looking fellow. His black hair was long and his bushy black beard met it on either side of his face. Add to this, full dark brows that had not recently, if ever, been trimmed and a black overcoat buttoned to the neck despite the warmth of the day and he cut such a peculiar figure that only the insouciance of the very young, surely, was responsible for the children playing about him and not running back to their nannies for succour.

'I'm fine,' he said. 'I apologise. It's just, you see, that someone has died.' His voice was a low rumble and rather lacking in the resonance that helps one place a stranger, via his vowels.

'Died?' I said. 'Recently?' For his dress suggested adherence to some strict Presbyterian sect, his hair and beard were soundly of the Old Testament and, overall, much about him pointed towards just the sort of man to go quoting Deuteronomy in reference to old forgotten crimes.

'Yesterday,' he said. 'My brother. My poor brother.'

'The—' I said, but stopped. I am sure if one is a Punch and Judy man, the term 'professor' does not strike one as inherently frivolous, but when discussing the death of a sibling it threatened to add a jaunty note I would rather avoid.

'Poor Bert,' the man said, and his voice finally broke. My womanly heart felt for him. My detective's mind wondered what Bert was short for.

'I was here,' I said. 'When it happened. I might be able to make you feel a little better.'

'You?' He stopped and swallowed.

'Yes, actually here,' I said. 'I was in his audience, watching the show. I've come back today to . . . pay respects, in my small way.' I hoped that Alec, behind me on the bench, was not chasing little scraps of batter around the newspaper with a wetted finger the way I had seen him do at times before.

'Thank you,' the man said. 'I didn't care to think of him dying among strangers.' His voice, now that he had said a little more, struck me as educated. Cultured, even. He spoke with a Scots burr, but then a Scots burr reaches much farther up the social scale than a Yorkshire whine or a Cornish chuckle. Even Hugh has something about his Rs, when he is speaking to his gamekeeper.

'I don't know what the police have told you,' I went on. 'I'm assuming you've spoken to the police?'

'They found me last night,' he said. 'Or yesterday evening anyway. They came and told me. Two constables. One too young for such a task but the other very kindly.' I wondered briefly if Constable Adams had been part of the expedition, or if Dundee perhaps had a plurality of kind and sensible bobbies. I hoped so. 'I'm afraid they told me too much for you to make me feel better now, though. They probably told me more than they told you. I know it's been kept out of the papers so far.'

'But really,' I said. 'It wasn't as bad as you're probably imagining.'

'I'm sorry but you are wrong,' said the man. 'I do thank you for your kindness and I don't want to share the details. You would never forget and might not sleep for a week either. Don't make me tell you.'

'I really do know,' I told him. 'The police didn't have to report on it. I saw him, you see. I found him. I know his throat—'

The man held up a shaking hand.

'Sorry,' I said. 'But let me say this: he was working his puppets one minute and, the next, there was stillness. There wasn't a sound. Not a cry. It was the merest moment.'

He said nothing, but gazed searchingly into my eyes, as if wanting to believe me but loath to let himself.

'We thought it was part of the show, at first,' I said. 'Some traditional pause of mysterious origin. It was only after a good long while that we wondered if he'd got distracted. Distracted, mind! We didn't expect any harm at all, even then.

When I and my – well, another person – walked round to the back it was more to complain than anything. And then, of course, there he was. His face was very peaceful. And there was no struggle, for we would have seen it. Through the canvas. Trust me, it was brutal and I feel terribly for you but he did not suffer. You can comfort yourself with that.'

Alec, seeing the interview going smoothly, had lost patience with the role of spectator and was now advancing.

'It is indeed a comfort,' the stranger said. 'And I thank you. I wish the police had told me that yesterday and saved me a wretched night. Oh dear.' He did not appear to have a handkerchief for, as emotion overcame him again, he covered his face with his hand, pressing fingers into one eye socket and thumb into the other as though to pinch his tear ducts closed before they could start up again. Alec stopped walking, but he was not going to escape the awkwardness if I could help it.

'Alec,' I said. 'This gentleman is the brother of the poor chap. Bert, I think you said, sir?'

'Albert. Albert Mackie.' He did not notice the look of dumbfounded bewilderment that passed between us.

'And so you are Mr Mackie also?' Alec said. 'Might I offer you my deepest sympathies then? On your loss.'

'Mr Mackie,' said the man. 'I suppose so.'

It was an odd remark, but I ignored it and pressed on. 'Did the police have any sort of explanation for you, Mr Mackie? Any kind of theory about why your brother was the victim of such a horrid attack?'

'Nothing,' he said. 'No answers. Only questions. And I had no answers to any of *them*. Oh dear.' He swayed and put a foot out to the side to steady himself. Alec stepped forward and cupped his hand under one of the man's elbows.

'Come, come,' he said. 'Let us buy you a cup of tea, Mr Mackie. Or perhaps we could take you home? Unless you came in your own car?'

'I don't run a motorcar,' the man said. 'I caught the train. From St Andrews. But I've a lot to do before I catch it home again. I don't even know where poor Bert was staying. I need to find his lodgings and . . . Well, to be frank, I don't know. But there must be things to do. There must be many things to be done and arrangements to be made. Wouldn't you think so?'

Alec looked at his feet. This, like every ticklish task, was evidently to be left up to me.

'Perhaps not,' I said. 'The police will be in charge for a while. Until the villain is arrested. And no doubt they'll be searching for your brother's lodgings. They've probably already found them, in fact. I mean, how did they find you?'

'Oh, that's easy,' said Mr Mackie. 'My address and telephone number were in his wallet. He always kept them there in case of mishap. In case of trouble.'

'He expected trouble?' said Alec.

Mr Mackie lifted his head and looked across the park at the distant view of the city and river, as though memories had overtaken him. 'He led a very different life from mine, Mr and Mrs . . .?'

'Gilver,' I said. 'And Osborne.'

I was sure I saw a flash of recognition in the dark and troubled eyes, but he said nothing about us. Instead he carried on as before. 'A very different life. A Punch and Judy show! I had become used to the idea after all these years but still it puzzled me.'

'So . . .' Alec began, then stopped. I knew what he was trying to ask. He wanted to determine whether the one brother had fallen below his station, or the other risen. There was no way to ask it politely, though, and he said no more.

'And he drank,' the poor man was now forced to say. 'He kept my telephone number about him in case of *that* kind of mishap. Not this. Nothing like this. Oh dear. Poor Bert. Thank God our mother is gone.'

It was a pitiful sort of bright side, but oddly enough instead of the thought bringing on fresh bouts of weeping, it seemed to serve as a finial. Mr Mackie shook his head, sniffed and turned a rather more stoic-looking face towards us. 'Right,' he said. 'The police have got the rig at the station, but ordinarily Bert would store it in the nearest theatre. The typical doorman will find an odd corner to stash almost anything, for a consideration. Or so Bert used to tell me.'

'*Is* there a theatre here in Dundee?' said Alec. 'The doorman might know his address, if so.'

'Her Majesty's,' Mr Mackie said.

'Can we walk with you?' said Alec.

'You are most kind,' said the man. 'However, if I might trespass on that kindness, and since we were lucky enough to meet, what I'd really like would be for you to go to the stage door in my place.'

Alec did his best not to look astonished. 'Certainly,' he said. 'Very happy to help you discover your brother's address.'

'Of course, I'll pay you for your time,' Mr Mackie said. 'First to find out his address and then to find out what happened to him. You see, I don't think the police will bother too much about a Punch and Judy man, do you? But you two, Gilver and Osborne, are renowned.'

'You've heard of us?' I said.

'In St Andrews? Certainly. I'm not a rich man, but I can afford to do right by poor Bert.'

'No need,' I began. Mr Mackie attempted to talk over me, but I held up a hand. 'Or rather, I should say, no possibility. We are already employed in the case. There was a question to be answered before yesterday's tragic events. And the lady who engaged our services is closely, deeply concerned in the murder.'

'Dandy,' Alec said, with a warning note in his voice. 'Have a care.'

'Yes, you're quite right,' I said. 'Mr Mackie, to speak plainly:

our client Miss Bissett is currently under arrest for your brother's murder. She didn't do it. It's absurd. Therefore we are determined to clear her name. So, we're going to solve your brother's murder as a matter of course, at no cost to you.'

Nine men out of ten would have had to have the matter explained in more detail and many repetitions, but Mr Mackie caught the thing at once. He blinked a couple of times and then nodded.

'Miss Bissett?' he said. 'I take it she and my brother were close friends? There's always a girl. In every town. Sometimes for the whole summer if he gets – got, oh dear – an engagement on a pier, but even by the week, I'm afraid to say there's always a girl. Tell me though, can this poor Miss Bissett afford to have you help her? Now that it's so much more than a breach of promise or whatever she was going after him for. She wouldn't be the first, you know.'

It was my turn to look at my feet. I thought it high time Alec did some of the unsettling bits. 'You mistake the matter, sir,' he said. 'Gilver and Osborne don't do that sort of work. And besides, Miss Bissett didn't know your brother at all. She was the owner of the copyright he was infringing. She's a publisher.'

'A publisher?' he said. 'Was she planning to put out a script? Don't tell me someone finally agreed to his terms?'

Alec and I must have looked as dumb as oxen. Mr Mackie carried on. 'Bert was quite impassioned about his show, you see. He stuck to the original words, and eschewed the modern additions. Not to mention the modern *omissions*. It's quite savage, in its old form, the humble, harmless Punch and Judy show.'

I had seen the beginning of the thing and could only agree, although Alec looked puzzled at the turn the talk had taken. 'How interesting that you should say that, Mr Mackie,' I said. 'I wonder if the recent developments are connected to your brother's death somehow. Because he was not by any means sticking to the pure form of the puppet show. He had added new characters for local interest, after the fashion of a pantomime. We didn't know it was a remarkable innovation but from what you're saying now, it warrants some attention.'

'It certainly does,' the man said. 'How very strange.'

'There are a number of strange elements to the matter,' Alec said.

'Oh?' said Mackie.

'Yes,' I agreed. 'It's not the first murder in the park, you see. There was another.'

'No!' he breathed. 'A mad man? A lunatic on a rampage? And poor Bert was caught up in his spree?'

I opened my mouth to set him right but he looked simultaneously so shocked and so relieved I had not the heart.

'But first things first,' Mackie said. 'Do you agree? I am no detective, but I thought if I – grieving brother – were to go to the stage door and ask questions about Bert's life, compassion or at least its everyday cousin convention would prevent the doorman from saying much at all. If you go, on the other hand, you might learn all manner of useful things. I do hope it's not a conflict of interest with your obligations to this Miss . . .?'

'Bisset,' I said. 'No, I hardly think so. Your concern, Miss Bissett's concern and ours would appear to be marching in step. So far anyway.'

We agreed to make for Her Majesty's Theatre together and drop Mr Mackie off at a convenient teashop if one presented itself along the way. Alec had suggested a public house, for it was just gone opening time, but the man looked shocked at the suggestion. Accordingly, we settled him at a corner table in the Sugarlump Café and, after some swift refreshment of our own, left him there with a word to the waitress that he was recently bereaved and she should take extra-special care of him until our return, with sweet milky tea and whatnot to soothe him.

'Thank you,' he said, as we were about to leave. 'I do thank you. I admit I feel a little drained by this day, after a sleepless night. I do hope I can get myself home tonight. I fear I might need to take a room and stay over until tomorrow.'

'If we find your brother's lodgings perhaps you could rest there,' I suggested.

Mr Mackie blinked again. I was beginning to understand that it was the outward sign of furious cogitation. 'I would be very surprised if poor Bert's digs would be suitable,' he said. 'I should far rather get back to my own rooms tonight. I shall no doubt miss dinner and have to give my apologies, but I'm committed to a reading in chapel in the morning, and I think it would be a comfort to give it. In memory of my poor brother.'

'Dinner?' I said. 'Chapel? Are you a schoolmaster, Mr Mackie?'

'A schoolmaster!' He looked amused for the first time since we had met him. 'I shall tell my cleaning lady you said so. She is forever chiding me that I am not dressed smartly enough. She irons and starches and mends endlessly, but she accuses me of being able to outwit any starch yet invented.' He had taken off the long black overcoat when he sat down at the café table, and I was inclined to agree with whoever this cleaning lady was, for his collar was frayed, his tie stained, and his coat bagged at the elbow.

'No,' he went on, with a bark of a laugh. 'My rooms are at the university. I, like my brother, am a professor.'

Chapter 10

'Talk about life's rich tapestry,' Alec said minutes later, as we made our way through the bustling streets towards the stage door at Her Majesty's. 'The Schwarzmann Professor of Psychology and a travelling puppeteer. I wonder how close to St Andrews the professor – I mean our professor, Professor Bert – used to go? That would cause a bit of a stir in the senior common room, would it not?'

'*I* wonder which one of them has travelled,' I said. 'Has the psychologist risen from humble beginnings or has "poor Bert" sunk and disgraced the name of Mackie?'

Dundee is not a large town, though. At least, its centre is compact, although like everywhere else it is spreading and spreading out through the countryside, engulfing farms and villages in an endless march of neat bungalows and parades of smart shops. Hugh has been known to shoot hunted looks out of the side motorcar windows as we drive through the outskirts of Perth, as though he fears that bunga-lows will soon be pressed against the walls of Gilverton. I could reassure him that unless building picks up a lively pace he will be dead long before the smoke from bungalow chim-neys can be seen from our escarpments, but one does not like to be unkind.

Given the small size of Dundee's civic centre, then, the drive to Her Majesty's Theatre did not leave much time to ponder the social standing of the Mackie family. In a very few more minutes, Alec and I were rumbling over the tram-lines in front of it and then over some very uneven cobbles in a narrow side street towards its stage door. This sat in marked contrast to the splendour of the public entrance. There, at the front of the building, were stone pediments, glittering brass, dazzling panes and polished wood. Here there was a battered door with paint only around the top edge, all the rest having been scuffed off by boots along the bottom, scraped off by bunches of keys at the lock or chipped away everywhere else as stagehands shouldered loads of planks and poles in and out.

There was a sign, not even so much as six inches square, proclaiming that this indeed was the stage door but that only theatre employees and invited guests were ever to be admitted. Above the sign, a gas lamp clung to the bricks at a sharp angle, looking like the best possible advertisement for electric street lighting. I eyed it warily as Alec banged hard on the wood below. One used to light gas lamps, lanterns and candles even, without a moment's thought, happily traipsing through the house with one's nightgown cuff an inch from the flame. We have grown soft in the luxury of recent years, I think, for this lamp, with its rusty screws and its threadbare mantel, struck me as a foolish hazard so close – attached, indeed! – to such a venerable old building.

But the door was opening and I fastened my attention on what it would reveal.

'Good morning,' Alec began, long before the person inside revealed himself. Herself, as it transpired.

'I'm not buying,' the door keeper said. She was a monumental figure, at least six feet tall and broad through the middle, although her shoulders sloped with age. Her legs, sticking out under a shapeless skirt, were swollen and visibly red even through thick stockings, and her feet were jammed into a pair of broken-down tartan carpet slippers, one of which had lost its pom-pom. All in all, she looked as though she were slowly melting and would one day soon become a puddle of herself around her former feet.

'I'm not—' Alec began.

'Whatever it is,' the woman went on, 'I've never bought so much as a clothes peg at this door. And I've never passed on a message to a chorus girl either, so you can put that right out of your nasty mind. No more have I ever spoken to the producer to get an audition for the likes of you, not even for ready money.' She fixed Alec with a stare. Above the collapse of her body, her head was still quite impressive. Her hair was rusty red, perhaps a choice informed by the reality of her youth, but quite outlandish these days as she passed into old age. Her brows were drawn on in haughty arcs of the same shade. She had large gold hoops hanging from her ears, and years of such things had dragged her lobes down until they resembled elephant ears. For all that, her cheekbones were sharp and expertly painted and her mouth, currently pursed in disapproval, had a bow above and a warm curve below. Her eyes flashed at Alec and their light managed to shine beyond the forest of blacked lashes and the ring of kohl pencil. When she narrowed them again, they were utterly invisible in the darkness.

'Well, thank you for the reassessment,' Alec said. 'From peg seller, to swain to budding thespian. Have you ever waved in a backer? What makes you think I'm not here to invest in a show?'

'Radio,' the woman said. 'Nobody with an ounce of sense is sticking his bob on variety these days, are they? You'd be putting your purse on a radio show. Or the talkies.'

'Thank you,' Alec said. 'An ounce of sense? Thank you kindly.'

The woman made a gesture so close to spitting as to make no odds and gave up on Alec, turning instead to me.

'Is it yours?' she said. 'Did you marry it? *There's* a slip I've never made anyway.'

I could not help but laugh. 'I did not marry it,' I said. 'Although I've got a specimen at home I'd like to hear your review of. I went into business with it, actually. We are private detectives. And we're currently looking for the last known whereabouts of a chap called Albert Mackie. We were told you might be able to help.'

'The professor?' the woman said. 'Yesterday, I'd have said one thing. For he's been leaving his rig at the back here for an obligement. Been doing the same every time he passed through Dundee for donkeys. Set your clock by him. But he's skipped town early this summer. He never turned up last night.'

'He didn't "skip town",' Alec said. 'He—'

Once again, and thankfully this time, she interrupted him. 'Oho!' she said. 'Had a better offer, has he? Well, there's gratitude for you. Years on end of me bending rules and giving him room for his messes and he's off to greener pastures, is he?'

She was angry, but her ire did not quite manage to cover the stew of other feelings. She was also hurt. Her red mouth trembled and she sniffed richly.

'Can we come inside?' I asked her. I had never seen anyone wear more black muck round her eyes. If she started crying through it, her poor face would be a wreckage and I hated to cause any woman – much less a fellow professional – to be brought that low in public.

She must have caught something in my tone, if not my words. For she grew still and watchful, a hare sitting up, twitching.

'What's your name?' I asked. 'Do you have a cubbyhole or a little place we can sit and chat?'

'Moll,' the woman said. 'They call me Her Majesty and they think it's funny, but my name's Moll. Come in.'

Stepping inside the back of a theatre was not something I had ever done before that moment. The state of the door should perhaps have prepared me, but I was not ready for the air that hit me like a gust from a bonfire when the wind changes. It was thick with myriad unfamiliar scents, all roiling together to form a cocktail that made me clear my throat and put a hand to my mouth to smother the cough I felt sure was coming. There was oil in the smell, lamp oil and motor oil, but the miasma held many other perfumes besides. At a guess, I would have said hair tonic and face paint, that sweet combination of powder and grease that emanates from Grant's box of tricks, only multiplied a hundredfold. Thick and many-layered as this perfume was, however, it did not hide the rank odour of hot human bodies, working hard and wearing the same costumes night after night. It was as though a vast cauldron of onions had been boiled up nearby and the mess left to rot there. Unspeakable. I knew Alec thought so too, because as we waited for Moll to unlock a nearby door I could hear him light a cigarette. He prefers his pipe, but it takes a while and clearly this was something of an emergency. I toughed it out and tried to distract myself by identifying the remaining notes that befouled Her Majesty's backstage air. There was dust, and damp, and the stink of sheer age. Some of the cellars at Gilverton have it clinging about them no matter how often the maids used to turn them out and air them. These days, when Becky cannot prevail upon the dailies to enter the cellars, much less scrub them, I daresay bits of my house smelled exactly like the room Moll was currently entering.

'Here's my little bolt-hole,' she said, revealing a tiny chamber, not eight feet square with a high barred window. There was a sofa and a chair squashed in somehow, and a makeshift table formed from a heap of playbills, crumbling at the edges and adding yet one more note the air did not need. Upon the table, a bottle of whisky and an electric kettle shared the space, a clutch of teacups evidently serving for either refreshment as required.

Moll went to what was obviously her usual spot – the far end of the sofa, worn into a hollow by years of her residence

– and let herself fall down. She then embarked upon the rest of her habitual movements, making to swing her swollen legs up onto the empty seat beside her, then remembered about the two of us and kept them on the floor. I sat hurriedly in the armchair, in preference to Moll's usual footstool. Alec gave me a look that told me the choice was not lost on him and sat gingerly, taking his hat off and looking around for an ashtray.

'Have you read the papers this morning, Moll?' I said.

'I have,' she said. 'And I've listened to the BBC too. Radio again. It'll kill the newspapers too in the end, you just see if it doesn't. Same as variety.' Then she seemed to realise that it was an oddity for me to ask and thought to say, 'Why?'

'Did you remark a story about an attack in Dudhope Park yesterday?' I said.

'He's never!' Moll said. 'Oh, the stupid fool that he is. He's never gone fighting and done someone a mischief, has he? Oh, look at your face! He has. And so he's been a night in the jail, has he? And me worried sick? And never thought to send a word to tell me where he was and let me rest easy. That's it. He's gone too far this time.'

'So Mr Mackie has been a fighting sort of a man before now?' Alec said, picking his words carefully. 'One doesn't think of it, somehow. A children's entertainer.'

'Best not let him hear that,' Moll said. 'Children's entertainer indeed. He'd swing for you and no mistake. If you've got an hour to spare ask him about the origins of his precious Punch and Judy, but only with an hour to spare, mind you. Not with a train to catch.' She glared at Alec, the proxy for her infuriating Bert, then she shook her head. 'Pour me a wee pour, would you?' she said. 'I'll just have a sip and then I'll get down to the jail and see what's what. Oh, that man!'

Alec leaned forward with alacrity and uncorked the bottle, selecting the daintiest and cleanest-looking teacup to provide Moll with her pick-me-up. He seemed to think this gesture would do for his part in the scene, leaving the rest – the breaking of the news – to me.

Never one to shirk, I cleared my throat and embarked upon it. 'Moll, you must prepare yourself for a shock, I'm afraid. Mr Mackie has indeed been caught up in a fight of some kind – perhaps better to say he was the victim of assault. He has been killed, my dear. I'm so sorry.'

Moll's blacked eyes searched my face as though she hoped to find, somewhere in my words or my look, a different interpretation of the bald fact I had forced her to hear. After a moment, she gave it up. Her eyelids dropped and she slumped back against the sofa cushions, slopping a little of the whisky from her teacup as she did so. The dash of liquid on her hand reminded her that sustenance was there, however, and she downed the remainder in a gulp.

'Killed?' she said. 'Who'd want to kill the silly old sod? Harmless, he was, for all his bluster.'

'Well,' I said, 'he had made enemies in town since he arrived. He was misusing characters he'd no right to, to add a bit of sparkle to his puppet show. He managed to get himself on the wrong side of some rather powerful people.'

'He'd never!' Moll said. She had paled, but now her colour rose again as she sprang to Bert's defence. 'He'd never steal a puppet. He wouldn't so much as buy one. He made his own. Whittled and painted and stitched. He'd talk your leg off about why too. And I mocked him. Oh, heartless woman I am. I teased him. Even though I could see they were beauts. Anyone could see that.'

I did not deem it worthwhile to explain copyright violations to Moll and so I merely nodded until she had said her piece. 'Now, do you know about the beauty of his puppets from watching his shows,' I said, 'or have you seen them in close quarters? Did he usually leave them behind with the tent?'

'Booth,' Moll said. 'No, the puppets were never out of his sight. If you told me he slept with them all lined up beside

102

him on his pillow I'd believe you. It was just the rig he left. It goes flat and it's made light for carrying but it's as tall as it is, if you see what I mean, and there's nothing to be done about it.'

'And about this pillow,' Alec said. 'Can you give us the address of his lodgings, while he was in Dundee? His brother doesn't know, but he's keen to find out, as you can imagine.'

'News to me he *had* a brother,' Moll said. 'But I'm glad to hear it now. Someone to make the arrangements. Can you make sure I hear when he's to be buried? And where? I'd not miss it. I shiver to think how many years we've been pals, Bert and me . . .' She fell into a reverie. 'Forty at least. He was a young man first time he came wheedling round asking favours.'

'Forty years is a fine friendship,' I said, thinking that I would not care to meet the chums of forty years back in my own life: grubby little boys who were forced to dance with me at parties and those pink-and-white china girls who never seemed to rip their stockings and who called me 'gypsy'. Alec, often less apt to be distracted, had made much more of her reminiscing.

'How long have you been here, Moll?' he said.

'At Her Majesty's?' she said. 'Fifty-two years come the start of the Christmas season. I was a hoofer, though you'd not believe it now, state of these gams.' She looked ruefully down at the swollen ankles above her carpet slippers. 'I never made it out of the chorus line and a few walk-ons in com- edies. But, those days, you could make a living on that, if you palled together with a few others to pay the rent or if you met a nice chap that didn't mind you dancing.' Her earlier bravado on the subject of men had quite melted away. 'I never did. I shifted over to ASM in my thirties and then fetched up here at the stage door, like I said, must be nearly forty years ago. I met Bert that first summer. He came and asked if he could leave his rig backstage, drop it off after curtains and pick it up before the matinee. He said he had nothing to pay me with until he'd done a few shows, but then he'd take me for a fish tea every Sunday and meantime he gave me this. Like an IOU. But I never gave it back.'

She had twisted round in her seat as she spoke and was now rummaging in a cluttered shelf cut into the wall behind her. There were framed photographs and playbills, naturally, but there was also a dizzying array of detritus, chocolate boxes and biscuit tins – empty I guessed from the way they fell about as she disturbed them – and there were fans both snapped shut and sprawling open, and more corsages and posies of silk flowers than I had ever seen in my life, including in the work room of a Dunfermline milliner whose path crossed mine once upon a time. This, I took it, was Moll's collection of tips and gifts from the many travelling players who had sought favours from her over the long years.

Her fingers found what she had been rootling for and she drew out something that looked at first glance like a chip of driftwood, tapered at each end. When she handed it to me, however, I saw that in fact it was a carving, a little fish, the twist of its body arising naturally out of the shape of the wood. Its fins, gills and tail were etched in impressionistic lines, but its face had been worked on. It wore an expression of comical detachment, inviting fellow feeling and offering the same. I smiled just to see it.

'See there now,' Moll said. 'I never thought much of it at the time. A plain wee thing, compared to some of the wax flowers and beadwork bags I was getting, but every time I show it to someone there's a smile. I've kept it all these years.'

'Forty years,' Alec said, putting his hand out for the fish, wanting to examine it. 'I'd like you to cast your mind back fifty years, Moll.'

'I wasn't on the door in those days. I was still dancing.'

'But you were here at Her Majesty's?'

'That I was. Those were grand days, when you could do

eight shows a week and still have tea with your granny on a Sunday. I'm lucky to be the age I am, really. Younger'n me and they were all at that Sunday trains to the next town. Repertory theatre!' Her voice dripped with scorn. 'Keeping the sales up and the wages down, that was. It was no life for girls. I've—' But with a glance at Alec she pressed her lips close together. 'Well, I'll just say this and not shock you, sir. Many's the time it did the girls good to have me here on the door, telling the stage-door johnnies to sling their hooks, instead of letting them into the dressing rooms, and looking the other way. And if it did all go wrong, well then me, being local, knew the area.'

'Yes, indeed,' Alec said. 'Well, speaking of fifty years ago, do you remember a killing in Dudhope Park? It didn't seem to cause a splash but we saw a snippet of news about it in the library this morning.'

'A murder in the park there?' Moll said. 'Fifty years back. I can't say that I do, no. I daresay I put it out of my mind. Murder's no thing to dwell on after all. Oh poor Bert. To think I'll never see his smiling face again. Face of an angel he had. Smile would light up an opera house and save the gas.'

'Poor Bert,' I agreed, trying hard not to remember the face as I had seen it. 'It was just that the particulars were very similar fifty years ago. It was a puppeteer, you see. A Punch and Judy man, like Bert. And he was set upon in his tent, like Bert. It's probably a coincidence, but it's an odd one.'

I half expected Moll to leap on the oddity and make it up into something macabre, having often found that the servant class adores nothing more than a whiff of the occult added to a scandal, but to my surprise, her face turned shrewd instead of awestruck.

'Ohhh yes,' she said. 'I mind it now. Yes, I mind it fine. It took a few years before any Punchinello man came back to Dundee after that, let me tell you. Bert was the first and that was a good ten years on. I'd forgotten it after all this time, but I mind it now you refresh me.'

'And his name—' I began, but Alec moved a hand. It looked as though he was simply passing the little fish back to me to return to Moll, but I knew that he meant to shush me. 'You called Bert a "Punchinello"?' I said, changing tack.

'He liked the old ways,' she told me. 'Poor Bert. He did like the old ways.'

'We shan't trespass on your hospitality much longer,' Alec said. He cocked his head towards the door where, indeed, sounds of activity indicated that the theatre was coming to life for the matinee. 'But if you would just give us the address of the lodgings? Bert's brother would be most grateful to be able to take care of his things.'

'Brother!' said Moll. 'I never thought there'd be one single thing that man hadn't talked my ear off about, but he never did mention a brother. I thought he was an only one. Same as me. Ah well, chances are he made out he *was* while he was wheedling round me, then afterwards it would be awkward to change the tale, wouldn't it?'

'A great incentive always to tell the truth,' I agreed. 'I have told my own two boys as much many times before now.'

'And there's my cue,' Moll said, as a bell clanged deafeningly just outside her room. I was astonished to hear such a noise backstage in a theatre; I should have imagined a muffled tinkle at most. 'It's just a step down Gellatly Street there to Dock Street,' she said as she was leaving. 'Corner of Candle Lane. Number seventy-four inside the building.'

Chapter 11

'Dock Street,' I repeated as we left the alley and turned down towards the water. 'I don't suppose there's any chance it's more salubrious than it sounds.'

'Less if anything,' Alec said. 'Or perhaps not, this early in the day.'

I puzzled over his words, wondering how a dockside could get worse as the day wore on into evening, thinking surely when the dockers had finished loading and unloading, the air would be lots less blue and once the fish were landed and the mongers had carted them off it would smell better. I supposed there might be a pub down there nice and handy. 'Drunks, do you mean?' I said. 'Might I remind you of that gang of louts and lost souls Teddy infected Gilverton with last summer. I saw *them* off. Besides, with sailors I needn't be diplomatic in case I meet their parents.'

Alec opened his mouth and shut it again. 'All right,' he said. 'Yes, why not? Let's say "drunks".'

'Well, what else?' I said. 'Dog fights? Bear baiting?'

'By all means,' said Alec, maddeningly.

'Well, what then?' I said, trying to think of something worse than bear baiting. When the penny dropped I halted my steps. 'Oh surely not!' I said. 'Not in Dundee!'

'You can wait with Brother Mackie back at the Sugarlump Café while I check,' Alec said. 'But to be honest, one wouldn't expect trade to have started at lunchtime and if it has, you can protect me.'

So it was with no little trepidation that I emerged onto

Dock Street. Had he not made the monstrous suggestion about the iniquity to be found there I might have thought the change of scene refreshing. The Overgate and Gellatly Street were both deeply shaded by tall buildings but on the dockside the sun shone unimpeded, sparkling on the choppy waters of the Tay and glinting on the chains and hooks of the great clanking machines that were currently plucking crates from the deck of a cargo ship and swinging them over onto the quayside. Across the river the green hills of Fife formed a calming background and the Newport ferry, halfway through its journey, bobbed and chuffed cheerfully in the middle distance. One understood why sketchers and watercolourists were drawn to harbours as one viewed the scene.

The smells were another matter. Seaweed, engine oil, coalsmoke and fish were a cocktail it would take effort to enjoy. I knew that prosperous brewers came to welcome the sour stink of their hop mash and the sweet pall of malt, symbolising as it did the barrels of beer that would be sold to swell their coffers. And Hugh loved nothing more than the fragrance of sheep pen, cattle press or even farrowing stall as evidence of the farming year rolling on in its endless fecundity. Perhaps if I were in shipping or owned the fleet of motor lorries, several of which were waiting to carry bounty from river to warehouse, from boat to market, these smells would be dear to me. As things stood, I put a glove to my face and breathed the sweet scent of Grant's careful laundering – lanolin soap and lavender water – trying not to notice Alec smiling at me.

We did not pass any pubs, as it happened, but only the front door of the Sailors' Home – a splendid edifice, looked over by a bust of Neptune – outside which some very elderly men, now in permanent dry dock, sat out the twilight of their years watching the passing show. It was only a few yards further on to Candle Lane and a gaunt tenement of five

108

floors directly opposite a dock and therefore directly in the path of the smoke belching from a ship there.

'Dear, dear,' Alec said, as we turned in at the open door. 'I do hope this is all single rooms for passing gents, don't you? This air would do no good for growing families.'

The perambulators parked in the lee of the staircase told us otherwise and as we rose up to the first floor, a glance out of the stair window to the back court showed a great many children playing happily under wagging washing lines, where nappies, cracking like flags, spoke of even smaller children still.

The numbering was straightforward, each door on a landing marked in turn, and I calculated that seventy-four must be right at the top. We were both puffing by the time we got there and we paused under the skylight before trying the door.

'Although it's almost certainly lock—' Alec was saying when the handle turned and the door swung open. 'Oh!'

Perhaps the late Mr Mackie did not see the point in giving himself all the trouble of keeping a key about him, I thought as I surveyed the apartment. There was nothing here that would cause a thief's fingers to twitch. It was a small room, even smaller than Moll's cubby, containing only a single bed with a thin mattress, an even thinner blanket and a pillow so thin as to be a gesture rather than a comfort. A kitchen chair served as a bedside table and an oval mat of cloth scraps appeared to complete the room's amenities. On the other hand, light poured in from a dormer window and the view was of blue sky, the tips of the highest cranes and the hazy Fife hills.

Alec had just stepped inside when we both learned that there was in fact more on offer at number seventy-four after all. A second door, hidden from where we stood, now opened and Professor Mackie, the brother of the deceased, came through it, his fists held up in front of his jaw like those of a boxer and a grim look on his face. When he saw it was us, he dropped his hands and leaned back in the doorway.

'I thought . . .' he said. 'I thought . . .'

'I'll bet you did,' Alec said. 'Sit down, sir. You've gone a rather funny colour.'

The man allowed Alec to lead him over to the bedside, where he sank onto the hard chair.

'I thought it was the killer,' Prof. Mackie said. 'I should have locked the door behind me. How did you find the place?'

'As we meant to,' I said. 'The stage door keeper at Her Majesty's knew the address. More to the point, how did *you* find the place?'

'Ha! Yes, indeed, madam. By a much more fortuitous circumstance, actually. Someone recognised me, in the tearoom. Someone – a young woman – came in, caught sight of me and looked as though she'd seen a ghost. The poor child. I daresay if Bert never spoke of me, she really did believe that she had seen him, calmly eating buns instead of lying in the mortuary. She went as white as a ghost herself. But what a game girl she is. Instead of running away and going to church, she came over. In the course of our conversation she shared poor Bert's address with me.'

'How fortunate,' I said. 'I wouldn't have thought you were particularly similar to your brother in appearance. Although . . .' I stopped myself from saying I had only seen Bert in death and Alec managed to dredge up a rather more suitable remark instead.

'Although,' he said, 'perhaps your likeness is in the turn of your expression or your regard. Dandy's husband and younger son are nothing like one another in photographs but at dinner they're a perfect mirror act, aren't they Dan?'

'What's a mirror act?' I said.

'I'm surprised you've heard of such a thing,' said the professor, so repressively I wondered if it was another case of Alec failing to protect my fragile womanhood from ugliness.

'Yes, they're dying out now,' Alec said. 'The best one I ever saw was in Paris, a little amuse-bouche in between the dancing girls. I've never forgotten it. Brrr.' He shivered and then grinned, but the grin fell away when he realised that Prof. Mackie was staring at him aghast. I did not believe that a professor of psychology in these shameless days would be shocked by a reference to a cancan show. I decided it was the easy chat about macabre confections that the man found unseemly.

Alec cleared his throat. 'Anyway,' he said. 'And so this girl knew your brother's address?'

'As I foresaw,' Prof. Mackie said. 'There was always a girl, every summer. And this summer's girl happened to come for her luncheon at the Sugarlump today. A stroke of luck. Unnecessary, as it turned out, since you found the place too, but I'll admit I was glad to have a moment here on my own to think about my brother.' He heaved a sigh and let his gaze travel over the bed, the mat, and the window.

'Did you find anything?' I said.

'A clue?' Prof. Mackie's eyebrows rose. They were luxurious eyebrows, still black – although the salt was beginning to win out over the pepper in his hair, and I could not help remembering the face of the man in the puppet tent, the sparse pale eyebrows in his white face.

'Not a clue,' I said. 'I meant a keepsake. Something of your brother's to take away and remember him by.'

'I'll take the rig and the players,' Mackie said. 'When the police are finished with them and let them go.' He flushed a little. 'I never did let poor Bert convince me about them. I wouldn't listen. I called them puppets. I called him a clown once when I was angry. But I'll take them back with me and set the thing up in my rooms to remember him by. I shall learn their names and perhaps I'll even learn a script.

The script, if Bert's to be believed. Such a stickler as he was.' He took a deep breath, let it out, and looked around himself. 'But there's nothing of him here. A razor. A toothbrush. A comb. I don't think he had so much as a change of linens. Perhaps he rinsed them out and stayed in bed while they dried or perhaps . . .' But he could not finish the surmise of how far his brother had fallen. He bit his lip and fell silent.

'Have you thrown everything away?' I said. 'I think perhaps they should be left until the police have looked at the room, you know.'

Mackie nodded his head at the second door. I had forgotten about it. I stepped over and opened it to reveal a little water closet with a lidded slop pail, a washstand with jug and ewer and a shelf, where sat indeed a toothbrush, a tin of tooth-powder, a cake of soap, a razor and a comb.

'It's all very neat,' I said. 'I don't think your brother had given up on the decencies of life at all. I mean he must have paid a premium for this convenience and there's no tap, is there? He would have had to lug water up all those stairs. And his things are clean as a new pin. I'd bet he went to the baths and did his clothes at the same time, wrung them out and hung them in the airing room.'

'Or maybe he had plenty of spares,' Alec said. 'If his rooms were never locked I daresay someone in need nipped in when they heard he'd died and pinched them. Could you take comfort in that, Professor Mackie? That perhaps your brother's vests and shirts are swaddling a baby and keeping it cosy? Perhaps his spare trousers are helping some poor chap look respectable enough to get a job today.'

'I didn't take you for a socialist,' Professor Mackie said. Alec's face was such a picture of astonishment that I am afraid I burst out into peals of laughter. Mackie joined in with a chuckle of his own. And it was, most unfortunately, at this moment that the door to the hallway opened to reveal the police inspector and a sergeant. We sobered but it was too late.

'Is this a private party?' the inspector said, waspishly.

'We are comforting the bereaved,' I said. 'This is Mr Mackie's brother.'

'Is it indeed?' said the inspector. 'And how did you find him? Why were you looking?'

'Mr Gilver and Mrs Osborne have been a great support to me this dark day,' Mackie said. I was glad he had not claimed long friendship, since he had got our names wrong.

'And did it not occur to any of you to keep out of here?' the inspector said.

'Out?' said Prof. Mackie. 'Of my poor brother's last home?'

'Until we'd been over it for prints,' said the sergeant.

'Well, no harm done,' the inspector added. 'We'll just have to take you all down to the station and get yours.'

'Get our what?' I said.

'Fingerprints,' the inspector said. 'For the purposes of elimination.'

'What?' I said. 'Elimination of what?'

'Mrs Gilver,' the inspector said, almost purring. 'For a self-proclaimed detective you don't seem very well versed in modern investigative methods. Naturally we're going to dust this room for fingerprints in case the rascal that killed Mr Mackie has been in here. In case we arrest him and he tries to claim he's never met the man, no idea where he lives and so on. But of course he'll have some clever-dick lawyer on his side, like they all do, and said clever-dick lawyer will no doubt argue that the possessor of some other set of prints is the real culprit. So we have to make sure we've got every set identified and accounted for. Exhibit one: interfering woman who should know better. Exhibit two: young man she's got round her little finger for some strange reason, who should definitely know better. Exhibit three: brother of the deceased. Exhibits four to whatever: girls and pals and the landlord no

113

doubt, but the point is there's always one set that shouldn't be here.'

It made perfect sense and, given how hard I had tried to stop Miss Bissett smudging useful prints with her own irrelevant ones, it was a wonder that I had never considered it before now, but then none of our cases before now had hinged on such things as fingerprints, thankfully.

'Very well then,' I said. 'Where *is* the police station? We shall wait there for you.'

'Excuse me,' said the sergeant, 'but we'll tell you what's to do, not the other way round, if you please.' He took a breath and then stopped and turned to the inspector. 'Sir?'

'You take them and send someone else to help me out here.'

'Take us?' said Alec. 'We might not be locals, but I've a marvellous sense of direction. We shan't get lost.'

'We need to make sure you don't skip,' the inspector said.

Alec simply gaped, but I stepped in. 'I was in full view of the entire Punch and Judy audience when Mr Mackie died,' I said. 'Quite forty people, all of whom stated as much. Prof. Mackie was at home in St Andrews. Are there witnesses to that, Professor?'

'The whole congregation of the university chapel was watching me sing a tenor role in the Bach chorus,' he said.

'And *I'd* never heard of the chap,' said Alec. 'I was at home, with a valet to vouch for me. And a telephone call.' Here he coloured slightly and I understood that Poppy had rung him up to bill and coo.

'Well see and go straight there,' the inspector said. 'Bell Street. We're too busy trying to solve the case to chase about after you.'

Some people, often men but my mother-in-law was notorious for it too, simply must have the last word in any exchange. Alec opened his mouth to make a bid for the prize but I grasped him firmly above the elbow and dragged him

114

away. The professor followed disconsolately behind us, muttering.

'What's that?' I said, as we began our long trudge back down the stairs.

'I'm finding the whole business so very grubby,' Mackie said. 'Not just Bert's rooms, although it breaks my heart to think of him living there. But such casual talk of "girls", and now I'm to walk through the door of a police station, for the first time in my life. At least it's not St Andrews and no one I know is likely to see me.'

'Oh, I shouldn't worry about it,' I said. 'I've been arrested twice before now and actually been locked up in a cell for hours during one of the two adventures. It's not such a serious matter, really.'

'I wish I could be so insouciant,' Mackie said. 'I am bitterly ashamed to admit it, now that he's gone, but when Bert passed through St Andrews I always made excuses not to see him. It was usually mid-June and I was always busy marking exams and then sitting on the boards of study, deciding the degrees, you know? But I'm sure he knew I was making excuses. Poor, poor Bert.'

I gave his arm a squeeze, but could not summon words of comfort. He would have to feel the regret until it faded; there was nothing I could do.

Alec managed rather better. 'Take a seat and rest, Professor,' he said. 'I'll just nip up to the top of the road and bring the car for you.'

The two of us sat on a low wall quite companionably until his return.

'Hop in, Professor,' Alec said. 'Take the front seat beside me. It's much more comfy. And, as Dandy just said, she's used to being carted around in the back on her journeys to the clink. Off we go.'

Dundee was changing, I thought as we edged out from the kerb and turned up towards the town. A few years back

115

we would have had to toot the horn to clear gossiping house-wives and gangs of skipping children out of the roadway, careful not to startle carthorses. Now, the challenge was to find a gap in the stream of motorvans and delivery bicycles into which we might insert ourselves. And, as we took the tight turn onto the Seagate and the High Street, omnibuses, private cars and even taxicabs joined the throng. The square ahead was choked up with the things.

'Bother this,' Alec said, stretching up for a view over the jammed traffic. 'Shortcut past the library, I think.' He pushed the pedal hard and shot up a quiet street that was relatively free of motorcars.

'Good idea,' I said, but then, as a second turn across the bottom of the library square saw us enter a street parallel to the busy High Street, I groaned. Here was not so much a traffic jam, where at least all the vehicles are headed in the same direction in orderly fashion, but a littering of little vans sitting at odd angles as if dropped by giants in a game of spillikins. Most of them seemed to have their back doors hanging open too.

'What on earth?' Alec said, throwing the motorcar into reverse.

I was leaning forward from the back seat wondering the same, then I noticed that all of the little vans were the same colour of battleship grey and all had the same painted sign on the side. I glanced up at the façade of the building that stretched along the north side of the street, and loomed over the square like a flagship, staring down the ecclesiastical library.

'D.C. Thomson,' Alec said, clearly reading along with me. 'Getting the late editions out for delivery. I'm surprised they're allowed to choke up a street this way. How very odd that they don't have a loading dock round the back somewhere.'

'They do,' said the professor, and added, 'One of my

116

colleagues in the architecture department waxes about it. There's a state-of-the-art . . . oh what did he call it? Some new-fangled jargon that made the classicists shudder every time he said it. "Through-put protocol"! That's it. He likened it to an organism, ideas in at the top and bales of newspaper out at the bottom.'

'Ugh,' I said. 'I see what you mean. I imagined dining with biologists might be a trial but I never thought of architects destroying one's appetite. Turn round, Alec. Quick, before someone boxes you in behind.'

But Alec was looking in his mirror. 'Too late,' he said, as a lorry wheezed to a standstill behind us and the driver leaned on a very loud town horn to make his views known. Evidently he was transporting spring lambs, for the horn set up a sustained and lusty bleating that added a painful top note to the sound of rumbling engines and the shouts of the drivers and warehouse men who were tossing bales of newspapers into the waiting vans.

'We're going to be stuck here for quite some time,' the professor said. 'I do hope that inspector doesn't take exception to the delay.'

'Too bad if he does,' Alec said. 'He'll surely hear about this muddle. It can't possibly be like this every day. Something extraordinary must be happening.'

That very moment, the evidence for the truth of his words was presented to us, for at the next street corner, beyond the clutch of idling motorvans, a police van sped past, klaxon wailing. We all heard the squeal of its brakes as it slowed to take a corner and then the booming echo of the klaxon reverberating off high walls as, presumably, the constable at the wheel drove along the very lane where all these newspapers should have been dropping out of the end of the architect's pride.

I caught Alec's eye in the mirror and knew that he was thinking precisely what I was thinking.

'Professor Mackie,' I said, 'would you be willing to wait here alone until the jam clears? You could give a little tootle-toot when the road's empty and we'll come back out again.'

'Gladly, dear lady,' Mackie said. 'I've had enough in the way of incident for today. Whatever's going on now, I'm quite happy to know nothing of it. I shall sit here and have a little think about a problem I've been tussling with.' He sighed. 'Or just enjoy some memories of boyhood perhaps. Poor Bert. He was a sweet child and a dear brother to me.'

I patted him on his arm and made that sickening face, with my head on one side, my eyebrows up, and smiling with my mouth closed, but I offered no words, in case he answered them. I was panting to find out what was happening at the other Dundee publisher's office this afternoon.

Alec was already through the revolving door when I finally scrambled out. It was an impressive entrance on the impressive frontage of an impressive building, but all I could think of was the plucky spirit of Miss Bissett's grandfather, sticking to his guns and keeping his magazines afloat despite this behemoth just round the corner. I shook the distracting thoughts out of my head and hurried after Alec, who was striding across acres of marble, towards a high mahogany desk, something like a judge's bench, where two telephonists and a uniformed watchman of some sort were sitting rather on the edge of their seats, torn between their duty to greet the guests approaching them and their natural desire to scurry to the back of the building and find out why that police klaxon had been sounding.

'What's going on?' Alec said, a stroke of communicative genius that allowed the trio to marry their two competing impulses and tell the guests – us – what they knew about the absorbing drama that had engulfed their work day.

'Oh, we're having a terrible time of it!' said one of the telephonists.

'A disgrace,' said the watchman. 'This isn't what we fought the war for. Lazy wastrels and their nonsense!'

'But what's happened?' I said, directing my question at the other telephonist.

'Someone has defaced our premises,' she said. 'A dreadful thing.'

I felt my shoulders slump and when Alec spoke his voice was rather lower than before too. 'Vandalism?' he said.

'Worse than that,' the security man said. 'A nasty profane threat, daubed all over the back wall in scarlet letters three feet high for the world to see.' Should 'the world' happen along a back lane in Dundee, I thought, but forbore to say.

'Do you know what it said?' I asked him. He cleared his throat and pushed his lips out.

'Step aside and tell me if it's not fit for the ladies,' said Alec.

Of course once they had withdrawn to the far side of the foyer, 'the ladies' were free to discuss it too. The flightier of the two telephonists got in first. 'It said "murdering B-words", madam. And then it said "Vengeance is mine".'

'Did it?' I said. I glanced over towards Alec, who had just heard the same for himself and was looking back over at me. 'Did it indeed? What a shocking thing. I hope the constables catch the rotter who did it.'

'It's got me all of a flutter,' said the other woman. 'And I try not to get het up about things. I get palpitations. Always have, since I was a child. I felt my heart going like a trapped sparrow when I heard, I can tell you.'

'I'm not surprised. Jolly nasty.'

Alec was making his way back. 'Deuteronomy,' he said in a low voice.

'Well and that's another thing,' the telephonist said. 'Quoting the Bible and using that word in the same breath.'

'Same daub,' the other girl said, speaking for the first time. 'Same difference, mind you.'

119

'Letters bigger than my head,' the watchman said. 'They'll never get the paint out of the stone. Or if they do, they'll never get it out of the mortar. Bright red paint. And right opposite a school playground too. Thank the Dear it's the summer holidays.'

At that very moment, a door opened onto the foyer and A Very Important Person came out to join us. I knew he was such not only because of his gold watch chain, gold tie pin, silk handkerchief and elegant shoes, but also because all three of the front-of-house staff straightened when they saw him and the girls refastened their attention on the switchboard, which was twinkling like a sequinned frock in a cha-cha.

'Must just get some air,' the man said. 'Can't go out the back. It's still . . . Need some air.'

He tottered towards the door. Alec, after a look, followed him and I agreed with the decision. This person, very important or not, was about to drop.

'Sir, whatever's wrong?' said the more voluble of the two girls.

He swung round and gave her an anguished look. 'It's not paint,' he said. 'It's blood.' And he fainted away.

Chapter 12

Alec, decades after his last afternoon on the rugby football pitch, nevertheless shot forward in something between a lunge and a curtsy and managed to get both arms under the gentleman, keeping his head from cracking against the floor.

The staff dithered and hopped about while Alec loosened the man's tie and collar stud and I rummaged in my bag for smelling salts. I took to carrying them a few years back during a case beset with both alarms and schoolgirls. I never used them at the time, the schoolgirls proving doughtier than imagined, but I was glad of them now. I waved them under the man's nose, which twitched. Then he frowned, sneezed and opened his eyes. He blinked a couple of times before, I surmised, Alec came into focus.

'Who are you?' he said.

'Detectives,' said Alec. 'Working on the Mackie case.'

'The what?'

'The puppet murder?'

'The *what*?' Colour was returning to the man's cheeks and annoyance was bringing him back to himself as nothing else, surely, could have. He sat up and tugged at his lapels to straighten his coat.

'The Punch and Judy man who copied your cartoons,' Alec said, throwing a worried glance my way. The chap had not hit his head but he was muddled, without question.

'Perhaps your boss didn't tell you,' I said.

'My boss?' He was struggling to his feet now, a comical sight given that he was using Alec as a support but still glowering at him, from inches away. 'I don't have a "boss". I *am* the boss. One of them.'

'Then you would know,' Alec said, 'if someone contravened your copyright. Presumably you would sign the letter telling him to cease and desist.'

'I most certainly would not,' he said. 'We have a reputable firm of solicitors to take care of such things. But I would have been the one to tell them to raise a letter. I have no idea what you're talking about.'

'Mr Thomson,' I said, hazarding a guess. He glared at me even harder, either because he did not care to hear his name from the lips of a strange woman or because he was not Mr Thomson and therefore did have a boss after all. 'Sir,' I said, in hasty exchange, 'there was a murder. On Monday. And there was a story impugning you – your company anyway – with a motive for it. And now the message on the wall. In blood, you say?'

He was back on his feet. He brushed down the seat of his trousers, smoothed back his hair, which had become disarranged in the tumble, and gave Alec a curt nod.

'Come with me,' he said. 'I want to hear more of this.'

'Will I get the nurse?' the more forward of the two telephonists called to his retreating back. 'Or a cup of tea at least.'

But the man paid her no heed. He marched through the building to a suite of offices I thought must overlook the back lane and strode towards an impressive desk. I could not help making a comparison with Miss Bissett's room, half the size and a quarter as richly furnished. Then I noticed that the man had stopped halfway across his Persian carpet.

'Would you just take a squint out of the window, there's a decent chap, and see what's going on?'

Alec managed not to look puzzled. He stepped to the window and pressed his cheek to the glass. 'A few bobbies milling about,' he said. 'They don't seem to be . . . ahhh . . . hosing or scrubbing or anything. There's nothing to see.'

'Thank you,' the man said. 'Much obliged. Were you over there?'

'I was,' said Alec. 'You needn't say more.'

They both glared at me, which was not fair, but I could hardly blame them.

'Now then,' the man said, 'what's this about a puppet show?'

We recounted what Miss Bissett had told me over the telephone, about Oor Wullie and Maw Broon and the letter sent to object to their misuse. We told him Mr Mackie had moved on to Rosie and Freckle and then had died in a crime, as yet unsolved.

'He might well have mocked up those two insipid girls,' the man said. 'And I should think Doig's would be grateful of the free publicity. But he did nothing of the sort with our beloved creations. Who told you this?'

'Miss Bissett,' I said. 'Funnily enough her cousin, the only remaining Doig as far as I know, agrees with you. About the publicity.'

'I suggest you go round to the Overgate and ask Miss Bissett where she got the tale.'

'She's not at work,' I said. 'She has been arrested, I'm afraid.'

'For the murder?'

'Yes, but—'

'And so one of her chums came round here to help her out by trying to throw suspicion on us, did he? Well, we'll see about that. I shall go— that is, once the wall has been cleaned. I don't suppose you would slip down there to the loading bay and tell the police, would you? Tell them the whole thing's a tarradiddle? We need to get back to normal before the morning editions go out tomorrow. That's a print run that would choke Doig's from midnight to lunchtime and I don't want to be slapped with a fine over city by-laws. There's a lot of envy among the councillors. Some of them

123

would like nothing better than to embarrass D.C. Thomson's and then see us have to report it on our own front page.'

'Happy to help,' Alec said. 'I'm almost glad we got caught up in it— Oh!'

'Oh no!' I said, as the same thought that had just struck him struck me. 'Mackie!'

We made hurried goodbyes and then bickered our way back to the foyer, each of us clamouring to take a message to the police and trying to ditch the much more boring task of going to soothe Professor Mackie and make apologies for abandoning him.

Alec won, by underhand means, I have to say. He pointed out that it was a man's work to explain to coppers that a fellow soldier had taken a fit of the heebie-jeebies at the blood, and that a woman such as me would only embarrass everyone.

We parted company and I stepped out into the street. The last few vans were having their doors slammed and engines revved and Prof. Mackie was peering out of the side window of Alec's motorcar, looking rather forlorn.

'I'm most awfully sorry,' I said, climbing in. 'We were over-taken by events. But the good news is that it's all pertinent to your brother's case, Professor.' I settled into the seat beside him and told him all about it, finishing with Deuteronomy.

He turned whiter and whiter as I delivered my report and by the end of it he was lying back in the seat, his chest lifting and hitching and his mouth trembling. 'Vengeance?' he muttered. 'Vengeance? But why would anyone seek revenge of poor Bert? For what? He led a blameless life for all it was a strange one and a disappointment to our father.'

'It's probably empty mischief,' I said. 'That is one of the Bible's most oft-used quotations.'

'It is, it is,' said Prof. Mackie. 'That's true. But it's not pertinent here, surely. Why would the killer scold a newspaper publisher about vengeance?'

'It might not have been the killer,' I said.

This appeared to upset the professor even more. 'Who else?' he demanded. 'What do you mean?'

'Perhaps it's someone who suspects the publishers of committing the crime,' I said. 'A murderer is exactly who needs to hear that verse. The thing that's troubling me is the next verse. It is far from being a popular choice. Its appearance is marked indeed.'

'The next? "Their feet shall" . . . what is it? "For their day of" something . . . Ha! I have proved your point, Mrs Gilver.'

'Slide,' I said. 'Calamity.'

'You don't mean to tell me that was written too?' Mackie was quite wringing his hands now and his colour was more grey than white.

'Not here,' I said. I was tussling with myself, for of course I should wait for Alec to share in what I was about to tell the professor. On the other hand, he had just grabbed a plum for himself, going to snoop on the message and talk to policemen. I was merely balancing the scales.

'The thing is,' I said, 'do you remember me referring to another murder? An earlier one? Well, it wasn't what you thought. It wasn't a rampage. You see, it's not the first time a Mr Mackie – a Mr Albert Mackie, no less – has died in Dudhope Park. It happened fifty years ago. An Albert Mackie, a Punch and Judy man, was killed in his tent by an unknown assailant.'

'That's preposterous!' The professor glared at me.

'Indeed it is. But it's true. It was in the "In Memoriam" column of yesterday's paper. With a biblical quotation. *That* quotation. From Deuteronomy.'

'Are you sure it's not a prank of some kind?' said the professor. He had gathered himself. 'A nasty twisted kind of prank, granted. Or perhaps they got the date wrong. The year. And it was meant to be a tribute to poor Bert. That must be it, surely.'

125

'You have a very logical mind,' I said. 'Even in grief. But I'm afraid not. You see, we saw the reports that went in at the time. Short snippets but unmistakable. There really was an Albert Mackie, puppeteer, killed in the same place as your brother, fifty years ago to the day. We wondered, Alec and I, if it was your father. Or even grandfather, I suppose.'

'Our father?' said Prof. Mackie. 'Good Lord in heaven.' The unfortunate echo of prayer struck me as comical. 'Howard was his name.' At that, I had to bite my cheeks. 'And he ran a billiards hall.' I was now forced to dig my nails into my palms to contain my hysteria. Until the oddness of it sobered me.

'An uncle?' I said.

'Fruiterers and joiners,' said Professor Mackie. 'One railway clerk, but he's on our mother's side.'

'Well, then I'm flummoxed,' I said. 'Utterly flummoxed. Might there have been a black sheep of an uncle that your brother knew about but whose tale you managed to miss?'

'I don't think so. I can't imagine so.'

'Is your father still alive, Professor? We could ask him.'

'My father?' he said again. 'Long gone. Quite a compliment, Mrs Gilver. I am sixty-six next month. My father died many years ago now.'

I have long believed that the academic life is quite the most comfortable existence for a single man, its only equal for women being a nunnery. In a closed order, that is; serving orders of nuns are simply nurses, teachers and laundrymaids with no nights off. Upon hearing that this man facing me from the other side of Alec's motorcar was sixty-five years old, I was more convinced than ever that living in rooms, with a scout, giving a couple of lectures a week and reading up on one's favourite subject every evening with an unlimited supply of college sherry was the sweetest of clover. Certainly it kept one in good training for bouts of deep thought. The professor was quite lost in contemplation of what I had told him.

126

Neither of us had made any headway with it, however, by the time Alec opened the back passenger door. 'You can drive, if you like, Dan,' he said. He was being magnanimous to make up for nabbing the better of the two tasks. He would regret it when he heard that I had plunged in and told the professor about the first murder.

'What happened?' I said. 'Did the coppers tell you anything?'

'It's an awful mess round there,' Alec said. 'It's not pure blood. The rotten devil mixed it up with a thin plaster of Paris to make it stick properly. It'll be a job to chip it off and the smell is indescribable.'

'But even mixed with plaster of Paris, Alec,' I said, 'where did the dauber get such a quantity of blood as all that, to make letters as large as that poor chap said? Unless they grew in his fevered mind, since it had upset him so.'

'No, no, none of that,' Alec said. 'The writing is simply enormous. Like the side of an omnibus. I should say our best bet is to ask the local butchers.'

'Won't the police do that?' said Prof. Mackie. 'Is there a need for you to duplicate their efforts?'

It was a puzzling volte-face from the man who had been so keen to be our client a few hours before. Perhaps he was simply exhausted with it all.

'Let's ask,' I said, as we drew in beside the Bell Street police station at long, long last and stepped down.

The stolid bobby on the desk, however, was either ignorant of the workings of his detective colleagues or had a poker face that could break the bank in Monte Carlo and no high regard for amateurs. He pushed his luxuriant moustaches out until they bristled and shook his head as, with slow determination, he lifted the desk and waved us through to a back room. Then, setting a little peaked printed notice upon his blotter to inform callers of his whereabouts, he followed and closed the door.

'I just need to get the matron for you, madam,' he said. 'We can't go manhandling *your* dainty fingers. I won't be a tick.' With that he left us. I half expected him to turn the key and lock us in there, shoot a bolt even, and although I do not generally suffer from that particular fear I was aware of a prickling under my collar.

It was a cheerless chamber and was not helped at all by the sight, in the corner of the room, of an enormous hulking shape covered in a brown tarpaulin. I could not help glancing at it, wondering what it might be, but it was Prof. Mackie who realised for which large object the Dundee police had suddenly been obliged to find house room. He went tottering over and tugged the canvas aside to reveal the tent, folded but still extremely bulky, and a pitiful little collection of puppets huddled on the floor beside it.

'Oh, oh!' Prof. Mackie said. 'Oh poor Bert. Look at it! Look at all he has to show for his life.' He lifted Mr Punch and turned him over in his hands, smoothing the rich stuff of his garments and even going so far as to stroke his bright wooden cheek.

'I don't know,' Alec said. 'They are rather fine. And Bert made them himself, did he? There's a great deal of artistry in them, if you ask me.'

'But look at the booth,' Prof. Mackie said. He lifted one of the flaps and let it drop again. 'Here's the proof that he was in dire straits. Patched and mended. Grubby.'

'Come away,' I said, worried that if he kept examining the striped canvas he would find a splash of his brother's blood and be overcome by grief and horror. 'Look at the puppets, not the kiosk. Look at the skill he put into them. Be proud of him for that.'

None of us had noticed the door opening and all three of us jumped when the bobby reappeared and barked at us. 'Here! Let that go! Put that down! What do you mean by pawing over that? That's evidence!'

'Oh come off it,' I said. 'You went off and left Professor Mackie in the room with his brother's most prized possession. What did you think would happen?'

'Private police evidence,' the bobby muttered. 'No one's possession but mine until I say otherwise.' But he knew he was in the wrong and he subsided soon enough. Having a little bad news to impart helped his mood; he was delighted to inform me that the police matron was out at the Home for Girls dealing with some other 'females'. Getting to mention me in the same breath as Dundee's fallen women quite restored his humour and he was whistling as he set about the business of our fingerprints.

'Now then,' he said, wheezing as he bent to the low shelves of a cupboard to extract a good deal of paper as well as a collection of ink, ink pads, stamps and a fearsome stapling gun – 'Ladies first.'

I am not sure whether he expected smiles in response to his sally. He got none from me. I did not need to be reminded that my presence in a police station and the taking of my fingerprints in a murder case would likely have killed my parents had they still been living and was no doubt making them right now spin in their blameless Northamptonshire graves. I fought resolutely not to let Nanny Palmer's face into my thoughts and started to remove my gloves, wishing heartily I had not removed them in Bert's rooms and so could have avoided this entire adventure.

I noticed that I was not the only one of the party who was ill at ease. Alec was busily filling his pipe and looked as relaxed as he would be by his own fireside after supper, but the professor was fidgety. It is often the case. Alec's position – his birth, family, estate and wealth – was secure. It would take more than a set of fingerprints on file in a police station to shake him. Professor Mackie on the other hand had risen from a start as the son of a billiards hall keeper to rooms and a scout – not to mention his chair – at Scotland's most venerable old university. He had clambered up and up while his brother, if anything, had sunk and sunk, and I was sure that this foray into what might be deemed his brother's world – of stage doors, dockside rooms and crime – was troubling him.

It was helping me, however. Sympathising with the professor helped me square both my jaw and my shoulders and I sailed through the ordeal without my lip trembling or my cheeks colouring. He did not do so well, shaking as the bobby grabbed him and hesitating on approach to the tray of ink. I saw the man's grip tighten and saw the professor's finger whiten at the knuckle and redden at the tip. And he jumped like a deer when the fearsome stapling gun was applied to the finished sheet. Alec gave him a friendly punch on the arm as they swapped places.

Finally, the bobby took a different bottle of ink from a higher shelf of his cupboard, and dipped his nib into it.

'Name?' he asked the professor.

'Leon Mackie,' came the reply.

'Leon!' It was almost a shout of glee. 'Middle initial?'

'B.'

'And you?' he said, turning to face me.

'Dandelion D. Gilver,' I said. 'D for Dahlia.' I have always loathed my name; only the feeble-minded could feel otherwise. I think that day in the Dundee police station was the first time I felt that perhaps I was growing into it. Certainly the bobby did not look up or otherwise indicate any interest in the label I had provided. He copied it down painstakingly.

'Address?' he said when he was done.

'Gilverton, Perthshire,' I said.

'Full address. Street name and number.' He frowned but kept his gaze on his on the paper.

'There is no street,' I said. 'There is no number. Gilverton is my husband's estate. That is my address. Mrs Hugh Gilver, Gilverton, Perthshire.'

The moustaches were bristling again. I rather thought the man wished he had treated us with greater deference now that our social standing was being laid out for him. I also rather thought Hugh was right about the effect of detecting on my deportment and demeanour, if it had taken the recitation of my address to show this man I was 'quality'.

'And Alexander Osborne, Dunelgar, Perthshire,' Alec said. 'Same do with me.'

Then there was a pause.

'And?' said the policeman, with a glance at the professor.

'My address?' the professor said. He cleared his throat. 'Certainly.' Then with a glance at Alec, he went on, 'Dunelgar—'

'Neighbours, are you all?' the bobby said.

'—37 Laurel Avenue, Bearsden, Glasgow.' He shook his shoulders as if struggling out from under something uncomfortable. Embarrassment, at a guess. 'I never did approve the habit of naming a house that stood on a street and had a number,' he said. 'I wouldn't have mentioned it if the constable here hadn't been so insistent on our "full" addresses. My parents went fishing on their honeymoon, Mr Osborne. It could easily have been Perthshire. I don't doubt it was your own ancestral lands that they chose to write on the fanlight of their villa in gold paint. I hope it doesn't offend you.'

'No ancestral lands involved here, my dear chap,' said Alec. 'I came into the estate through the man who was supposed to become my father-in-law if his daughter hadn't been killed before the wedding. The case was all in the family. A hell of a stain on the place, actually. I daresay your ancestral villa in Glasgow is much more respectable.'

He is the kindest of men.

With that we were done. We all ruined our handkerchiefs scrubbing at the ink as we stepped out onto the street again.

'I was surprised you didn't give your college address,' Alec said.

'Thank you for not mentioning it in there,' the professor said. He still sounded rattled. In fact, if anything he sounded more rattled than ever. 'I couldn't face the thought of them turning up at the university asking for me and everyone hearing. The vice-chancellor! Oh Lord the undergraduates! So. I've a tenant in the house, been there years now and all very satisfactory. He forwards any post that turns up for me. Of course, if a policeman comes sniffing round he might decide he doesn't want to live there any more and I'll have to get myself a new tenant, but better that than the porters and cleaners and my fellow . . . There's nowhere like a college for gossip, Mrs Gilver.'

'I can believe that,' I said. 'My younger son came down after his three years a perfect ghoul for scandal.'

'Down from St Andrews?' Mackie said, still sounding wan. 'Gilver? Gilver?' he added musingly.

'Gosh no. Oxford,' I said, before I could stop myself. It was hardly polite after all to express surprise at the notion. 'I'm English,' I added, thinking that might explain the outburst and lessen the insult. It did not.

'Plenty English come up to St Andrews,' said Mackie.

I said nothing. I knew that all sorts of second-class brains trudged north to Durham, Edinburgh and yes even St Andrews when the universities' doors slammed in their faces. Hugh tuts and mutters when I say so. He nags me not to say 'the universities' when I mean only two of the many. He would; he went to Aberdeen.

Alec was attempting to smooth the ruffled air that had whipped up between us. 'When did your parents retire to Glasgow?' he said. 'I'm something of a scholar of Scottish tongues and I detected no twang in you. So I deduce that you didn't live in the Bearsden villa as a boy.'

This was a failure too. Mackie got a rigidity about his jaw and steely look in his eye as he replied. 'No, indeed, Mr Osborne. We lived over the billiards hall in Lanark all through my boyhood. "Dunelgar" was a fond memory and a daydream for many's a long year. Only Bert ever stayed there, and that not for long. He was a wanderer as soon as he was out of the schoolroom.'

'He was much younger than you then?' I said.

'Five years,' said Mackie. 'Poor Bert. Sixty-one years old and in his grave. Far too soon for him to go to his rest.'

It was a conventional phrase, of course. Still it startled me that he would use it. For we all knew very well that Bert was not in his grave and would not be for quite some time. We knew that Bert was in the mortuary, awaiting, undergoing, or showing the effects of the police surgeon's attentions. Anything less restful could hardly be imagined.

'You will stick with it, won't you?' the professor said. He spoke as if about to take his leave. 'You'll get to the bottom of this? I can't believe a publisher of a ladies' magazine has got anything to do with it. Even in spite of the copyright squabble. What was he thinking? After all these years to suddenly start adding new puppets? I wish I understood what kind of trouble he was in to panic and start messing around with his show that way. And the blood? The writing? That kind of nastiness makes me think there's something really malevolent at work, doesn't it you? Not a nice young girl trying to keep a magazine afloat. You'll get to the foot of it, won't you?'

'We will,' Alec said. 'We will get to the truth no matter what that truth is. No matter where the facts lead, we will follow. That's our company motto, isn't it Dandy?'

'We are servants of truth,' I said, nodding.

'Splendid,' said Mackie. 'And you'll write to me? Tell me about your progress?'

'We will need to speak to Miss Bissett about that,' Alec said. 'She's our client. But I can't see her making any trouble about Mr Mackie's brother being informed of progress on the case.'

'Do you think we'll be able to get in to see her?' I asked him. 'Do we even know where she is? Are there cells for women in every jail? Will she have been carted off somewhere? Edinburgh? Glasgow?'

I was still standing on the top step of the police station, facing the street, and I looked over my shoulder then, considering another visit to the stolid bobby to ask him. What I saw made my jaw drop open. Miss Bissett had not been carted off to one of the cities to be handed over to a police matron. She had been held in the very station where we had just produced our fingerprints and she had been released. She was walking towards us right now, scowling, and plucking at her cuffs and belt as though her things had only just been returned to her and she was still wriggling into them.

'Oh!' I said, delight in my voice. 'Here she is! They've let her go!'

'I'm going to slip away,' the professor said. 'I know what I just told you and I think she's probably not guilty. Almost certainly. But just in case, I don't want to meet poor Bert's killer. If it's all the same with you two, I'm going to just slip away.'

Chapter 13

It was hours before Alec and I managed to do the same. Night had fallen by the time we found ourselves trundling westward along the banks of the Tay. The river was a different beast once the town was behind us: no more docks, railways and ferry boats; here, the dark fields sloped down to rocky beaches and the water glittered in the light of a waning moon almost snuffed out to nothing, leaving the stars to dazzle in the black sky.

We pulled over at one point to allow a lorry to pass us and, afterwards, Alec disengaged his gears and switched off the engine.

'What a day,' he said, stepping out. 'Let's have a smoke in the quiet, shall we?'

Since I was not driving, I could have enjoyed a quiet smoke on the road, and I was dog-tired too. The day had begun with the foolish Doig receptionist, and taken in Miss Bissett, the puppets, the lipsticked glass, Cousin Johnny Doig the printer, Mrs Miller the char, the library reading room, Dudhope Park and the devasted Prof. Mackie, Moll at the stage door, the lodgings, the poor squeamish chap at Thomson's and the writing in blood, and finally the police station and the astonishing appearance of the released prisoner . . . all had taken their toll.

Miss Bissett had been little the worse for her sojourn. She had even managed a feeble joke. 'It's an ill wind, isn't it?' she said. 'I can now write an exposé of the Dundee jail.' She jerked her head at the building we had just left. 'Don't let

135

the pillars and portico fool you. The cells are Hogarthian. I've a good mind to do it. Write the convict's eye-view. Like . . . who was it?'

'George Orwell,' said Alec.

'That was destitution, not incarceration,' I said. 'You mean Oscar Wilde, Miss Bissett.'

'Do I?' she said. 'Oh dear. Perhaps best not then.'

'Are you – forgive me the bald question – but are you out on bail?' I asked her, as Alec guided her, with an outstretched arm, towards his motorcar.

'Good heavens, no,' said Miss Bissett. 'I wouldn't know how to begin to organise anything like that. Could you have done it for me? Out of interest?' She was still determined not to pay a solicitor, it seemed. First the cease and desist attempt, which was far outside our usual remit, and now this. I hesitated before answering and thankfully she swept on. 'No, I am released without a stain on my character. My alibi was investigated and has been deemed sturdy.'

'Where shall I drop you?' Alec said. We were all installed now.

'I'm dying for a bath and a drink,' said Miss Bissett. 'But I suppose I should go back to soothe the staff. What a spectacle I made of myself this morning!'

'What *was* your alibi?' I asked, as Alec swung towards the Overgate again.

'Ha! It could hardly have been improved upon if I'd known in advance I'd need it and ordered it from a catalogue,' said Miss Bissett. She had pulled a compact from her bag and was inspecting her face and hair. 'Ugh. I look dreadful.' With a snap, the compact was closed again and stowed away. 'I was golfing on the links over in St Andrews. Just a friendly game with chums. But ahead of us were the Fiscal and some bigwigs he was trying to impress and behind us were a pair of historians from the university. Both sets of old fossils despised our presence there, as you can imagine. We quite ruined their day. And I'm afraid the devil took me and I called out to the Fiscal, "You should have stuck to the club, sir. We wouldn't have been let in there!" My chum punched me in the arm and told me to grow up but I'm very glad I said it now. Was there ever a better alibi?'

'There was not,' Alec said, exchanging a look with me. Unfortunately, Miss Bissett caught it.

'What?' she said. 'What?'

'Just the possibility of an accomplice,' I ventured, once Alec had indicated by extreme concentration on the road that he was not going to say anything. 'An alibi quite so perfect as all that would raise my suspicions rather than allay them. Are the police going to look for someone? Given the motive?'

'You must excuse Mrs Gilver,' Alec said smoothly. 'She is speaking very plainly but theoretically, I assure you. *We* don't suspect you. We are simply used to being devil's advocates.'

Now it was my turn to say nothing. He who declines to speak should refrain from criticising the speech of others, if anyone asked me.

'The police don't seem to think much of the motive, thank goodness,' said Miss Bissett. 'Copyright and infractions thereof mean little to Inspector Daunt.'

'Daunt!' I said. 'One would think he'd bandy that about a bit more freely. Daunt? Golly.'

'What about the puppets and the lipstick?' Alec asked.

'Ah,' said Miss Bissett. 'Much as it pains me to admit it, I've been lucky enough to ride to safety on exalted coat-tails when it comes to those. The mischief at Doig's wasn't the only mischief today, you see.'

'Aha!' said Alec. We had reached our destination and so he was able to turn and give Miss Bissett his full attention as he delivered the next remark. 'The daubed message at Thomson's has persuaded the coppers that both firms were being "framed" eh?'

'Gosh, you *are* good,' said Miss Bissett. She gave Alec a

look that made him blush. 'You're certainly quick on the uptake.'

It was hardly a conundrum of any great challenge, and the solving of it hardly evidence of a towering intellect.

'We have been detecting for fifteen years,' I said, repressively. 'One does pick up this and that.' Then I heard how sour I sounded and cast about for a further contribution that I could deliver more sweetly. 'We are very happy to bring those fifteen years of experience to help you now, Miss Bissett. If you would like us to continue.'

'Um,' she said but, before she could finish the thought and report her decision, the front door of Doig's burst open and Mr Syme of the Art department ventured out all of a tumble, as though he had been pushed from behind.

'It's *you*!' he said, peering into the interior of the motorcar. 'I drew the short straw to come and see who was idling at the kerb and what they wanted.' He twisted round and shouted to someone inside. 'It's Miss Bissett.'

'Why such an excess of vigilance?' she asked him.

'Oh we're all of a-twitter inside,' said Mr Syme. 'He came back!'

'Who came back?' Miss Bissett said. Her voice was filled with dread and I am sure she, like I, was thinking wildly of ghosts, in particular the ghost of one Albert Mackie.

'The florist,' said Mr Syme.

'Who?' began Miss Bissett, but she had not run a successful business all these years for nothing and she cut off the reply. 'Inside,' she said. 'Marshall your thoughts, Mr Syme, and tell me inside. Mrs Gilver? Mr Osborne? Follow me.'

Alec gave a mocking salute behind her back as she left his motorcar and followed her employee into the building, but he made good time after her.

'He came back!' young Fiona was saying as I entered the foyer. A crowd of colleagues was gathered around her, muttering their confirmation. 'The man with the parcel that looked like flowers, Miss Bissett. I saw him upstairs. Never saw him come in and never saw him leave, but he was here.'

'As are you,' I said. 'I thought you'd gone.'

'Upstairs where?' said Miss Bissett.

'Home and Garden,' Mr Syme and Fiona said in chorus. Then Fiona continued: 'Mrs Priest *saw* him.'

Miss Bissett raked the gathered crowd with a shrewd look. 'Is she here?'

'She's had to lie *down*,' Fiona said. 'Nurse McKee said she didn't like her colour.'

'I didn't like her colour,' piped up a woman in a navy uniform, stepping forward. 'I'm going to recommend you send her home once she's had a wee rest, Miss Bissett.'

'What did he want in Home and Garden?' Miss Bissett said, more to herself than the others.

'Has it been searched?' said Alec. 'To see if anything's missing?'

As he spoke, we all heard footsteps approaching down the stairs and watched a pair of trousered legs pass on the far side of the iron lift. 'Nothing's missing,' came a voice, and Johnny Doig appeared, rather white in the face. He strode into the middle of our little group and banged down what appeared to be a gallon paint tin. My nose wrinkled. 'He left this behind though. I didn't notice it on my first pass through. There are always such a lot of oddities up there: clever new hand tools and kitchen aids and what have you. It was on Graham Alexander's desk. As if he was going to write about it or test it or something. But it occurred to me that no manufacturer would send such a lot of it, would he? He'd send a little sample. The cost of the postage alone.'

'I admit it's odd,' Alec said, 'but do you have any other— Oh!' He stopped and bent close to the front of the tin where the label was pasted. His nose was wrinkling too and young Fiona, quite unconsciously, had put her hand up so that her cuff covered her nostrils.

I had gone to stand beside Alec and read the label by myself. The lettering struck me as horribly familiar.

Plenty more where
this came from.
It is not over.

'Does anyone have a stout penknife?' Alec asked and one was thrust into his hand, already opened. He kneeled and, very carefully, touching only the knife handle and not the tin, worked his way round prising up the lid. When it came away, the crowd, who had inched forward, all fell back, crying with a single voice in protest at the smell. I had been ready for it and so, holding my breath, I leaned over and peered in. The tin was almost empty, just a sludge of blood and plaster clinging around the bottom.

'Is that . . . Is that . . .?' Miss Bissett said.

'Yes, but probably from the butcher,' Alec said. 'Not human.' He was trying to help.

'*Human?*' squeaked Mr Syme as Fiona yelped '*Probably?*'

Alec refitted the lid and pressed it down hard with the butt of the penknife. He proffered the knife back to its owner but the gentleman shrank away, shaking his head.

'Should I ring the police?' said Miss Bissett. 'I can't say I'm keen to be dragged off again. Once is enough for today.'

'The thing about ringing the police,' I said, 'is that, strictly speaking Mr Doig, you oughtn't to have moved it.'

'I'll put it back,' Johnny Doig said. 'To be rediscovered later and left severely alone.'

I was not happy about the plan but he was gone before I could muster a coherent counter-argument. Besides, Miss Bissett had hit her stride.

'Mr Syme, have a nip of brandy from the bottle in your office. You look peaky. Nurse McKee, could you check on Mrs Priest and see if she's fit to journey home. If she is, please ring up a cab for her. The rest of you should all have

140

a cup of sweet tea and a biscuit. No doubt Mrs Miller will make another round. Fiona, could you bring mine upstairs and a cup each for Mr Osborne and Mrs Gilver? To the boardroom, please. Meanwhile, I shall ring up the police station and tell them about our grisly find. Remember everyone: Mrs Priest found it and came to tell me and I rang the police. That's the tale and we must stick to it.'

'No,' Fiona said. The rest of the staff had started to disperse but that brought them to a standstill. 'No, I won't. I won't stick to tales and I won't bring your tea. I'm not going up those stairs when we don't know who's in here or why. And I'm not sitting on this desk to see if he comes back in right past me with another bucket of blood. My mum never wanted me to take a job and my young man's asked me twice to marry him. I should never have come back after this morning and this time I'm done.' She had been rummaging on the low shelf under her desk as she spoke and, once she had extracted her handbag, her cardigan, her umbrella and her picture magazine, she strode out with her chin in the air.

'Anyone else?' said Miss Bissett.

'Pfft,' said one of the young women in the brown overalls. I took her to be a packer. 'She was always a flighty bit. And about as much use as a chocolate teapot on her best day.'

'Well, well,' said Miss Bissett. Then, in response to a distant clank and jingle: 'Here comes Mrs Miller with the tea.'

So it was that by the time Alec and I pulled off the road for a smoke on the way home, the plan was hatched for our return to Dundee the next day: I was to sit at the front desk at Doig's and await the possible return of the man we had apparently agreed to call 'the florist', while Alec was to haunt the back door in case the man made his approach from there. We had argued stoutly that we should be free to follow wherever the case took us. But Miss Bissett had pointed out, not unreasonably, that she was our client and she wanted us to guard the building.

141

'Of course, I'll only need to be there when deliveries are expected or vans are going out,' Alec said. 'I can come and relieve you otherwise, Dandy. Let you get round the staff asking questions.'

'Or you can do it,' I said. 'I don't mind. I'm rather looking forward to learning how to put through telephone calls, if I'm honest. I've never had a "job" before.'

'What about the convalescent home?' said Alec. 'That was work.'

'I was never a nurse,' I said. 'It was more like duty visits to a relation, except that we weren't related and they were one after another all day. Poor things.'

'Hm,' said Alec. 'You've said rather too much about your tasks before now for me to believe that.' He sounded considerably annoyed, which struck me as unfair. One is required to land on a pinhead with him, some days. One can't mention the war or the fallen, or even the upsetting scenes in which one played a part. But one cannot finesse them out of the record either. One path is unfeeling and the other patronising. It is impossible. And it is impossible to complain about too. I said nothing, for that reason, but merely smoked in silence.

'Sorry,' he said, gruffly, after a while.

'Nonsense,' I said, and equilibrium was restored. 'What worries me more than who gets to lark about with the notebook and who has to stick to his – or her – post is whether we'll miss the meat of the case if we're stranded at Doig's altogether.'

'The police certainly think so, thank God,' Alec said.

'And all His angels,' I agreed.

The police had come to fetch away the bucket of blood, in the person of Constable Adams from Dudhope Park on Monday. He had confirmed what a sensible fellow he was by responding, having seen the bucket and read the message: 'Someone's got it in for you, Miss Bissett. You should be very careful this next wee while.'

'But if not at Doig's,' I asked Alec now, 'then where *are* the answers to be found?'

'The answers to which questions?' Before I could furnish them, he replied himself. 'Whodunnit, naturally. How did he get away without being seen. How did he arrive without being seen. Why did he pick such a ridiculous venue for the crime. What do the puppets, the blood and the lipstick have to do with it? Is the florist the murderer? Is the biblical dauber the murderer? What does Bert Mackie's murder have to do with the killing fifty years ago! How on earth do the two men come to have the same name, for the love of God!' What had begun as a list of questions turned into questions proper and ended as an outburst straight from the heart. In disgust, Alec threw his fag end away into the grass; then, in even more of a temper, he trotted over to stamp it out. His Dorset childhood had left him with the indelible belief that discarded fags and matches might cause a fire. Perthshire is in no danger of going up in a blaze, in August or any other month, but I find it endearing and have never mentioned it to him.

'Let's take it to a board meeting,' he said as he came back, and I could see the glint of his teeth in the darkness as he grinned.

I was grinning myself as we tucked ourselves back into the seats and set off on our way. Gilver and Osborne is still a two-man operation and I do not foresee any expansion into typists and the like. We would have to desert our only principle – as Alec likes to call it – and take on divorce work if we had our hearts set on an office in town and a pool of underlings. Things have not come to it yet, thankfully. That said, first my husband and then my maid had over the years offered help – both helpful help and the kind of help it is a bother to avoid – and each now felt that they were deeply concerned in Gilver and Osborne, almost to the point of wanting recognition in the form of a mention on our business cards. We skirted that ignominy by not having any of the things. Alec was against them outright, feeling that they were déclassé and smacked of the grubbier end of commerce. I held out on more practical grounds; I could not imagine ever fishing one out of a pocket or bag and managing to hand it over without making a muck of it somehow: mistiming the thing so that I had to watch it being read and evaluated; pressing it too eagerly where it was not wanted and offending the pressee; or simply dropping it in a puddle. I had never mastered the art of giving tips from hand to hand, once the world changed from the place where I had been born, into one where such acts became a social necessity. I still far preferred the old days when tipping was something one did to other people's servants in envelopes after one was gone, or to one's own servants at Christmas in the form of dress lengths and bottles of brandy. Tipping cabbies, waiters and shop girls is a rigmarole I shall never find easy.

'Tomorrow,' I said to Alec. 'Let's lay it out to them and see if hearing it all of a lump makes it clear.'

'I hope not, if I'm frank,' Alec said. 'They are both insufferable in their separate ways when they see through a tangle that we've been caught up in.'

'*They're* insufferable!' I said. '*They* are!'

'We are too,' said Alec, which set me spluttering. 'Oh all right then, *I* am. But why not? Why shouldn't we have fun with it, if the competition keeps us up to the mark?'

'Because of poor Bert,' I said. 'You didn't see him, Alec. Crumpled on the grass in that tent, with his throat slit. It's hard for me to think of this case as any kind of fun. His face will haunt me.'

'I do feel somewhat different about it, actually, from not having seen him,' Alec said. 'I thought it was the endless variety of witnesses today and the deluge of facts to be taken in that was making things seem so . . .'

'Muddled?'

'Muffled. But now you mention it, it could well be from

144

not being there at the moment of crisis. He seems missing from things. No, I don't mean "gone"; I know he's gone. But he seems . . . I can't catch at him, somehow. Nothing Moll said, nor even his brother, brought him to life much. What do we know of this chap who was born to new respectability in a Glasgow villa—'

'Dunelgar!' I said, remembering.

'Indeed. Born into this new respectability and then squandered it entirely by plunging into the life of a wandering puppeteer. Such a vertiginous descent, while the other brother rose.'

'He wasn't quite without intellect either,' I said. 'He was interested in the history of the form. A purist. A scholar, one might almost say.'

'Did you believe that?' said Alec. 'I wondered if his brother was trying to add a little gloss to his reputation.'

'Moll said something similar,' I reminded him.

'But still,' Alec insisted. 'Something about the claim struck me as terrifically bogus.'

'Don—' I began, then bit my lip. I had been going to tell him not to say 'bogus' the way I did my sons, even Donald, though his marriage and fatherhood should have stopped me.

'Sorry, Mummy,' said Alec, and the moment when we might have hit upon the pertinent fact was lost in laughter.

Chapter 14

Grant, on the following morning, could scarcely be made to care about the case, from the detecting point of view, so charmed was she by the prospect of fitting me out as an office girl.

'You can't wear your diamond,' she said, referring to my engagement ring, as if it was my habit to swan around blinding everyone with a duck egg. 'And I wouldn't think make-up would be allowed either, madam.'

'Oh no,' I said. 'No, no, no. You are not plonking me down in daylight and a grey coat and skirt without a bit of paint on my face. Besides, Miss Bissett wears scarlet lipstick and lash black and young Fiona, whose job I'm stepping into, had suspiciously rosy cheeks for her colouring too.'

'What grey coat and skirt?' was all Grant said. 'Have you bought something off the peg in Dundee, madam? Where did you put it when you came in last night?' I withered her with a look. 'Good. I can't bear cheap clothes. I'm going to add collar and cuffs to that navy dress you never liked. If I take up the hem I can put some belt loops in and it'll look very suitable. You could tuck a hanky into your waistband.'

I shook my head and left her standing in the middle of my bedroom floor while I went for my bath. Bunty, darling dotty dog, was waiting in the bathroom for me, wagging her whole back half in her delight at my return. I wondered if a company as eccentric as Doig's would let a receptionist keep a Dalmatian under the desk, but decided it was better not to chance it.

'Come on then,' I told her as I lowered myself into the

bathwater. She put her paws on the side, submerged her muzzle and drank noisily and deeply. She never does it while the water waits for me and won't touch the stuff after I'm done, but I seem to make a bath full of hot water into her favourite kind of soup with my presence, and the challenge is to stop her drinking so much of it that I have to run in more. The other problem is that I have had to give up bath salts, but, as I used to think in the early years of my marriage, our soft peaty water came out of the taps – actually upstairs in tall jugs in those days – ready salted.

'Will you need spectacles?' said Grant, rejoining me. 'She'll be sick if she keeps golloping down hot water like that, madam.'

'I'm sure she'll turn away,' I said. 'Why would I need spectacles?'

'To complete your disguise,' Grant said. 'To perch on the end of your nose while you take dictation.'

'I shan't be taking dictation.'

'It would help the effect overall.'

'Not if someone who can actually take dictation looked at the bird scratches I'd made and I was undone as the fraud I am.'

'You'll have to type,' Grant said. 'What if someone sees *those* bird scratches.'

'I shan't have to type at all,' I said. 'There are typists, in a pool. I shall have to smile, answer the telephone and intercept intruders.'

'*I* can type,' Grant said, rather wistfully. Clearly she was embarking on a campaign to join us.

'What colour of collar and cuffs were you thinking?' I said. One can always deflect Grant with talk of fashion.

'Not white,' she said. 'Too stark for your colouring. Perhaps a sky blue or a pale pink. I'll surprise you.'

The deflection did not survive the board meeting, most unfortunately. The four of us gathered in my sitting room

147

after breakfast and Bunty's walk; Alec, Grant, Hugh and I. I sighed about the inevitable lack of refreshment: Pallister, our butler, can just about countenance Grant sitting with us and pitching in her thoughts on the matter of the day, but if he were asked to serve her with coffee, much less sherry, he might give his notice and open a country pub.

Alec took the floor to fill in the other two. That is always to be preferred, since Hugh listens to him more attentively and Grant interrupts him quite a bit less.

'It's a beaut of a case,' he began. 'The impossible crime, carried out by the invisible man, under the gaze of twenty-five strangers. And fifty years to the day after another man of the same name and doing the same job – no relation, mind you – was killed in the same spot.'

'Who are the principal players?' said Grant, drawing a sheet of paper towards her.

'The deceased himself,' Alec said. 'Albert Mackie, an itinerant Punch and Judy man. He seems to have had a great deal of interest in the history of the form, even to the extent of sticking with the old characters, whether or not they were likely to entertain children.' He shuddered.

'That chap with the extending neck was pretty gruesome,' I agreed.

'He had a Scaramouche?' said Hugh.

'And no crocodile or sausages,' said Alec. 'So that's Bert. He came from a middlingly respectable family, or one that improved itself anyway, and his brother has done terribly well, but Bert – suspending requirements not to speak ill of the dead – was a bit of a drinker, and wont to throw his fists about when in his cups. He lived in a style below modest, in the barest, humblest rooms down by the docks while he was in Dundee and, I suppose, in much the same manner in the other towns. He also had an understanding with one "Moll" at the stage door of Her Majesty's Theatre and similar understandings with similar women elsewhere.'

'Similar to Moll?' I put in. 'She's a one-off, surely.'

'We had the good fortune to see over his rooms before the police got to them,' Alec said, ignoring me, 'but there was nothing by way of a clue. Nothing much at all, actually.'

'A clue in its own right, perhaps,' said Grant, which was a good point. I cast my mind back to consider whether Mackie's rooms were simply tidy or whether they had been stripped.

'Who next?' Alec said. 'There are two publishers of newspapers and magazines in Dundee. Thomson's, very much the Goliath to the local David, which goes by the name of Doig's. Thomson's publishes the daily and Sunday papers and a slew of successful magazines, including comic strips.' Hugh sighed and frowned at the same time. He is one of the few people who can pull this off. I tried it and found the sigh ruined and the frown ineffective. 'There is a point to my including that detail, Hugh,' Alec said. 'We were engaged, Dandy and I, by Doig's, very small beer compared with Thomson's but also in the comic strip game. Now, here's the case we were handed: Bert Mackie, newly arrived in Dundee, added the beloved cartoon characters of Thomson's to his Punch and Judy show without permission. Briefly, until the solicitors scolded him out of it.'

'Are you sure that's true?' said Grant.

'Very perspicacious of you,' Alec said. 'As it turned out, it was a tarradiddle. But how did you guess?'

'It's obvious,' said Grant, annoyingly.

'But we *do* know that he added the characters from the Doig stable,' Alec said. 'One Rosie Cheeke and one Freckle.'

'Do we?' said Grant.

'Of course,' Alec said. 'After all, that's precisely why Miss Bissett engaged us.'

'But Alec,' I said. 'Grant's right. I mean, *do* we actually know that Mackie did what he's accused of? The puppets weren't in the show, as the two of us, Becky and Mrs Tilling

149

can all attest. Granted, the man was dead before the end of the first act, but Rosie and Freckle weren't even in the tent.'

'They were there in the boardroom at Doig's the next morning, though,' Alec said. 'They certainly exist.'

'Yes, but—' I began before Hugh interrupted me.

'Don't start arguing yet,' he said. 'Let's lay it all out first. Carry on, Osborne.'

'The next morning, at Doig's, in the boardroom, the two puppets were propped up on chairs. And there was a note, written in red lipstick on Miss Bissett's private cloakroom glass. "That's the way to do it".' He shuddered again. 'Nasty. Nasty enough for Miss Bissett to be dragged off to the police station in handcuffs and thrown in a cell. She's out now, thankfully, because at the time the murder took place, she was golfing at St Andrews in sight of a full deck of bigwigs.'

'But if it's an impossible crime carried out by an invisible man,' said Grant, 'why not add an unbreakable alibi?'

'More to the point,' I said, 'while Miss Bissett was in chains, someone daubed a message on the back wall of Thomson's. Not lipstick this time, but just as red. It was blood. And, also while Miss Bissett was under lock and key, someone strolled into Doig's and put the almost emptied bucket of blood on the desk of the poor blameless Home and Garden editor and just about gave her heart failure.'

'And now for the strangest thing of all,' said Alec, seizing the floor back from me with the smooth look that is his version of Hugh's frown and sigh. 'The death fifty years ago was commemorated in the paper on Monday with a verse from Deuteronomy.'

'Vengeance?' said Grant.

'Vengeance,' Alec confirmed. 'And the *next* verse was what was daubed on the wall at Thomson's. Along with the accusation that the inhabitants of the building were murderers.'

'And then the paint was left in Doig's?' said Grant. She certainly did have a good grasp of the affair.

'Exactly,' Alec said. He paused for a moment, then started filling his pipe. 'Any time you want to reveal the solution we've missed, go ahead.'

As Hugh drew breath to speak I was aware of feeling quite dejected. He has never admitted that the clear summation of the problem given by us to him is in any part responsible for the brainwaves he has. He would crow about it for days if he had done it again.

'Clearly, this Miss Bissett had an accomplice,' he said. 'To carry out the actual crime and to go capering about with buckets of blood. I daresay she was delighted to be hauled off. You couldn't really ask for a better alibi than being in a jail cell.'

'She didn't look delighted,' I said. 'And are you forgetting, Hugh, that she employed us? It was down to her that I was there on Monday when Bert died and that we were both there yesterday when the puppets and lipstick came to light. Our witnessing the blood at Thomson's was a lucky accident, but otherwise she orchestrated the presence of detectives.'

'Cocky,' said Hugh.

Alec and I had entertained the notion before now that our client had engaged us to augment an air of innocence, but we had never been right and I was far from convinced that this time was the exception. Hugh had not seen the woman, or heard her anguish.

'"Cocky" would be an understatement,' Alec said. 'Rash, foolhardy, demented. Dandy, did you get the impression she was speaking with a forked tongue when she rang you on Sunday?'

'I believed completely that she wanted the puppets out of the show and wanted me to make it happen,' I said. 'And the puppets exist. We saw them. What do you mean?'

'We saw them at Doig's,' Alec said. 'Just as Grant said. Not in the puppet show.'

'I don't know why you're suddenly so doubtful,' I said.

151

'But we must be thorough, I suppose. We can find out who actually saw the puppets and how Miss Bissett found out about them.'

'Let's turn to the fifty-year anniversary now,' Hugh said. Cheated of the first point he had tried to win he would be even more determined to carry this new one. 'Same name, same job, same scene and same crime?'

'We don't know how the first Mr Mackie was killed, but yes to the rest.'

'Maybe he wasn't,' Hugh said. 'Maybe it was a mistake, or more mischief. Was it reported at the time?'

'It was in the *Dundee Advertiser* of 1887,' I said.

'Well then, either this new Mr Mackie is related or was operating under a pseudonym. Let's consider which is more likely.'

'Neither are at all likely,' I said.

Hugh ignored me. 'If he inherited his tent and puppets from a father, that helps explain why they're so old-fashioned.'

'Yes, but he didn't,' I said. 'His brother is the most respectable man you could imagine, Hugh. A professor at St Andrews and terribly embarrassed by poor Bert, not to mention distressed at his embarrassment. Anyway, he furnished us with the information that their father was the manager of a billiards hall and that they have no uncles, and no ancestors in the puppet game at all. He was utterly mystified by the coincidence. As am I.'

'Hm,' Hugh said. 'The professor brother rather gets in the way of my "stage name" theory too, doesn't he?' It was a significant concession from my husband. I rewarded him with a smile and he looked away.

'Why don't we ask around?' said Grant.

'Around where?' said Alec. 'Ask who?'

'You said understandings with women who work in theatres,' Grant said. 'Moll at Dundee and similar women elsewhere? Do you know where, by any chance?'

'No,' said Alec. 'But we could surely find out. And then, do you think we could go and ask what these women know about Bert's family? Moll didn't even know he had a brother.'

'St Andrews,' I said. 'His brother mentioned St Andrews in mid-June. Golly, when you think about it like that, he was probably even in Perth at some point.'

'Might I use the telephone, madam?' said Grant. 'Theatre people are among the hardiest in the land, as you know. They never stop. So there's a fighting chance that Sidney Hasting is still on the door of the Majestic. And if there was an understanding between a Punchinello and anyone there, Sid would know. He was always the world's worst backstage gossip. Saw everything and would tell anyone for the price of a Guinness.'

I gestured towards the telephone. 'Be my guest,' I said. 'But do hang up quickly if Pallister approaches, won't you?' I added, then felt rather shabby as all three of the others smiled. Pallister is a man of dignity and should not be smiled about behind his back.

Grant needed no urging. She was a master with the modern exchange too and before another minute had passed she was hailing someone on the other end of the line.

'Yes, yes indeed, really and truly. I've no idea – twenty years anyway. What? Oh, they're fine. Still at it. Wouldn't have it any other way. Me?' Here she shot me a look and cupped her hand more closely around the earpiece to shield me from what was passing. 'Oh, well, you know. It's not so bad really. I've no complaints.' She had the grace to blush as I raised my eyebrows. 'Now, Sid, I'll tell you why I've popped up out of the blue like a genie through a trapdoor. What? I *do* remember! How could I forget? Six weeks in traction, if my memory serves. But I suppose the place has been redone since then. New ropes and pulleys? No? Well, you wouldn't catch me up on a wire.' She caught Hugh's eye then, and seemed to come back to herself. 'I've got a name for you, Sid.

I need you to go through that address book you carry between your ears and tell me if it means anything. No, not a girl. No, I wouldn't. Did you? Are you? Fifteen years? Well, congratulations. Me? No. Not yet anyway. I'm still Miss Grant, and I daresay I'll stay Miss Grant till I die. No, this is a man. A Punchinello man. Traveller. Name of Albert Mackie. Only we think that might be a fake—' She held up a hand as though we had been chattering in the background and distracting her. 'Really? Well, there's a turn-up. I don't think . . . I mean, there's no need . . . I wouldn't want . . .'

Then she swallowed hard and passed the telephone to me. 'One of the dressers, madam. Tilly. Sid said she and Bert had been "close friends" for over a decade. He's gone to fetch her.'

'Grant!' I said. 'Why should it fall to me to tell the poor thing what's happened to him? Here, take it back. Don't be such a sweep! And stop laughing, you two.' For Alec and Hugh were finding this development immensely entertaining. I waved a hand at them to shut up as I heard echoing footsteps; a woman was approaching the stage-door telephone in that far-off theatre.

'Bertie?' came her voice after the usual thumps and rustles from the mouthpiece and earpiece being adjusted. 'Where have you got to? You were supposed to be back by now.'

'Oh dear,' I said. 'I rather think the message has been garbled. Mr Hasting – was it? – didn't mean Mr Mackie was on the line for you. But someone with news of him. And you are? Matilda?'

'Theresa,' she said. 'Tilly for everyday. Who are you? You sound a right posh bit. How have you got your claws into Bert?'

'Oh my goodness!' I said. 'It's not that at all. Heavens, no. I'm a married woman, for one thing.'

Hugh's mouth dropped open. 'What the devil's she saying to you?' he asked in a fierce whisper.

154

'So?' said Tilly. 'Lots of women walk down the aisle and still find themselves alone and needing a cuddle. Actress, are you? You've got the plums in your gob for it.'

'Good grief!' I said. Alec, even though he could hear none of this, was nevertheless hugging himself and rocking to and fro with silent mirth. 'I am a detective, young lady.'

'Bully for you. And I'm fifty-three, by the way.'

'Oh. Well, I'm still a detective, my . . . good woman. A private detective, and I'm afraid I've got some bad news for you about your friend.' I paused, hoping she would guess, but after a moment's silence I was forced to carry on. 'I'm sorry to have to tell you that he has met with misfortune. He was set upon, on Monday, in Dundee. In fact, my . . . dear, I'm afraid he has been killed.'

'But,' said Tilly, quite humbled by this shocking news. Her voice had lost all its bluster. 'But he's supposed to be back here. I've got his trunk. I've got all his worldly belongings, except the rig. What am I supposed to do with it all?'

'His brother should receive his . . . estate, by rights,' I said.

'Oh yes. He mentioned a brother once or twice,' Tilly said. 'But I wouldn'tknow where to start to find him.'

'He's a Professor Leon B. Mackie,' I said. 'And he's rather at hand too, since his chair is at St Andrews University. He's in the psychology department. I can let him know to expect a letter from you. Or my associate and I could make a visit and pick the things up. Deliver them for you.'

'No, no,' said Tilly. She was rallying. 'No, no, no. I'm not handing all Bert's traps over to a stranger to pick over and blame me for what's gone missing. I'll handle it myself. Leon, eh?'

'Professor Mackie,' I said, regretting that I had let the poor man in for more upset, once this bumptious individual tracked him down. 'And please do remember that he has had a terrible shock and is grieving.'

155

'Don't you worry about that, missus,' came the reply, oddly vehement. 'I know how to behave.'

Without so much as a word of leave-taking, she hung up and left me open-mouthed like a goldfish.

'Oh, Alec,' I said. 'Poor Professor Mackie. That dreadful woman is going to beard him at the university and . . . well, I couldn't work out if she's going to ask for a hand-out plain and simple or hold the brother's belongings to ransom and make the poor chap buy them back.'

'We could hot-foot it down there and try to stop her,' Alec said. 'Or tell the Dundee police that we've found the man's effects and then *they'll* stop her.'

'That's a much better idea,' I said. 'Hand it to the police and let's us concentrate on *our* case, for *our* client. Miss Bissett wants us watching out for the possible return of this "florist". That's what we shall do.'

Conscientiousness and good manners had been dinned into me by Nanny Palmer, my governess and Mlle Toulemonde at my finishing school. Even my mother had helped, by way of frowning her displeasure should my behaviour ever fall short. In middle age I was still unable to let the sun go down on an unanswered letter, let a thank you note stay unwritten, and let a paying client go hang while I truffled off after more exciting prey than the result that paying client desired. So it was that, with all four of us paying attention, I decided to ignore the alarm 'Tilly' had set off, and return to Dundee.

Chapter 15

Grant got her way, infuriating as it is to relate, because it made good plain sense to have someone manning the front desk, pretending to be a receptionist, someone manning the staff entrance downstairs at the back, pretending to be an odd-job man or perhaps one of the printers on a perpetual tea break, and someone left over to roam the various offices, conducting interviews. At least I got to be *that* one and did not have to suffer Grant swanning about and stopping by with updates only when it suited her. Besides, as luck would have it, I happened to be there at hand in the foyer when the matter became pressing.

Miss Bissett had recomposed herself after her ordeal. She was already in her office when I climbed the stairs, suited and lipsticked as ever, with her hair freshly set and her high-heeled shoes propped on the edge of her desk as she swung to and fro on her revolving chair.

'Do be careful,' I said. 'Is it one of the ones that tilts as well as spins?'

'I've been sitting in this chair since my legs were too short for my feet to reach the floor,' said Miss Bissett. 'Now, I shall have to leave you to it, Mrs Gilver. We've lost a lot of ground and we can't afford to put out a light issue. I'll be paying overtime all week as it is.'

'Oh, I don't know,' I said. 'I always prefer the more cheerful articles in any magazine I pick up at the station. Would it hurt for once?'

Miss Bissett looked at me as though I were a grub on a lettuce leaf. 'Light,' she said, 'means short of pages. Thinner than usual. It knocks out the printing, the paper reams, the packers, the orders, the loading of the deliveries. We need forty copies to a box or the whole caboodle will be like a ball of wool when a kitten gets it.'

'Ah,' I said. 'And I suppose there's no way to reuse old material? The *Good Housekeeping* do it all the time.'

'Mrs Priest has not returned to her post after the shock yesterday,' said Mrs Bissett. 'So even if that were an option, we are without the very woman who could make it happen. Besides, it isn't an option. The *Good Housekeeping* can freely reprint from their unassailable position. They are not standing in the shadow of a predator.'

'You could use bigger writing perhaps?'

'Bigger writing,' said Miss Bissett. It was not a question. It was an expression of stupefied disbelief.

'Or,' I said, feeling sure that finally I had hit upon a sensible suggestion, 'you could offer some enticements to your advertisers.' I was very proud of the way these words tripped off my tongue.

'Mrs Gilver,' said Miss Bissett, 'if I were to instruct the good men in my advertising department to drop our prices, then the manufacturer of every vanishing cream, gripe water, cigarette and floor polish in Scotland would conclude that the *Cheek* was going under and would pull all their advertisements before the pall of failure could stick.'

'Really?' I said. 'Golly, they sound flightier than the stock exchange. Gripe water? You do surprise me.'

'And so I must conjure up a walk on the monk's way from the landing at Cockburnspath and persuade Mrs Hodge to write three recipes instead of two, and publish them without testing first, and persuade Mr Gould in Letters to cover for us if the recipes go wrong and we are flooded with complaints.' She drew a ragged breath. 'And meanwhile you must . . . do whatever it is you want to do to help me in the way you promised to help me only yesterday.'

My eyebrows had climbed my forehead as she expended all of that and my mouth had pursed. She was, when all was said and done, a slip of a girl and I was not accustomed to being addressed that way.

'Don't glare at me,' she said. 'You are not my Aunt Maud.' Then she gave a bark of laughter. 'Speaking of which, thank God Uncle John is safely in Bournemouth. At least I shan't have to deal with his "help". Now, if he would just stop ringing up Johnny in the middle of the working day, when he's far too busy to break off . . .' She sighed. 'What is it you want to ask me?'

'I have a very few questions,' I said. 'They won't take more than a minute.' None of them was a request for the name of her nanny or governess so I could pass them on to my daughter-in-law in the hope that one day my own little granddaughter would achieve these heights of insolence. 'Who saw the puppet show with your characters in it?'

Miss Bissett frowned. 'What do you mean?' she said. 'Everyone did. The audience in the park did.'

'But how do you know?' I said. 'Were some of your staff in the park?'

'No, of course not. They were all at work. It was a Friday afternoon. Oh, I see what you're asking. One of our readers congratulated us on it. She was charmed by the appearance of her favourites and she stopped in afterwards to praise us for the innovation.'

'You spoke to her?' I said.

'Good heavens, of course not,' said Miss Bissett. 'We constantly have our valued readers stopping in at the desk to share their thoughts. I'd get nothing done if I went flying down every time. No, Fiona rang for Mr Gould. Letters.'

'Letters?' I said. Of all the departments I might have expected her to mention that was near the last of them.

'I'll let Mr Gould himself explain why,' said Miss Bissett. 'I prefer to draw a veil.'

Of course, that was like waving a lollipop in front of a toddler. Wherever a veil has been drawn I, in my detective's role, must withdraw it again.

'And where would I find Mr Gould?' I asked.

'What's this all about?' she said.

I wondered how to answer her. 'It's just that the tale of the Oor Wullie and Maw Broon puppets isn't true,' I said in the end. 'Thomson's knew nothing about it. They didn't get their lawyer to stop it.'

Miss Bissett looked suitably startled.

'And so we're wondering if any more of the story would dissolve if one blew on it. If perhaps the whole thing is an attempt—'

'At a "frame-up"?' she said. 'To make it look as though I had a motive?'

'Exactly.'

'Down one flight and all the way to the end then through the double doors,' she said. 'But don't keep him talking all morning if you can help it.' As I rose, she put out a hand. 'I'm not being callous. I hope you find out who killed Mackie. It's just that it was no one here who did it and it would do no good for us to slip and go under through an excess of fine feeling.'

I thought, as I took myself down the stairs, trying not to clatter since so many people were evidently working hard all around me, that I had no idea magazine publishing was such a high-wire act. To be frank, I had never considered it at all before Miss Bissett's telephone call and my introduction to Doig's. As I turned the pages of a picture paper on a train journey or flipped through *Tatler* at someone's house to while away a shooting party, I had never given a thought to the army of men and women who beavered away to get out the issues. For this reason, when I had found the double doors behind which Mr Gould ran the Letters department, I knocked quite diffidently and arranged a supplicating expression on my face.

The expansive call to 'come in, come in, whoever you are!' was a surprise, and when I entered I found a large, egg-shaped gentleman with a head of a smaller but otherwise identical egg shape, sitting behind a cluttered desk with a napkin tucked in at his neck. 'Oh!' he said, on sighting me. 'Well, I suppose I can't complain, but I thought you were Mrs Miller with the coffee and buns. It's Eccles day today. Quite delicious but terribly flaky.' He twitched the napkin away and refolded it on a small plate that sat waiting on his desktop. He seemed to have pushed aside a mountain of papers to give it room.

'Mr Gould, I don't think we met downstairs and I don't seem to remember you being in the foyer when . . . well, yesterday.'

'I know!' he said, archly. 'I was at the dentist and missed everything. Just my luck. But I'm going to take a wild stab in the dark and guess that you are Mrs Gilver.' I nodded. 'Where's Mr Osborne?'

'He's stationed at the back door,' I said. 'In case the florist comes back. The chap with the bucket of—'

Mr Gould held up a hand. 'Please, don't. Ghastly.'

'Miss Bissett just told me you were the first one to hear the news about the puppets. I'd be very grateful if you'd relay it to me. There seems to be some muddle about it round at Thomson's, so I'm double-checking here. No offence intended.'

Mr Gould, far from taking offence, flapped his hands and sighed elaborately. 'Oh, I wouldn't be at all surprised,' he said. 'I'd have to be much more of a fusspot than I am to keep all this in apple-pie order. Muddle threatens me at every turn. Muddle looms at my elbow and breathes down my neck. I mean to say: Letters, you see. But are they, Mrs Gilver? Are they? Are they letters per se?' He waved a hand over the piles of paper on his desk, which I now saw *were* letters. Mr Gould snatched up a handful from the nearest pile. 'Take these!' he cried. 'They're complaining about

161

recipes. As complaints they should be answered individually. But then they carry on to suggest improvements, making them letters per se. So they should go to the "Good Neighbour" column on the Letters page. Only they suggest something easier and tastier altogether, quite often, so they should be sent down to Mrs Hodge for testing.

'Or what about this lot?' He let the recipe complaints drop, scattering them far and wide, and snatched up a new handful. 'Are they expressing appreciation of the article on early married life? A triumph of delicacy, I must say. We don't answer thank you letters with thank you letters of our own, or where would it end? But perhaps they're not thank you letters. Perhaps they are letters per se, whose writers really mean the details they include to be printed on the Letters page. Or perhaps they are Questions to be Answered. Because even though the *Cheek* has never had a Questions Answered page, and is not about to start one now, it doesn't stop battalions of readers sending pleas every month as though we were their mothers, or their ministers. Or,' he paused and finished his outpouring in a near whisper 'their doctors. Believe me.'

'Dear dear,' I said.

'I say "believe me" but you wouldn't even if I told you,' said Mr Gould. 'Everything from "My husband uses too much hair oil and I can't get the pillow slips clean for my life" to "My sister's fiancé has asked me to a dance, what should I do?" And much worse, as I indicated, but I won't go into details.'

'It must be quite an undertaking every month,' I said. 'I see what you mean about the taxonomy. If that's the word I mean.'

'Taxonomy?' said Mr Gould. 'Winnowing, I call it. How to shovel enough of it off my desk onto the desks of others so that I've got some faint hope of managing.'

'Ah, now we come to it,' I said. 'Given how busy you are, why were you summoned downstairs to deal with the matter of the puppets at all? It doesn't seem to me to be within the purview of your department.'

'Thank you for saying so,' Mr Gould said with grave courtesy. He even bowed. 'Here's the thing though. When they come in, as they do – sometimes they bring the results of their attempts to follow our recipes. Not when it's worked – they eat *that* – usually when it's stuck to the pan or run out of the case or what have you. But when they come in, I go down and have a little chat and then tell them that their concerns will be addressed in the next issue, on the Letters page. Then I make a bit of space somewhere and say "To the young lady who lightened the editor's day with a visit, we say thank you for your . . ." quick thinking, or household acumen, or principled arguments, depending on what bee she might have had in her bonnet, ". . . you are the heart, soul, sinew and crowning glory of the *Rosy Cheek* and we salute you." They love it. Lap it up.'

'Don't they notice that you say it every month?' I said.

'I don't know,' said Mr Gould, wonderingly. 'I'm never sure if they only scour the Letters page when they've popped in, or if they read the Salutes in every issue.'

'Or if they read the "Salutes" and want to feature in one so badly they drum up excuses to come and pester you,' I said.

'Now that is a sobering thought,' said Mr Gould. 'Imagine if our ploy to deal with the stoppers-in was actually making work for poor old me! That's a very sobering thought indeed.'

'Well, I'm glad that the policy is currently in place,' I said. 'For that means that it was someone of your stature who dealt with this particular woman and not young Fiona, who struck me as rather less . . .' he had narrowed his eyes, '. . . attentive,' I finished.

'I feared you were going to say mature, Mrs Gilver. It was Friday afternoon.' He had swept into the meat of the conversation without any further preamble and I found myself scrabbling for my notebook and my propelling pencil. 'Fiona – no loss, that girl, if she's really gone; she wasn't nearly decorative enough to excuse her incompetence. Don't quote me – she rang up on the internal telephone, without dropping the connection or cutting off any other calls while she was at it. For once. And so I went tripping down there, cuffs buttoned, coat on, hair combed.' I had been looking down at my pad to hide the expression I feared I might be wearing, since Mr Gould's waspishness was beginning to grate on me. I was glad of it now – I could not have helped a glance at the shining top of his egg-like head if I had been facing him. 'She was waiting in the front entrance with her two little daughters. Quite an ordinary sort of woman. Late forties, I'd say. Neat coat, sturdy shoes, capacious bag, hat too far back on her head. Not a follower of fashion. In short, she was our typical reader. But she was not, for a wonder, clutching a blackened grill pan or a half-knitted disaster and a receipt for the wool. She looked excited. As though she were bubbling over with something. Yes, that's exactly what she was like: an ill-chilled bottle of champagne. One twist of the wire and it's everywhere.

'I asked her how I could help and she was off. "Oh, I'm thrilled for you. I'm tickled pink. You could have knocked me down with a straw. I've just been in Dudhope Park with my two little girls watching the Punch and Judy, and we couldn't believe our eyes. Rosie and Freckle right there on the stage with Mr Punch and all the rest of them! I gasped aloud, I'm not ashamed to say it. And the lady who was in the next-door deckchair to me said she was pleased to see it too. And she told me that they had tried something else first but it didn't go well." She broke off then, Mrs Gilver, and she dipped her head as if she was uncertain. "Thomson's," she said, so low it was almost a whisper. "They started out with you-know-who from the *Sunday Post* but Thomson's would have none of it." And then she congratulated Doig's on being more forward-thinking and not so stuffy. She went on in that vein for longer than you'd believe, Mrs Gilver. I can't abide people who can't give a report without a lot of waffle.' Once again, I was mightily glad I was looking down at my notebook. 'It took me a good ten minutes to get rid of her and I was dying to. I took it straight up to Miss Bissett and said, "What do you think of this for cheek?" and told her about the rascal and what he was up to and how he'd got short shrift from our illustrious cousins round on Meadowside and now he thought he would make free with Doig's as if we were lambs for the slaughter.'

'And Miss Bissett took your view of it?' I said.

'Of course! What other view would she take? That rattle of a woman did us a favour.'

'Only Johnny Doig thought it would be good publicity,' I said. 'He would have happily run off some hand bills or coupons or what have you and passed them out.'

'I'm sure,' said Mr Gould, so sourly the words whistled through his pursed lips. 'That wouldn't surprise me at all. He'd hawk bruised sheets round the pubs if you let him.'

'Bruised sheets?'

'Damaged pages that have to be discarded in the printing. It was bruised sheets that got him started. The print foreman was a master of his craft. Never cut a corner, never put out less than perfection, you see what I mean?'

'Not really,' I said. I have found that sometimes honesty can be disarming.

'He was going to put us out of business, one beautifully aligned, all-colour, tag-free high-gloss issue at a time. He wouldn't countenance changing the stock to something cheaper, you see. But it was when he junked an entire run over one illustration with the red wash the tiniest hair out of true with the green wash . . . An entire run! A night's work! So it wasn't just the paper and the ink and the men on the printing floor, it was the vans and the drivers and then the loss of goodwill at the newsagents, not to mention our fuming readership. There's no use getting your magazine on a Wednesday if you read it at the hairdressers on a Tuesday, now is there?

'I can imagine not,' I said. 'And so the print foreman was sacked and Mr Doig took over?'

'Mr Johnny,' said Mr Gould. 'I remember him when he was Master Johnny! But it saves confusion with Mr Doig Sr, when he's here. As to the foreman, he stormed out; he didn't need sacking. Said he would be ashamed to say where he worked if an issue like that went out under his name. Then Miss Bissett reminded him that it didn't – it went out under *her* name – and he said quite a lot about how much he liked working for a "chit of a girl" – not much, it'll come as no surprise to hear – and off he flounced. Miss Bissett was at her wits' end. But she's a very determined young lady. And she got straight on the blower to the black sheep cousin – well, no, that's not fair – to the cousin, and waved some cash in front of him. She's paying him peanuts, but he's got an annuity – not that the staff is supposed to know their private family business – and he more or less does it as a lark. And a tease.'

'A tease,' I repeated. 'Teasing whom?' But as soon as I had asked the question I knew the answer. 'Thomson's.'

Mr Gould rewarded me with a grave nod, eyes closed and mouth pulled into a tight rosette; an expression that rendered him quite comical. He could have gone on in any repertory theatre as a snooty butler, without any make-up at all.

'And so Mr Johnny, with an eye on the balance sheet, wouldn't be likely to turn down free publicity,' Mr Gould said. 'While Miss Bissett, who feels herself deep in the shadow of Thomson's, made an over-hasty decision that if Punch and Judy was an insult to Oor Wullie then it was an insult to Rosie too.

'At which point, Mr Mackie gets his knickers in a twist . . . excuse me, Mrs Gilver.'

166

I shook my head and tushed a bit, but his cheeks continued to flame. 'Truly, Mr Gould,' I said. 'I have two sons and their slang makes me weep when I think of their school fees. I've heard everything.'

He inclined his head graciously, but still took another run at it, with some rephrasing. 'At which point, the professor *sees red* and decides to write nasty notes and slosh blood around.'

'No,' I said. 'The puppets and lipstick were left behind in Miss Bissett's office long after Mr Mackie was dead. Not to mention the bucket of blood showing up back here again. These things weren't done from beyond the grave, Mr Gould.'

'What makes you so sure?' said Mr Gould, more from a dislike of being contradicted than anything else, I rather thought.

'Mrs Miller assured us there was nothing in the boardroom when she was cleaning early on Tuesday morning,' I said.

'Oh, Mrs Miller! If that's all.'

'But the mess in the back lane round at Meadowside couldn't have been missed. It was still wet when it was found. Whoever did that it wasn't the victim.'

'Pity,' said Mr Gould, 'since that's the only thing that makes any sense, isn't it? Nasty notes and daubed obscenities on two respectable publishers whose only connection to the professor was that they scolded him about his puppets. And leaving the puppets propped up on chairs in the boardroom's all of a piece. "Won't let me use them? Well, here they are then. And I hope they choke you." That makes sense. Nothing else does.'

I stared at him. Of course, it was impossible. And yet, and yet. I opened my mouth to speak, then realised that Mr Gould would not fit the case. I needed Alec.

Chapter 16

Alec was delighted to see me. He had read his newspaper, enjoyed his pipe, gazed in through the doorway at the print-works and was now, before elevenses on the first day, thoroughly bored with his billet there on a hard chair just inside the back basement entrance.

'Those printers have made me feel an absolute pansy,' he said. 'Swishing about in their overalls and asking me if the noise was bothering me.'

''Twas ever the curse of the philosopher to be scorned by the ploughman,' I said. 'Detective, in this case, but it amounts to the same thing. Don't pout, Alec dear. I'm not in there asking the burly printers to help unpick this pretty knot that's formed in my head, am I? I'm here asking you. Cerebral, intellectual, imaginative you.'

'If they heard all that they'd really take against me,' Alec said.

'Or if they heard you say they "swish",' I pointed out.

Alec grinned. 'And the printing machines do make a god-awful racket, as it happens. Now stop wittering and show me the knot.'

He listened avidly to what had passed between Mr Gould and me.

'Your report is below par,' he said, when I was done. 'For a start, it's not a good idea to call both brothers "the professor". I was quite misled there for a moment.'

'Mr Mackie and Professor Mackie?' I said. 'Hardly better.'

'Bert and Leon,' said Alec. 'Poor Leon, being saddled with that, after Trotsky.'

'No!' I said, startling him. 'I'm afraid poor Bert is established in my mental firmament as Poor Bert, so poor Leon can't be Poor Leon. Now then, Mr Gould's best attempt at an explanation for the puppets in the boardroom requires a ghost.' Alec raised his eyebrows. 'So, clearly, we need a better explanation. Obviously, it was supposed to look as though Bert brought them round here, pinned them to chairs, wrote a note of sarcastic capitulation – a hat tip, if you will – on Miss Bissett's glass and went back to the park to do the show without the local colour. Only Mrs Miller says the note wasn't on the mirror on Tuesday morning.'

'Perhaps it was two different people,' Alec said. 'In fact, it must have been two different people, mustn't it?'

'Must it?'

'The writing on the tin of blood and plaster was the same as the writing on Miss Bissett's mirror,' he said. 'Bert was dead by the time of the daubing and the bucket turning up here.'

'But the person who daubed might not be the person who wrote the label.'

'That's what I'm saying.' Alec gave me an exasperated look. 'There are two people in it. The florist – possibly Bert – at five o'clock on Friday and someone else, with a yen for Deuteronomy, on Tuesday morning here and on Tuesday afternoon round at Thomson's.'

'*If* the florist brought the puppets to the boardroom,' I said. '*If* Bert had the puppets in the show. They weren't in the tent when Grant and I looked inside.'

'Well of course they weren't,' Alec said. 'Because the only way they could have got from Dudhope Park to Doig's was if the murderer, once he had cut Bert's throat, took them away with him.'

'That's actually a much better account of the thing, isn't it?' I said. 'Someone murders Bert, steals the puppets and uses them to point the finger at Miss Bissett?'

'So,' Alec said, 'cast your mind back. Were there spaces for missing puppets in that tent, Dandy?'

I screwed my eyes up very tight in a way that would have made Grant want to smack me and tried my best to conjure the scene in my mind: the damp closeness of the tent, its red stripes giving it a pink glow as the sun shone through the canvas; the smell of crushed grass and boot black; the row of leering faces ranged along the shelf below the stage, and the slumped figure of Mackie, looking as still as a sack of meal although, in fact, he was gradually settling, settling, and in a minute was about to fall flat on his back with his terrible, stricken face out there on the grass for all those unfortunate children to see and to dream about for months to come, undoubtedly.

'Mr Punch and his wife were onstage with horrible Scaramouche,' I said. 'And I'm pretty sure there were only three gaps on the shelf. Mind you, two late additions perhaps didn't have a place with the regular cast.'

'But if Bert was in the habit of making local puppets wherever he roamed, these two *would* be regular cast members,' Alec said, 'only with different finishes to meet the occasion.'

'That's another thing that troubles me,' I said. 'The "finishes", as you put it.'

'But, surely, if Bert was painting the things afresh for every town, they would be crude, wouldn't they?'

'No, it's not that,' I said. 'They *weren't* crude. They were modern, but they were rather fine for all that. Recognisably Rosie and Freckle. Nicely done.'

'But that's hardly surprising, given what we know about Bert's artistic sensibility,' Alec said.

'Artistic sensibility,' I said. 'No, I'm not mocking you. I know what you mean. And your saying it is relevant.'

'To what?' Alec said, when I had been silent a while.

'Something,' I said. I could see that it was not the most

170

helpful contribution and I did not blame Alec for the steady look he gave me. It is a look I know well; he employs it whenever it is a great effort not to roll his eyes and snort. 'Something about Bert's skill and handiwork.'

'We never actually heard that he had any,' Alec said. 'What we heard was that he had an interest in— Aha!' He saw the flash in my eyes at the same moment as the thought occurred to him. I smiled and let him have the moment. 'The professor – Leon, I mean – told us, didn't he? Bert was a traditionalist, a scholar of the form.'

'No sausages, no crocodile,' I added.

'So why would he suddenly put Oor Wullie in his show?'

'He wouldn't. Not in a month of Sundays.' I sat back. 'And I think Grant saw that right away. How tiresome.'

'So what was she up to?' Alec said. 'Not Grant, I mean. The approving reader of the *Rosy Cheek* who made a special trip from the park to Doig's—'

'With two little girls in tow,' I said. 'Mr Gould said so and, perhaps you don't know, but a child dragged away from a park with a puppet show and made to trail after Mummy along a boring street to a boring office would be a grizzling whining monster. What was she up to indeed?'

'Setting up a motive for the owners and staff of Thomson's and Doig's,' Alec said. 'To throw suspicion off herself?'

'Impossible!' I said. 'You mean to suggest that the real killer is a woman?' Before Alec could confirm or deny it, I swept on: 'Besides, I think the tale about the Thomson's puppets was served up to Doig's alone. It was supposed to stop Miss Bissett from thinking the Rosie and Freckle puppets were a good idea. And it worked.'

'But,' Alec said, frowning deeply, 'Thomson's was involved somehow, wasn't it? Or why the message written in blood?'

'True,' I said. 'Unless . . .'

'Yes,' said Alec. 'I agree. The daubing and the hiding of the bucket in the cupboard here is more of the same animus that lay behind the dolls and the lipstick. Diversion. Distraction. And nasty with it, in that there's enough bad blood between the two publishers to stop them being able to shrug it off. Miss Bissett won't say, "Our friends, the Thomsons? Tush! We have neighbouring boxes at the theatre for the winter season".'

'At Her Majesty's? Not likely.'

'It was just an example. And Mr Thompson isn't in a position to say, "Young Sandy Bissett? Why, she's been my bridge partner these last four years".'

'And as well as pointing fingers at two respectable family firms instead of the real culprit,' I said, 'the mischief served greatly to suggest that illicit puppets are the reason Mackie died, thus obscuring the real motive.'

'Whatever that motive is, it's not copyright.'

'Well, of course it's not copyright!' I said. 'Of course not. How, after all, could copyright have anything to do with the *first* murder? The first Albert Mackie, fifty years ago. Or with Deuteronomy.'

We sat for a while, each hoping inspiration would strike the other. When nothing struck anyone, at last Alec heaved a sigh and got to his feet. 'I'm going to step away and wash my hands, Dan. Would you hold the fort here a moment?'

'Of course,' I said. 'And then I'm going to begin my interviews in systematic earnest. I don't believe that florist got in here at the close of business on Friday and again yesterday, both times carrying bulky items, without someone seeing him except Fiona.'

But it takes a good deal more than a vehement announcement of belief to bend this careless world to one's own desires. I did indeed ask everyone in Doig's over the course of the morning and early afternoon, with a short break at luncheon time for a rough sandwich in the boardroom, and I received precisely nothing useful for my efforts. A junior clerk in the Payroll and Accounts office had heard footsteps; a stout lady in Knitting said she thought someone had stolen some of the wool manufacturers' samples she had been sent for testing; and two of the printers, large red-faced men who spoke at a shout even when not in the printing room with the machines running, told me when I caught them having a fag break in the lane beyond the staff door that they didn't believe in the florist at all.

'Naw,' one of them said, the sound booming like a foghorn, 'not on Friday. We started our weekend early, didn't we? We had a kickabout in the lane here. There's no way he got past us.'

'Hm,' I said. 'And he didn't come in the front door because Mrs Miller was sitting on a bench in the church garden having a bit of a rest and watching the door, all set to come back over and start shutting up for the holiday as soon as everyone was out.'

'Is that right?' the other one said. 'Is that what she told you?'

'Butter wouldn't melt,' put in his friend.

'Well, she admitted to a smoke too,' I said.

'The devil! She never!' the first man roared, laughing heartily and winking at his friend. I dropped my cigarette and stepped towards it, but the laughing man had put his foot on top of it and ground it out before I had a chance. 'Let me, madam,' he said. 'I don't like to see a lady ruining her good shoes on a fag end. I hope Mrs Miller's got a nice wee wall she stubs hers out on, beside her bench there. In the church garden.'

'I don't know what you're getting at,' I said. 'I'd be very grateful if you'd tell me.'

Both them laughed even harder and, although I wouldn't have imagined it possible, even louder. 'Not us,' the smaller one said. 'We're keeping out of it. We know what side our bread's buttered.'

'And I don't know what you mean by that either,' I said. 'It's very irritating.'

Only a stop-off in the foyer to talk to Grant soothed me for, purposeless and annoying as my day had been, hers had been worse. She had been beset with what she called 'silly women' in a steady stream, and had caught not so much as a glimpse of the stranger who had threatened his return.

'Silly in what way?' I said.

'Every way imaginable,' she replied. 'One brought a story she thought could be published. Well, I took one look at the first page and I was able to tell her it wouldn't do.'

'You didn't!'

'It wasn't even typed, madam. Written out in ink and blotted and splotched all over at that. Then some chit came in with a pineapple cake that was stuck to the tin. She hadn't lined it. She said the recipe didn't say to line it. I said I bet the recipe didn't say not to hit herself over the head with it either.'

'Grant, for goodness' sake,' I said. 'If Doig's have a spate of cancelled submissions after today, Miss Bissett would be well within her rights to take them off our bill.'

'There weren't enough visitors to make a dent in their submissions,' she said. I felt my shoulders drop in relief. 'Most of them just rang up.'

'And what have you been saying to *them*?'

'I've got up to a marvellous run average,' she said, ominously to my ears.

'Meaning?'

'I've hardly had to put any calls through at all. I've managed to deal with almost everything myself.'

'Oh God,' I said. 'Can you give me an example?'

'I can give you eleven examples,' said Grant. 'I only had to put through a chap from the bank who wondered whether Miss Bissett would like her new chequebook sent round or whether she'd be calling in. I told him she could probably do with the exercise and he could keep it there for her, but he insisted on getting it straight from the horse's mouth.'

174

'What a stickler,' I said, but sarcasm is quite lost on Grant, usually.

'What this magazine needs is a page of "Problems for Auntie". There have been two women – well, one of them was just a girl – this morning alone, hoping for advice.'

'"Problems for Auntie"?'

'I've been entertaining myself thinking of names for it,' she said. 'That's the best one so far.'

'Now, look,' I said, 'Doig's has a Letters department and it has a policy. You can't steam in and start inventing magazine pages when you're here for a day on quite other business.'

'I don't agree,' Grant said. 'I don't think Doig's can put out a paper like the *Cheek*, and have a character like Rosie who makes out she's a friend, and tells them what to wear and eat and read, who then has nothing to say when they find themselves in a spot of trouble. I don't think that's fair.'

I could see what she meant. To save her from getting even more insufferable, however, I said nothing. I merely tutted and left her, taking myself off out onto the Overgate and into the sunshine.

For I had an idea and now that the afternoon was at its peak, it was time to set it in motion. Most people are creatures of settled habits, and no more so than the very young. (My parents, in their enthusiasm for Pre-Raphaelite life, with its linens and wildflowers and general air of skipping unfettered through meadows, were rather down on the notion of regular habits, even for small children. Thankfully, Nanny Palmer was well able to nod and smile at my mother's suggestions and then go her own sweet way when she and I were back upstairs in the nursery alone. I shudder to think what kind of ninny I might have turned into otherwise. My sister Mavis was none too stalwart even with Nanny's help to balance the nonsense.) And if infants and toddlers keep settled hours in their daily round, then the greatly aged could be used to set clocks. Meals, naps and, most importantly for me, constitutionals are laid down in the diary of the pensioner like the prayers of a cloistered sister.

For these reasons, it had occurred to me that whoever was in Dudhope Park on Friday afternoon to see or not see the innovations in the Punch and Judy show would also be there today. I got to the park gates at just gone three and strode forward to the main lawns like a lion on the savannah.

My hunch bore heavy fruit. There on all the benches were spindly old ladies with stockings falling into spirals around their twiggy ankles, and stout old ladies with jowls overhanging their collars. There too were comfortable old gentlemen with hands clasped on the crest of their frontages, looking like Dickens illustrations, and withered old gentlemen wrapped up in scarves despite the sunshine, having outlived their own flesh and so being left with nothing against the breeze of this August day.

In the middle of the grass, the children played, as I had expected. Girls of eight and up had organised themselves for skipping, while the boys played a game of chase. They were, I assumed, strictly forbidden from kicking footballs, for park keepers are such spoilsports, always railing about the flowerbeds, when in fact the type of summer bedding municipal parks go in for could not be much harmed by a rugby scrum. Dudhope Park was no different: the begonias were fearsome fleshy things and the salvia spikes were so robust that, if it came to it, I would put my money on them to burst the bladder rather than the bladder to flatten the blooms. I squared my shoulders and approached the nearest clutch of young mothers to ask my questions. I was willing to admire their grubby offspring – runny noses, scraped knees and all – if I had to.

Chapter 17

There, with the young mothers, my luck ran out rather. They *had* all been here on Friday afternoon, as I expected, and of course they had seen the Punch and Judy tent, as how could they not, but of the show's content they were unable to apprise me.

'I cannae afford to pay for a deckchair. There's free benches everywhere.'

'But did you happen to glance over?' I persisted.

'Not me! In case some wee man came round with his cap out asking for coppers.'

'You needn't have given him any,' I pointed out.

'Is that right? I thought you had to pay to watch it.'

'Naw,' said her friend. 'You're allowed to watch from the back. How could they stop you? It's a free country.'

'And a public park,' I agreed. 'Did *you* watch then? From the back?'

'No fear,' said the young woman. 'I caught a wee keek when he was here at Easter and thon puppet with the neck gave me the willies. Thank Mercy the bairns never saw him. My wee girl's got too much imagination at the best of times. That would have been a do.'

'Scaramouche,' I said. 'I'm with your little girl. He gave me the willies too. In fact . . .' The thought breaking over me was new but irresistible.

'In fact whit?' said one of the waiting women. I had left them hanging.

'Yes, I think that's exactly when it happened,' I said. 'That's

177

how the rascal got away unseen. It would be beyond human capability not to watch that hideous neck stretching and stretching.'

'Like when your dog brings up a worm,' one of the mothers put in, to a chorus of disgust but, I noticed, no disagreement.

Then I remembered, with a slump, that there had been one individual looking out for her friend who was late arriving. She had been adamant that no one had left the vicinity of the tent, but her assurances had been in the jumbled immediate after-math of the crime and, besides, I would wager that the police had not mentioned Scaramouche to her particularly. They would not have known to, since Constable Adams did not appear on the scene until afterwards. I should go and tell him, if I could find him, or even dour Inspector Daunt at a push, that here was a way to double-check the woman's evidence.

Of course, people being what they were she would deny it stoutly, but she could be tricked into openness if the approach was sufficiently sneaky. With a wry guess at how the inspector would like being told how to hone his approach, I took leave of the mothers and made my way to the park gates. The elderly on their benches could wait. I was bound for Doig's to offer the task to Alec, who would demur, and then to Grant, who would grab with both hands the chance to interfere with an inquiry, put police backs up and invite scorn, all in the hope of nudging one of the many impossibilities of this benighted case over to somewhere less bewildering. We would still have the fifty-year-old echo of the Mackie murder, which was nothing to be sniffed at, as well as the Bible verses and the invisible florist, but it was a start.

I never made it as far as the Overgate. Cutting down Lindsay Street, I caught sight of a cherry-bedecked straw hat, glinting in the sunshine, and turned in time to see the apron strings of what must surely be Mrs Miller, disappearing into a darkened doorway opposite the church. Remembering the smiles and arch looks of the printers when I spoke of her rests in the holy garden, I followed her. I did not pause to look at the sign above the darkened doorway; it did not occur to me there was any reason to hesitate before following a fellow woman wherever it was she was bound. I had become inured to public bars, miners' institutes, circus performers' caravans, convents and mental asylums in the course of my work over the years and I would not have said there was an establishment left that would shock me, excepting perhaps the possibility Alec had foreseen down on Dock Street.

I was wrong. Following Mrs Miller, who of course no more sat in church gardens in her odd minutes than I did, I found myself for the first time in my life entering the tobacco-tinged, desperate, dissolute, shabby and shameless precincts of a bookmaker.

The silence that greeted my appearance there was of a depth and duration one would have thought required a director to enforce it. One by one the men, young and old, stopped studying their *Racing Times*, stopped sucking on pipes and fags, stopped arguing about form, stopped counting out coins and flicking through bundles of notes, and all turned towards me. The clerks – if that is the term for them – stopped their adding and subtracting, stopped their chalking up of results and their rubbing off of odds at the large blackboards that covered one wall. Even a whippet, unnerved by the sudden stillness, stopped scratching his ear with his hind paw and sat up to look at me. The only living soul in the whole place who did not look at me was Mrs Miller. She stared stolidly in the other direction, the fruit on her hat not stirring and her apron strings hanging down as though in defeat.

'Carry on, chaps,' I said, at last. 'Don't mind me.'

At the sound of my voice, Mrs Miller turned at last. 'I thought I saw you, madam,' she said. 'I wasn't sure you'd seen me.'

'Ah well,' I said. 'Not to worry. Might I ask you a question or two, Mrs Miller?'

She glanced at the clerk waiting to take her bet.

'By all means place it,' I said. 'I'd hate to be responsible for a loss. Who do you fancy? Where are they running today?'

One of the men let out a laugh and taking that as a cue the bookies began slowly to come back to life.

'Ayr, is it?' I said. 'I've never been to the races at Ayr. Musselburgh, once or twice. Ascot of course, as a girl. My papa used to give me a ten-shilling note and let me make a day of it. So, you see, you have no need to hide your little treat from me.'

'I'm hiding nothing,' Mrs Miller said. Her business had been contracted, a mystifying exchange of remarks having passed between the bookie's clerk and her. She took the slip handed to her and tucked it into her apron pocket.

'I'm not sure I can agree with that,' I said. 'You bore witness to me that you were watching the front door of Doig's on Friday and would have seen the mysterious stranger entering. I'm assuming that in fact you were nowhere of the kind and wouldn't have seen a regiment of florists and a Greek chorus of puppeteers storm the place.'

'You've a way with words,' said Mrs Miller. 'I'll say that much for you.'

'And while we're on the subject of squaring untidy corners into neat points,' I said, 'did you dust behind the door of Miss Bissett's cloakroom?'

'What?' Mrs Miller was somewhat distracted by the results now being relayed from the track, via a telephone in the corner. I pressed my advantage.

'Did you clean the glass in Miss Bissett's cloakroom on Tuesday morning?'

'There's only her uses it and she doesn't wear hair tonic.' I took that to be a no.

'Did you even clean the boardroom chairs on Friday?'

'There's only suits ever hit those chairs,' she said. 'Never an oily overall or a set of shorts a wee boy's been sliding about the muddy park in. I reckon you can over-clean good furniture. Wears it out. Carpets too.'

I took that to be another no.

It was a theory I had never heard when we had a staff of residential maids, none of whom would want their employer to conclude that the house was too clean and did not warrant so many girls with rooms in the attic and four square meals a day laid out in the servants' hall. Since the advent of the daily char, however, I have heard little else. Not only furniture and carpets, but also parquet, silver and even lavatorial china has been dragged forward to exemplify the kind of delicate artefact to be nursed tenderly and not annihilated with a scrubbing brush or a duster.

'Hm,' was all I said to Mrs Miller on the matter. 'So you have no idea when the puppets hit the chairs or the lipstick the glass. And you can't, after all, help with the question of when the florist got in.'

'You muddled me up with all your questions,' she had the gall to say, straight-faced.

'Hm,' I said again. 'Good luck with your horse.'

'Dog,' said Mrs Miller, making me feel very foolish for my talk of Ascot and Musselburgh. To smirks all round, for the men had naturally been listening, I departed what I expected to be the only bookmakers I would frequent in my life, looking forward to telling Alec about my adventure, and determining never to mention it to Hugh.

I was following the woman for a good five hundred yards before I noticed her. As I rounded the end of the spurned church nothing was in my mind except the question of how to narrow down the florist's arrival time without Mrs Miller's evidence. In my defence, there was nothing remarkable about her. She had no shiny hat with red fruit, nor any apron strings to flutter as she went on her way. In fact, I daresay if she had not repeatedly glanced over her shoulder towards me I would have got to the corner of the Overgate and turned in without ever seeing her. As it was, I wondered if she was looking for a taxi. The way she kept hurrying along, flinging looks behind her, suggested she was hoping for a cabbie but far from sure she would find one and so had decided to make progress on foot in the meantime. The puzzle was that she was headed straight for the river, which made no sense, or perhaps straight for the Tay Bridge railway station, which made little more. Any cabbie who picked her up here for a five-minute fare to the station would be rightly outraged.

So I was mildly interested in her when she threw the next look my way, and that was when I recognised her. She had been in the park on Sunday, waiting for her friend, assuring the police and me that no one arrived at the Punch and Judy tent before the murder, nor left it afterwards. I surged forward, close to breaking out into a jog myself, and I caught up with her on Union Street almost opposite the station, where we were both obliged to stop while first a tram rattled by and then a dray horse clopped past impossibly slowly, the cart behind it creaking under its weight of beer barrels.

'Just you today?' I said cheerfully as I drew up beside her. Her chest was rising and falling, not rapidly, but quite far, each breath making her puff out like a pouter pigeon.

'I beg your pardon?' she said. 'I don't believe I've had the pleasure.'

'Oh, don't you remember me?' I said. 'Well, it was rather a distressing day when we met. I was in the park, for the Punch and Judy show. We spoke briefly.'

'Did we,' she said. The lack of any upward inflection turned it insolent somehow, and I drew my chin back into my neck.

'Did your friend ever turn up?' I said. She blinked and turned the corners of her mouth down, but said nothing.

'The buses are dreadful on bank holidays,' I went on. 'I see you've decided to take the train instead today.' This was a guess. 'Do you have far to go?' And that merely an excuse to keep talking, to see if the source of her extreme displeasure might be revealed. It was not. Instead the displeasure itself dissolved, light breaking over her features and a flush – one assumes at her rudeness – creeping up her neck.

'The bank holiday!' she said. 'Why yes of course. I remember you now. As you said, it was a terribly distressing day. That poor poor man.'

'Tell me,' I said, 'did the police welcome your evidence? I've found at times in the past that unwelcome facts are subject to dismissal when they come from us ladies. I hope you weren't disparaged.'

'At times . . . in the past?' she said faintly. 'Have you had frequent dealings with the police then?' She had drawn away from me, somewhat understandably. With her navy-blue coat and skirt, capacious handbag and well-cared-for high heels, she looked just the sort of respectable type who would shudder at such things. As would I have, a few years previously. I gave her what I hoped would be a reassuring smile.

'I'm not a jailbird,' I said. 'I'm a private detective.'

But that revelation served only to increase her look of alarm.

'A detective?' she echoed, her voice no more than a whisper. She looked me all over rapidly, as though checking for revolvers and chewed cigars, although after a moment I decided, more sensibly, that she was digesting the surprise that a woman like me, who reeked of minor aristocracy, would have any job at all, much less this one. I found a second to regret that Grant had not, in the end, kitted me out in the dress with collar and cuffs; evidently my tweeds and amusing little hat were in conflict with her view of my profession.

'Indeed,' I said. 'A gumshoe, a private eye, a dick – my sons have taught me every term for it, down the years. Confidential enquiries undertaken.'

'And you were working at the puppet show on Monday?' she said, swallowing. 'Was trouble expected then?'

'I was,' I said. 'But it wasn't. Well, some trouble was expected but not what happened. Heavens, no. Or I'd have been on the other side of the tent, waiting for the killer to make his move. Not sitting out front watching.'

'Would you?' she said. She seemed to be of a terribly nervous disposition; she was turning pale as I described this utterly hypothetical scenario.

'No,' I said. 'My partner – a gentleman – would have taken it on. And actually, if we had had a tip-off about a murder, we would have handed it over to the police in advance. I'm giving myself airs, pretending I ever do anything so swash-buckling.' I grinned at her and she had sufficiently recovered to give me a wan smile back. 'Mind you, I wish I *had* been lurking under a tree to see him sneak in and sneak out again. It's terribly unlucky that the one person who was watching the approach didn't see him.'

'Me?' she said. 'Do you mean me?'

I frowned. 'I'm sorry,' I said. 'I might be mistaken. I thought you were looking out for your friend, who'd missed her bus, and you said that no one approached the back of the kiosk in all the time the show lasted?'

'The police think I'm lying,' she said. 'They kept me for ages, going on and on. I was ill the next day. It was all terribly upsetting. But I stuck to my guns – I wasn't brought up to tell stories, even to escape that terrible inspector and that sordid little room.'

'They took you to the station?' I said.

'I couldn't believe it. You could have knocked me down with a straw when they said I had to go with them. And I've had nightmares every night since.'

'You know what's been giving *me* horrid dreams?' I said. I was lying, but I had seen a chance and was taking it. 'Scaramouche. He was hideous. He has got himself mixed up with poor Bert in my mind, at least after midnight.'

I waited.

184

'Scaramouche?' she said.

'With the neck.'

She shrugged. 'Was he part of the show?' she said. 'Is that what the dog's called? Scaramouche?'

'You really *were* looking out for your friend then,' I said, then hastily added, 'I do apologise! I didn't mean to doubt you. I only marvel that you could resist the sight of him. He was mesmerising. Like—' But I broke off before referencing a dog with a worm, guessing that this dainty individual, so upset by a police station and so anxious even at a friend's late arrival, would take a dim view. 'Scaramouche was the puppet who was centre stage when poor Bert Mackie had his throat cut. He has a peculiar neck. It stretches until his head is lost above the proscenium arch. Most unsettling and all the more so for seeming to have no purpose. I mean to say, there must be an explanation, lost in the mists of time. Perhaps he's a warning to Mr Punch to behave or be hanged. Perhaps it's meant to indicate divine judgement – looking down from on high— I say, I'm sorry. I don't mean to upset you.'

She had paled even paler this time and had stepped away from me, stumbling on the kerb and almost falling into the road. I put a hand out and hauled her back up again.

'My dear woman, I could kick myself,' I said. 'My husband says my sensibilities have been coarsened and my finer feelings blunted by the work I do, but I've never made anyone faint before. I'm terribly sorry. Would you let me buy you a cup of tea?'

She shook her head and, with a troubled look down at where my hand gripped her elbow, she obliged me to let it go. 'I need to catch my train,' she said. 'I'm expected at home.'

'Well, at least let me walk you to your platform and see you safely aboard,' I said, but she was shaking her head hard.

'I wouldn't hear of it,' she said. 'I'm quite fine. I shall be perfectly fine.' And with that she was gone, hurrying over the road and in under the glass porch affair that sheltered the entrance. I was still unhappy, though: racked with guilt and genuinely concerned about her hurrying up a station platform and climbing aboard a train. If she fell, her bruises and sprains would be down to me. Accordingly, I waited a moment or two and then followed her. She had her ticket, evidently, for she breezed past the counter and straight out into the belly of the station, where she moved smartly and – I was relieved to see – steadily towards the waiting Fife circle train. Jolly good, I thought. A soothing journey back around the coastline through all those charming fishing towns would settle her spirits again. She would be fine. It was I who had been left with a disturbing reality to be managed somehow.

For if that woman truly was watching carefully for her friend then, given the absence of a handy blind spot, how the devil *did* the killer come and go?

As I left the station again, I saw a movement to my side and turned, only flinching a little, to see a shabby stranger, holding out a crudely coloured little pamphlet in one hand and a tin collecting box in the other.

'Do you love the Lord, your God, with all your heart?' he asked me, as urgently as might well be imagined.

I took one of his pamphlets, thinking him an old soldier who needed a shilling more than I. When I looked down, however, this is what I saw:

And thou shalt grope at noonday, as the blind gropeth in darkness, and thou shalt not prosper in thy ways: and thou shalt only be oppressed and spoiled evermore, and no man shall save thee. Deuteronomy, 28:29

'Him again!' I said, scandalising the old soldier. I thrust the paper back into his hands before fleeing.

Chapter 18

As a concerned citizen with useful, if unwelcome, information to impart, there was no reason for me not to march to the police station in expectation of a civil welcome. My nerve failed me, however, and I scurried past with my head down, en route back to Doig's to pick up Alec and take him with me as a second, should the vile inspector pooh-pooh my report.

'Anything happen?' I asked Grant, as I swung into the foyer. 'Any sign of him?'

'Not a peep,' Grant said. 'Not a sausage. Just as well. Mrs Priest – her that saw him and swooned yesterday – has come back in to do the afternoon. Plucky. Dedicated. No thought for anything but her work. I'd like to give her a little treat as a reward for her courage.'

'What's wrong with her?' I said, for Grant did not fool me. She had clearly been offended by something in the woman's appearance and was all set to barge in and offer to correct it. Treat, indeed!

'Hair like a floor mop and eyebrows you could train beans up,' Grant said. 'I'd be doing her a kindness.'

'I'll take over here, if you like,' I said, feeling my magnanimity like a light shining out of me. 'Let you get started right away.'

'Hardly,' said Grant. 'Madam. I've put in the long boring day and I'm determined to stick with it until it bears fruit. I'll fit Mrs Priest in somewhere. I thought ladies who worked at magazines would be chic, didn't you? Even Miss Bissett—'

I quelled her with a glare. 'It didn't sound boring when

you described what you'd been up to earlier,' I said. 'How are the submissions going this afternoon? Have you offended anyone new?' I was through in the stairwell now and she had to follow me to the doorway and shout as I descended.

'I haven't offended anyone at all,' she called. 'People are sick of being pandered to. Straight talking is a welcome change. I wouldn't be surprised if I'm offered a permanent position at the end of this.' Then I passed through the doors to the bowels of the building where the printing was done.

'Is that your maid bellowing like a costermonger?' said Johnny Doig, appearing with a newspaper under his arm and a cup of tea in his hand. 'She's an original, isn't she?'

'You're being kind,' I said. 'But how on earth did you find out that she's my maid when she's got her assistant detective hat jammed so firmly on her head?'

'I overheard her dishing out advice on washing a christening gown over the telephone and I forgot myself so far as to question her credentials.'

I laughed. One has to laugh, with Grant. 'Where's Alec got himself to?' I said, spying the empty seat by the back door.

'Cricket in the lane,' Johnny Doig said, and indeed as he spoke the words, there was a thump as a ball hit the other side of the door, a chorus of 'Howzat?' went up.

'Now where has he found cricketing chaps this far north?' I said. It was one of Alec's few complaints about Scottish life. I have heard him mourn the waste of a stretch of hard sand at low tide before now, when no one had employed it as a cricket pitch on a sunny afternoon.

'Oh, that was me,' said Johnny. 'I didn't mind dropping everything to help out Sandy, but there are limits to my sacrifice. I've just about managed to bear it with a spot of cricket at lunchtime.'

I gave him a smile, but truth be told he was just the sort of man who rather puts my back up. I have met dilettantes of many stripes in my time – the louche brother of a lady doctor in Moffat, a trio of sisters who dabbled in a nunnery – and without exceptions they made pests of themselves. I was sure that Miss Sandy Bissett would have been able to find the wages for a printer if she scraped around hard enough, and then a decent working man would have had a job in these dreadful times, instead of Johnny Doig making his staff learn cricket and putting them all behindhand.

'One must make one's own fun,' I said blandly enough, to my way of thinking. I was surprised to notice Doig giving me a sharp look.

'How is the case going?' he said. 'Have you grubbed anything up?'

I was not sure whether he meant it to be as condescending as it sounded. 'We haven't had to grub,' I said. 'Clues are falling on us like the gentle rain from heaven. There's an embarrassment of the things.'

'Really?' said Doig. 'But isn't that good? You sound glum about it.'

'One would think. But actually it makes it hard to see what's what. Some of the discoveries we've made are so peculiar they distract while we think of them and as soon as we turn away they fade again. One can't seem to knit them together to make a whole.'

'Really?' he said again. He seemed oddly pleased by the notion. 'For instance?'

'An invisible killer, an impossible connection across fifty years, non-existent puppets. Witnesses who are beyond reasonable reproach yet who must be lying.' I was thinking of the woman in the park waiting for her friend, and the woman who came to tell Doig's about the puppets. I had no idea who Johnny Doig was thinking of, but he was no longer pleased. His face was a mask of bland watchfulness.

'Who is lying?' he said. 'You don't mean someone at Doig's, do you?'

I hurried to assure him I did not, but I thought furiously the while. What an odd assumption. Who did *he* imagine might be lying? And about what? I must have been watching him as I pondered these questions and, under my gaze, he shifted from foot to foot and a flush passed over his cheeks. An idea crept into my head as though an imp on one shoulder had whispered it in my ear. And I knew exactly how to check if I was right about it. 'Grant tells me Mrs Priest is back in the saddle,' I said. The man's eyes widened until I could see the whites all around. 'I missed her earlier. I think I shall go and have a chat, for the sake of neatness, don't you know.'

I opened the back door and rather gingerly looked out, not desiring to be struck by a cricket ball. Thankfully, I had happened to intrude on one of the many longueurs with which the game is beset.

'Hold up, lads,' Alec said. 'Intruder on the crease.'

'Would you like to come with me?' I asked him.

'Your expression suggests that I would,' Alec said, picking up his coat from the wall behind him and jogging towards me. 'What are you up to?'

'Forgive me spoiling your fun,' I said to the rest of the men in the lane. To Alec, I said, 'A hunch. Indulge it with me?'

'Where are we going?' Alec asked as we passed in through the door to the passageway again. Johnny Doig was nowhere to be seen. 'I shouldn't leave my post.'

'Well, that's the thing,' I said. 'Let's see.'

Home and Garden was somewhat more organised than Letters, surprisingly since it had swatches, crafts, gadgets and all manner of household accoutrements under its purview. I gazed around the long room, lined with shelves and lit from skylights above, my glance resting briefly on each of the four desks that formed a square in the middle, and wondered how on earth the rest of the staff had ever believed an intruder to have infiltrated the place and left behind him a bucket of blood.

Three of the desks were empty. At the fourth, a formidable woman with perfectly normal-looking curly hair and perfectly normal-looking groomed eyebrows sat knitting. One was, however, reminded of Madame Defarge rather than of a kindly grandmother. One was certainly not easily persuaded that this creature had taken leave of herself over a stray bucket, grisly contents notwithstanding.

'Mrs Priest?' I said, and I heard Alec utter a faint 'ohhhhh' beside me.

'Shh,' she said. 'I'm counting.' She continued to stare at us with her lips moving until she reached some waystation in the knitting process that was impenetrable to me, then she dropped the square of wool in her lap and bent to examine it.

'Shoddy,' she said. 'Poorly tensioned. I shan't be recommending it for the next pattern, no matter how much the rep tries to get round me.'

'Does he visit you?' I said. 'Or send parcels?'

'He takes me out for plates of sandwiches,' Mrs Priest said. 'But it'll do no good.' She was now ripping out the knitted-up wool and re-forming it into a ball. This she secured by sticking the needles through it, as though she were D'Artagnan.

'I was just wondering, you see,' I went on, 'if there was an habitual procession of men dropping things off in your department.'

She narrowed her eyes. Perhaps Grant had a point about her brows after all; they bristled with the change in her expression.

'You're talking about the stranger who violated Miss Bissett's office and the boardroom and Thomson's and then tried to put the blame on us here, aren't you?' she said, all of a rush. She had been coached but had no natural talent for the business.

'Indeed,' I said. 'Now then, where was everyone when the chap came and left the paint tin?'

'I don't know when it was,' said Mrs Priest, stoutly, lifting her chin. 'I've no idea where any of us were, for we are in and out all day long, and who's to say when the thing was done?'

'We can narrow it down a fair bit,' said Alec. 'Thankfully. The message was daubed on the wall at Meadowside round about two o'clock, and the tin was discovered here just an hour later. That's not too much time to account for. Do you keep a detailed diary, Mrs Priest?'

'I write in a journal every night and have done from childhood, but it is private. I'm shocked that you would even think of such a thing.'

'Not that sort of diary,' I said. 'An appointment book. Something that might let us know when the office was empty that day.'

'If the bucket dropped off here even was the leftovers from the daubing,' Alec said. Both Mrs Priest and I turned to hear more. 'It just occurred to me this minute that, if he always meant to cast blame on Doig's, he might have paid the two visits in either order. In fact, it wouldn't be a good idea at all for him to have been strolling – even scurrying – about the streets once the deed was done. If I were going to embark on such an escapade, I'd drop off a bucket with enough blood to make an impact here first and then go a-painting with a different bucket afterwards.'

'And do what with the second bucket?' I asked.

'Throw it in the river,' said Alec. 'Or nip up a close and stuff it into a midden. Anything.'

'But what do you know about it?' said Mrs Priest. 'You're building castles in Spain. You've made that up out of whole cloth about two buckets, or two tins or whatever you want to call them. I say if a man has the nerve to do what was done round the corner at Thomson's, then he has the nerve to get rid of the evidence by playing a trick on us. It's part and parcel, if you ask me.'

'You don't sound angry,' I said. 'You sound, in fact, almost admiring.'

She started to splutter.

'Or perhaps indulgent is a better word,' I said. 'Affectionate. How long have you worked here, Mrs Priest?'

'Since the old man's time,' she said. 'I started as a packer at the age of fifteen. Miss Molton I was then. I never stopped. We never had any kiddies and Mr Priest is very forward-thinking. He's always been proud of me.'

'Good for Mr Priest,' I said. 'Jolly glad to hear it. And if you never had any children of your own, that explains the affectionate indulgence even more. How old was he when you first met him?'

'I've no idea what you're talking about,' she said, giving it a great deal of emphasis, unfortunately with a voice not quite steady.

'He told me,' I said, and at my words all her breath came out in a rush and she slumped so far down that the ball of wool dropped off her lap, needles and all, and lay unnoticed on the floor at her feet.

'Well, why didn't you say that instead of trying to trip me up?'

'He didn't know he'd told me,' I said. 'He gave it away, like you.'

'Well, I call that a low trick!' said Mrs Priest.

'Low?' I replied. 'I do feel I've cleared the bar set by Mr Doig and his bucket of blood. Pig's blood, was it? Do you happen to know?'

Before she could answer, we all heard advancing footsteps and Alec and I turned in time to see the arrival of Johnny Doig at the open door.

'Drat it all,' he said. 'Are you permitted inside casinos, Mrs Gilver? You would break them with that poker face of yours. She's on to us, Mrs Priest. We are undone.' He picked up a hard chair on his way to Mrs Priest's desk and swung it round to allow him to sit astride it, his arms resting on its back. 'Go on, then,' he said. 'Have at me.'

'We'd got as far as the blood,' Alec said. His voice was cold and Johnny Doig withered rather under his stare. 'Pig?'

'Lamb,' said Doig. 'Which, now I think of it, is a little blasphemous as a medium for daubing up Bible verses. But it's all the butcher had to spare.'

'We'll need the butcher's name,' said Alec and, when Doig started to bluster, added, 'Either us or the bobbies. Your choice, of course.'

Doig subsided, with no more than a muttered 'no harm done'.

'Great harm done, actually,' Alec said. 'And of a most insidious kind too. I take it that you got back from wherever you were without any shell shock? Well, Mr . . . someone at Thomson's wasn't so lucky and the smell of all that blood where he wasn't expecting it put him flat out in a faint.'

'How was I expected to foresee that?' Doig said. His drawl had quite gone. He sounded like a child, caught doing wrong and not about to admit it. It was a tone I knew well from Donald and Teddy's early days. I had always thought Hugh a bit of a dragon about it, storming and spanking when they were no more than children, but to hear it in the mouth of a man in his thirties made me send a silent message of thanks across the miles to Perthshire.

'How were you expected to know that this city is full of men not best able to withstand nasty shocks?' Alec said. 'Hardly a great feat of imagination.'

He said no more. Doig's mouth was shut so firmly his lips had gone white. They simply stared at one another, while Mrs Priest stared at me, as though somehow it was my job to pour oil on the troubled waters. It was not. My job was to find out who killed Bert Mackie, and if troubled waters got even more so, too bad.

'Might one ask why?' I said, as a first step.

'Why do you think?' Johnny Doig was clearly one of those men who was only pleasant when pleased. Displeased, he had turned brusque to the point of rudeness. I lifted an eyebrow and thus managed to shake a grudging apology out of him before he carried on. 'Sandy had been hauled off by the peelers,' he said. 'I was angry and not a little scared. I knew she hadn't done anything so I thought I'd muddy the waters a bit and throw some suspicion elsewhere.'

'And why the Bible?' I said. 'Why Deuteronomy?'

'It hit the right note, I thought,' Doig said. 'Vengeance, you know. I could hardly leave a limerick if I wanted to put the willies up them. Only, after I'd done it, I realised that even if the paint on the wall cast suspicion for the murder onto someone at Thomson's, the suspicion for the paint was still in need of a resting place. And, perhaps I'm not cut out for that sort of adventure after all, but when my anger passed and I found myself walking back here with the empty tin I felt I'd been rather a chump. So I decided to try a double bluff, if you see what I mean. I wrote a few words on a label, trying to match the letters on Sandy's mirror, then I left the bucket to be found.'

'Thinking the last thing a guilty person would do is put evidence where it would incriminate him?'

'Exactly,' said Doig.

'And where did you come in, Mrs Priest?' I said turning to her, hoping to catch her off guard.

'I offered to help,' she said. 'I was happy to help. I'd do it again.'

I nodded, thinking it over. 'You said you saw the florist and that set off a search, which turned up the paint bucket,' I said. 'Very clever. Much cleverer than pretending simply to see the bucket. Hardly helpful to anyone trying to get at the truth, however. Your claim to see this stranger, added to

195

Mrs Miller's claim *not* to have seen him, has given us a lot of bother when we were rather busy anyway, you know.'

'I'd do it again,' Mrs Priest repeated, even louder. 'It's nothing to do with us. None of it is anything to do with us. What business could we here at Doig's have with that sort of man? The lowest kind of cheap entertainment, one step up from a beggar with a mouth organ.'

'It's actually a tradition with a long and quite illustrious history,' Alec said.

'And as I know from Monday afternoon,' I added, 'genuinely rather diverting. Not to mention harmless. Good grief, Mrs Priest, where would we be if Punch and Judy and mouth organs were banished from our streets? What next? Donkey rides? Hurdy-gurdies?'

'Picture papers?' Alec added, wickedly.

'Tchah,' said Mrs Priest. 'It's all very well for you living there on your estate never troubled by them all with their noise and their mess. It's another thing when you can't walk through a park without being pestered for a shilling. Dundee never used to be that sort of place, and it was the better for it.'

I thought of Moll at Her Majesty's and the rumours of the sort of business conducted after dark down on Dock Street, and it occurred to me that the Dundee of Mrs Priest's fond memories was more than likely a place that existed only in her wishes.

She was still describing this mythic Dundee, a place where people knew one another and strangers had to watch their step. A place where a nice tea could be got for a reasonable price in any number of temperance hotels instead of ladies like herself being forced to walk past public houses and billiards halls only to fetch up in a grubby teashop and pay through the nose.

But I was barely listening. For the teashops, strangers and entertainments had become whisked up together in

196

my mind and had formed something slightly less solid than an idea, but more solid than a notion. I smiled, rose and murmured my goodbyes, desperate to get out of the room before the emulsion curdled into its separate elements again and drained away.

Chapter 19

'Go on then,' Alec said, as we descended in the lift. 'You're bursting with something. What is it?'

'Not bursting,' I said. 'Not at all. I'm courting a wisp of an idea more fragile than a syllabub.'

Alec pulled the handle, stranding us between floors. When the lift's gears stopped grinding there was perfect silence. 'Speak,' Alec said. 'I'll try to catch the end of it.'

'I'm thinking of a theatre company,' I said. 'People are playing two parts, saving money. Banquo, the doctor, a soldier and a courtier all played by the same exhausted actor. And I'm wondering if it's the same here. Do you see?'

'Not yet,' said Alec kindly. 'Keep talking.'

'Well, it's all these women,' I said. 'The woman from the park with the two little girls. I ran into her again. She was rushing for her train but I don't think that's the only reason she was keen to get away from me.'

'What two little girls?' said Alec.

I tutted at my mistake. 'See what I mean? You're right. *She* didn't have two little girls. That was someone else. She had a late friend she was looking out for. But then it's what I was just saying to Mrs Priest. The Punch and Judy show wasn't a silly tawdry little nothing. I saw it. It was rich and strange and impossible to look away from. Scaramouche, Alec, was mesmerising. And I just wondered whether the woman who was watching for her friend managed not to give him so much as a glance because she'd seen it all before. Because she knew Bert.'

'It's a bit of a thin thread,' Alec said.

'On its own, certainly,' I said. 'But there's something else. Oh, what a relief! There's something else and it has finally come into focus.' I grinned at him. 'It's about the *third* woman. Remember what Leon said about meeting her in the teashop, and how she told him where his brother lived?'

'Oh!' said Alec. 'Yes. *She* knew Bert. Is that what you mean? She was a friend of Bert's, a close enough friend to know his address, a thing his own brother didn't know. But what makes you think she's the same woman you met in the park? *She* could have any number of reasons for being uncomfortable when you ran into her again.'

'For one thing, I didn't run into her. I caught up with her when a flurry of trams prevented her from crossing the road. And it was a lucky thing because until they did she had been fleeing. She kept looking over her shoulder. I thought she was after a taxi. But that wasn't it. She was trying to get away from me.'

'Yes, but—' Alec said.

'You're going to kick yourself.' I could not resist teasing him; he would have done the same to me – *had* done the same to me countless times, in fact.

'I give up. Or give me a hint anyway.'

'The woman who gave Bert's address to Leon in the teashop, while we were at Her Majesty's . . . Leon was waiting for us to come back and she came in and . . . Do you remember?'

'Leon told us that she turned white, because she thought she'd seen a ghost. So she knew where he rented rooms . . . but she didn't know anything about his family?' Alec frowned. 'Is that it?'

'Come on!' I said. 'Think! It's right there, Alec. Can't you see it?'

'Give me another hint.'

'There are no other hints to be given. You've just said it yourself.' I waited. Alec shrugged. 'She knew . . .'

'Bert's address?'

'Oh, this is unbearable. Do you give in?'

'I give in.'

'She turned white because . . . she knew Bert was dead.'

Alec's reaction was extremely gratifying. He groaned, smacked himself in the head, and gave me a short round of applause. I bowed.

'She did, didn't she?' he said. 'She thought *she'd seen the ghost of Bert*, when she saw his brother. She knew Bert was dead!'

'And knew pretty early on too,' I said. 'Before Moll heard it from us.'

'So how did she find out?' said Alec. 'His name wasn't in the paper, was it?'

'There's one way to know a man is dead before anyone else knows,' I said. 'And you'd certainly be shocked at the sight of a brother in that case, wouldn't you? In a state of heightened awareness caused by guilt? Because it still puzzles me that she recognised Leon so readily. They're far from doubles, the two of them.'

'It's a possibility,' Alec said. 'But I'm sorry, Dan, I still think it's thin. Unless you're saving the clincher for last.'

'Not exactly. Although there is *something*. I know there is. You know how sometimes you know there is?'

Alec nodded.

'I'm not absolutely clutching at straws,' I said.

'I'm not suggesting that you're clutching at straws,' Alec said. 'I believe there's another bit of the puzzle floating around in that mind of yours and history suggests that sooner or later you will get it in your fist.'

'Thank you,' I said. I waited to see if the wisp would drift by while I was watching for it, but of course I was not afforded that good fortune. 'Can you get this thing moving again, Alec please? We need to go to the police station, much as I would happily never have to meet that awful inspector again.'

There was a surprise waiting for us at the Bell Street station, however. Inspector Daunt had been humbled by an onslaught of news, some of it unhelpful, some of it downright abysmal and some of it – this is the news I am sure had broken him – simply mystifying. He had spent his morning floundering in full view of his staff and, by the time we enquired of today's sergeant whether he was at home to friends, he was ready to call on seaside psychics nevermind a pair of slightly annoying detectives.

So we were ushered into the sanctum. Truth be told I softened to him when I saw the place. The tumultuous disorder of papers, files, notes, old newspapers and crumb-strewn sandwich plates spoke of either a job so fraught and busy it would overwhelm the best of men or of a man so unequal to his job that he was slowly drowning. Either way, one would have been a stone not to feel a pang of pity.

'Come in,' he said. 'Come in and sit down. Shift that stuff off that seat there, Mr Osborne. Just put it anywhere.' Alec hesitated and I did not blame him; the shoving of a tottering pile of papers 'just anywhere' did not strike me as a useful development in the economy of the inspector's office. In the end, Alec sat clutching it to his breast, all set to replace it when he stood. 'And are you here with questions or information?' the inspector said.

'Both,' I said. 'You needn't answer the one but we would urge you to listen to the other.'

'We've done the post-mortem,' was his reply. 'There was no question of the cause of death, obviously. The man was cut through to his spine with a short blade, very sharp. A clean cut. He was practically exsanguinated – Mrs Gilver, I trust you don't mind hearing these details?'

I assured him that I was not about to swoon and disarrange his chaotic office even further.

'Apart from that he seemed to be in moderately fair health. Better health than he deserved. For he had not taken good care of himself. The doctor said he'd have put the man's age at much more than sixty. He would have believed seventy.'

'Well, it's a hard life tramping the roads,' I began.

'Tramping the roads doesn't get your liver in that state,' said the inspector. 'He hadn't had as hard a life as many that end up on the post-mortem table. He was well-enough nourished, and his teeth would have seen out his natural span. A touch of arthritis in his fingers, mind you.'

'Poor Bert,' I said. 'Manipulating those puppets all day long with arthritic fingers can't have been much fun.'

'One wonders that the pair we found at Doig's were so well finished,' Alec said. 'I'd have expected them to be rougher than the others.'

'And when did you see the others, sir?' said the inspector.

'The day we came to have our fingerprints taken,' Alec said. 'Oh, did that policeman not happen to mention he left the three of us alone in the room with the tent? Didn't you wonder how the professor's prints got all over it?'

'Indeed I did,' said the inspector, his face darkening. 'That's one of the many things that've been making me scratch my head. But I couldn't make head nor tail of it. Otherwise we wouldn't have let the brother take them away.'

'Did you?' I said. 'When was this? He never mentioned to us that he intended to pick them up. Or not to me. Did he say anything to you, Alec?'

'He was very keen,' the inspector said. 'A memento, I think, more than anything. He came mooning over them and took the whole caboodle: puppets, tent and everything. Which was helpful to us here, actually. It took up quite a bit of space and those dolls were upsetting our little girl who works in the canteen. She said they were creepy and refused to take the tea round. We were glad to see the back of it all. There were no prints to be had off any of it, besides the brother's.'

'None?' I said. 'Absolutely none? That's surprising, isn't it?'

'Oho!' Daunt said. 'That's just the start of it. Wait till you hear the rest. There were no fingerprints on the puppets or the tent, meaning that the killer wore gloves, and also meaning that Bert Mackie must have cleaned everything before the show on Monday. It was the same at his rooms. Your prints were there, both of you, and the brother again, but of Mackie's own there was nary a smudge. Nothing. The wee bathroom was clean enough to eat your dinner out of the sink. Notice I don't say off the floor. The floor was filthy. Dust, dog hair, flakes of tobacco – raw and ash – spills of salt and tea leaves. But setting the floor apart it was almost like a new pin.'

'Puzzling,' I said. 'But lots of people have blind spots when it comes to housekeeping and hygiene. My younger son, when he was small, hated to have sticky hands. He would shriek if an ice dripped onto his knuckles. But I could have grown potatoes behind his ears.'

I had missed it but Alec had noticed the salient word in all of the inspector's outpouring. 'Almost?' he said.

The inspector rewarded him with an approving nod. 'Almost. There was a lady's handprint and five perfect little fingertips on the inside of the cupboard door in the bedroom.'

'Odd,' I said. 'How small was it? Might it have been a child playing hide and seek?'

'It might,' said the inspector, 'except that the dust was worse in that there cupboard than anywhere else in the place and there were footprints too. Small feet.' He held up a hand to cut off my interruption before I could make it. 'In high heels. So there's a woman in the case somewhere. That much we do know.'

It was the perfect opening to the news we had brought him. Alec stared hard at me, sending the message that it was my job to deliver it.

'There *is* a woman in the case, Inspector,' I said. 'Several. There's Moll at Her Majesty's stage door, for a start. She stored the tent and puppets when Bert wasn't using them. She might be responsible for the cleaning of them. Although she didn't strike me as the fastidious sort.'

'Her Majesty Moll McGraw?' said the inspector, with the nearest thing to a twinkle I had ever seen on his face. 'I should say not. She's not got a neat wee pair of feet in a set of high heels either. Or a dainty hand.'

Alec let out a guffaw and even I had to smile when I remembered Moll's swollen ankles hanging over her slippers.

'But as well as Moll,' I went on, 'there's a female friend of Bert's who ran into his brother, Leon, in a teashop on Tuesday. She got the fright of her life, thinking she was looking at Bert's ghost. Professor Mackie didn't describe her, but we think there's a chance she's the same woman I met in the park on Sunday. She was a neat little thing. I'm trying to remember her shoes . . . and yes, I think she was tripping along the road on fairly silly heels.'

'The road?' said the inspector. 'You said the park.'

'I ran into her on Lindsay Street, when she was rushing to the station. Or so she said. I think, in truth, she was rushing to get away from me. You'll have her name, you know. She was questioned as a witness on Monday afternoon. She'll be on the list.'

The inspector had perked up a little. One could see that finding the owner of that handprint inside Bert's bedroom cupboard would mean a great deal to him.

'And then there's the mother of two little girls who came into Doig's on Friday and told them that Bert had Rosie and Freckle in his show,' Alec said. 'Which we are far from sure he actually did, by the way.'

'The same one again?' said the inspector hopefully. He had taken to the notion of this single woman playing multiple parts with great enthusiasm.

'No idea,' said Alec, causing the inspector's shoulders to slump. 'We thought she was a reader of the magazines come to congratulate the publisher on a clever notion but—'

'Maybe that was a ploy, though,' the inspector chipped in. 'Maybe she gushed with praise, knowing damned – excuse me, Mrs Gilver – knowing fine well the Doigs would be affronted by Mackie's cheek. She was trying to bring the Doigs's wrath upon him! And, if that's her handprint, she hid in his rooms! I don't wonder she thought she'd seen a ghost, do you? The man she killed come back to life and sitting drinking tea?'

'She didn't kill him,' I said. 'She was sitting next to me. She was in the next deckchair. She was the one who wasn't watching the tent and was therefore able to confirm who came and went. To wit, no one.'

'Why wasn't she watching the tent?'

'She was looking out for her friend,' said Alec.

'While everyone else was watching the show?' said the inspector.

I nodded.

'Riveted?'

I nodded once more.

'No attention to spare for anyone slipping away and bearing down on the kiosk with murderous intent.'

'That's a thought,' Alec said. 'Dan, would you have noticed her leaving and returning?'

'For it's only her word,' the inspector said. 'She's the only one making the claim that turns this case into a pain in my neck with an invisible killer and an impossible crime!'

He was cleverer than I had given him credit for. That was a neat piece of arguing. I tried to cast my mind back to the moment: Scaramouche alone in the centre of the little stage, his neck stretching and stretching. Would I have noticed the woman in the deckchair beside me slipping away? Surely.

'There is a more mundane explanation,' Alec said. 'We have no proof but hear me out. Bert had a girlfriend in every town. This we know. We thought his Dundee lady love was Moll.'

The inspector snorted.

'Yes, she's no oil painting, but she seems a good sort. Well, what if the woman in the park wasn't distracted by her friend's expected arrival so much as by the fact that she had seen the show a hundred times and it no longer interested her? What if she was Bert's Dundee girlfriend, in other words. That would also explain her almost swooning when she saw his brother in the teashop. And it might explain her reporting his new puppets to Doig's to . . .'

'To what?' said the inspector.

Alec, having had all the glory of delivering the easy bit of our theory, now turned beseechingly to me.

'To sound them out about the publicity stunt, perhaps,' I said. 'Or to see if they might cough up to make him stop. Even to make mischief for him, if they had had a falling out.'

The inspector perked up again at that. 'A falling out,' he said. 'That brings us back to the notion of her nipping round the back with a knife, doesn't it? In which case I can well see why she'd scurry away from you in the street, Mrs Gilver.'

'This is the wildest speculation, though,' I said. 'And I'm not sure how we – one, I mean, you, rather, the police – I'm not sure how any of it could be checked.'

'That's the easiest thing in the world,' the inspector said. 'You describe the woman to me and I send one of my men round – the café, Doig's, the neighbours on Dock Street – and see if the description matches. And if she's a Dundee lass, someone will know her. What does she look like, Mrs Gilver?'

'She's small,' I said.

'Dainty handprint,' said the inspector.

'Quite. That doesn't mean it was her, hiding in Bert's rooms, but it doesn't let her out. I'd put her in her late forties. Rather young for Bert.'

'Not if he has a high opinion of himself,' said Alec. 'Exactly the kind of man who would happily keep a woman in every

206

town. Or perhaps she is looking after herself rather better than Bert did and she's a well-preserved fifty-odd to his reckless sixty.'

'It's distinctly possible,' I said. 'Her hair was neatly set, her hat was chic and clinging to one side of her head like an alpine mountaineer. Her gloves were very clean and very tight. And she was tripping along on high heels, as I mentioned before. Flawless stocking seams too. I happened to notice, since I was following her.'

'To the station,' Alec said. He was grimacing.

'What?' I said. 'What are you thinking?'

'Sorry, Dandy, but it occurs to me that there's a much less helpful explanation for all of this. Someone scurrying towards the station *is* probably catching a train. And someone so anxious and keyed up about a late friend is exactly the sort to be equally keyed up about missing a train, and distraught to see an acquaintance who might slow her down.'

I felt a slump as my airy confection began to break into fragments and drift away. The inspector too looked rather flattened.

'Good point, Alec,' I said. 'We really have been adding two and two and making five, haven't we? There's actually *no* reason to think there's only one woman in this case rather than three.'

'Four,' said the inspector. 'The one in the park, watching for her friend. The one at Doig's reporting the puppets. The one with the dainty hand, hiding in a cupboard. The one who saw Leon in the teashop.'

'Five,' said Alec. 'Bert's Dundee girlfriend. If it's not Moll.'

'Which it might be,' I said. 'I could ask Grant for a description of his St Andrews girlfriend, to see what Bert's standards were, if that's not too brutish a way to describe it.'

'But we really are clutching at straws,' Alec said. 'Wouldn't you say?'

I stared at him. 'That's the second time you've said that

207

to me today. And the second time it's bothered me. I wish I could work out why.'

'Ah well,' the inspector said. 'It was nice while it lasted. It would be very satisfying if we could say there's one woman and one man in this case. A man to kill and a woman to cloud the waters. But it's not to be.'

'You were going even further, Inspector,' Alec reminded him. 'One woman in the case and no man at all. Except the deceased.'

'And his brother,' I said. 'And that other Mackie from fifty years ago. What do the police make of that, Inspector? For I'll freely admit it's got us stumped.'

'Has it?' said the inspector. 'Why, what do you reckon it could mean?'

'Nothing very sensible,' I said. 'My first thought was that Bert Mackie came from a line of Punch and Judy men, but his brother supplied the family history that quashed that. Then we wondered if chose his "stage name" in honour of this earlier Mackie, but then the professor – the real professor – is Mackie too. So once again, no. After that, we had only coincidence to rely on and it's most dissatisfactory. But what else?'

'Why are you looking at us as if we're a pair of chumps, Inspector?' Alec said. 'What have we missed?'

'The only possible explanation,' the inspector said. One could forgive him for indulging a long pause there, the better to enjoy the glory of revealing it to us, besting both of us with his insights. The pause outlasted my patience however and I had heaved a mighty sigh before he spoke again.

'Simply this,' he said. 'A little boy by the name of Albert Mackie sees a Punch and Judy show and finds out that the puppeteer's name is none other than . . . Albert Mackie!'

I groaned. 'Of course,' I said. 'I can absolutely believe the ambition to be a Punchinello started that way. In fact, we were puzzled by how a man from Mackie's background ever ended up where he did. This explains it all.'

'Leaving only the question of who killed him and why and how,' Alec pointed out.

'A man,' said the inspector. 'Let's at least go back to that as a working assumption. Even if I could bring myself to believe that a dainty little woman could wield that knife, I couldn't see her daubing blood and plaster on the walls at Thompson's in broad daylight. Apart from anything else, the letters were too high. She'd have had to stand on a bucket.'

'Ah,' said Alec. 'That brings us to the other small matter we've got to tell you.'

Chapter 20

'It still doesn't explain the fifty-year echo,' I said. 'Nothing the inspector said explains that.' Alec and I had left him recovered from his outrage at Johnny Doig's tricks and back to scratching his head again. We had come out for a stroll to scratch ours.

'I keep thinking about old Millie,' Alec said. Millie had been his spaniel, a dog of little sense but great sweetness, the lifelong friend of the first Bunty until *her* death and the long-suffering playmate of the second Bunty. I always thought my new puppy had brought cheer into Millie's arthritic, blind, deaf and toothless dotage. Alec, I suspected, blamed the excesses of the puppy for Millie's finally wearing out. We do not speak of it.

'What about her?' I said.

'Remember the bull?' he said. I nodded. Millie had been a friend to every dog, cat and sheep she ever met, although rather a fiend to anything smaller, the helpless captive of generations of breeding that had led her to view rabbits, mice, one unfortunate parrot of Alec's houseguest and every brush that tried to escape into its dustpan in her presence as a pheasant to be retrieved. It was when she met her first bull, though, that her behaviour mystified Alec and me. She ignored it. She walked under it, sniffed at a tussock, sat down and scratched her ear.

'It's too big,' Alec had said at the time. 'She can't see it. She can smell something, but that object is simply too enormous to register as a fellow creature. What a daffy dog!'

'I think this double murder fifty years apart has taken the police the same way,' he said now. 'It's too odd. Too inexplicable. Too macabre. They can't fit it into their view of the world in any way that makes sense and so they are ignoring it. Like Millie and the bull.'

'Are we any better?' I asked. 'What do *you* make of it?'

'It's not a coincidence,' Alec said. 'I know that for sure. Even if Deuteronomy has turned out to be irrelevant.'

'Has it?'

'I think so. Talk of vengeance after murder is perhaps to be expected, not to be remarked.'

'Perhaps,' I agreed. 'But whether or not the fifty-year echo is coincidence I don't see what we can do with it. So I suppose, reluctantly, I conclude the same as the police. Rather than make ourselves dizzy over something utterly bewildering, we look at other aspects of the case in hopes that pulling on any string at all will make the whole thing unravel.' I thought for a moment and went on: 'What string do you fancy pulling?'

'The nearest,' Alec said. He looked up at where we had strolled to and then took off at a more purposeful pace. 'Let's go and ask at the Sugarlump Café whether the woman who came in and spoke to Leon was short and neat with a fancy little hat. It's only round the corner.'

This first string-tugging failed. We recognised the waitress who had served the three of us but as far as she was concerned we two were perfect strangers. She gave only the barest of polite nods as we entered, looked blank at Alec's cheery 'Back again, you see!' and went as far as to sigh when we asked her for a moment of her time to ask a few questions.

'As long as it *is* just a moment,' she said. She wore a wristwatch, of course. Every smart little waitress and shop girl wears a wristwatch these days, I have noticed. But she twisted right round and gave a pointed look at the wall clock instead of glancing at it.

'Do you remember us from yesterday?' I said.

The girl shrugged.

'We were here around lunchtime with another gentleman. He was rather upset. He'd had bad news. I asked for extra milk for his tea.'

'We keep our milk jugs well filled,' said the girl. 'I'm sorry you had to ask. But if we'd been very busy, we might have got behind ourselves briefly.' She looked down and her expression hardened to see only a puddle of rather blue milk at the bottom of the jug on our table. This was unfortunate, I thought. She would blame us for her feeling foolish and be all the more determined to thwart us in whatever we hoped to gain.

'We're not complaining,' I said. 'Gosh, I couldn't begin to do what you do all day every day. It's a marvel you don't simply shoo us out and lock the door at any given minute. Fussy, demanding, ungrateful wretches that we are. Never mind when we waylay you with all these questions.'

This outrageous sucking up mollified her. It always mollified people, whenever I wheeled it out; a depressing thought. Just once I should like to see an arched eyebrow and a request for me to stop being so patronising, but clearly today was not the day.

Despite *my* having buttered her up, Alec pressed the advantage. 'Do you really not remember us?' he said, twinkling disgracefully at the girl. 'Three of us came in. We two left about twenty minutes later, but our friend – tall chap, dark hair and beard, long dark overcoat and, as we said, upset after some bad news – stayed quite a while longer. I'd have thought you would have time to start wishing you could get his table back. Don't you begin to notice lingerers and wish they would buy something else or leave?'

This didn't go down as well as my flattery, strangely. Perhaps the girl resented Alec's trying to suggest he could see behind the curtain.

'I daresay he did buy something else, when his brother's

acquaintance arrived,' I said. 'She would have needed a reviving cup of tea and certainly they sat and talked.'

'Hang on,' said the waitress, cutting across me rather rudely. 'Do you mean to say this chap came in with you two, then you left, then another female came in and joined him?'

'Exactly,' Alec said. 'I knew you'd remember.'

'I *would* remember,' the waitress said emphatically. She retied her apron strings as she spoke and reaffixed her cap by means of a couple of hair-pin jabs. The overall effect was of readying herself for battle. 'We don't allow that sort of thing. Someone would certainly have stopped *that* from happening.'

'Stopped what—' I began.

'It's the docks,' the woman said. 'The sailors. They're on to them down there now so they've started in on respectable establishments like ours. Only we don't let them.'

'Oh!' I said. 'No, no, no. We don't mean anything like that. We rather think this was a woman in her forties in tweeds and a smart hat.'

'You'd be surprised,' said the waitress. 'They're clever enough to hide what they really are. And there's no way any transaction like that passed in this establishment yesterday. I'd thank you not to go around suggesting it did. Now, did you want to order anything?' She took her order pad from her deep apron pocket and stood with pencil poised over it. These were her sword and shield, she seemed to say, and we could do our worst.

Not caring to sit and drink tea under the eye of a person who thought us to be mixed up in immoral earnings, however, Alec pressed a tip into her hand and we beat a retreat.

'I had no idea such affairs were conducted in teashops where the doilies are starched beyond usefulness,' I said. 'I'm having visions of her breaking up married couples who arrive separately and throwing nannies out on their ears if they come in alone out of uniform.'

'Hm,' Alec said. 'Given that she missed the professor and Bert's friend meeting, I should think people are quite safe. The policy is more trumpeted than enforced. Still odd though.'

'Perhaps she sat down at a neighbouring table instead of joining him.'

'Even more suspicious, wouldn't you say? Like all those spies who stare straight ahead and talk to the chap beside them on a park bench.'

'Then leave a newspaper to be picked up after they've gone,' I agreed. 'I wonder how often a spy has some kindly stranger running along after him shouting "Sir, sir, your *Evening News!*" and has to start again on another bench.'

'Or perhaps when the professor said she ran into him at the teashop, he meant as he was leaving. In the doorway, or even on the street.'

I shook my head. 'But he wasn't leaving. He was waiting for us to return. It was when he met the woman that he decided to go to Bert's rooms instead.'

'True,' Alec said. 'Well then that waitress must be mistaken. And we shall have to attack this little puzzle from the other end. Ring up the professor and ask him to describe her. We should have done that in the first place, probably.'

But it proved a great deal more complicated than we could ever have imagined. At least we were not reduced to standing in the corner of a post office, since we had the use of the telephones at Doig's, still being officially in Miss Bissett's employ until the killer was caught and the good name of her family firm was washed of the taint from its proximity to the murder.

And Grant was delighted to help. After a day in charge of the meagre switchboard at Doig's, with its one outside line and its little board of a dozen inside extensions, she felt herself quite the telephonist. If she could have got a headpiece with earphones and a wire bending around her jaw to hold

214

a speaking device to her lips she would have been in seventh heaven.

'St Andrews University,' she said to the operator in clipped tones, one professional woman to another. 'Department of Psychology.' Then she frowned and listened. 'Well then the main switchboard, of course,' she said when there was a break in the flow of talk on the other end of the line. 'We're very busy people. It shouldn't be beyond you.' There was another outburst of quacking from inside the telephone. Then a long pause, during which Grant said only 'Thank you.'

While a distant bell finally rang, Grant covered the mouthpiece with her hand and said to Alec and me, 'The girl on the exchange doesn't know all the departments, clearly. She said we should have looked it up in the directory if we were as fussy as all that. Can you believe it? No way to talk to customers.' I said nothing and even forbore to give Grant a look.

When someone eventually answered the telephone in St Andrews, however, there was little more satisfaction to be had, for there did not appear to *be* a Department of Psychology, and when Grant asked for Professor Mackie by name there was only a long silence.

'Give me the telephone,' I whispered. She did so with rather ill grace.

'This is Mrs Gilver, of Gilverton in Perthshire,' I said into the receiver. It still works sometimes and it was working now. The voice on the other end took on a more subdued note and asked how its owner could be of assistance to me. 'As my colleague mentioned,' I said, 'we urgently need to speak to Professor Mackie. Would you be so kind as to put us through? Professor Leon Mackie. Psychology.'

'Yes but you see the thing is, madam,' said the subdued voice, 'that we don't have a psychology department. We have schools, here at St Andrews.'

I sighed. 'Well, the Psychology School then.'

'We don't have one. And our professors don't have their

215

own telephones in their rooms so we don't have a directory by name. There's no need for it. You'd be better writing to Professor Mackie.'

'Couldn't someone take a message to him and get him to come to the telephone?' I said.

'But you don't know where he is, madam,' the voice said. It was taking on a patient tinge.

'Surely the porters know where everyone is,' I said. 'I mean, where would the letter be delivered if we were to write?'

'We don't deliver letters to professors' rooms, madam,' said the voice. 'We put letters in their pigeonholes in the school.'

'But we don't kn—' I began, then took a deep breath and reconsidered. 'If a letter came to the university with no depar— *school* named, where would it go?'

'To the main porter's lodge,' said the voice.

'And do they have a telephone? Might I speak to them?'

'That's who you are speaking to, madam,' the voice said. 'I'm sorry I can't be of more help to you.'

'Professor Leon Mackie,' I said again. 'He holds a chair in psychology, department or no department, school or no school. I can't remember the name of it off hand, I'm afraid. But, from the top of my head, that means he could be in the School of Medicine, he could be in anthropology . . .'

'Philosophy,' Alec chipped in. I relayed it.

'He might even be an economist,' said Grant, who can always surprise me.

But we had lost the goodwill of whoever it was who answered the telephone at the main porter's lodge at St Andrews. With a second and rather peremptory suggestion that we look up Mackie in the directory, and the information – almost reaching the level of a scolding – that there were not enough porters to go to five different places on wild goose chases, the voice declined to be of further help. 'He might be a visiting professor,' she said. 'Or too new for us to know yet.'

216

I thanked her, unsure what I was thanking her for exactly, and hung up.

'How odd,' said Alec. 'How beyond odd, actually. He's not new. He definitely said he'd been living in his rooms there for years on end. And surely if that telephone girl was new she'd have asked a colleague of longer standing. How very, very odd.'

'If he were a woman,' said Grant, 'he might have been using his maiden name. Bluestockings do that, just like film actresses.'

'We're making far too much of this,' I said. 'An incompetent and unhelpful employee in a porter's lodge, that's all. She might even have been lying. Perhaps she didn't want to go chasing around the quad, up and downstairs, delivering notes. It's turning into a filthy night after all. I say we do as we were instructed and consult a directory. To the library!'

'Not me, madam,' said Grant. 'I'm going to find a nice teashop with comfortable chairs and refresh myself there until you're ready to go home. It's nearly five now and I can't see any use in holding my post. That florist isn't going to break in after hours.'

Alec and shared a guilty look. We had quite forgotten to tell her that 'the florist' had not been anywhere near Doig's since Fiona glimpsed him on Friday. She had been sitting long hours at her post for nothing.

As we made our way back to the library, I was aware of a troubled feeling, one familiar to me and always unwelcome. 'We're missing something, Alec,' I said. 'We've missed something somewhere. That porter or telephone operator or whatever she was should have said, "Professor Mackie? Why certainly, let me run along and tap on his door." Or at least, "Let me pop a note into his pigeonhole. What number should he ring you on?"'

'I agree,' Alec said. We were briefly separated from one

another by a tide of workers flooding along the street. It was after five now and the offices of Dundee were emptying as every clerk and teller, every manager and office boy, hurried for the buses, trams and trains that would take them home. Each seemed to have at least one brown paper parcel of something under one arm and of course they each had an umbrella hooked over the other so that they were ungainly, unwieldy and a menace to one's elbows.

Still, with all of that, Alec was the real danger to the orderly procession of commuters. For he suddenly stopped dead in his tracks and stared straight ahead, causing a collision directly behind him, a flusterment to either side and an outbreak of loud tutting. I tucked myself in close to his side and looked up into his face.

'What?' I said. 'Have you had a brainwave? Have you cracked it?'

Alec screwed his face up. 'It's within reach,' he said, his voice as strained as his grimace. 'She should have known who Professor Mackie was. Of course she should. Now, I know we've been entertaining the notion that Bert Mackie simply happened to have the same name as the Punchinello from fifty years ago, given that Mackie Sr wasn't a Punch and Judy man.'

'But rather the owner of a billiards hall,' I put in.

'Ah but that's the thing,' Alec said. 'Was he, Dan? Place your bet and follow me to the library.'

As annoying as the periodicals librarian had found us when we were asking for yesterday's newspapers, it was nothing to the level of irritation she achieved when we asked her for the Lanark Post Office Directory from sixty years ago.

'Sixty?' she said, appalled.

'At a guess,' said Alec. 'We'll try a few years in either direction. How many can you carry at once?'

This, naturally, put her in something of a quandary. On

the one hand she would find inconveniencing us hugely gratifying, and the forms one had to fill in to request material from the collection were thorough to say the least. On the other hand, it was she who would be making the trip up to and down from whatever stack housed such neglected volumes as the Lanarkshire Almanacks of the 1870s. In the end, she brought us three at a time, but very slowly.

'Mackie, Mackie, Mackie,' Alec said, fluttering the pages of alphabetic names. 'Here we go: Geo. Mackie, chemist; Mrs Annette Mackie, spinner; Wm. Mackie, surveyor. No mention of a Leon or an Albert or any kind of Mackie at all who kept a billiards hall.'

'It's rather a louche calling,' I said. 'Not perhaps the kind of chap who cared much for the directory.'

'Mrs Annette was only a spinner,' Alec said.

'Ah, but Mrs Annette might have been in more comfortable straits when her husband was alive,' I said. 'She might have been accustomed to an entry and found it hard to give up.'

'Well, well. Let's not argue,' said Alec, as he sometimes does when he is losing. 'Let's check under "Halls, billiards" and see if he gets a mention there.'

'Won't you tell me why?' I said.

But Alec only waggled his eyebrows and started leafing through the little book again.

It was remarkably tricky to find the entries and we were close to agreeing that such lowly establishments did not bother having one, but we kept finding public baths, greyhound breeders and the like and did not feel certain enough to give up.

'Ha,' Alec said, after another ten minutes. 'Archery clubs, curling clubs, bowling greens and eureka! Billiards halls. Here we go.'

'I bet the curlers are affronted, being lumped in with that lot,' I said. 'Is he there? Mackie?'

Alec sat back and let all his breath out in a sharp puff

that made the librarian look up. 'He is not. But at least we know where to look in the other years now.'

When we had checked every year from 1850 to 1900, when – according to Leon – his father was safely retired to 'Dunelgar' in Glasgow, and the librarian was ready to throw us both out of the window, or at least give us permission to go down to the stacks ourselves and get our own clothes covered in book dust, Alec clapped his hands together and gave me a broad grin.

'Right then,' he said. 'Now that I have a bit of evidence to support my theory, I'm ready to present it to you.'

I waited.

'Albert Mackie changed his name.' Alec pronounced this in tones of such ringing pride that the librarian came rocketing over to throw us out as she had long been itching to. We only went as far as the top of the stairs, where a handy balustrade offered us somewhere to lean and the velvet curtain muffled the noise of our talking. It was distinctly chilly, libraries being second only to churches when it comes to staying cold all summer and only turning stuffy when there is snow on the ground.

'Changed it to what?' I asked, once we were settled.

'Changed it to Albert Mackie,' Alec said. 'Really, Dandy. I expected more of you. Can't you see it yet? What I'm seeing.'

I shook my head. I really could not see 'it' and even if I did and stole Alec's thunder he would sulk all the way home.

'He has the same name as the first Punchinello,' Alec said. 'But we thought his brother being Mackie too meant it must be his real name and not a choice he made when he took up puppeteering. But think about it, Dan. We can't find "Professor Mackie" at St Andrews. They've never heard of him. And we can't find this billiards hall owner from Lanark either.' He tutted suddenly and looked back at the door of the periodicals room. 'We should have checked Glasgow for Mackies too. Oh well. We can do it later perhaps, if you need more persuading.'

'Which I most certainly do so far,' I said. 'Why would Albert Mackie change his name to that of a murdered man?'

'Any number of reasons,' Alec said. 'He might not know the man was murdered. He might have bought the show from a widow who wanted her late husband's name to live on. Or it might simply have been that it said "Albert Mackie" on the tent and he couldn't afford to have it repainted. Or perhaps . . .' here Alec paused, and I sensed that whatever came next was the heart of his idea '. . . perhaps the name of a murdered man was preferable to the name he gave up. I think that's it.'

'Why?' I asked. 'It didn't say Mackie on the tent, by the way.'

'It might have, originally,' said Alec. 'And as to why: because of what Leon did. We were both there to see him give the name "Mackie" to the police and sign it, but I'm quite sure now that's not his real surname. How do you account for that?'

I put my head in my hands, thinking furiously. 'So,' I said, raising my head again at last, 'Leon has kept the family name in academic circles but did not want to let the police hear it? Or at least did not want the police to hear a different name and wonder how that came to be and conclude – or even remember! – a scandal.'

'A scandal so serious,' Alec said, 'that it would be better to have the name of a murdered man.'

We beamed at one another. It was neat and plausible and explained a great deal. Alec's smile dimmed at the same moment as mine. 'It doesn't explain the second murder,' he said. 'Fifty years to the day.'

'Nothing does,' I said. 'Nothing could. But this perhaps gets us a few little paces closer.'

Chapter 21

We were so very pleased with ourselves that, determined to go and show off to our client – we called it a report of progress but it was showing off of the most egregious kind – we strolled out of the library, the exact spot we needed to be to ascertain the usefulness of the theory and convert it into solid information.

Instead we swanned back to Doig's and got a printer, out for a smoke, to let us in at the back door.

'Just in time,' he said. 'Mrs Miller's doing an extra round, since Editorial's stopping on till six.' We took the lift up to Miss Bissett's office, arriving neck and neck with the trolley.

Mrs Miller, as is the way of human nature, now despised me like poison, since I had made her feel and look foolish. She scowled at me, gave me a chipped cup, slopped tea in the saucer and searched out the smallest flattest teacake to hand over to me. Alec, just as much a part of the operation that had caused her humiliation as I was, nevertheless got quite the plumpest cake, dripping with butter, and got it with a smile. I could hardly judge her: feeding Alec is a simple joy, like feeding a dog.

'We have made considerable advances,' I told Miss Bissett. She was sitting at a desk, all but obscured by a perfect bazaar of odd objects. Three members of her staff I knew to be attached to the *Freckle* were ranged on its other side looking expectant, the two young men desperately earnest and the woman leaning forward apparently from the ankles in her eagerness. Miss Bissett nodded at me, but then returned her attention to the jumble on her desktop. It reminded me of nothing so much as a nativity, except that it seemed to be fashioned out of those natty coloured-paper drinking straws one sees at ice cream emporia at the seaside.

'Is that a nativity?' I said, taking a closer look at the figures gathered around what might be a footstool with a wobbly top or might equally be a manger.

'Yes,' said Miss Bissett. 'What do you think?'

'We're putting together the Christmas issue,' said one of the supplicants who awaited Miss Bissett's judgement.

'On time-and-a-half?' Alec muttered. I had given up hoping to understand the magazine publishing calendar and said nothing.

'We always have a Craft,' the supplicant went on, capital letter clearly audible.

'And it's always seasonal,' said her colleague.

'Only we weren't sure if we could improve on last year's flaked-soap snowman. They loved that, didn't they? The kiddies.'

'Although the mummies sent a letter or two,' Miss Bissett murmured, evidently crushing the last speaker, whose shoulders slumped. The first supplicant leapt to the defence.

'And so this year, you see,' she said, 'we thought we'd use something the children would need to seek out for themselves rather than pinch from the household supply.'

'While, at the same time, making sure the raw materials are not beyond the kiddies' pockets,' the third chap chipped in.

Miss Bissett raised her eyes to Alec and me. 'Good or bad?' she said. 'The advances.'

Alec cleared his throat. 'Good, for Doig's,' he said. 'Tremendous for Doig's. The case is no less peculiar but all of its peculiarities point away from you, Miss Bissett.'

She bestowed a smile on him. 'Such as?'

'There's more than likely some scandal in Mackie's past,' Alec said. 'His family's past, that is. And we rather think there

223

is a woman mixed up in the very heart of it, responsible for making it look as though you and Thomson's were both involved. And perhaps she's responsible for the failure of the police to make inroads into the method of the crime itself.'

'Busy girl,' said the less earnest of the two young men.

'Indeed,' I said. I began to have an inkling that felt useful, but before I could pursue it, Miss Bissett broke into my thoughts.

'I'm still not sure,' she said. 'I'd far rather it was Father Christmas on his sleigh.'

'The reindeer were impossible,' the young woman said. 'The antlers. They all looked like cattle. Actually that ox *is* one of them.' She pointed at tangle of straws that did, granted, have four legs but could have been anything from a cat to a rhino.

'I worry that it's blasphemous,' Miss Bissett said. 'Baby Jesus made of drinking straws? St Joseph? The Virgin?'

'Oh, but part of what makes it so perfect is that the straws make such wonderful halos,' the earnest young man said.

'Why didn't you make the Saviour?' said Miss Bissett, pointing at the manger. It was indeed empty. I daresay I would not otherwise have mistaken it for a footstool.

'Well,' said the chap, shifting. 'We didn't like to.'

'Precisely!' said Miss Bissett. 'Straws!'

'No, not at all,' said his earthier friend. 'It was more than we wouldn't know what to do with it afterwards. It didn't seem right to throw it into the wastepaper basket. But when the children make them, they'll treasure them. They'll be carefully laid away in tissue paper year after year and handed down.'

I tried not to look askance at the collection of stick figures as he spoke.

'If we want that,' said Miss Bissett, 'we should at least suggest pipe cleaners.'

Alec was breathing heavily and I knew he was trying not

to giggle. I could not have looked at him for a pension, for this solemn discussion of the merits of straws and pipe cleaners and the blasphemy of putting the Christ child in a wastepaper basket or in a box in the attic was the most ludicrous thing I could ever remember hearing.

'But then the kiddies will be pilfering again,' said the earnest man. 'From their daddies.'

'I could see cancelled subscriptions if a chap comes home from work on Christmas Eve and can't clean his pipe until after Boxing Day,' said the earthy man.

'Imagine if he dismantled the nativity,' said the woman. 'For a smoke!'

Alec was beginning to clear his throat and there was a dangerous-sounding warble about it.

'No daddy would start with the Baby Jesus!' the earnest man said. 'The pipe cleaners would be rolled up tight. He'd take a shepherd's crook, surely.'

'Did you hear of snowmen being dissolved in the wash last year?' I said. Alec snorted. 'Is it likely to be a widespread problem?'

'That's not what's bothering me,' said Miss Bissett. 'It's that rude saying. I thought it and now I can't get it out of my head.'

'What rude saying?' said the young woman.

'Stick that in your pipe,' said Miss Bissett.

'Ohhhh, yes,' said the earthier man. 'And smoke it. Yes, I see. I think you're right. That's rather unseemly.'

The woman had got two spots of colour high on her cheeks. 'Straws are worse,' she said. '"Couldn't give a straw".'

'Is that worse?' Alec said. He had recovered. 'It might be, depending on context, of course. Or it might be perfectly proper if the thing one doesn't care about is trivial. "I couldn't give a straw about my puppy chewing my slippers," for instance. "There are more important things in life".'

'And I'm sure there are lots more sayings about straws

that are neutral,' I said. '"Knock me down with a straw", for instance. There's even a biblical one. "The straw that broke the camel's back". Not a happy quotation, but no one could say the Bible has no place at the nativity.'

'Feather,' said the earnest man.

I frowned.

'Knock me down with a *feather*,' he said. 'That's the saying.'

I opened my mouth to argue with him, then realised it was true. I swivelled away to meet Alec's gaze.

'We need to confer, Miss Bissett,' he said. 'We'll leave you to it, in the matter of straws and pipe cleaners. If it were up to me I'd make a bid for a pine cone forest, but I daresay that's much too pedestrian. Come along, Dandy.'

We crossed the landing and entered the boardroom, where Alec closed the door at his back and turned upon me a look of avid attention.

'We're right,' I said. 'We're dead right about one bit of it anyway. Mrs Late Friend is the same person as Mrs Two Little Girls. Beyond doubt.'

'Good,' Alec said. 'I'm glad to hear it. Because while that lot were wittering on about the blasphemy of housekeeping supplies, I realised that we missed our chance to make short work of another bit of the puzzle. But you go first.'

It did not take long to tell him about Mr Gould quoting 'Mrs Two Little Girls' and my hearing 'Mrs Late Friend' using the same odd phrase after she had failed to escape me en route to the station.

'They both said "knock me down with a straw",' I concluded. 'Instead of "a feather". Too idiosyncratic a phrase to be used by two separate people, wouldn't you say?'

Alec gave me a short round of applause, then his face fell and he heaved a sigh. 'Now for my much less welcome realisation,' he said. 'We really shouldn't have left the library. We should have marched back into the reference department and ruined that chilly librarian's day. And not by looking for Mackies in Glasgow.'

I waited for enlightenment.

'Think about it, Dandy,' he said. 'How many villas called Dunelgar do you suppose there are in Bearsden?'

I groaned. 'Of course!' I said. 'We could have found out Leon and Bert's real name.'

'If we're right about the scandal and the name-change,' Alec said. 'At the very least we could check to see if we *are* right.'

'Only, I don't think the POD includes those fanciful names picked out in gold paint on the fanlight,' I said. 'I can't remember ever having seen any.'

'No matter,' Alec said. 'There's another way to come at it. Bearsden *and* Lanark. See?'

'How clever you are,' I said. 'Of course, we could cross-refer between Bearsden villas and Lanark billiards halls and find the name that pops up in both places.'

'Then ring back to that porter – who, it turns out, isn't unhelpful at all; rather polite, given how much drivel we were talking about a "Professor Mackie" – and ask to be put through to the man using his real name.'

'Well, we can do it tomorrow,' I said. 'Leon's not going to go stale overnight. Or come to any harm.'

'I hope not,' Alec said. 'I really do hope that's true, Dandy.'
'But?'

'But you ran into the woman hurrying to the station, for the Fife train. And she wasn't best pleased to see you, was she? I've got a nasty wriggling feeling eating away at me that she was headed to St Andrews. To make mischief there. She's made all the mischief she could possibly make in Dundee already, hasn't she? Misleading the police about an invisible man and throwing suspicion on Miss Bissett.'

'Your concern for Leon is credit to your good heart,' I said, 'after he lied to us about his name. But we're building castles in the air now, Alec. We've got no real reason to think he's in danger because a woman got on a train.'

'But what if Mrs Two Little Girls and Mrs Late Friend is also Mrs Teashop?' Alec said. 'That means she revealed her acquaintanceship with Bert to his brother Leon,' he went on. 'She revealed that she knew Bert's address. If that is her handprint inside the cupboard in Bert's Dock Street rooms, she has every reason – *every* reason – to want Leon unable to bear witness against her.'

My brows had climbed my forehead as he spoke.

He nodded in answer to what I had not said. 'Quite. He's not the only one. You should keep an eye peeled, Dandy. If you see her again, don't go running after her. Promise me you'll take care of yourself.'

'No need,' I said. 'You can take care of me. I'm coming with you, Alec, and you needn't try to argue me out of it.'

'Coming?' said Alec. 'Where are we going?'

'To St Andrews. To the university. To find Leon and see that he's all right. If we read through a comprehensive list of Chairs, I'm sure the name of his will jump out at us. Or if we describe him surely someone will be able to tell us his name. Tall, bearded, glowering, dressed in black.'

'He's Scottish too,' said Alec. 'Which is far from a given, in a university of that standing. Don't tell Hugh I said so though. *And* he was away from college for the last couple of days. Even if he hasn't told anyone he had a brother and that the brother died. What a mess pride makes of us all, Dan.'

'That wasn't pride,' I said. 'It was shame. Still he seems to have recovered from it. At least as far as—'

'At least as far as what?' Alec said. 'You look like the cat that got the canary.'

'I was going to say at least as far as not being ashamed to take the Punch and Judy tent away with him,' I said. '*That's* how we'll find him, isn't it? There can't be more than one professor at St Andrews who has had the porters deliver a miniature theatre and cast of puppets to his rooms. Not in the last week or so.'

'And we're going tonight, are we?' Alec said.

'I think we should,' I said. 'I really do have the most dreadful feeling about all of this, Alec. And didn't Leon say something about dinner in the senior common room? I have a feeling he lives quietly and evening might the best time to find him at home. I'll take a turn behind the wheel, by all means.'

I had gone too far at that, of course. Alec accepts me driving my own little motorcar even when he is in it, but as to my taking over and driving his? Unless he was currying favour, such a thing would not be countenanced. He might even take the scenic route back to Perthshire at the end of the evening simply to make the point that he was not tired and could, if he needed to, drive all night.

Grant at the front desk had finished her tea and was delighted at the thought of a trip to St Andrews, although the university was not of any great interest.

'You could drop me at the theatre,' she said. 'I could do a bit more sniffing around. See if I can pick up any more information about Bert from Sid and Tilly.'

I had all but forgotten who Sid and Tilly were, such was the proliferation of characters in this case.

'Bert's girl,' Grant said, clearly reading my thoughts from my face. 'And my old pal who let him stash the puppet booth.'

'Thank God for the booth,' Alec said. 'If Bert had done card tricks or even juggled clubs we'd never find his brother now. Thank God for the bulk of the booth.' At Grant's quizzical look, he added, 'Let me explain.'

Our discoveries and the theories we had built upon them carried us all the way across the Tay Bridge and through the countryside to the outskirts of the ancient town of St Andrews. I had been married to Hugh long enough to enjoy the passing scene, for the chief distinction of Fife when set against Perthshire was that instead of steep valleys, wooded and useless, Fife was a patchwork quilt of rich pillowy fields, the soil as black as caviar and the crops it produced monstrous in their health and bounty. Now, in mid-August, the potato crop was at its peak, blight free and simply squeaking with goodness. The occasional corn field was deeply golden as though to set off the endless green like a finial and, when we happened to pass by a pasture meadow full of poppies, cornflower and campion, even Alec broke off to remark that this was good land and he wondered who owned it.

Since he had paused, Grant jumped in. It must have been a trial to her to remain quiet as long as she had. 'I was hoping you'd touch on the fifty-year anniversary murder,' she said. 'That's the thing that still makes no sense to me.'

'You're not alone,' I said. 'It makes no sense to us either. A Punch and Judy man called Albert Mackie is killed in his tent in a park in Dundee. The killer is never caught. A young man who wants to be a puppeteer, and also wants to escape the scandal of his family name, buys the outfit, changes his name to Albert Mackie, and is killed in the same park in the same town fifty years later to the day, either by an impossible invisible killer or by a visible killer with an accomplice who swears he wasn't there.'

'The latter,' Grant said. 'The killer can't be invisible and must be possible. It was misdirection. Scaramouche's neck keeping our eyes glued on the front of the booth and then that one woman saying she was watching the park, when she wasn't, just as she said she saw the Freckle and Rosie puppets when she didn't.'

'And we think she told the professor – Leon, I mean; the real professor – where Bert lived. And possibly she visited the rooms herself, if it's her handprint. But we have no proof of that. Yet. It's pure conjecture until we can track Leon down and ask for a description. The teashop woman might be a second woman. The one with the handprint might be a third. And the handprint might be innocent, of course.'

'I don't think so,' Grant said. 'What innocent reason would there be for someone to be inside a cupboard with a hand flat against the door?'

'But if it's all the same woman,' Alec said, 'then she can't be the killer. She was sitting out front in a deckchair when Bert was murdered.'

'Also,' I said, 'surely it was the killer who cleaned all the prints from every surface in Bert's room. Who else after all? And the woman would know she'd been in the cupboard, wouldn't she? On the other hand, it wouldn't occur to a different person. It wouldn't occur to *me* to wipe the inside of a cupboard.'

'So it's perhaps one woman, perhaps two, and perhaps three, but none of them are the killer?' said Grant. 'No, that's not right, is it? If it's two, then one of them might be although the other's not. And if it's three, then two of them aren't and one of them could be.'

'Stop!' I said. 'You're making my head ache. I can't believe any woman did what was done to Bert. You saw it, Grant. Can *you*?'

'At least if it is a woman there's a motive,' she said. 'If he really was the faithless philanderer that Sid says he was. One of his women might have decided she'd had enough.'

'Or perhaps all of them did,' Alec said. 'If they found out about one another. A monstrous regiment. One to kick up a dust storm with the local papers, one to do the deed, one to say no one did the deed, one to hide in a cupboard for some reason.'

'And one more to get the fright of her life when she saw Leon,' I said. 'It makes a clever story, Alec, but it's not the sort of thing that really happens.'

'Even if it did,' said Grant, who often prefers to believe that life is as dramatic as storybooks, picture shows and the grimmer fairytales, 'the motive would dissolve, wouldn't it? If you were married to a man – well, I mean to say, you are, madam – and you found out about just one other woman stashed away somewhere, you might be angry enough to contemplate murder, between the two of you. But if you had an understanding with a travelling puppet man, and you found out you were one of a crowd, you might feel foolish, but you'd feel even more foolish if you murdered him over it.'

'And it still wouldn't help make sense of the fiftieth anniversary,' Alec said. 'Right then, Grant. Where's this theatre?' For we were in the outskirts of St Andrews now. 'If you can get Tilly on her own for a chat, you'll be able to tell if she's in deep mourning or recovering from a murderous rage or whatever, won't you? Then ring up the main porter's lodge at the university when you're done and we'll come and pick you up.'

It was unfortunate timing. We had been speaking quite desultorily, almost playing with the thing, but we had managed to drift within sight of the solution. If St Andrews had been just a little further from Dundee, or Alec had been a slower driver, or even if he had known where to find the theatre and so had not needed to break into the musing to ask for directions, we might have got there. But, by the time Grant's instructions had brought us to the stage door of the Majestic, the vague shapes we had conjured had once again faded away without us ever seeing them for the truths they were.

Chapter 22

'Of course, this place is on its last legs now,' Grant said as Alec drew in at the kerb on a bustling street of shops and pubs. I craned out of the side window and could only agree. The sort of repertory theatre where a Punch and Judy man might store his tent when he passed through town was never going to put anyone in mind of Drury Lane, but the cruelly named Majestic was particularly down at heel. The posters to either side of its door were barely visible behind cracked and clouded glass and the gilding was coming off the various painted curlicues in great fat flakes that no one had swept up very recently.

'Why "of course"?' I said.

'The New Picture House, for one thing,' said Grant. 'And the Byre. A brand-new theatre taking over. If you like sitting on a meal sack on the floor and watching Swedish people sniping at one another with no scenery.'

'Norwegian,' I said mildly, 'unless you mean Danish.'

'I do not!' said Grant, truly shocked. All these years after she gave up treading the boards and still the very thought of casting aspersions at *Hamlet* was anathema to her. Shakespeare might, I took a moment to muse, be the only individual, living or dead, at whom she could not bring herself to pitch criticism. I had, after all, once heard her take issue with Moses.

'Sad all the same,' I said. 'To see a thriving tradition start to fade away.' The truth was I had never been to a variety theatre while they were in their pomp and I young enough to find the entertainments amusing. I had always assumed they would be similar to the Paris shows, only with less glamour, and even Paris glamour was largely derived from not being able to understand the words. Still, as one ages one finds it easier and easier to regret the trappings of a youth one never quite lived.

Grant gave me a satisfied nod, as though I had managed to get back in her good books, and stepped down from the motorcar, leaving Alec and me to navigate the narrow streets of the ancient town towards the university.

The porter's lodge by St Salvator's had the dishevelled but cosy air of all porters' lodges, butlers' pantries, cabbies' shelters, and as we now knew, stage door keepers' cubbyholes: there were old armchairs around a battered table; tea-making equipment with a remarkable number of biscuit tins; and the whole thing enveloped in a fug of bottled gas.

Our welcome was as warm as the lodge for we had inadvertently picked an excellent time to come badgering the gatekeepers: just as the legitimate business of the college day was winding down and the only duty ahead was the booking in of tipsy undergraduates returning from town. The porter on duty had his coat buttons open and his tie pulled down, but his cap was hooked over the handle of a drawer under his sliding window, ready to whip back onto his head should a senior fellow pass by.

'We spoke to one of your colleagues a little earlier today,' Alec said. 'She—'

'*She*?' said the porter. His lodge was too well stuffed with old flyers and directories for the word to ring out but it was pretty loud. 'There are no female porters here. No offence meant, madam.'

I shrugged. The chap had given up the best armchair for me and I have always believed that we ladies cannot expect chivalry and equality at the same time. Alec was leaning

234

awkwardly on the edge of a dresser, just avoiding the drawer knobs. I was quite happy.

'It was about four o'clock,' I said. 'But it was definitely a woman we spoke to. Perhaps she was a secretary.'

'Oh,' said the porter, colouring a little. 'Well, that was more than likely my wife. She brings my dinner in when I've got a long shift and I did just step away a moment. She did wrong to answer the telephone. I'm sick of telling her.'

I suppressed a sigh. I agreed with his assessment. If that silly woman had admitted she was not in the employ of the university, we would have pressed her to connect our call to someone who knew the professor and we would have saved ourselves a trip.

'No harm done as far as we're concerned,' Alec said. 'In fact, it's good news. You will no doubt be able to help us with our enquiry.' I flashed my eyes at him as he began this unfortunate phrase. The porter had drawn down his brows upon hearing it.

'Who are you?' he said. 'I took you to be parents.'

'Of a student?' said Alec, rather squeaky. It was unclear whether he was annoyed at being thought old enough to have a child at university, being thought old enough to be married to me, or being thought the kind of parent who would chum up with a porter in the long vac for no discernible reason.

'Do parents often beard you in your den?' I said, quelling my smiles.

'In the summer, certainly,' the porter said. 'Just about now is when it starts. Rooms you see, for next term. I have a little influence and somehow some parents have managed to find out.'

In other words, he had broadcast the fact that good rooms were in his gift and was making a nice living on the side from the parental pockets of spoiled children.

'Hence, one assumes, your unwillingness to break off for

235

meals and leave the lodge unattended,' I said. 'But surely your wife answering the telephone is the point, isn't it?'

'She's only supposed to take messages,' the man said. 'Not go plunging in.'

'No matter, no matter,' Alec insisted. 'We're on the trail of one of your professors. We don't know his name, unfortunately, but he's the something professor of psychology, and we thought if we looked at your directories – fingers crossed they're arranged by rank and not in alphabetical order – we'd find him.'

'By school in order of age, by rank inside the school, by seniority inside the ranks,' the porter said. Good old academic snobbery, I thought quietly to myself. It would be well-nigh impossible to find anyone by name. 'But there's no Department of Psychology here at St Andrews.'

'So your w— So we heard,' I said. 'But he might be in any number of departments: divinity, theology, philosophy, history even.'

'And as I'm sitting here thinking over our professors,' the porter went on, 'I can't say as I can bring him to mind. Are you sure it was psychology? Philosophy, now! A named chair in philosophy we can do you, no trouble at all.' He sounded like a market gardener offering pears although the peaches had gone over.

I tried to cast my mind back to meeting Leon in the park. I had been reeling from the news that he was Bert's brother and that he was a professor at all. I might easily have misheard the less remarkable bit of his title. I nodded. 'It could have been zoology,' I said. The porter shook his head. 'Psychiatry?' Another shake. 'Sociology?' A third shake and a frown to go with it.

'Seismology,' said Alec. It had a more similar sound than any I had suggested, but got only a glare.

'Well let's start with the directories,' I said. 'Philosophy and theology, perhaps. It wasn't French or art or law. We heard him say the word, didn't we Alec?'

'That's a lot of looking up,' the porter said.

'Perhaps not,' said Alec. 'We might be able to come at it from another direction. We happen to know that this professor had a large parcel delivered yesterday or today. Or perhaps gave word of it coming tomorrow.'

'Pff,' said the porter. 'That won't pick him out of the crowd. They're always having packages delivered. Mostly books and these books are not dainty. Some of the volumes of ancient art are enough to put your back out.'

'Larger than a book,' I said. 'Larger than the largest volume of reproduced paintings ever published. Even folded, it would be . . . what would you say, Alec?'

'Four feet by six and a big box along with it,' Alec said. 'It came from Dundee.'

The porter took a moment to think but then shook his head with his lips pushed out.

'So back to finding him by his chair,' Alec said. 'Philology, phonology . . .'

'Aha!' I said. 'I've just remembered. The name of the man who endowed the chair was German.'

The porter frowned.

'Perhaps not,' Alec put in hastily. 'Perhaps Austrian.' It did not help. 'Or simply Jewish. Might have been a Scottish chap for all we know, mightn't it Dandy?'

'We don't have any chairs named for Jews,' the porter said. I felt my shoulders climb in expectation of nastiness, but the man surprised me. 'They've more to worry about than endowing chairs on the Fife coast. I'm getting so I don't like to open a newspaper. I expect you're the same.'

'Swiss?' I suggested, the alarming moment seemingly behind us.

'Oh!' said the porter. 'You don't mean the Schwarzmann Chair of Soteriology, do you?'

'Schwarzmann!' Alec and I sang out in chorus. Then he went on to say, 'Of *what*?'

237

'Soteriology, sir,' said the porter. 'It's the study of salvation. School of Divinity, although it's comparative theology, properly speaking. And you're in luck. Very, very few of our professors actually live in the university, you know. Most, well-nigh all, have houses or lodgings in the town. Professor Dennis is an exception. Top of the stairs on the second door round the quad counter-clockwise. I know he's in too, because he came and dropped off his letters not half an hour ago and he was in his cardigan sleeves and carpet slippers.'

'He didn't mention an enormous parcel on its way from Dundee?' I said. He had not.

'Thank you,' was all Alec said as he slipped the man a folded note. He did not speak again until we were out on the gravel at the edge of the grassy quad, making a beeline for the second staircase.

'Salvation, eh?' Alec said. 'I am led to wonder how blasphemous we were in Leon's hearing, aren't you Dan?'

'I'm sorry to say it was the first thought that sprang into my mind,' I agreed. 'But then comparative theology is very different from ordinary divinity and he didn't do any soul-saving around us in the time we were together.' After that I saved my breath for climbing the stairs. There is nothing like the dank air of a Scottish stone stairway open at the bottom for quenching the breath one needs as one ascends. Tenements and ancient turrets are just the same.

We knocked on the door at the top of the stairs and immediately heard the kerfuffle, from beyond it, of books and papers being laid aside and chair legs moving. A bolt was drawn and the door opened. Alec and I, looking at where we expected Leon's face to appear, found ourselves gazing into an empty room. With a blink, I dropped my eyes until they rested upon the man who stood there, smiling gently and waiting for us to speak.

'Hello,' I said. 'Um, we're looking for Professor Dennis.'

'Yes,' said the little man. He had long white hair that spilled

238

over the shoulders of his cardigan like candy floss and although he was clean shaven he sported a pair of spectacular white eyebrows that threatened to interfere with the half-moon glasses over which he was peering at us.

'Is he in?' Alec said.

The little man looked down at his feet and up again. 'He is liminal, currently,' he said. 'How can I help you?'

'Professor Dennis, the Schwarzmann Chair of . . .' I had forgotten the unfamiliar word again already.

'Soteriology, yes,' the little man said. 'I am thinking of asking to change it to "Salvation Studies" like my American colleagues. It packs them in to the lecture halls, my transatlantic friends tell me. Salvation Studies! What could be more thrilling?'

'Excuse me,' I said. 'Do you mean *you* are Professor Dennis?'

He nodded. 'You are at an advantage,' he said, with a kindly smile.

'And I don't suppose someone has tried to deliver a Punch and Judy show to you today?' said Alec.

That took him a little longer to digest. 'You are quite correct,' he said at last. 'Should I wait in for one tomorrow?'

'I don't know,' I said. 'That's the plain truth, Professor Dennis. I simply don't know.'

'But we're sorry to have troubled you so late in the evening,' Alec said. 'We'll let you get back to your studies.'

'Late?' said Professor Dennis. 'It's not late. I've got two hours till I'll be nipping out for last orders at the Central. Until then I'm reading a western. I do love a western. So soothing to find such moral clarity, don't you think? I don't know how my fellow scholars in the School of Literature can bear to spend their evenings with the sort of people they're writing novels about in England now. Scotland too, I daresay.'

Alec and I nodded and smiled and managed to make our

goodbyes without further rudeness but we were both in the same mental state, minds reeling and thoughts whirling.

Alec broke the silence as we emerged from the bottom of the stairwell back into the quad. 'Westerns, eh?'

'Yes. Shades of Professor Mackie and his down-on-their-luck theatres.'

'Except he's not a professor and he's not called Mackie,' Alec said.

'Do you suppose he's even Bert Mackie's brother?'

'My word, that's a thought,' said Alec. 'Surely the police didn't just take him at his own reckoning?'

'They took *us*,' I said. 'We stated our names and addresses, gave them our prints and skipped out again.'

Before Alec could reply, however he meant to reply to this possibility – and I was not sure *I* knew what to make of it – we heard a loud halloo-ing and turned to see the porter, still without his cap and with his coat flapping behind him, come scurrying across the grass, ignoring the many signs forbidding just that, calling to us.

'A Miss Grant rang the lodge for you,' he said. 'You never told me you were famous detectives. No trouble, I hope? Is Professor Dennis all right? Nothing fishy about this package that's coming for him, is there? It's me that signs for all the parcels and I wouldn't like to put my name to something I shouldn't.'

'We made a mistake,' I said. 'There won't be a parcel after all. Did Miss Grant leave a message?' I wanted to finish with 'of any useful substance', but forbore.

'Oh yes indeed,' said the porter. 'She summoned you to the Majestic as soon as you can get there.'

'Those were her exact words?' I said.

'Post-haste, I think she said,' the porter told me after a moment's thought. 'Your boss, is she? Tell me about it. My boss is just the same.'

'If only he were wrong,' I said to Alec as we beetled off

back to the motorcar. 'And before you say anything, remember I know your Barrow.'

'My Barrow is a termagant right enough,' Alec said, but his mind had left me and raced ahead to Grant. He had the motor running before I was properly in my seat and he dashed through the narrow streets with not a care to the burghers out for an evening stroll nor the frame of the machine as we bounced over the cobbles.

Grant was outside at the Majestic watching for us, as close to wringing her hands as I had ever seen her.

'What is it?' I said through the open window as we drew up.

'Tilly's gone missing,' Grant said. 'They're all up to ninety in there.' She jerked her chin back at the open door behind her. 'Partly because she's the only dresser left – if you can believe it – and they're doing the *Arabian Nights*!'

'No one wears very much in that surely,' I said. 'A scrap of chiffon over the face and some pyjamas. It would be much worse if it was a Restoration comedy, with all the girls in corsets and panniers.'

'You're quite wrong,' said Grant. 'The sturdier the costume the easier it is to get into and out of, especially in a quick wing change. Scraps of chiffon are the very devil. And then there's the body paint. The cast can do their own fronts but what about their backs?'

Alec was flapping his hands at her. 'All right, all right,' he said. 'Partly the costume changes, but partly what else?'

'They're worried she's come to harm,' Grant said. 'She's been anxious and distracted, Sid says, and she's had a lot of furtive phone calls too. One night he said she definitely had someone in here, stowed away in the scenery bay. She kept going to talk to him during the acts and one of the chorus heard raised voices.'

'What night?' I said. 'Look, let's go inside and talk to this "Sid" of yours in an organised fashion, shall we?'

241

'Sunday,' Grant said. 'Sid said she hasn't been herself for a good while, but Sunday was the worst of all.'

She had drawn us into a sort of alley at the side of the theatre, closed off from the street by a door but open to the skies above except where some tarpaulins had been stretched over various stacks of theatrical flats evidently being stored there. It was not a sensible solution to an overcrowded backstage, not in Scotland, and some of the flats were beginning to look rather tatty as the nails rusted and the canvas, from soaking and drying, began to shrink away from the frames. I rather thought they were rotting; there was a most unpleasant smell that grew and grew the deeper we went into the alley.

'Tilly not herself on Sunday night is most intriguing,' I said as we edged around the stacks and in at a side door, where we were instantly plunged into the blackest gloom, not to mention a choking stink. 'What is *that*?' I said, putting my finger along my upper lip, as though affecting a moustache. I was taught, as a child, that this was the most ladylike way to block my nose against unpleasant smells and even this was only to be used when I was without a handkerchief to hold to my face. Alec, free of such concerns, was holding the end of his nose firmly between his thumb and forefinger knuckle.

'What *is* that stedge?' he said.

'Stench?' said Grant. 'Oh. Camels. One camel, anyway. I told you: *Arabian Nights*.'

'A mixture of *Arabian Nights*, desperation and an old pal who happened to own one,' said a lugubrious voice from deeper inside the theatre. 'And so here we are, eyes watering and stomachs heaving.'

He stepped forward and the lugubrious voice was joined by a hang-dog expression and a slouching posture. 'Sid,' he said. 'Majestic door keeper and stable hand.'

'A live cabel,' Alec said, in tones of adenoidal wonderment. 'Golly. I'd thick they could spell it frob the stalls. Will it really help with tickets?'

'It might,' said Sid. He fished in his trouser pockets and brought out a packet of the nastiest, foulest little cigarettes ever peddled by a third-rate backstreet tobacconist and offered them around. Needless to say we all took one. 'Unless it pegs out on stage and we have to send for the knackerman to winch it off and drag it to the glue factory.'

'It's not in the first flush of youth then?' Alec said.

'It's not even in the first flush of dotage,' Sid said. 'We had a camel before once, for *Aladdin* in panto season, and it didn't smell nearly as bad. Poor Humphrey.'

I could not help a giggle escaping me, but the extra blast of stink that came along as I breathed in after it sobered me up again.

'Is there anywhere to get away from the smell?' I said. 'We'd very much like to ask you about Tilly. You're worried?'

'We are,' Sid said. 'Come out front. We've half an hour till the doors open and the bums – excuse me – hit the seats.'

He led us through a warren of passageways. I thought we were leaving the camel behind us at first, but just as I took a deep breath in celebration we rounded a corner and some airshaft or open door delivered another noxious waft of the terrible odour. I sent a silent apology up to Nanny Palmer and grabbed my nose with my glove. It was a great deal more effective than the finger moustache.

Sid was right, however: when we emerged from the wings onto the bare stage we were met by a welcome counter-draught of fresh air coming down the aisles, and by the time we were settled side by side in the front row of the stalls the air was merely musty, nothing worse.

'Sunday evening then—' I began. But I was interrupted by a loud voice shouting from somewhere behind the stage. 'Delia? Si-id? Where have you go to? Oh to hell with that camel. What a bloody pong! Dee-lee-yah?'

'Out front,' Sid shouted back. And in a moment or two a young woman dressed like a tomboy in wide cambric trousers and a checked shirt, with her hair tied up in a rag, came out onto the stage. She was clutching a large square object to her chest.

'Sid, the smell back there is beyond a joke,' she said. 'Can't we put him out in the alley between shows? Or at least give him a charcoal biscuit?'

'You found it,' Grant said. 'Madam, Mr Osborne, this is Betty the ASM. She's tracked down the album of open and closers.'

'What are they?' I said. We had taken the side stairs from the stage to the stalls but Betty clambered over the footlights and dropped down in front of us like a boy vaulting a gate.

'Opening and closing night parties,' she said. 'Photographs. There's bound to be some of Tilly in here. She's been here longer than that camel's been alive.'

'Humphrey,' I said and laughed again.

'We had a leopard called Dot once,' Betty said. 'And a tartan zebra.' She giggled. 'Just an ordinary zebra with a bit of extra paint, but it was quite effective, or so they tell me. That was before my time.'

'It was in *my* time,' said Sid. 'Back when I had hair on my head and a bend in my knees.'

'And no young wife to wear you out,' said Betty, then to my astonishment she dropped a ringing kiss on his bald head and sat on his lap.

Grant was leafing through the photograph album. The pages threatened to crumble as she turned them, and several of the wax-paper corner fixers had given up the ghost as their glue dried out, so that half the photographs slipped out into her lap. She gathered these into a handful and passed them over, some to me and some to Betty.

'Why are we looking for a picture of Tilly?' I said.

Grant gave me a puzzled frown and spoke patiently. 'Because she wasn't here on Monday afternoon and you never know.'

'And on Sunday?' I said, trying again. 'She had a visitor?'

'We hope,' Betty said. 'Never thought anything of it at the time. She usually does a shift in the Central Bar on a Sunday night when we're dark here, but – you've smelled the camel; we're struggling – so we've got permission from the Burgh Council to have shows on Sundays, matinees and evening, for the summer. Only Tilly's favourites round at the bar weren't best pleased. She's a big draw, I think. And we reckoned it was one of her beaus – oh, she's a girl! Isn't she, Sid? – come round pining.'

'Did anyone see him?' I said. I was thinking that Prof. Dennis had mentioned a regular pint of beer at the Central Bar and it was a vague connection in this case, which was so sparsely supplied with them.

'In the distance,' said Sid. 'Miserable-looking cove. Shoulders all bent over as if he had the weight of the world on them.'

Betty's dancing eyes caught mine and she winked at me.

'Tall, short, thin, fat?' I said, after an answering wink.

'Tall,' said Sid. 'Can't say about his figure because he was in a raincoat. Weather on Sunday night! There we go grovelling to the council for a Sunday show and would you like to know the number of dry Sundays we've had? Three. Since Midsummer's Day. Three, as true as I'm sitting here.'

'Tall,' I repeated. That let Prof. Dennis out then.

'It might have been Bert,' Grant said. 'Would Bert Mackie have dropped in on anyone else except Tilly if he'd popped down from Dundee?'

'Bert would know better,' Sid said. 'Him and Tilly's understanding relied on him not springing up when he wasn't expected. The weekend before Easter, a week in June and again for half-term if the weather holds. Then he's off on his travels and Tilly's looking for the next one.'

'Gosh,' I could not help saying, although I try to be modern.

'Sinbad wasn't through the dressing room door before she

245

picked him off, this run,' Betty said. 'I warned her about him but she can't help herself. Can she, Sid?'

'Never could,' Sid said.

'Bingo,' Betty said, 'if you'll pardon my vulgarity.' She was holding up a photograph that appeared to depict a bacchanalia, or at least a heap of tangled humanity, half of them dressed in bedsheets and wearing olive crowns. 'That's Tilly.'

I leaned over and found myself looking into the laughing face of the woman I had last seen hurrying away from me in the street in Dundee, terrified that I would remember her from the scene in the park at the Punch and Judy show.

Chapter 23

It was a glimmer of a motive at long, long last. An argument, caused by Bert Mackie coming back to St Andrews when he should have been safely in Dundee for the bank holiday weekend, and discovering Tilly in the arms of another, might very well light a touch paper to a powder keg.

'Because it has not been my experience,' I said, 'that a man with a girl in every port accepts those girls welcoming a man off every ship. I'm sorry, you two, but it's true.' Alec shrugged. He is not a saint and can readily take offence when I pronounce about 'men' in general, but seldom when the particular focus is affairs of the heart, as opposed to a sense of direction, say, or prowess with a shotgun. Sid also shrugged. Perhaps he knew he was lucky to have got a cheerful pretty young wife, perched this minute upon his knee, and wisely sought not to rock his steady little boat.

'So you're saying that Bert came back to St Andrews for some reason and found out his girl was two-timing him? Why would that get him killed?'

'Let me think,' I said. 'I'm close to it. Give me a minute.'

'And why was Tilly in the park on Monday afternoon watching the show?' Grant added, completely ignoring my plea.

'Never!' said Sid. We all turned to find out the nature of the objection. 'Tilly spending a shilling on a deckchair to watch Bert Mackie's puppet show?' he said. 'Never in a month of Sundays. She's a professional.'

Betty shushed him but he persevered.

'You should know that, Delia,' he said to Grant. 'A dresser wouldn't sit and waste her time watching a show. No more than a circus clown would laugh at a slip on a peel. We see behind, we see the wires and hear the cogs. We're not gullible enough to— No offence.'

'She wasn't actually watching the show,' I said. 'She never claimed to be. She was watching the gates. And I'm not offended. I happen to know you're right, Mr . . . Sid. The circus clowns of my acquaintance would nod in approval at a neat addition to an act, but I never saw a single one of them laughing. That was for jossers.'

'Well, well, well,' Sid said, giving me an appraising look. 'You've done well for yourself, haven't you girl?' I gave a self-deprecating simper. Of course, I had only moved in circus circles for a few weeks one winter while investigating a case, but I dislike being patronised.

'I've just thought of something else too, Dandy,' Alec said. 'We took it on its face value because we had no reason not to, but why would that woman – Tilly, it transpires – have all her attention glued to the park gates simply because her friend was late off her bus? She wouldn't, no matter how anxious her nature. The friend could hardly miss the striped tent and Tilly was saving a seat. We were fools to swallow it.'

I nodded. 'We were. She wasn't doing that at all. And I've managed to lay my hands on the idea I was chasing.' I glared at Grant as if to say *no thanks to you*. 'Bert discovering Tilly in Sinbad's arms wouldn't get him killed. But . . . Sinbad discovering the existence of Bert might, if he was of the right violent temperament.'

'And Bert Mackie had a way of grinning at you, like a wolf, that would make a monk want to lamp him,' said Sid.

'More like the cat that got the cream,' Betty said. 'A right mucky grin he had, a laugh to match.'

'So he might have put Sinbad's back up?' I said. 'And if Tilly knew that Sinbad's plan was to go to Dundee and have it out with Bert, then she might very well scuttle off up there herself.'

'And in that case she'd be well advised to keep her eyes trained on the park gate and the approach to the tent in case Sinbad came steaming in!' Alec said.

'Can anyone account for Sinbad's movements on Monday afternoon?' I said. 'Is he part of the current show?'

Betty, Sid and Grant all gave me an incredulous look. It was Alec who spoke up, though. 'He's Sinbad in the current show, Dandy.' He turned to the others. 'What's the actor's name?'

'Douglas,' Betty said. 'And we've no idea where he was on Monday daytime. Ordinarily we'd have had a matinee on a holiday, but what with the Sundays this summer, they need a bit of a rest at least one day a week. He could have been anywhere.'

'Where is he now?' I said.

Sid took a pocket watch from his waistcoat and opened it. 'Dressing room if he knows what's good for him. And we need to be shifting ourselves. The early coaches will be in soon. These Mothers' Union trips always take their seats sharpish. None of them drink for one thing and it gets the weight off their corns.'

Sid was needed at the stage door to let in what he called 'the chorus and hoofers', and so Betty showed us to the dressing rooms. The stink of camel, stronger than ever it seemed to me, followed us through a warren of awkward passageways and up and down myriad little staircases until eventually she knocked on a door.

'I smell no smoke,' said a booming voice from behind it.

'Sorry, Douglas,' Betty said. 'But this is important.' Then she opened the door and shoved the three of us through it, before melting away.

'Smoke?' I said.

'Because the only reason to disturb me before curtain-up

is the theatre on fire,' said the man who sat at a dressing table in the cluttered little room, glaring at us in the glass. He was wearing nothing but a towel around his slim hips, perhaps to let the paint on his body dry. His face, arms, shoulders and the outer rim of his back were done, but there was an egg-shape in the middle, reaching from shoulder blades to waist, that needed attention.

'Here. Let me,' Grant said. She surged forward and lifted an enormous pot of something with a sponge sitting in it. She scoured the sponge around and then, without asking for permission, began to dab the man's back, as he leaned forward and smeared black around his eyes.

'Tilly's really gone then?' he said. 'I don't suppose you're free after to wipe it all off again, are you?'

Grant swatted him with the sponge and told him, quite mildly in my view, to behave himself.

'You don't seem concerned,' I said, as the man rose from his chair and stepped, thankfully, behind a dressing screen set up across the corner of the room. 'About Tilly.'

'I'm annoyed,' the man said. 'The dresser taking off in the middle of a run is nearly as annoying as the smell of that damned camel. I told Aladdin and Scheherazade not to come to St Andrews. They looked at a map, saw the seaside, and thought of Eastbourne. Now they're shivering the summer away. But even I couldn't have predicted the camel. Should I be? Concerned about Tilly?'

His rapid change of topic took us a moment.

'Everyone else is worried,' Alec said, when he had caught up. 'There's a chance – actually, we've confirmed it now – that Tilly is mixed up with something rather nasty. And she may well have come to harm.'

The towel had appeared, thrown over the top of the screen, and now the man emerged again, wearing a short, glittering waistcoat and a pair of striped satin trousers that stopped at mid-calf. His facial expression was nigh impossible to determine underneath the face paint. That is to say, his eyes looked surprised but then he had lines of black and white around them to make them appear larger than life. And he might have been flushed under the rouge or pale under the panstick. Who could tell?

'Where were you on Monday?' Alec said. 'Monday afternoon.'

'Tilly was still here on Monday night,' he said. 'She dressed both houses on Tuesday.'

'Still,' Alec said. 'Where were you? About half past two, wasn't it Dandy?'

'I don't see what business it is of yours,' Sinbad said. He had sat back down at his dressing table and was now winding a length of cloth around his head to form a turban. 'But I was in Dundee, as it happens.'

Actor that he was, he knew immediately that he had made a deep impression with his words. He stopped winding the turban and said: 'Why?'

'You took the word out of my mouth,' Grant said. 'Why were you in Dundee? If St Andrews isn't seaside enough for you.'

'I was at Her Majesty's,' he said.

'Go on,' I urged him.

'I'd had a telegram. It came to my digs first thing Sunday morning. And I fell for it. Big enough and ugly enough to know better, but there it is. I fell for the oldest trick in the book.'

'You never did!' Grant said. Sinbad hung his head.

'The telegram said an impresario had seen my performance on Saturday night and wanted to audition me for a new show. If I would present myself at the stage door and so on and so on.'

'Never,' Grant said. 'They're still playing that old "impresario" wheeze? And you didn't see through it?'

'It's that camel making me light-headed,' Sinbad said. 'But I'm telling you the truth.'

'Who did you speak to there?' I said. 'At Her Majesty's.'

251

'An old girl on the door,' Sinbad said.

'Moll,' said Alec. 'Yes, we know Moll. We can easily check with her. And we shall.'

'Look,' said Sinbad, then stopped speaking as a loud bell rang out just beyond his dressing room door. 'What's this about?' he said when the ringing had died away. 'That's five minutes and I need to prepare.'

'Bert Mackie,' I said, watching as carefully as I could the face behind the make-up. I saw no flash of recognition but I reminded myself that he was an actor as well as being currently masked by paint. Besides that, if he was mixed up in Bert's death the name would come as no surprise. 'Punch and Judy man. A friend of Tilly's.'

'She's not fussy,' he said, with a sneer.

'You didn't happen to see him on Sunday night when he might have come to visit her?'

'I knew she *had* a visitor,' Sinbad said. 'Everyone knew. They were in the paint shop arguing hammer and tongs. I stayed out of it. She's a nice girl. Good dancer, doesn't cling, but she's nothing to me when all's said and done.'

'Not much of a write-up,' said Alec, who cannot bear lapses in chivalry.

'Bert Mackie was murdered on Monday afternoon,' I said. 'In Dundee, and we think perhaps Tilly was there. We think perhaps she saw whoever it was who did it.' I glanced at Alec and Grant. 'At least that's what I'm coming round to.' Each of them considered the notion and then nodded. 'And now she's disappeared. Our worry is that whoever killed Bert found out she witnessed the crime and has now . . .'

'Tied up the loose ends,' said Grant, sepulchrally. Of course, this was very far from true since it did not address the problem of Bert's disappearing brother, the puppets in the Doig's boardroom, or the fiftieth anniversary of the first murder, but it was an effective ploy. It put the willies up Sinbad, certainly. He started babbling.

'I've never heard of Bert Mackie. I'd sooner have a girl who's got other chaps, if I'm honest. I don't want them getting ideas about me. I've a wife and three boys in Helensburgh. I don't want any complications. My wife's father wants me to drive a taxi. I've got the telegram still. I saved it. I was summoned to Her Majesty's and I didn't kill anyone while I was there.'

'He wasn't killed at the theatre,' I said. It was a point in Sinbad's favour that he genuinely did not seem to know that. 'He was killed during his puppet show, right there in the kiosk.'

Sinbad ran a hand over his mouth, smearing his face paint. 'Moll, you said?' His voice was strained. 'Moll will tell you I was at Her Majesty's and my railway tickets are still in my pocket. My jacket's hanging on the back of the door there. I never went near the pier and I never saw any Punchinello.'

'What pier?' I said.

'Or prom or beach or wherever the show was put up,' he said. 'You have to believe me. I don't know what Tilly's playing at and I don't know where she's disappeared to but I didn't kill anyone on Monday or anytime.'

'We believe you,' Grant said. 'It was a park. Dudhope Park. Not a prom or a beach. So either you really didn't know that, or you're a good actor.'

He stared at her a moment until he saw the joke, then he sank back in his chair, convulsed with helpless laughter. Alec was rootling around in the pockets of the coat hanging on the back of the door and jumped as someone banged on the other side of it.

'Beginners,' a voice shouted.

'I'm on,' said Sinbad. 'Thank God for Betty on the book. I've never been more sure to forget my lines in my life. Come round,' he went on, relief making him expansive. 'Come and watch. It's a decent show, if I'm being fair, and you can't smell that bloody camel out front.'

He stood very still for a moment, statue-still, and seemed to grow a little taller before turning and sweeping out.

'He'd be wasted in a taxi,' Grant said after he had gone and the blast of camel occasioned by the opening of the door had died down again. 'I wouldn't mind slipping into a back row to watch him do his stuff, if it's all the same to you.'

'Why not?' said Alec. 'We still need to ask the rest of the company and stagehands where Tilly might be and we're not going to get anywhere with that until afterwards.'

Sid's world weariness had receded somewhat. He went as far as to twinkle at us when we presented ourselves to be ushered to a run of three spare seats in the front of the balcony. He was still proud of his troupe and their show, the twinkle said. And despite his disparaging words about the Mothers' Union, the audience was gratifyingly ready to be charmed by the hoary old tale and the glistering baubles the cast had donned to tell it. When Scheherazade danced the little dance, not quite a ballet, that marked her entrance, the crowd gave her a round of applause, and when the camel appeared at the end of the first act the resulting uproar threatened to stop the show ahead of the curtain.

As the audience – courting couples, families, and the ladies from the charabancs – drained away to buy ices, Grant, Alec and I stretched out in our seats. The house lights were not fully up, the magic not quite done away with and replaced by threadbare carpet, flattened velvet and damp-stained stucco. In the half-light, spinning tales seemed warranted. And the three of us spun.

'Tilly,' Grant said. 'She's mixed up in it all. No question about it. But how? Is she distracting us from what we should be seeing or is she what we should be looking at?'

'Like Johnny Doig with the bucket of lamb's blood,' Alec said. 'That was a masterful bit of distraction, if you please.'

'It took nerve,' I agreed. 'The puppets and lipstick look bad? Well, here comes Johnny Doig, far from hiding the

254

connection, adding more and more until the whole thing is too ludicrous to be taken seriously. I mean, if it was just the puppets and lipstick it would be more suspicious than those letters three feet high. And they're less suspicious with the bucket stashed in Home and Garden than without.'

'But we think the puppets and lipstick were a distraction in themselves,' said Grant. 'Don't we?'

'Which makes Johnny's visit to Thomson's a double bluff and the bucket on Mrs Priest's desk a triple bluff,' Alec said.

'And what about poor Professor Dennis?' I said. 'How did he get mixed up in any of this? Why did Leon Mackie pretend that he held Dennis's chair?'

'If Leon's real job is something he wouldn't want us to know,' Alec said, 'perhaps he plucked "Schwarzmann Professor of Soteriology" out of thin air.'

Grant snorted.

'Not exactly out of thin air,' I said. 'There's a slight connection after all. Tilly works – I hope it's present tense – in the Central Bar where the professor toddles off to for last orders.'

'But Leon doesn't know Tilly,' said Alec. 'She was Bert's friend.'

I groaned. The audience, ices in hand, were beginning to trickle back in. I overheard a pair of stout ladies sharing a whispered conversation.

'It's fresh enough in here,' one said. 'It must be the drains. And it might be the gents, but who's to say it's not the ladies?'

'Well, I'm not checking. I'll wait and go at home.'

'Sshhh,' said her friend, digging hard into the other's ribs. 'I can't take you anywhere. Don't be so coarse.'

When they had passed by, I heaved a sigh. 'I disagree. About coarseness. I think a bit of plain speaking is needed here. I don't think the puppets matter. I don't think the publishers matter. I don't even think Leon's little fibs about his job matter. I think Tilly matters a certain amount – she is the only witness, who for some reason misled the police and has gone missing.

255

But the main thing we can't ignore any longer is that someone killed Bert Mackie. We don't know who and we don't know why but we do know it was fifty years to the day after someone killed another Bert Mackie, in the same place, by the same means. The rest of it is just . . .'

'Business,' said Grant. 'Like a camel or a mirror act.'

'What *is* a mirror act?' I said. 'You mentioned such a thing, Alec, and never explained it to me.'

'Wait and see,' said Grant. 'For there's one coming up in act two.'

'Really?' said Alec. 'What a treat.'

'I wondered why they'd bothered with Dunyazadiad, but it makes sense now.'

'Who?' I said.

'Scheherazade's sister,' said Grant. 'She's one of the easiest to cut to keep the cast down. But look at the programme: Bella and Bertha Borthwick. Sisters. If they don't do a mirror act, I'll eat my hat. And it explains how Bertha got the female lead too. She's not an actress and goodness knows she's not a dancer.'

'You are mean, Grant,' I said. 'I thought she was charming.'

'Same name as the director,' said Grant. 'Arthur Borthwick. He must be their father. Well, I suppose it keeps the wage bill down, but I wouldn't be in their shoes. The chorus must despise the pair of them.'

'Grant!' I said. 'You were in your parents' company from when you could toddle. There's nothing unseemly about a family business. Don't be such a—'

'Sssshhhhh,' said Grant, with enormous impertinence, as the lights went down and the curtain rose. I sighed and sat back, wondering how long it would be until the finale. We had had Aladdin and Ali Baba in the first half and I saw nothing much to look forward to in the remainder of the evening – the camel and a mirror act, whatever that was, notwithstanding.

Chapter 24

How wrong I was. Over the course of the next hour I came to wonder why Aladdin and Ali Baba were the stars of the show at all, for the tale of the three princes, bringing magic carpets, magic looking glasses and magic apples to woo their princess, struck me as a great deal more entertaining.

'I wonder why the brothers Grimm never bothered pinching the carpet,' Alec whispered. 'They scooped up the mirror and the apple all right, didn't they?'

'Far too cold in Germany,' I whispered back.

'Ssshhh,' said Grant again.

When Prince Ahmed had taken his bow and left the stage, Scheherazade came creeping back on, staring at the looking glass left over from the tale. She put a puzzled look on her face and appealed to the audience, who tittered, more comfortable with the style of a pantomime than a play even as unserious as this most unserious production.

'Now you'll see it,' Grant said, barely whispering at all, clearly not bound by the same rules as Alec and me.

Scheherazade stepped toward the mirror, which was angled just so, and peered into it at her reflection. She preened a little, danced a few steps and, taking a jewelled comb out of a hidden pocket, she settled with her legs to one side, like a mermaid, and proceeded to comb her long black hair.

Just when the audience began to grow restive, for it was hardly a spectacle, something rather eerie began to happen. I could not have put a finger on the inkling that something was wrong with the reflection in the magic mirror; only that the girl sitting on the stage and the girl in the glass gradually seemed to be sparring with one another, egging one another on, growing frenzied as they yanked at their hair and panted, scrabbling for purchase on the boards of the stage with their bare feet, until the girl on the stage flung the jewelled comb from her, sending it skittering down towards the footlights. There was a gasp from the audience as the comb in the mirror, instead of disappearing backwards, came through the 'glass', past Scheherazade and stopped beside its mate, just upstage of the edge, where immediately a spot was trained upon it.

Scheherazade, astonished, turned her head slowly and stared at the pair of combs. The audience let out an unearthly moan as they watched the 'reflection' *not* turn but keep looking at the other girl with a cold devilish gaze.

'Watch out!' someone called from the audience, surely a plant but effective all the same. Scheherazade looked up, with flashing eyes, then whipped her head back around, hair fanning out in a shining black arc, just in time to see the girl in the glass look away.

Most of the audience were thrilled, making that noise halfway between a giggle and a whisper, although somewhere in the stalls a child began to weep softly. On the stage, Scheherazade reached out, hand trembling and hesitating, and tapped the reflection on her shoulder.

The infinitely slow way the other girl turned back, like an automaton, her cold smile slowly revealed as her face came back into view, made me shudder.

The child's weeping grew louder and another child joined in. Even Alec, I saw at a glance, was pole-axed, sitting bolt upright with his hands clamped on his knees and his chin drawn back into his neck. Only Grant was unperturbed.

'Not bad,' she whispered. 'But let's see how they land the finish.'

Scheherazade reached out again as though to touch her

reflection's face, but when her fingers were an inch away, the other girl's hand shot up like a lizard's tongue, grasped her by the wrist and twisted. To shouts of dismay from the crowd – and I had to bite my lip to stop myself from joining in with them – the other girl kept twisting until Scheherazade's hand was up between her shoulder blades and she was bent double with her face near the floor. But then she kicked out, one foot flashing so quickly that the jewels on her slippers dazzled, and that kick sent the other girl sprawling backwards, to cheers from the audience, who had picked their heroine and their villain and were joining the fight with gusto.

What a fight it was! Never crossing to the other side of the mirror frame, each girl yet managed to land punches and kicks, to pull hair and slap bare limbs, and while I knew it was stagecraft, and could hear Grant's murmurs of approval at my side, still it was absolutely convincing, the smacks ringing out and both girls gasping when blows hit their middles. I had not noticed the music starting, but it was now doing its bit to add tension to the melee, rising in a crescendo as the fighting grew more and more desperate until each girl had the other by her shoulders and was shaking the life out of her.

That was when the mirror frame started to turn, slowly at first, then faster, until the girls were running in circles to keep up with it, one girl and then the other flying into the air, feet straight out, as they spun, hanging on grimly with both hands, so that the pair of them made a whirligig going ever faster until, as the music grew higher and higher and the mirror spun to a blur, suddenly there was a cymbal crash and they flew apart. Scheherazade was thrown downstage and landed sprawled on her back with her chest heaving, while her reflection stood in the mirror, face stark with horror.

Scheherazade, for we still believed it was she, groped blindly and found one of the combs still lying on the stage where it had landed, then threw it with all her might. It hit the mirror dead centre, shattering the glass into a thousand sparkling chips. The girl in the frame screamed but when the glass chips fell away they revealed only empty darkness.

The girl sitting on the stage turned her head, very slowly, gave the audience a familiar cold glittering smile and laughed one last time.

'I say!' Alec said, then he was on his feet like the rest of the audience, myself included, cheering and stamping as the vanquished girl joined her sister for a bow.

'Quite well done,' said Grant as we took our seats again.

'Oh come off it,' I said. 'That was astonishingly good.'

'When you've never seen it and don't know what to expect,' Grant said, 'I suppose it is convincing.'

Then we were loudly shushed by the row behind and we subsided to pay attention to whatever poor member of the company was charged with following *that*. The camel, I saw, as Humphrey lumbered in from stage left; perhaps the only creature who could command attention right now.

I am sorry to say he did not command mine. I could not get the whirling girls out of my mind. So clever, such confidence in where we would be looking: to swap the empty frame for a pane of sugar glass as we all watched 'Scheherazade' tumble across the stage towards the drop! So clever the way they revealed the final twist, just Scheherazade's scream to find herself trapped in the glass and the other girl's icy smile.

If Alec had clutched my arm a minute earlier I would have jumped out of my skin, but when I felt his fingers digging into me and turned to see his face, eyes wide and mouth hanging open, I was already where he was and I simply nodded and jerked a look to the side door, urging him to let me out and follow me.

'Are you sure?' he said when we were in the dark passageway that led up the edge of the auditorium, back to the foyer.

'Dead certain.'

'What's going on?' said Grant, arriving beside us. 'Are you

upset, madam? It's only an act. When you've seen it as many times as I have it's nothing troubling any more.'

'Grant,' I said, hurrying towards the foyer door, 'when you've seen it as often as you have it's not only not troubling; it's too familiar to be helpful. But that mirror act has just made Mr Osborne and me look beyond the wood and see at least one, and I think two, very sturdy trees.'

Thankfully, there was no one at front-of-house. Even the ice-cream stand was closed and empty. We could let ourselves out and make our hasty way to the motorcar unmolested.

'What is it?' Grant said. 'What did you think you saw in the Borthwicks' act?'

'Two where there should be one,' Alec said. 'And then the wrong one, the other, gone God knows where.'

Grant screwed up her face in just the way she tells me never to screw up mine or risk becoming a wrinkled crone beyond the reach of face cream, but in the end she had to give in and beg for enlightenment.

'No one knows who killed Bert Mackie,' I said. 'The villain came and went unseen. More than unseen. With a witness ready to swear he didn't exist.'

'And there's no motive that anyone can fathom,' Alec said.

'And his brother – whom he never mentioned to Moll, if you remember – is not a professor at St Andrews, and has disappeared. For no earthly reason that we can see.'

'Oh God, Dandy,' Alec said. 'A professor!'

'That's disgraceful,' I said. 'To thumb his nose that way. To mock that way.'

'I still don't know what you're talking about,' said Grant, with more asperity than I had ever heard her use before, for she does have some faint glimmer of memory from the days when she wore a cap and bobbed a curtsy in my presence.

'Think about the mirror act,' I told her. 'Swap them round.'

She was a silent a moment. Then she let out a gasp to

rival a whole charabanc full of Mothers' Union. 'Bert Mackie wasn't murdered!' she said. 'Bert Mackie was the murderer!'

'And he really didn't – doesn't, I mean – have a brother,' Alec added. 'There is no such person as Leon B. Mackie. He was dreamed up by Bert to allow him to revisit the scene of the crime.'

'And Bert made him a professor as some kind of pun?' Grant said. 'I agree, madam, that *is* shocking. That's just cheek.'

'And then to add a bit of detail,' I went on, 'they gave him a chair.'

'They?' said Alec.

'Oh yes, most definitely,' I said. 'They only knew about the Schwarzmann Professor of Soteriology because he is in the habit of wandering into the Central Bar for a late pint of ale. And Tilly works there. Definitely they: Bert and Tilly, who have now both completely disappeared.'

'But she didn't know what soteriology was,' said Alec. 'So Professor Mackie became a psychologist. No matter that St Andrews has no such thing.'

We were barrelling through the streets now, in the gloaming, Alec gripping the wheel tightly and sitting so far forward that I feared for his hat brim if he should have to stop suddenly for any reason.

'Where are we going?' I said.

Alec opened his mouth and then laughed. 'I don't know!' he said, 'which I suppose means I can slow down a bit without any great repercussions.'

'Surely we're going to the police station in Dundee,' Grant said. 'To tell that snooty inspector that we – you, madam, and Mr Osborne, with my help to get you started – have worked out who committed the murder.'

'Right you are,' Alec said and I could feel the motorcar beginning to speed up again.

'Of course, in any ordinary case,' Grant went on, 'working

out who did the deed means the end of the mystery. This is a novelty, though, isn't it?'

'That is a remarkable understatement,' I said. 'But I take your point. We can tell the police that they should be on the trail of Bert Mackie and Tilly . . .?'

'Ohhhhhhh,' said Grant. 'Now you've got me but we can telephone to Sid once we're at the police station and ask him.'

'And Bert Mackie is his real name?' said Alec. 'Is it actually safe to believe anything "Leon" said to us?'

'Oh, I think Bert Mackie is his real name,' I said.

'Why?' said Alec. 'You sound very sure.'

'Because of the anniversary,' Grant said.

'But I don't think I fully understand that yet,' said Alec. 'I don't see the connection just as I don't see a motive. Granted, we've cracked the crime, and named the murderer, but we don't know who the victim is. I can't imagine ever feeling less satisfaction than I do now.'

Grant was giving Alec a perplexed look from the back seat of the motorcar, and I felt the same puzzlement. 'Are you serious?' I said. 'You don't see the motive? You still don't see the connection? You don't know who the corpse was?'

Alec smiled. 'I wish I wasn't driving,' he said. 'I'd like to light my pipe and enjoy what's coming. Go on then, make me kick myself.'

'Do you want me to tell you or give you a hint and let you work it out?'

'I don't mind telling you, Mr Osborne,' Grant said, but I shushed her.

'One hint,' said Alec. 'Then you can draw straws for who gets to tell me.'

'One hint each,' said Grant. 'You first, madam.'

'Billiards hall,' I said.

'How very cryptic,' said Alec. 'Your turn, Grant.'

'Deuteronomy,' she said. It was an excellent hint and I wished I had thought of it.

Alec said nothing for a while, then smacked his hands against the steering wheel and let out an exasperated snort. 'I've got it,' he said. 'Good grief. You have my permission to take me to a doctor and have my head examined, Dandy. Ask him to see if there's any sign of a brain in there. Albert Mackie senior did not run a billiards hall in Lanark, nor retire to a villa in Bearsden. Dunelgar indeed! You can't accuse him of lacking nerve, can you? Albert Mackie senior was a Punch and Judy man and he was murdered fifty years ago in Dudhope Park in Dundee, leaving his kiosk and his puppets to his only son, who carried on the family trade.'

'Booth,' said Grant. 'Art.'

'And now Albert Mackie junior has killed someone, fifty years to the day. The obvious motive is revenge. The murdered man is whoever killed his father.'

'Exactly,' I said. I felt as though little bombs were detonating in my mind, or if not bombs then at least missiles of some kind: perhaps the rocks my sons used to heave into lakes as children, hoping to be soaked in the resulting deluge; strange are the ways of small boys. 'For didn't the post-mortem report say the doctor thought the man much older than Bert Mackie's reported age? And here's another thing. It explains why Leon wanted his brother's puppets back, doesn't it? Because they're *his* puppets and he's attached to them. Oh! And something else too. *That's* why the woman in the teashop thought she'd seen a ghost even though one "brother" has a head of black hair and a long black beard and the other "brother" was fair. That always bothered me.'

'Talk sense, Dan,' Alec said. 'The woman in the teashop doesn't exist. Leon – oh drat it! – *Bert* didn't need someone to come and tell him the address of the rooms. He knew it, for he'd been living there.'

'But if he'd been living there why was he so keen to go back? And if he was keen to go back why did he not just come with us?'

'Perhaps he wanted to get into the rooms in the guise of Leon, in front of witnesses, in case he'd left fingerprints somewhere,' Alec said. 'Tilly did, after all. Or perhaps he couldn't bear the thought of us being there without him. As to why he didn't come with us . . . perhaps he didn't expect us to winkle the address out of Moll and he meant to peddle the "woman who saw a ghost" story upon our return so we could all go together.'

'Or,' said Grant, 'he preferred to sit in a cosy teashop instead of tramping the back streets of Dundee to get an address he knew already.'

'We are fools,' I said. '*I* know why he couldn't come to the stage door of Her Majesty's with us while we asked Moll if she knew his address.'

'Ohhhhhh, so we are,' said Alec. 'The false beard and the long dark overcoat might fool strangers and mild acquaintances but Moll has known him for years. Of course she'd recognise him if he turned up in her little den and sat drinking tea.'

'We're not fools at all,' said Grant. 'We really have cracked this case wide open, haven't we? Oh, I'm so glad I'm going to be there to tell the police. I don't know if you realise it, madam, but I very often get left out of the most rewarding tasks in any case. A long day sitting at that reception desk while you dashed about is only the most recent example.'

'Grant, you were absolutely in clover behind that desk,' I said. 'You had the time of your life. Don't tell stories that aren't true. But, to show how wrong you are, when we get to the police station, you may take the floor.'

'Thank you madam,' Grant said. 'I accept. Not that it'll take long to say "Bert Mackie killed the man who killed his father". It's very simple really, now we're looking at it the right way. It even makes a kind of sense. I mean, revenge is understandable.'

'And thou shalt grope at noonday, as the blind gropeth in

265

darkness, and thou shalt not prosper in thy ways: and thou shalt only be oppressed and spoiled evermore, and no man shall save thee,' I said.

Alec puffed out his cheeks and let his breath rattle along the sides of his teeth. 'Hard to argue,' he said. 'When you put it that way.'

Chapter 25

We never made it to the police station.

'Lights on at Doig's,' Alec said as we drove along the Overgate.

'Printing the *Freckle*,' said Grant. 'They're probably behind from all the goings-on.'

'Well, if they're behind anyway,' I said, 'why don't we stop off there and give them an update? I'd rather like it to be horrendously late when we get to Bell Street. I'd rather like to be sent on my way and have that inspector come toiling up to Gilverton tomorrow if he wants to talk to us.'

'Hear, hear,' Alec said, and guessing that the front door would be locked and bolted he reversed up the street a little until he could nose the car down the alley at the side of the building, and turn into the back lane.

'Although I don't want to keep you out too late, Alec darling,' I said. 'Isn't it tomorrow she arrives?'

'Who arrives?' said Alec, turning the steering wheel and inching forward.

'Or is it Friday?'

'Is what Friday?' He was distracted by the closeness of the stone wall to the wing of his Daimler, it is true, but Grant and I still shared a panicked look.

'Poppy,' I said, and added 'you goose!' in a jocular tone as though forgetting the very existence of one's betrothed was a matter to be teased about and not an enormity.

Alec stopped the car and climbed out in silence. 'I hope it's open,' he said, as the three of us approached the back door. 'They'll never hear us knocking with the racket of the printing machines going on.'

'There's a light,' Grant said. 'A red light goes off at the presses if there's someone at the door.'

But it was open anyway, and we let ourselves in. I braced against the noise, *Götterdämmerung* going at it again worse than ever, unless it was the contrast with the stillness of the late evening out in the lane, for Dundee is no carnival on a Wednesday night, even in fine weather.

Thankfully, we did not have to breach the heart of the beast itself by opening the printing-room door, for just as we arrived, one of the men came out and saw us in the passageway.

'Fright of my life!' he said. 'I didn't see the bell light.'

'It's open,' said Grant.

'Is it, by Jove?' said the man. He had pushed his blue cotton cap onto the back of his head to wipe his forehead with a spotted handkerchief and now he plucked a cigarette from an open packet in the breast pocket of his overalls. 'I won't tell if you don't,' he said. 'Whoever had the last fag break cannot have locked up again. Let's just say I met you in the lane there and let you in. Save anyone getting in bother.'

'Of course,' I said. 'Is Mr Doig really such a stickler?'

'Mr Doig's not here,' said the chap, with a laugh. '*He's* no stickler. And neither's Mr Johnny. Just in a bad mood tonight. And he'll not be best pleased if I stretch my smoke either so . . . if you'll excuse me.'

'Of course,' I said. 'We've got the most tremendous news, but perhaps we'd better come back in the morning when Miss Bissett's here anyway. If Johnny's grumpy.'

'Miss Sandy?' said the printer. 'She's here. Up in her office in case we need another driver when the run's through and packed. But she's just waiting meantime. She'd be glad of the company, like as not.'

He left us then, scraping his match on the brick wall outside before the door was closed behind him, while we made for the basement stairs, the cage lift and the cluttered little office where the case began.

'Johnny?' Miss Bissett said in a groggy voice at my knock. 'Have you recovered your temper?'

'It's us, Miss Bissett,' I said, taking her words nevertheless as permission to enter. 'All three of us. Forgive the late hour but we've got some staggering news for you.'

Miss Bissett had been reclining on the elderly sofa but she swung her feet to the floor at my words and rose, groaning. 'Let's have a toast then,' she said. 'I keep a bottle of whisky in my drawer, as did my Uncle John and my grandfather before me. My father would be scandalised, but I hardly ever drink any of it. And besides, he's not here to judge me, is he?'

As she spoke she had poured whisky into a pair of glasses, a teacup and a little stone pot that looked as though it might be a bud vase. I grabbed this last: I loathe whisky and she would not be able to tell through the thick stone sides that I had not drunk it.

'Are you prepared for a surprise, Miss Bissett?' Alec said. She smiled at him.

'Bert Mackie is not dead.'

'He . . . he recovered?' she said, with a troubled look at me. 'But you told me his throat was slit.'

'No. A throat was slit. Bert Mackie slit it. The dead man in the Punch and Judy tent was not the puppet man. He was someone else entirely.'

'Who?' she said.

'We don't know,' I admitted. 'But we can leave it to the police to find out, when they catch Bert.'

'If they catch him,' Grant said. 'He's on the run, Miss Bissett.'

'But you're sure he did it?'

'There's no question,' said Grant. 'He did it.'

'But that means we're out from under the cloud!' Miss Bissett's voice began to rise and fall in her delight. She sounded more Scottish than ever. 'We're not going to keep on being suspected and struggling against a scandal? We're going to weather it? Oh, that is the most tremendous news!'

'It certainly is,' I said. I raised my bud vase, but Miss Bissett's face was already falling.

'So are you saying it was all just a coincidence?' she said. 'The Rosie and Freckle puppets? Do you know the police have given them back, by the way?'

'To you?' I said. 'Don't they belong to the estate— Oh, well, I mean to Bert Mackie.'

'I'd have thought so,' Miss Bissett said. 'But the sergeant brought them round and said Mr Mackie's brother had asked for the kiosk and the real Punchinello puppets to be sent to his home but wanted the two new ones to come to me, to put things right. They're in that brown paper parcel on my desk. I have to admit I can't bear to look at them. But I don't know what to do with them. Put them on the fire, I suppose. Only – you'll think I'm silly, but – one of them is supposed to be my mother and the other one is supposed to be me and I don't particularly want to see them turned to ash.'

'Quite understandable,' Grant said. 'I couldn't destroy a doll even if it was nothing to do with my family.'

'Johnny thinks I shouldn't have let the sergeant leave them,' Miss Bissett said. 'That's what put him in such a temper. He was angrier than I've ever seen him and we've known each other since we were tiny children. Practically brother and sister rather than cousins really.'

'I've never seen them,' Grant said. 'Do you mind if I unwrap them now and have a look?'

Miss Bissett waved a hand in permission and Grant went over to the desk and started in on the brown paper.

'As to coincidence,' Alec said, 'I don't think so. I rather think it was a deliberate attempt at distraction. It's quite remarkable how different everything looks with Mackie as murderer rather than victim.'

'And do you really not know who the victim is?' said Miss Bissett.

'Yes and no,' Alec said. 'We think he was the target of Mackie's murderous intent because he – the victim of the current murder – was the perpetrator of the earlier murder. We think the first murder, fifty years ago, was of Mackie's father.'

'Oh my,' said Miss Bissett. 'That's rather . . . I don't know that I could hit on the right word, actually.'

'Shakespearean?' I suggested. I glanced quickly at Grant but she was so engrossed in unwrapping her parcel that she did not remark on my use of a name that would ordinarily have had her whiskers quivering.

'And so the new puppets and all the wrangling about copyright were to distract from the motive of revenge?' Miss Bissett said.

'I can't see any other explanation,' I said. 'Things only began to make sense when we turned it on its ear and looked at it from the other end, if you see what I mean. Bert Mackie not killed but killing, for instance. But there's no way to turn two new puppets and a threat of copyright violation on its head. At least not that I can see. What is it, Grant?' I added, for she was back from the desk with a puppet in each hand. She was holding them forward, showing them to Alec, Miss Bissett and me. I had to glance away from their vacant leering faces.

'These aren't right,' she said. 'These aren't new.'

'No, we know they're not,' I told her. 'We think they're spares, repainted and re-dressed. The dolls themselves are probably as old as the others.'

'I never believed a man who used Scaramouche and didn't use the crocodile would paint over puppets as modern characters, though,' Grant said. 'I've thought that from the off. And he didn't.'

'Probably not,' Alec said. 'He probably never meant to use

271

them in the show. He only meant them to scare Doig's and Thomson's. *That's* why he knocked them up – to make Thomson's and Doig's look guilty. Distraction, as you said.'

'Not Thomson's, if you remember,' I said to him. 'Mr Thomson knew nothing about it.'

'Just Doig's then,' said Alec. 'He made up this whole tarra-diddle and painted up a pair of old puppets to cause mischief for Doig's and hide his crime. He must have loved how well it worked, Miss Bissett, when you were arrested.'

'You're not listening,' said Grant. At our looks she went on: 'He didn't daub a bit of new paint on a pair of old puppets. That's what I'm trying to tell you. This red paint for their hair and the stitching on Rosie's frock and Freckle's jersey is not new. The paint's worn and chipped and the fabric is faded in its folds. The stitches are rotted away in places. Cheap thread that was never meant to last this long. I'd say it's fifty years old, roughly.'

The silence lasted long enough for Miss Bissett to drink all of her whisky in three long gulps. When she had put her glass down, she said: 'You were right, Mrs Gilver. It has to be turned on its head to make sense, you said.'

As she spoke, we could all hear footsteps pounding up the stairs. He started calling out while he was on the last flight. 'Sandy? Someone said those detectives were back. Don't speak to them! Don't say a word about anything!'

Alec was on his feet when Johnny Doig came bursting in through the door. 'Steady on,' he said. 'There's no need to go crashing about.'

Johnny Doig stood, panting and ragged, his face haggard with defeat. Then a ghost of his old smile hooked itself up at one side. 'You're right,' he said. 'What's needed is a calm report of the facts. What's needed, at long last, is a reckoning. Pour me a whisky, Sandy, won't you?'

When he was settled, he began. He all but started with once upon a time. 'Grandfather Doig,' he said, 'started the

272

picture papers. Both of them with his daughter's likeness on the cover, woman and girl. But *my* father was always credited with the notion that was right at the heart of the magazines' success, the idea that Rosie Cheek and Freckle shouldn't just be faces on the cover, but real characters inside, with fresh stories every week. Someone for the readers to take a friendly interest in. It was his one useful contribution, and it offset a great deal of waste and nonsense.' He took a sip of whisky. 'Only, you see, it wasn't his contribution. Not his idea. It was Albert Mackie's. Who knows how it began. Maybe they met in a pub – a puppeteer and a publisher – or maybe my father saw a Punch and Judy show in the park one sunny afternoon. One way or another, Mackie gave my father the idea that let the Doigs flourish.

'But it was hard in the early years. There was no money to pay anyone royalties on a copyright. If Mackie had sued for them, it would all have been over.'

'Just so I'm sure I've got this straight,' I said, 'you mean that your father—'

'Uncle John?' said Miss Bissett. 'I don't believe it.' She was searching his face with her eyes and her cheeks had paled, leaving her freckles standing out like filings on her skin. 'Did you know?'

'I suspected,' said Johnny Doig. 'I remember Pa talking when I was a kid. About the family business and the importance of a steely purpose, the ends and the means. It didn't fit with the way he lived or the way he worked and so it stuck in my mind. It puzzled me.'

'And how did you solve the puzzle?' Alec said.

'He hated that Punchinello,' Doig said. 'I never knew why. *Now* I understand. It must have seemed macabre beyond belief when an Albert Mackie came back to Dundee, with the same show. My father avoided the park all summer. It was in case he caught sight of the thing. When that woman came round on Friday squawking about

273

new characters in the puppet show, it must have been like a waking nightmare.'

'She really did then?' I said. 'We wondered if it was part of your distraction. If you had told someone to say so.'

'Oh she came,' said Doig. 'Trying to get my father to go and see for himself. Which he did. I don't know what he thought he was going to achieve, going round to face the man down on Monday afternoon. Maybe he meant to do it again. He can't have known . . . He can't even have suspected . . . Or maybe he did. Maybe he was sick of the whole thing and didn't care how it ended, as long as it ended. But for two days, I thought he'd done the murder. Killed the son as he killed the father.'

'But he didn't?' said Miss Bissett, whiter than ever. 'Who did? And who was killed?'

'It took until Wednesday for me to . . .'

'Swap them round,' Grant said, earning a grateful smile from Doig.

'Swap . . .?' said Miss Bissett. 'Do you mean to say the man who died, the man who was killed in the puppet tent, was Uncle John?'

'Who else?' said Johnny Doig. 'I'm sorry it's coming as a shock to you, Sandy. It came as an enormous relief to me.'

'Relief?' said his cousin, her voice a squeak.

'Of course, relief,' he said. 'From Monday to Wednesday I believed what everyone was saying. That Albert Mackie was dead. And I thought my father had done it again and this time run away. It was hell, Sandy. Sheer hell. I never slept a wink and all day every day I was listening for the police klaxons coming up the street.'

'But you . . . you daubed blood at Thomson's,' said Miss Bissett. 'You put the bucket on Mrs Priest's desk.'

'Yes,' said Johnny. 'And I put two puppets in the boardroom and lipstick on the mirror and I told Fiona to say she'd seen a stranger at nine o'clock on Tuesday morning as we were opening – which she got wrong, fool that she is; and Mrs Miller didn't help with all *her* tales – and I told Mrs Priest to say she'd seen him again. Meanwhile I put it out that Pa had gone to the seaside and that he had rung me up and nagged about the margins. Yes. I covered for him. Even when I thought he had killed for the second time. I covered for him. Even when you got arrested, Sandy. So when I realised the truth, I felt *nothing* but relief. I still haven't felt a wisp of grief. I suppose I'll grieve one day – he was my father, after all – but not today.'

'But I don't understand,' said Miss Bissett. 'When you realised he'd been killed why didn't you tell someone? Why didn't you go to the police? I'm no lawyer but covering up in case something had happened when in fact it hadn't doesn't sound like a crime to me. And the paint round at Thomson's was mischief. Malicious damage, at worst. Why didn't you want justice for your father, Johnny?'

'Because he'd already got it,' Doig said. 'At long last, fifty years later, he finally *got* justice. I didn't see the point of carrying it into a new round. I was weary. If the police found Mackie and hanged him then his son would hate me, and he might exact revenge and then my son would hate him. I reckoned it was better to let it end here.'

'He doesn't have a son,' I said.

'True,' said Doig. 'Although he has two daughters. He sent me their pictures along with that dammed kiosk and all the puppets. They live – well, I suppose, they're on the run now, but until this week they lived – over in Fife, in St Andrews. His wife is something in the theatre there and works in a pub to make ends meet while he's been on the road all these years, biding his time, trying to discover who killed his father.'

'Tilly?' said Grant. 'He and Tilly are married?'

'Why would that be a secret?' I said.

'Part of Bert Mackie's exceedingly long game,' Doig said. 'He was shielding them against the day they'd all have to run. But secret or not, I don't want to make a widow, much less two orphans. Not when it's all my fault.'

'How is it your fault?' I said, at the same time as Grant said, 'How *did* Mackie find out all these years later?'

'I was having a clear-out,' Johnny Doig said. 'And I found these two puppets. I asked my father why he had them when he loathed puppet shows. He flew into a rage and stormed off to get drunk. And once he was drunk, when he came home, while I was pulling off his boots and loosening his tie, he mumbled a name: Bert Mackie.'

'Oh Johnny,' said Miss Bissett.

'So when I saw the flyers for Albert Mackie's puppet show, I went round there. I went to the park on Thursday and said to the chap, "I think I've got something of yours, old man. I don't know why, but would you like them back?"'

'And that was enough?' I said. 'Tilly, his wife, came here and said the puppets were in the show, hoping that your father would be . . .'

'Foolish,' said Johnny Doig.

'. . . enough to go to the park and see for himself.'

'Which he was,' said Doig. 'Which he did. And he paid the bill outstanding.'

'How do you think it was managed?' I said.

'I imagine,' said Alec, 'that Bert invited your father to step into the booth before the show and—'

'We needn't go into that,' I said. 'I meant how did Bert get away?'

'As we always thought,' said Grant. 'He stretched out Scaramouche's neck and then, when everyone was watching, he left the tent and headed for the trees.'

'Bold,' I said. 'Beyond reckless.'

'No,' said Grant. 'Misdirection. Pure theatre. Like every card trick and shell game and mirror act there ever was.'

Alec was nodding. 'No one could see the back of the tent. And no one was looking at the grass beyond.'

'And if anyone on the benches had happened to glance that way and seen a man simply walking across the park, they wouldn't have turned a hair. He'd have been long gone before the alarm was raised.'

'No doubt,' said Johnny Doig. 'But never mind what happened then. What happens now is the thing. What now? Do we let the whole sorry history end there? Let Doig's survive. Let all the people who work in this building keep their jobs. Or do we help the law to hang a man for avenging his father? It's my father who died but I know what I think. What think you, Mrs Gilver, Mr Osborne? And Miss Grant too.'

I looked at Alec, then at Grant. I could not begin to imagine what either of them made of this. 'It's late,' I said. 'And we have a long journey home. We'll discuss it. We'll tell you tomorrow.'

Johnny Doig stood up from where he was leaning against a bookcase and Miss Bissett got to her feet too and slipped her shoes on. 'The print run's finished,' she said. She was right; the deep bass rumble from the bowels of the building had ceased without our noticing. 'So even if this scandal destroys us and this is to be the last *Freckle* we ever publish, it will be in the shops on time tomorrow.'

As the pair of them left the room, Alec, Grant and I remained facing one another. And I rather thought that both of them felt exactly the same as me, all of us hoping someone else would speak first.

We were almost back at Gilverton before anyone spoke at all.

'It's not on, is it?' Alec said. 'I mean, I'm sure Johnny Doig does feel a sense of responsibility to all those printers and packers and recipe writers, and I suppose if anyone has the right to pardon his father's murder, he does. But . . .'

'But *does* anyone have that right?' I said.

'Who's to say the *Cheek* and *Freckle* will fold anyway?' said

277

Grant. 'Miss Bissett's the boss and she did nothing wrong. In fact, you never know: a little notoriety might . . .'

'Besides,' I said. 'It's not as if Bert took the only way out of some tragic moral labyrinth. He could have told the police. John Doig could have been tried in front of a jury.'

'Could have been and should have been,' Alec said. 'Look, we're all going to have to decide where we stand, aren't we? In the next year or two. We're all going to be asked whether we're willing to close our eyes for a quiet life or whether we're willing to . . . Well, one doesn't want to be a prig.'

'"One's" probably going to have to not mind being a prig,' said Grant. 'Given the alternative. Might as well start now.'

'Agreed,' I said. 'I'll ring the police in the morning.' Doubts began immediately to form again in the corners of my mind, but I shook my head to dispel them. 'If Hugh is right – and deep down I know he is – then I shall be sending my boys off to fight for justice and honour before too long. That will be hard. This is easy.'

THE END

Facts and Fictions

I've tried my best to set the story in the real Dundee of 1937, although I was forced into a few tweaks here and there. Her Majesty's Theatre closed in 1919, signaling the beginning of twenty dark years in Dundee, but I have kept it open, just, so that Moll can work there. The Delnevos did own a fish restaurant at 25 Overgate in 1937, before the family moved to the Venice Café at No. 15, but I've got no reason to think Mrs Delnevo would sell the very chip papers on a busy lunchtime. Thomson had some competition in the newspaper business in Dundee in the early days but, by the turn of the twentieth century, a Mr Thomson was in overall charge at Meadowside, consolidating and expanding the publishing empire that flourishes today. The Doigs and their magazines are imaginary.

I've made even more free with St Andrews. There was no professor of soteriology, Schwarzmann or otherwise, and even if there had been, he would not have lived in college. And the Majestic Theatre is imaginary, although the Byre is real and does not deserve any of Grant's sniffiness.

Acknowledgements

I would like to thank: Lisa Moylett, Zoë Apostolides, Elena Langtry, and all at CMM Lit Agency; Francine Toon, Joe Hall, Sarah Christie, Kate Keehan, and all at Hodder and Stoughton; all the readers, bloggers, reviewers, booksellers, and librarians who support Dandy and me; and my friends and family who might be wishing I'd give it a rest but never tell me.